# ROUGH EDGE

LAUREN LANDISH

Edited by

VALORIE CLIFTON

Edited by

STACI ETHERIDGE

Photography by Wander Aguiar.
Edited by Valorie Clifton & Staci Etheridge.



The following story contains mature themes, strong language and sexual situations. It is intended for mature readers.

## ALSO BY LAUREN LANDISH

*Bennett Boys Ranch:*

Buck Wild || Riding Hard || Racing Hearts

The Tannen Boys:

Rough Love || Rough Edge || Rough Country

Standalones

My Big Fat Fake Wedding || Filthy Riches || Scorpio

*Dirty Fairy Tales:*

Beauty and the Billionaire || Not So Prince Charming || Happily Never After

*Get Dirty*:

Dirty Talk || Dirty Laundry || Dirty Deeds || Dirty Secrets

*Irresistible Bachelor*s:

Anaconda || Mr. Fiance || Heartstopper

Stud Muffin || Mr. Fixit || Matchmaker

Motorhead || Baby Daddy || Untamed

# CHAPTER 1

## BRODY

"Well, as I live and breathe. Is that you, Brody Tannen? I haven't seen you in ages, boy!"

Mrs. Perkinson squints her rheumy eyes at me and I do my best not to cringe. It's not that she's unkind, but she's at least the fifth person to tell me the same thing this afternoon alone. You'd think I hide out on the ranch and never see the light of day in town. There might be some truth to it, but I don't need people pointing it out left and right all damn day.

"Good afternoon, ma'am." It's the bare minimum of words to not be accused of rudeness. I'd know because I've tested it over the years. My preference was a simple 'hello', one word and done, but apparently, that made me sound like a grunting ass and didn't meet the requirements of respecting my elders. So the needlessly complicated 'good fill-in-the-blank' and 'ma'am' or 'sir' is what I've gone with.

So far, so good. And I'm almost done with deliveries of my sister's homemade, high-demand seasonal treats, not only for the day, but for the entire week. No more pies, no more jellies and jams, no more soaps, and best of all, no more people. I can't wait to not have to *people*. Yes, that's a verb, because again, it's simpler to say 'people' than 'I don't prefer to socialize, thank you very much' because who needs all those useless words when one will get the same message across just fine?

"Get your hiney on into my kitchen and let me feed you. Skin and bones, you are!" Mrs. Perkinson's bony finger juts out, poking at the thick slab of muscle on my chest.

Great. She's obviously gone blind as a bat if she thinks I'm skinny. Most people cross the street when they see me coming—too tall, too broad, too brooding, too asshole, with a reputation of kicking ass first and asking questions never. I'm too busy being busy to give a shit with consequences unless they affect my family.

"As much as I'd like that, ma'am, Shayanne would have my hide," I say with as much 'aw shucks' as I can muster, not a single fuck given that I'm throwing my sister under the bus, but I can't help scratching at my lip with my thumb as the lie passes between them. "I'm on her schedule, you see."

She takes the jar of lemon curd from my hand, signaling the end of this conversation. Or at least I hope it does, but I've still got to say polite goodbyes and whatnot or she'll be tattling on me to Shay for sure.

"Well, that girl works her tailfeathers off, so I won't begrudge her requiring the same of you lot. Only way to keep you hellions in check is a firm hand. Glad to hear she's got one." Sweet Mrs. Perkinson becomes a bitchy old biddy right before my eyes, and I'm no longer willing to uphold niceties when she's insulting me and my brothers, even if she is one of Shay's customers.

Without so much as a goodbye, because I ain't wasting words when I don't have to, I turn and shuffle down the two steps of her porch. I climb into our old farm truck and peel out of her driveway. She probably thinks I just proved her point, that I'm a rude motherfucker with no proper manners despite my poor sister's attempts to housebreak me, but I don't care.

If anything, I raised Shayanne, not the other way around. Little thing was just thirteen when Mom passed. She took over that role without a fuss, but she needed some guidance growing up, and that responsibility fell to me as the man of the house, because Dad sure as hell wasn't.

Not that I'm thinking of him.

May the Devil himself be pissing on his soul down in hell.

I hear Mom scolding me in my head and sigh heavily as the speedometer creeps up to sixty on the old country road. "Fine, Mom. I hope Dad's resting *comfortably* in hell, does that work for you? Because we both know he ain't up there with you. When you were here, maybe it could've gone that way. But you know how it was later, so don't be rewriting history now because it's rude to speak ill of the dead."

I turn the radio up to drown out the voices in my head. I don't hear them very often anymore, not Mom's sweet assurances that I'm doing okay and definitely not Dad's harsh bites that I'm fucking everything up. Truth be told, they're both right in some ways.

But the growl of the old diesel engine drowns them both out easily, and they float away on the wind blowing through the open window. Along with any preconceived notions Mrs. Perkinson has.

For a moment, I'm free.

Wind in my hair, Johnny Cash on the radio, a thermos of diesel-strong black coffee in the seat beside me, and the blessedly open road before me. The speedometer cranks higher, and there are no responsibilities weighing on my shoulders like stones, no expectations gripping with tight fingers to hold me in place.

I'm Brody Tannen. I'm myself, but also not.

I'm nothing and no one. I'm free. And it's bliss.

Right up until the old truck jerks, slowing down even though I never let up on the pedal.

"Shit, Bessie! What the fuck are you doing? At least hold it together until we get to town." Okay, so I'm sweet-talking the truck like the girl I took to the senior homecoming game, and perhaps more relevant, the afterparty where she got drunk as a skunk and nearly puked in my truck.

Bessie—the truck, not the girl—sputters but rallies and keeps chugging along, down to twenty-five now. The ride is rough and jerky, but we're so close to town, I can see signs rising high in the sky. I rub at the dash encouragingly instead of pulling over. "See . . . just up ahead, girl."

I scan, looking for a parking lot I can pull over into, not as familiar with the main drag on this side of the mountain. When Shayanne expanded the delivery radius of her homemade treat business to this side of the mountain, I'd told her to go for it, thinking it'd be our brothers, Brutal and Bobby, doing the deliveries, or hell, even Shayanne herself when she could. I didn't give a shit. I didn't plan on coming to the far side myself, and I definitely didn't plan on getting stuck over here. But that was then, and here I am now.

Like a beacon rising in the sky, I see a white sign ahead. *Cole Automotive.*

Son of a bitch, must be my lucky day in some twisted sort of way. It'd be damn better if Bessie were running smooth as butter, but I'll take a mechanic shop over parking in some pot-hole-riddled, abandoned lot of a closed dollar store. Anywhere better than that would probably call the police on me for abandoning a piece of shit like this.

*Sorry, Bessie, but you know it's true.*

I jerk my way into the lot, cranking the engine off as soon as possible. "Fuck!" The bark of frustration is timed perfectly with the bang of my fist on the steering wheel. The sentiment is repeated as I slam the door.

I turn toward the bay doors of the garage, thankful that they're still open at least. The sun's starting to move down in the sky, foretelling a hell of a sunset, but that'll be a few hours away with the long spring days. It takes a second for my eyes to adjust to the dimmer light inside and my ears to adjust to the absolutely blaring heavy metal music.

"Motherfucker." The murmur isn't silent, but no one would know that because of the music's volume.

I see a small coverall-clad figure standing on a stool, ass in the air and head buried in the engine compartment of a truck. "Hey, kid!"

No response. Not even a flinch.

"Hey! Kid!"

I step to the side, reaching out to tap the kid on the shoulder. But instead of the 'good afternoon, sir' that manners and customer service require, according to Shay, I get greeted by a wrench swinging up in an arc from inside the vehicle to aim right at my head. My hand shoots out automatically, catching the kid's wrist to stop the attack. "What the fuck?"

The kid's wrist twists in my hand, some looping motion that breaks it free, and at the same time, a steel-toed boot connects with my gut and pushes me back.

Pushes *me* back, all two hundred pounds of don't-fuck-with-me warning-labeled asshole actually moving from the kid's shove.

"Get your fucking hands off me, motherfucker."

The response is threatening and more of a lip reading, but the message is loud and clear. It also comes accompanied with a press of the wrench to my throat that keeps me off-balance after the not-quite kick.

"Hey, hey . . . sorry . . . just trying to get your attention." Every bit of my apology is yelled at volume eleven in an attempt to be heard over the music and drown out my own instincts to instantly fight back.

And something suddenly becomes real fucking crystal clear. It's not a kid in front of me. It's a woman. A gorgeous one.

She's tiny, maybe five feet tall at most, and swallowed by her navy-blue coveralls, which are rolled up at the arms and the ankles.

There's a thick knot of dark hair piled on her head and a map's worth of freckles across her nose and cheeks, along with a few smudges of black grease. Her dark chocolate-brown eyes are blasted through with gold, not like some pretty poetry shit but like she's about to start shooting fire right at me.

"Alexa, turn down the music." The deafening music quiets, leaving only the ringing in my ears. "What did you say?"

The urge to swallow against the wrench rides me hard, but I don't dare, not willing to admit to her or myself that I'm at her mercy. "Sorry, didn't mean to scare you. Wanted to see if someone could look at my truck."

The wrench drops to her side. "Then you knock on the damn door like a normal fucking human being. You don't touch me, or anyone, without permission or without their even knowing you're fucking here."

I don't know that I've ever met someone who curses as much as I do. And I curse a fucking lot, which is saying something considering I don't speak much. I think I just fell in love a little bit with this wisp of a woman. Not seriously, of course, but that big mouth is kinda fun in a surprising way. A very small percentage of folks stand up to Brody Tannen, and an even smaller percentage of women ever gives me sass. Insults, yes, but smartass back-talk? This might be a first.

"Hell of a way of getting customers—blasting metal, attacking people, and cussing them out when they're just trying to hire you to do your damn job," I deadpan, only half joking.

She's shit for customer service. I'm shit at being a customer. Match made in heaven, we are.

"Waltzing in here like you own the place, putting hands on people, and somehow thinking you're in the right." She ticks off my shortcomings on her greasy fingers with the wrench and enough attitude that she should be ten feet tall and bulletproof. "Fuck off. We're closed." Somehow, the movement of dismissal she makes with the wrench feels like she just flipped me off. Makes no sense, but it's the truth, and there's talent in that, I suppose.

Lil Bit—that's what I've decided to call this pretty stick of dynamite because one, I think it'd piss her off and that sounds like twisted fun, and two, she seems full of sparks and danger—turns her back on me, spinning in place and stepping back onto her footstool, which puts her roughly at the same height as me.

I'm stuck here with Bessie misbehaving the way she is and a woman who damned near took my head off with a Craftsman tool. Luckily, just my actual head, not my cock because it's feeling some quick stirrings of ideas it wants to accomplish before I start pushing up daisies.

"So can someone take a look at my truck or not?"

"Nope. Shit outta luck, Cowboy." The words echo in the engine compartment of the truck, but I can hear her victory in shutting me down.

"How'd you know I'm a cowboy?" I curl the brim of my hat out of habit, not admitting that I'm double-checking myself that I don't have my cowboy hat on, because it'd be just my luck to challenge her when I'm wearing something that makes it real obvious what I do for a living.

With echoing words again, she says, "Dirty boots, dirty jeans, dirty shirt, dirty hands, and you smell like cow shit."

My lips quirk of their own volition. I barely notice that last one anymore. "Seems like you checked me out pretty good while you were sizing me up as a threat. No worries. I was checking you out too."

My flirting is rusty, like a tractor left to rot in a field for a few years' worth of rain and snow, and comes out more threatening than complimentary. Lil Bit makes not a peep of noise under the hood.

Something interesting occurs to me, and the question pops out before I can stop it. "How'dya know what cow shit smells like? As opposed to horse shit, dog shit, or people shit?"

What the hell am I doing? Why am I talking about shit?

Before she answers, or maybe she's not planning to anyway because who wants to talk about shit, a door opens and my eyes are pulled away from her ass. I figured I could try to suss out what was under those coveralls without her noticing. Hadn't planned on someone else catching me, though.

Two guys come into the garage, also clad in navy blue coveralls, and I make the mental jump that they work here too. The first guy is tall, not like me, but compared to the short and stocky other guy, he seems to think he's the hotshot here. The tall guy crosses his arms, trying to widen his rangy frame. Posting up to me ain't a good move, man.

Once upon a time, that challenge in his eyes is all it would've taken for me to start throwing haymakers. I've gotten better now, more stable, more thoughtful. Not because I'm getting soft in my old age, but I don't have the same rage boiling in me like I used to when I was constantly dealing with Dad's shit.

The chest patch on the lucky bastard I'm not beating up says *Reed*. The other guy's says *Manuel*.

"What can we do you for?" Reed says. His narrow eyes measure my height, width, and the distance from me to Lil Bit's ass. I don't move.

"Truck started acting up. Think it's the transmission, thought *someone* might take a look at it."

I'm still talking to Lil Bit, even though she's tits-deep under that hood, but Reed's eyes light up when I say transmission. I don't know much about trucks, but I know it's an expensive repair, and a shop would have to be stupid to turn down a sure job with the vehicle sitting like a stone in the lot.

"Yeah, sure," Reed agrees easily.

That echoey voice calls out again. "Touch that truck and you're fired, Reed."

He licks his lips like it pains him to tell me, "Sorry, no can do, man."

I take a deep breath, hold it, and then exhale loudly, knowing I sound like I'm accepting defeat. I'm not. I get in one more dig. "Mind if I leave it in the lot overnight 'til I can get it towed somewhere else that wants to take my money?"

She grunts. I'm fluent in them, though, known for speaking the language myself, so I hear her permission to leave Bessie overnight. I'm also planning to be here when the tow service comes to get Bessie, just so I can get another eyeful of Lil Bit. Maybe see if she's as ornery when I haven't scared the shit out of her right out of the gates.

I nod to Reed and Manuel and step toward the open bay door to dig my phone out of my back pocket.

I could hit up one of the guys at the ranch to come get me, but it's a long drive over the mountain, and Katelyn, my boss's wife, is at the resort right between me and home. She'll be heading toward the ranch shortly when she gets off work, so I shoot her a text thinking it'll consolidate trips, if nothing else.

*Me: Bessie died. Stuck at Cole Automotive. Need a ride home.*

Yeah, not so much on the manners, but of anyone, she's the most used to it since she's married to Mark. Mark is, to put it as kindly as possible, an utter asshole and even quieter than me. Once upon a time, we'd been sworn enemies, but he'd come through for us Tannens when the shit hit the fan, and I'll be forever grateful for that, even if I have to work for the motherfucker now.

*Katelyn: Busy. Will send Marla. Hang tight. Mark loves that truck.*

See? She's accustomed to it. And she's giving me fair warning that Mark is going to kick my ass for being the unlucky son of a bitch who was driving Bessie when she finally gave out. She's had a good life, though, and hopefully isn't ready to be sent to scrap. She just needs a good mechanic. One not at Cole Automotive.

Not meaning to, I overhear Reed. "Hey, you wanna grab a bite tonight?"

He's nervous, the question weighted with intention beyond grabbing a burger with a coworker. His possessive look comes back to me, and I realize something. Reed is sweet on the ball-busting, wrench-wielding woman and doing his best to flirt with her. I chuckle under my breath. "Good fucking luck, man."

Anybody who ever tells you women are the gossipy ones ain't never spent time with men. We might not sit around and gab about shit like women are wont to do, but we have our own ways. Like me right now, leaning against the doorframe, hat pulled down low so it seems like my eyes are on my phone. But I'm watching everything go down like a bored housewife at church on Sunday.

Lil Bit ain't having it. She's wiping down something under the hood with zero interest in, or even the slightest awareness of, Reed. "Nah, heading home early to catch the game tonight."

He shoots, but instead of scoring, he goes down in a blazing ball of flames. But he's not done.

"We could watch together?" Give the man points for gumption and perseverance. I don't, but somebody should.

"You don't know the first thing about baseball, and I'm not spending three hours explaining shit to you, Reed." She manages to make it sound like he's not worth the spit it'd take to explain a strike-out, but then she laughs, softening the insult like it's something they've done a thousand times before.

From my undercover vantage, I see Reed shake it off. Manuel looks back and forth, from her to him, and then he follows Reed out the door like a catty hen ready to get to clucking about the situation.

See? Gossipy guys are the worst.

I wait a few minutes in silence, examining Lil Bit's ass in those coveralls, and when that doesn't yield any useful information, I scan the rest of the shop. It looks busy, several vehicles in the lot and every bay filled. There's a long workbench along the front with organized tools arranged on a wall of pegboard. The left side of the garage holds an old refrigerator, a cheap pressed wood cabinet with a hanging door that's topped with a small microwave and a coffee maker, and a desk piled high with file folders. It reminds me of Mark's office, bare-boned and functional, nothing that's not useful and necessary. It tells me something about the woman who's still busy working under that hood.

"What's wrong with your truck?"

"Oh, she speaks."

Sarcasm drips from my lips because I know she heard me tell Reed about the transmission. Apparently, I'm a recent convert to masochism because I'm looking forward to her vitriol-filled comeback, but Lil Bit doesn't respond. Eventually, I give in. "Bessie was doing fine, then started jerking. Seemed like the tranny was slipping."

"Bessie? What is she?"

I swear I hear a smile, but when her head pops up, her lips are pressed straight. But trucks seem to be an interest, so I indulge her. "Ninety-six Ford F-250, Power Stroke diesel."

Lil Bit hops off her stool, her thick-soled boots making a small thud. Her hands go to her coverall pockets as she eyes me. I'm not sure what measure she's taking this time, but I'm eye-fucking the shit out of her. She moves toward me, and my cock stands up at hopeful attention. But she simply frees one hand, holding it out palm-up. "Keys?"

I don't question it, just drop them into her outstretched hand as she passes me by. She pulls open Bessie's door and literally hops inside. Vaguely, I wonder how many things she has to hop up on and down from in a day.

A second later, the loud engine breaks the silence. Lil Bit looks thoughtful, and I realize she's listening to the chug-chug-chug sounds as if they hold the secrets of the world. Hell, maybe to her, they do. To me, it sounds like a truck. Loud and ready to work, except I know Bessie ain't doing so well once she gets in drive.

A four-door sedan pulls into the lot, drawing my eye. I can see Marla, Katelyn's assistant, waving at me. She's a good helper for Katelyn, though I know more of her from Katelyn's stories than I actually know Marla. This makes the third time I've ever met her face-to-face. Luckily, the other two times, she rambled nonstop about her husband and twin girls, and I assume today will hold more of the same and I won't have to say a word.

I lift two fingers in a wave to Marla and the truck silences.

Lil Bit hops down again, walking toward me already talking. "I'll take a look at her. It'll be a couple of days before I can get to it, though. Once I've done diagnostics, I'll call before I fix anything to get approval on the charges. Number?"

She puts the keys in her pocket, smart businesswoman taking the truck hostage until I agree. But I'm desperate and she knows it.

I'm not usually one to be at a disadvantage with anything, and certainly not with women. But damned if she doesn't have me dead to rights intrigued, and she seems wholly unaffected by me.

"Sure. There's a business card for my boss in the visor. Call him to approve the money stuff."

Lil Bit nods and keeps on walking, past me and right back into the garage. She grabs a chain off a hook and the door rolls down between us. A loud click sounds out, letting me know she's locked the door. It reassures something in me that she's locked safely away for the night to watch the baseball game she didn't want to explain to Reed.

Dismissed and striking out just as badly as Reed, I amble toward Marla's car. Just before I get in, heavy metal music starts blaring again and I look up to see Lil Bit watching me leave through the row of glass windows in the blue garage door. Maybe not a complete strikeout, then?

I expect her to jump, maybe act like I didn't bust her clear as day looking at me. She does nothing of the sort. She simply stares at me as I fold my long legs into Marla's sedan.

# CHAPTER 2

## BRODY

"Thanks, Marla." I'm back to one-word responses with bare pleasantries. I was right. She talked about her girls and husband the whole time so they're literally the first words I've said to her.

"No problem, Brody. Katelyn is finishing the setup for the breakfast meeting in the morning, so she might be a while. Grab a beer and dinner in the bar. I'll let her know where you're parked." She hustles off, and I can almost see her tick off the item on her mental to-do list. Pick up Brody . . . check. Deliver to resort . . . check.

I pull my cap off, curling the brim, and slam it back on my head. I'm not dressed for the resort bar. It's not what most folks would consider fancy, but around here, it's as fancy as it gets. And as Lil Bit reminded me, I'm wearing dirt like an accessory from head to toe. Deciding I don't give a fuck because a beer sounds good, I head in and find a stool off to the far edge of the room where I can watch the comings and goings and not be easily seen in the shadows.

The bartender starts listing off drink specials, the first of which is something called a Great Falls Flyer, which sounds like a shitty name for a ski resort drink to me. Not that anybody asked me. I hold up a hand, stopping his recitation of fancy mixed drinks, and slide a fifty across the bar. "Bud. Bottle. Start a tab."

He blinks, his face a mask of 'yes sir', and grabs me a bottle. He sets a frosted mug down beside it, the question in his eyes asking if I'd like to pour it myself or have him do it. I pick up the bottle and take a swig from it, skipping the mug completely. He dips his chin and disappears, taking the mug with him.

Finally alone.

Yeah, in a bar. But with a beer in hand, no one to talk to, and no expectations to be polite. I can just sit and be alone.

Most folks probably think I spend a lot of my time alone. They'd be wrong. I spend all day, every day with a thousand head of cattle. Those animals are my friends. I know when one's feeling aggressive, I see when they're favoring a leg or ready to get inseminated, I see the friendships between the big creatures as they group together among the larger herd. They might not talk to me in English, but they say plenty. Same goes for me. I might not say much, but I say a lot if you know how to listen.

But now, I don't have to watch the cows or talk to family or anything, really. I can just sit here anonymously in peace and quiet.

After a bit, I order a burger, which comes out huge and delicious. I nod my thanks at the bartender, who's picked up on my silence and twenty minutes later, quietly takes away my empty plate and delivers another Bud.

The bar starts to fill up as it gets later and the sun goes down. It gets louder, and I start to people watch. There's a noisy table in the corner, some sort of bachelorette party or girl's night out, I think, because it's a group of women dressed to the nines for the resort bar. I might be underdressed, but they're overdressed from what I can see.

The group shifts around the table as some pop song I don't care to know comes on. They're singing and have their arms around each other's shoulders, swaying like it means something.

And then I see her.

A dark-haired stunner amid the group. She's got on ridiculously high heels but seems to know exactly how to move in them because the pseudo-dance doesn't make her wobble a bit. Her skirt is so short, I'd bet it measures in the single-digits for length, her flat chest is barely covered by a thin scrap of cotton that does nothing to hide the little perks of her nipples, and her face is expertly painted with smoky eyes and a bright red lipstick.

There's something vaguely familiar about her, but she's not the sort that runs with dirty cowboys. Still, I try to place her as I watch her hold court over her group of friends.

Maybe she was a previous resort fling? It's not something I've done often, but there's a certain type of woman who likes a one-night vacation when they come to town. And occasionally, a night of no-strings-attached is a release of a too-tight valve for me.

But that doesn't seem right about her.

She's obviously the ringleader, loud and happy as the other women follow her cue. Hell, maybe it's her birthday or she's the bachelorette?

I scan the rest of the room, but as the women take to the floor to start dancing, she pulls my eye again. It's not that I'm attracted to her, exactly. It's that it's irritating the hell out of me that I can't figure out where I know her from.

Suddenly, it hits me.

It's Lil Bit. But sure not looking like she was before in those dirty coveralls, steel-toed boots, and grease.

I take another appraising look at Automotive Barbie on the dance floor. I wouldn't have thought Lil Bit's hair was that long, but it's brushing far down her back, almost to her ass. Her freckles, which I wanted to count earlier, are all but invisible in the thick makeup she's got on. Her body's tiny and tight, barely a curve to be seen, but she moves with womanly grace. At least she is now when she's not threatening my life with a wrench.

The difference is remarkable.

At the shop, she'd been all-business and snappy like a rabid raccoon. Now, she's flirty and girly. But the idea jolts something inside me other than my cock.

I think I prefer the way she was before when she was about to take my head off. I can't help but watch, fascinated at the difference.

A cheer goes up across the bar, and I turn to see what the ruckus is about. The baseball game is on, and Lil Bit didn't even so much as glance toward the TV. 'Watching the game,' my ass. I can't help but cringe a bit at her giving Reed the brushoff and then coming out with her girls to dance the night away. Kinda shitty to just not say 'hey, dude, never happening' and let the chips fall where they may. She'd seemed that type before, but I guess not.

I feel a bit like one of those old guys on National Geographic, in the natural habitat of these people but not a part of it. I'm just a sideline observer of it all—the guys watching the game, the girls on the dance floor swaying to get their attention, even Lil Bit's transformation. All woefully unfamiliar to me. Not that I suddenly want to become a native.

No, thank you. I'll be heading home soon to my family, where I know what makes everyone tick, what buttons to push, and when I'm stepping too close to the line. Where things make sense.

I flag the bartender down and order a third beer, not giving a shit because Katelyn's driving home. As I take that first cold swallow, I feel someone sit down next to me.

"I'll take another one of those Flyers," a sweet voice says to the bartender.

Ah, shit, here we go. Lil Bit's seen me. Hell, she probably saw me looking at her and is coming over here to threaten my life again. Might be warranted this time, at least.

"I saw you over here by yourself and thought I'd come say hi, so . . . hi."

I swear to God I was given a brain at birth, and have even been known to be decent with ladies. But I'm so confused at the complete one-eighty of her personality and appearance that what comes out of my mouth is, "Huh?"

She blushes, nibbling at her lower lip, the white of her teeth bright against the red lipstick. "I just wanted to say hi."

Not sure this isn't a trick, I drawl out, "Okay, well . . . hi to you too."

The bartender sets down a pink frozen drink in a swervy glass. Lil Bit takes a sip and moans happily. "Mmm, this is so good. Though I should probably stop because it's my third. Don't want to make too many bad decisions." She sounds like I'm a bad decision she really wants to make, and a couple of hours ago, I would've indulged that choice with at least three orgasms. Now, my cock is damn near shriveled up in revolt. "Want a taste?" She holds the straw my way, and what strikes me the most is how clean her hands are.

Stupid, but the truth. I glance to my own rough, dirty hands, knowing I'll see the jagged, stained cuticles, short nails, and scarred skin. I'd expect a mechanic to have similar hands from all the hard work, but Lil Bit's are as clean as a whistle and look soft as a baby's ass.

"What soap do you use?" I lift my chin, indicating her hands.

Her brows fall together. "What? Oh, uhm . . . lavender vanilla. Do you like it?" She pulls her hair over her shoulder, and I get a whiff of something floral and light. Guess that's what she's talking about.

I wonder if the flower shit does something for the skin? I should tell Shay about that. Maybe she could add it to her recipes for her goat milk soap business because if it'd get our hands that clean, all of us ranch guys would use it, even if we did smell like floral crap twenty-four seven.

She's looking at me expectantly, and I realize she asked me a question. I don't remember what it was, so I go to my default grunt.

My phone buzzes against the counter, the screen bright in the now dimmer bar. I glance down.

*Shayanne: You missed dinner, asshole.*

Shay speaks my language. What she means is 'I missed you at dinner, are you okay? Because I'm worried.'

I send her a middle finger emoji, which she'll take to mean, 'I'm fine, home soon,' even though what I really mean is 'fuck off.'

Lil Bit seems to be reading over my shoulder because she asks, "That your wife?"

I look at her through narrowed eyes, not happy that she's all up in my business. Hell, I don't let Shay get in my business and she *is* my business. Though now that she's married to Luke Bennett, I pawn her off on him as much as I can because he signed up for that gig with a diamond ring. *She's his problem now*, I think happily. Shay did good with him, much as I hate to admit it.

"Family business." The implication is clear.

She seems to hear me say 'no', though, as in I'm single, because she goes right back into some smiley, hair-twirling version of flirting.

And it's doing nothing for me. Earlier, I'd thought she was hot as she was handing me my balls for daring to disturb her. Now, this whole getup and flirty thing feels like a split-personality show. I don't like it. Fake and filtered makes my bullshit meter go off. And it's clanging in my head like a damn siren bell. It's a pity because her flirting like this earlier would've been more than welcome. Maybe it's because she was at work?

Off the clock, she's doing all the right things, sending me every damn signal she can—laughing even when I don't say anything funny, touching my arm . . . and nothing. I'm not encouraging her in the least, have barely grunted at this point, but still, she's trying.

I'm mostly thinking she's got Bessie and I shouldn't piss her off, so I sit here sullenly and let her gush girliness all over me, knowing I'm gonna need a shower later. And not to jack off, but just to get the fake off. And maybe to try to figure out which is the real Lil Bit. Not that it matters to me.

As long as she can fix the truck, it'll be just fine. And I won't even have to see her again. Hell, I'll send Mark to pick it up and not even have to see her then.

The bartender walks over, looking hesitant to interrupt, but he knocks on the bar in front of me like it's a damn door. I meet his eyes and he lifts his chin toward the door. I turn and see Katelyn waiting for me.

She raises one eyebrow in question. "You still need a ride?" that eyebrow says.

"Gotta go," I tell Lil Bit, or the bartender, or maybe no one, I don't know. I pick up my beer and chug the rest of it. "Keep the change." That was to the bartender for sure.

Lil Bit pouts, her bottom lip poking out in a move that has probably gotten her what she wants countless times. "Already?" She takes the liberty to trace a short-nailed finger along the tattoo on my bicep, so much in those three syllables.

I blink, looking at her and remembering her earlier. And just like that, I forget Lil Bit ever existed and my cock agrees whole-dickedly.

I get up from the bar, walking toward Katelyn without a word.

Katelyn looks over my shoulder. "Who's that?"

"No one. Let's go." I hold an arm out, motioning for her to walk in front of me because I'm a damn gentleman despite the tattoos, rough hands, and fuck it attitude I wear like badges of honor.

Katelyn says quietly, "Looked like someone to me. She was eye-sexing you when I walked in, and she watched every swaggering step of you leaving. I think you've got yourself a fan, Brody Tannen."

---

"WHAT'D YOU DO?" MARK'S GROWL WOULD STOP MOST ANY BAR fight in its tracks.

He's a big motherfucker and has a presence about him that says he'd just as soon knock your head off your shoulders as look at your stupid face. In most cases, that's true. Much as I hate to say it, it's one of the things I like best about him. We're two peas in the same pod, and because we understand each other, we do our best not to step on each other's toes.

Not too long ago, I would've told you that me and the oldest Bennett being anything but enemies was damn near impossible, that it'd be more likely for my cows to sprout wings and start flying around the field like birds than for us to be cordial, much less friends.

I'd have lost that bet.

The transition when the Bennetts bought our ranch wasn't all rainbows and cupcakes, more like fists and insults, but the cows are still mooing and Mark's a good friend now.

That don't mean the accusation doesn't sting like a bitch, though.

"Not a thing and you know it." My growl back is equal in measure, one of the things I think Mark likes about me too. It took awhile for him to get used to someone calling him on his shit because he was accustomed to his word being law as the oldest. Well, except for one person, who rides herd on us all.

Damned if I'm not the same way, both of us having spent years running our family ranches. We were like two bulls ramming into each other for a while, but we've got a good stasis now. It's just a whole lotta fun to test it sometimes.

Luckily, in this family, it's just another normal evening, so those bar-fight-stopping growls don't give anyone the slightest pause. The swoosh of a beanbag against wood keeps right on sounding out in the evening air as Brutal and Cooper play cornhole on the set they built as a father-son project.

I should've seen that coming as soon as Brutal told me his girl, Allyson, had a son, but I hadn't been prepared to add a smart-mouthed nine-year-old to our family. But we did, and Cooper's just another one of us now. A tiny version, but family. Brutal, my monster of a brother, is like the hard-shell coating on an ice cream sundae, totally ooey-gooey messy underneath that tough exterior, and he's taken to fatherhood like it was his life's purpose all along. His latest fascination is teaching Cooper all about hand tools, hence our newfound evening routine of cornhole after dinner.

"Sit down and tell us all about it, Brody." Mama Louise's kind offer of a chair beside her is topped off with a glass of her special sweet tea. It's special because it's got more bourbon than sugar, and if you've ever had sweet tea, you know it's got a shit ton of sugar. I make a note to take it easy because we've all had Mama Louise's tea set us on our ass unexpectedly. It goes down so smoothly, you're drunker than a skunk before you know it. And I'm already three beers in tonight.

I sit down beside Mama Louise, take the offered tea, and have myself a healthy swallow before I say a word. I take the moment to look over my glass at our mish-mash, motley crew of a family.

The Bennetts. Mark, Luke, and James, the three boys who were once enemies and are now pseudo-brothers, though I'd deny that if asked, and Mama Louise, their mother by birth and ours by forced adoption when we were grown—but the woman won't take no for an answer—are sitting around the yard in old handmade wooden chairs.

And the Tannens. My brother, Bobby, and my sister, Shayanne, are watching Brutal and Cooper play as Allyson watches on like only a mother can. Pretty sure they're all cheering for Cooper at this point, and Brutal's shit out of luck.

Katelyn's gone to sit on Mark's lap since we got here, where she is half the time you lay eyes on them. And Sophie, James's wife, has a full-sized goat in her lap, mindlessly scratching under its chin, which means their daughter, Cindy Lou, must be inside asleep already.

It's not the family I ever thought I'd have, but I'm damn thankful for it. There's a saying about family, something about it giving you roots and wings. That's what this right here does for me. I've always had roots—to this land, to our herd, to my family. But for a while, I had no wings. I was as landlocked as my cows are. Weighed down by Dad, by bills, by expectations.

When we'd been forced to sell our ranch to the Bennetts in the wake of Dad's death, and came on as the hired help, I'd fought stubbornly against it. I'd been so arrogant and prideful. Don't get me wrong. I miss being the one to shine if it's all good, and even the one to rage if it all goes to hell, but it's been nice to just work and go home, rinse, and repeat. It's freeing in a way, finally giving me those wings in a way I didn't expect.

Mark's eyeing me, telling me to get on with explaining what happened. If Katelyn wasn't running her fingers through the hair at the base of his scalp, he'd probably still be growling. As it is, with her magic, he's almost purring. And glaring, but purring and glaring is a damn sight better than growling and glaring.

I take one more sip of my tea before I start, just to irk him because I like stomping all over that line where he goes from okay to aggravated. "Did Shay's deliveries, had old ladies telling me all day that I was too skinny." Mama Louise snorts, probably because she's the one who makes food for all of us and knows how much we can put away in one meal. "I know, right?" I pat my flat belly in confusion. "But Bessie was doing fine until she wasn't. Felt like the transmission, but I made it to a mechanic shop. They're going to look at it and call you with an estimate before they do any work."

Mark grunts. Could mean 'good job', could mean 'I'm gonna beat the shit out of you behind the barn later'—no way to tell for sure. I choose to take it as the former.

Katelyn smiles, never missing a loop on Mark's hair. "He's skipping the best part."

Mark leans in and acts like he's whispering to her, even though we can all hear him just fine. With an amused tilt of his lips, he asks her, "What's the best part of my truck needing a couple thousand dollars' worth of work, Princess?"

"Where'd you go after the mechanic's, Brody?" I swear, she's almost sing-songing the question.

"Resort bar." Another sip of tea.

"What'd you do there?" More singing. She might as well be turning into a damn Disney princess—*Princess Katelyn of the Redneck Ranch*, coming soon to a theater near you.

"Drank beer. Ate a burger. Watched the game." Too soon to take another drink, but I lick my lips and press them together, telling her she's getting nothing out of me.

"And who was your friend?"

"Ain't got any."

Mark scoffs at that. "Think again, asshole. Look around you."

Mama Louise points. "Language."

Mark apologizes to Mama Louise with a good-natured dip of his chin, but his eyes say he meant what he said. "Who'd you meet at the bar?"

Shit. Damn nosy cowboys, worse than gossipy hens. Katelyn threw me under the bus on this one, probably karmic retribution for my using Shay as an excuse earlier. And a quick scan tells me that everyone's listening now. Even Cooper has stopped tossing his beanbags to listen to me explain my 'not friend'. Guess my protesting was a bit overplayed.

"Just some woman who was chatting me up. No big deal."

But the women scent blood in the water. My blood.

With Bobby and me being the only single ones left in our group, the women have decided to take us on as projects. They've tried matching us up for blind dates, which I refuse, of course, accidentally running into people when we're in town and I suddenly remember that I need wire from the feed store, and trying to give us quizzes from some magazine website. That one was actually fun because I answered truthfully and it'd all but said that I was going to die alone. I'd celebrated, not the being alone part, but that I'd fucked with the girls' big plans to find my soulmate or some shit.

Truth be told, I don't want that.

Shay had it tough when Mom died, but she was young enough that I tried my damnedest to protect her from the worst of it. But me? I was the oldest, the one who had to deal with everything. I saw Mom and Dad, deep in love and happy one day, and Dad absolutely gutted the next.

The day Mom took her last breath, our whole family died too. She'd been the glue and we'd all been too young and stupid to notice. Until she was gone.

Dad crumbled, but he didn't go down easily. No, he crash landed, taking out as many innocent bystanders as possible. Mainly me. I lost count of the times I had to go pick him up at the bar, the casino the next county over, or a few times, at the jail for drunken and disorderly charges. Hell, I had to add a *bail* line item to the family budget, though I called it a *contingency fund* so Shayanne wouldn't know what I used the money for when she balanced the books.

And he was angry, so fucking angry. I've been in a lot of fights in my life, but I've never thrown fists like Dad did. And usually at me. I don't know why he chose me to take out his fury on because I certainly hadn't gone easy on him in return, once punching him in the gut so hard I'd had to drive him to the hospital to get checked out. He'd insulted my wimpy-ass punch the whole way, and the nurse had rolled her eyes at his bruised gut and my swollen jaw. I'd felt guilty, and he'd felt righteous that I should've somehow magically adjusted the market price on cattle so he could get the money he needed to pay his gambling debts.

That's what love does to you—gives you false hope and happiness and then rips it away, absolutely ruining you.

Even Mama Louise, a woman I admire for her strength, still walks around talking to her dead husband like he's sitting here on the porch with us. And that's supposed to be considered a healthy coping mechanism?

I don't get it, don't want it.

I'll keep my heart locked away behind my chest, take care of the physical side when I need to, and get back to doing what I do best—getting up before dawn, working my ass off all day, raising my family and crops, and keeping all the animals healthy to get to market.

Rinse and repeat.

I sit here, looking at the happy couples all around me, feeling like they're ticking time bombs about to go off at any minute and knowing I won't ever willingly strap one of those explosives to myself.

And definitely not with Lil Bit, the *Presto Change-O* woman.

"What was her name?" I don't even know which of them asks because they're like a hive mind right now—one will, one way.

"Dunno."

"Did you like her?" Shay asks that one, at least having my best interests in mind, I think.

I think about that. I did like Lil Bit at the shop. She seemed fun and challenging, even badass. Definitely interesting, but not interested. But at the bar? She was fine, but not for me.

For most guys, I suspect it'd be the opposite. A woman flirting pretty hard-core, wearing barely a stitch of clothing, and looking gorgeous should be a slam dunk. But no.

I think about how to answer. "At the bar? No." See, the truth, just a little slick.

"So you're not going to see her again?" Katelyn asks that one, and I know she's wondering if she'll see the dark-haired woman. Since Katelyn works as the event planner at the resort, and the area has grown so much, so fast, with tourists coming in and out, she sees a whole different crowd than we do way out here in the country.

The only way I'd see Lil Bit is if I go get the truck, but I can work my way around that. 'Busy, busy, busy with the cattle and goats, can't go to the far side of the mountain today. Sorry, Mark. Send Brutal.' I frown. That's a good plan, actually. I don't consider why I want to send my scary as fuck brother who's head over heels for Allyson and not my single brother, Bobby. Nope, don't think about that at all.

"Nah, won't see her. Just a bar conversation."

Katelyn sags, pouting. Mark looks at me like I kicked his puppy. He doesn't even have a puppy, but he's pissed at me for making Katelyn sad. I swallow the rest of my tea in one smooth gulp, knowing I'll regret it at five a.m.

"I got winner," I call to Brutal and Cooper.

The boy hoots so I know exactly who's winning. He always wins. At first, we let him. Now, he's just that good. Like one of those kids who can do angles and arcs and wind drag in his head, and adjust his throw accordingly.

I get up and make a show of stretching out my arms, windmilling them back and forth. "You're going down, kid."

He stands as tall and wide as his skinny frame will allow. "Bring it on, Uncle Brody."

He does a damn fine impression of Brutal's low grumble. Hell, of any of us. We're cowboys, the real deal, through and through. And though Cooper might not have had a father for a long time, he's got a hell of a one in Brutal and a herd of uncles who are making sure he's flush with male role models. Maybe not the best ones, but he's got 'em, nevertheless.

"It's on."

"My money's on Cooper." James's shit-eating grin says he knows exactly who's going to win this game. And it's not me.

"Nobody's gonna take that bet, Son. We all know Cooper's a shoo-in." Mama Louise laughs at James, but I hear her instruction to me as clear as if she were the mob boss of a redneck mafia . . . the boy wins one way or another. She's a Grandma-Bear, that one. Definitely glue, which scares the shit out of me. I already lost one mom. Can't bear to lose another.

# CHAPTER 3

## BRODY

"How did I end up getting stuck with this job? Should've sent Brutal."

I know the grumbling makes me sound like a whiny ass, but when Shay radioed that someone from Cole Automotive called and said Bessie was ready, I went into defensive mode. Unfortunately, Brutal has plans with Allyson tonight and woman trumps truck. Asshole.

I'd tried James without luck, but before I could attempt a sweet-talking deal with Luke, the girls had figured out there was something I was trying to get out of and Mark had stuck me with the assignment. He'd said it was because it was my fault Bessie was on the other side of the mountain, but I'm near certain Shay was conspiring.

And she doesn't even know about Lil Bit. But she knows me.

So here I sit in the passenger seat of Sophie's big brown truck, heading to the far side of the mountain. She got wrangled into this fair and square, at least. She's delivering a foster goat back to its owner. Right now, Vincent van Goat is in the back of the truck in a kennel cage large enough that he could stand up and prance around, but he's curled up in the hay, enjoying the wind in his hair.

"Vincent doing better?"

Should be an easy enough question, but Sophie looks at me out of the corner of her eye. "This what we're doing? Talking shop?"

I pull my hat off, curl the brim, and put it back on again, which must be some kind of tell because Sophie smiles like I just spilled my deepest, darkest secrets.

"Vincent's doing fine. His ear's all healed up, and he's ready to get back to his herd. Thankfully, he seems to be hearing just fine." She chuckles at her own Van Gogh-slash-goat joke.

Vincent van Goat came to us a couple of weeks ago after a coyote got onto his owner's land. Vincent's ear had been the only serious injury thanks to the rancher's herd dog, but it'd been pretty serious at first. If Vincent hadn't been the rancher's daughter's pet, he probably would've been sent to *greener pastures*, but Sophie promised the girl to save him, and somehow, she did.

"You did good with him."

"Thank you. I felt like it was a bit of a test, but Doc seems proud and I think Vincent is going to dance around when he sees his girls."

Sophie only recently finished veterinary school and became official, but she's been Doc Jones's right hand for a while now. She's good with animals of all sorts, humans included. So as we get closer to Cole Automotive, I decide to tempt fate.

"Can I ask you something?"

"No, you're not my favorite Tannen. That's Shay, followed by Brutal because have you seen him with Cooper? You and Bobby are tied for third." I grunt, not amused. Or at least not letting her know that I am. "Fine, sorry. Ask away."

"It's about you girls." She clears her throat pointedly. "Sorry, *women*. But I don't get my feathers ruffled when you call us 'the boys' even though we're all men. Except for James. Always goofing off and doing something stupid."

She snorts at my dig at her husband, but he is the most playful of any of us. Hell, even Cooper has told him he's immature when

James gets to pranking us. "I like him silly and doing stupid shit. Keeps me on my toes and makes the day fun. But I don't think that was your question, now was it?"

I hum under my breath, some tune Bobby's been picking at on his guitar that's already gotten in my head, trying to decide if I should back out of this conversation. Hell, James does stupid shit, so why not me too?

"Shay's country, through and through. She's always been like that, a tomboy more into dirt and animals than anything stereotypically girly. Katelyn is basically the opposite, all feminine and frilly. And you . . . you fall somewhere in the middle."

I pause and she interjects. "I have no idea where you're going with this, but I can't wait to find out." She's nearly vibrating in anticipation of my spilling my guts, something I literally never do.

This is such a bad idea, but I force the words out anyway. "You do this." I gesture to her muddy clothes, bedhead hair that was braided and forgotten hours ago, and bare face. "And then, you get all dolled up too, in fancy outfits and makeup and stuff. How do you flip-flop and still feel like yourself? Doesn't it feel fake?"

Her hands tighten on the steering wheel. "Wow, there's a lot to unpack there, but thanks for the armchair psychoanalysis and observation." She fidgets with her braid now that I've drawn attention to it.

"Never mind, sorry. I shouldn't have said anything." I try to backpedal, hating that I made her uncomfortable because that wasn't my intention.

But she's thinking, formulating an answer. "No, it's okay. I know what you mean . . . kinda . . . or I think I do. They're both me, the gritty vet version and the fancier stuff too. Just different sides, if that makes sense? I grew up in the city, didn't fall in love with this kind of life until college. My brother thought I was nuts when I said I wanted to be a livestock vet. He'd never seen me without a manicure, much less with dirt under my nails. But it just fit, you know? I'm still that girl, but just this one too." She tosses her braid over her shoulder dismissively. "Everyone's got different facets like that. I mean, Shay has been known to dress up in actual heels and a dress before, and Katelyn dresses down in sweats and stuff. But I don't know if that's exactly what you mean, is it?"

She's picking at the edge of the tape holding me together, or at least holding my lips closed. I huff out in annoyance, but it's a front. I started this and I'm gonna finish it. "I met a woman—"

She squeals and kicks her feet in the floorboard, making the truck slow down suddenly. Luckily, when I look behind us, Vincent hasn't so much as shifted in his sleep in the hay. Sophie points at me, her finger dangerously close to my nose. "I knew it. Is this about the woman Katelyn saw you with at the bar? I knew there was more to that than you were saying."

"There was. I met her earlier that day, at the mechanic shop," I admit slowly. Sophie's brows jump hopefully as she realizes where we're heading now, but I shut that down with a glower. "At the garage, she was different—like one of the guys." I leave out that I wanted to fuck her against the nearest flat surface, something I've never felt about any guy I've ever known. "But an hour later, she's prancing around and girling out and flirting."

Sophie dances in her seat, her butt wiggling around like a happy goat. "I like it! Sounds like someone's in-ter-est-ed!" She ends on a singing, drawled-out note.

I shake my head, examining my dirty hands and remembering Lil Bit's clean ones. "Nah, not like that. It was just confusing, you know? I'm a no-filter, what-you-see-is-what-you-get guy. I was trying to make sense of it, for science."

"For science?" Sophie snorts. "Let's start here, Mr. Psychoanalyst . . . you are the furthest thing from a *was-ee-wig* guy and you know it. Hell, you play it up when the mood suits you." She looks over, waving her hand over me like I did to her. "*This* says redneck cowboy. Rough, tough, stoic, and quiet. You have literally growled at strangers at the grocery store, and people are scared of you because you have a reputation as a brooding asshole."

"Thanks."

She backhands my shoulder. They weren't compliments. "On the flip side, you're trying to figure this woman out. You're aware, watchful, and observant like Brutal is. And not that you'd let anyone know it, but you're smart as a whip. What was the last book you read, Brody?"

Shit. She's right. That's not exactly something I go around advertising. It's not that I want people to think I'm stupid, but it's not my job to avail them of their own preconceived stereotypes about ranchers. "*Midnight in Chernobyl*. It's about the nuclear disaster there."

Her brows knit together even as her eyes widen. "What the . . . see? Nobody's going to think some ranch riding cowboy like you is devouring stuff like that as light bedtime reading with a Jack Daniels nightcap. You're this hard exterior, but there's more to you, Brody. So much more."

We're both silent for a moment, her words floating through the cab of the truck. I'm wishing I hadn't started this conversation. I meant to figure out Lil Bit, not have Sophie figuring out all my pieces and parts. But I guess in a way, she did help me figure out something about Lil Bit, about how she can go from one extreme to another.

"So you going to ask her out when we get to the garage? When do we meet her? She'll have to pass the family test, and it's damn near impossible to get our approval." I wish I could say she was lying, but we are a persnickety and prickly bunch.

Though I could probably roll in with just about anyone and they'd throw a parade in celebration. I don't exactly go around advertising my one-night stands, so they are under the mistaken impression that I'm lonely.

"Nah, it ain't like that. Just for science, like I said." I smirk, knowing Sophie's well aware that I'm full of shit. I'm not exactly interested in Lil Bit, or at least not anymore, but I am still a bit confused how one version of her could have me rock hard and thirsty and the other could leave me so cold and uninterested.

Sophie hums, not convinced in the least. "Science? Yeah,

biology and chemistry. Bow-chicka-bow-wow." She wiggles in her seat again.

I return the shoulder backhand, though decidedly gentler than her smack.

# CHAPTER 4

## ERICA

"Rix, whatcha want me to do with the Toyota?" Reed yells across the garage even though the music is barely loud enough to hear. "It's all done and ready to roll."

I don't move from my perch beneath the truck I'm working on. Sighing, I bite out sarcastically, "Gee, I don't know, Reed. If it's all done, why don't we just scoot it over to the side and use it as a place to take mid-afternoon naps?"

"*Okay* then . . . guess I'll go call the owner?" Reed is still asking, like there's any other reasonable option.

I hum agreement, never stopping work. But that's nothing new. I'm always working. Twenty-four seven, three-hundred and sixty-five since the day I turned fourteen and Dad let me start working with him in the garage.

Back then, I played tool bitch, fetching this and that only to return it to its proper place when Dad was done. And I watched, and I learned, and I fell in love . . . hard. With engines. Tinkering and tweaking and making them purr.

I use the simmering frustration at Reed to crank the wrench a little harder, and it gives like I knew it would. The door to the break area opens and Manuel comes out, wiping his hands on a rag. "Where you want me, Boss?"

That's what I like to hear. Manuel's ready to work, and once I set him on a course, he's solid until the job's done. Phone call to the customer and all.

"Hit the blue truck next. Needs brake pads and rotors," I call over my shoulder, keeping a mental tally of what we need to accomplish today.

"On it." Manuel's voice is already disappearing from behind me, and a moment later, I hear the truck start up, pull into bay three, and then he gets to work.

And all is well for a moment. Work being done, money being made, and grease on my hands. Life is pretty much perfect.

It's not the norm, a female running a mechanic shop, but running Cole Automotive is what I always knew I'd do, even before I started helping here. I used to listen to Dad talk shop with the guys and hang on every word, read *Car & Driver* instead of *Vogue* like other girls my age, and sneak out to the garage at home to work on the lawnmower engine for practice.

At this point, I can hold my own against any penis-dragger who thinks he knows more about cars than I do because of his dick-birthright. I know everything there is to know about engines, even a few things more than Dad at this point.

"Oh, my God! I met him! The man of my dreams." Emily's voice is loud and high-pitched, ending my moment of peaceful bliss as I work. I love her but she's . . . a lot.

Still under the truck, my voice echoes. "Again?"

My wry response isn't meant to belittle her pronouncement of a happily ever after. It's just that I've heard it before. Several times, in fact. Emily isn't prone to giving her whole heart that readily, but she's enamored with the idea of love and basically walks through life thinking it's everywhere, all around her, free for the taking whenever she's inclined.

My cynical heart tends to disagree.

*Cowboy was free for the taking*, a hushed little voice says, and my pussy perks up, agreeing wholeheartedly. Good Lord, he'd been something.

Tall and broad and dirty. I know most women wouldn't be turned on by filth, preferring their men clean-cut and showered, probably wearing khakis or a suit. I am not most women, and work-earned dirt on a sexy man is like my kryptonite, instantly flooding my basement.

"He's so hot and sexy and broody." Her voice lowers on the last bit, which makes me laugh a little inside. Like she has to sound broody to describe it. "Why are moody assholes so addicting?"

I duck out from under the truck, giving the shorthand version of a conversation we've had before. "It's not. You're just mental. FUBARed in the brain, Em."

I meet her scowl with a smile. "Rude, Rix. But you didn't see him. He was so sexy, and we talked and flirted. Did I mention hot?"

I use my screwdriver to clean the grease from under my nails. "Where'd you meet this one?"

"Not this one, *The One*. And at the resort bar a couple of nights ago. I was just dancing around with the girls, and like the sea parting" —she mimes parting the Red Sea like she's Moses of Morristown— "and there he was, watching me. He tried to play it cool, but Mama didn't raise no fool, so I went on over to him."

"Is this the part where you fell madly in love with him?" I might not be the romantic type like Emily, but she's entertaining when she gets like this. Which is relatively often.

"No, this is the part where we flirted."

She delves into the details of their conversation, and I swear I mean to listen, but my attention is haphazard at best as I let my eyes check on Manuel, who's working hard on the brake job, and then to Reed as he walks back into the shop and gets to work on a Dodge Viper that needs an oil change. I know he pulled that ticket because he wants to listen to that thing growl up close.

I know because I was thinking the same thing. Reed and I might butt heads sometimes since he's been here as long as I have and is basically the son Dad always wanted, but there's one thing we agree on every time.

Engines.

Yeah, while Dad was training me to be his legacy at the garage, he was teaching Reed too. Reed is Dad's best friend's son, and we grew up together. Hell, I call Reed's dad 'Uncle Smitty,' though we're not actually related, but that's what Dad told me to call him and I've just always gone along with it.

But not the rest of the plans they have concocted.

"And then he left with her, so I don't know what that's about." Emily's story is wrapping up, and though I haven't been paying attention, this part catches my ear.

"Wait. He got a text from one woman and then left with another, all while sitting there, flirting with you?" I repeat her own words in a harsh tone, hoping she hears how ridiculous that sounds. "Em, you know better than that! If he's a player, you're going to end up hurt. Even if he left this other woman for you—which let's be clear, is disgusting and cheating and a myriad of other things that end in fucked up and wrong—he'll do the same thing to you when he sees a greener pasture."

I'm not known for sugar-coating hard shit. Emily, however, is a believer in the power of love, gifted with a heart of gold, and sees the best in everyone and everything, even when they're no-good, cheating assholes.

"It wasn't like that. It might've been his sister or something, I don't know. What if it's fate that we met? What if we're meant to be?" Her plea for me to understand falls on deaf ears, and I wish I could get her to hear herself the way I hear her. Naïve, charming to a fault, and so full of goodness, it makes my teeth hurt.

We couldn't be more different if we tried. For her every softness, I'm sharp; her sweetness, I'm bitter; her trusting nature, I'm cynical to the point of jaded. For as rough as I am, she's baby's butt smooth. I'm dirty and greasy, and she's clean and prissy.

I raise one brow, glaring at her in disappointment. "Then you'd meet when you're both single."

She sighs grumpily, deflating. "Not like I'm going to see him again, anyway. I didn't even get his name and the bartender wouldn't give it to me. He said he didn't know it, but I could tell . . . he knew." She points at her eyes like she could read this bartender's mind.

"You didn't even get Dream Guy's name and number, Em? Shit, he might as well be a figment of your imagination then. Maybe you did dream him up."

"Nope, and we're going to the resort bar for a drink tonight after you close up the shop."

The laugh pops out of my mouth before I can stop it, sounding like a loud bark. "No fucking way am I going drinking at the resort." Coming from my mouth, 'resort' sounds like 'hell' because to me, it basically is. Fancy and expensive, and not my couch with a cold beer.

"Come on, Rix." It's not begging, but more teasing encouragement because she knows she's going to get her way. She always does, but I have to at least put up a fight to maintain appearances. And because maybe this will be the time I will get out of doing what she wants. Because the resort? Fuck that.

Before I can say no a little more clearly, something along the lines of 'fuck no, never gonna happen,' Emily's phone rings.

"Oops, I need to take this. Back in a sec." She's digging her phone out of her tiny purse—what does she keep in a bag that small, anyway—as she hustles toward the breakroom, disappearing behind the door.

Reed meets my eyes. "If you're getting drinks tonight, I'd be happy to drive so everyone stays safe. I'll make sure no one bothers you." He might as well try sticking a flag in my ass, claiming me as his. Just one big problem with that . . . I'm not.

"We're not getting drinks, and even if we did, I don't drink to be impaired, you know that." I can put away my fair share of beer, having earned my alcohol tolerance the hard way . . . in the military against guys twice my height and width, with livers to match. But I'm responsible, always.

Reed shrugs. "Offer stands anytime, Rix."

I smile, just a little one, because it's hard to be mean to someone when they're being that nice, but I also don't want to lead Reed on. I know he's onboard with our dads' grand idea and is patiently waiting for me to come to my senses and marry him.

Which isn't going to happen. Ever.

An old brown midsize truck pulls into the lot. "Incoming," I warn Reed and Manuel. You never know what type of job or what type of person is going to pull up, and I love that moment before I find out. Maybe it'll be an engine repair or something easy like an oil change? Maybe it'll be a little old lady who needs help or an asshole I can overcharge with the 'putting up with you' service fee?

The old truck has seen better days and seems to be hauling . . . a goat in the back? Not the weirdest thing I've seen around here, but definitely not a common sighting, either. It comes to a quiet stop, so not brakes, and the engine sounds smooth, so not that either. The passenger door opens and then slams shut on the far side.

As the truck pulls away, I see him.

Cowboy.

Damned if he didn't piss me off the other day when he brought Bessie in. I had almost taken his head off with that wrench, not just brandishing it, but a bare breath away from swinging it at him. I'm not usually that jumpy, but he'd scared the bejesus out of me by touching my shoulder. But he hadn't been the least bit scared of me. No, I'd been holding that tool to his neck, his huge hand wrapped around my tiny wrist, and he'd almost smirked about it, his lips temptingly full in the middle of a day's worth of scruffy beard growth. Like I'd surprised him, and more importantly, like he liked that.

For a moment, the air had felt charged like we were unexpectedly caught in the middle of foreplay. I'd almost kissed that look right off his smug face right then and there just to shock him even more. Hell, I'd wanted to see those brown eyes open wide in surprise and then close as I kissed the shit out of him. I've never had that type of instant reaction to someone before, though I'd hid it pretty well with snark and venom.

He'd pissed me off even more when we were chatting each other up. Though I'll never admit it, later it occurred to me that he had been the highlight of my day. Sparring and glaring, neither of us backing down, had been exciting. And he's hot, not like some cute bad boy Emily has deemed her flavor of the month but in a barely restrained, molten lava way. The fire inside Cowboy isn't like a warm bonfire you want to snuggle up to. It's fiery and destructive wildfire you know will scorch you to ashes, but you can't help but want to touch it anyway.

And don't I sound just as FUBARed as Emily? She'd laugh her ass off at me if I admitted that, not that I plan to.

"Hey, Cowboy, you here to get Bessie?"

His dark eyes lock on me, freezing me in place. I watch as he boldly scans me head to toe in slow motion. Ballsy, cocky bastard. Usually, that'd be enough to have my middle finger flying his way, but this feels different somehow. Oh, he's checking me out for sure, but there's a hint of confusion swirling in those dark eyes.

I don't fit in boxes the way other women do, which confuses people. Rough, dirty, and foul-mouthed are not your typical feminine traits.

But for some reason, I didn't want to be confusing to him. Even though I'm filthy, sweaty, and messy, I guess I wanted him to still find me . . . interesting. I won't admit, not even to myself, that I want him to be attracted to me. Because after our little incident the other day, I went to bed thinking about him, another thing I wouldn't dream of admitting to anyone but George, my purple vibrator with rabbit ears. He knows things about me no one else ever will.

"Hey, Lil Bit," Cowboy drawls out slow and low, smiling as he says it. It makes little sun-kissed crinkles pop out next to his eyes, and I realize he's nicknamed me too.

I hate it.

Okay, I don't. But I hate that I don't hate it.

He's watching for my reaction, so I give him the one he expects and scratch at my cheek with my middle finger. He chuckles and steps closer, lifting his hand slowly, the question of whether I'm going to stop him in his laser-locked gaze. I don't say a word. Hell, I don't think I even breathe, too curious about what he's doing.

"You missed it. That smudge is right here." He cups my jaw, swiping at my cheekbone with a delicacy I wouldn't have expected from such a rough and gruff guy. I feel singed heat in the wake of his gentle thumb, and I'm not ashamed to admit that I tilt into his touch, wanting even more of his fire.

Our eyes meet across the distance from mine down low to his, a good foot above me. I swear I hear his chest rattling like he's growling. No, humming. He's humming under his breath, but it's tuneless, just unrelated notes, and I decide that's the sound of his hunger. Like a growling stomach tells you when it's time to eat, this humming is Cowboy's version of 'it's on like Donkey Kong.'

He's going to kiss me.

I know it with every fiber of my being.

I want him to.

I know that just as well.

I lick my lips in preparation, enjoying the way his eyes track the movement, and feel myself lean forward to get closer to him.

I'm not this girl. Not by a long shot.

I'm not the girl in a late-night romance movie who lifts to her toes to reach some guy whose real name I don't even know, especially when I'm wearing steel-toed work boots and shapeless coveralls.

But here I am. And here he is.

And damned if I don't want to kiss him stupid. That cocky confidence tells me he knows what he's doing, and I want to treat myself to a man who knows how to work my body and his own. It's been way too long, and I need orgasms like I need air, I decide. And while a kiss isn't gonna get me there, it'd be a good litmus test to see if I'm right about Cowboy's skills.

He leans down in slow-motion, and I feel surrounded by him,

engulfed not only by his size but his presence. An unsuspecting fish caught in his net.

We're a sliver away, so close I can taste the wet heat of his breath, feel the electricity buzzing between us, that last moment before we both succumb to the base desires running through our bloodstreams.

A loud whirring breaks the moment, and I rock back on my heels, getting an inch of space to breathe my own oxygen instead of Cowboy's. I look over and see that Reed and Manuel have been watching the whole show we are putting on. Not that it was a show, or at least it wasn't yet, but it was definitely something.

Reed's holding an automatic drill in his hand, one he needlessly hit the trigger on to break up my moment, and his eyes are bright with fury and hurt.

*What just happened here?*

Somewhere in the deep, dark recesses of my mind, I already know that I'd be tiny beneath his wide chest, that his thick arms could hold me and toss me around in a *Kama Sutra*'s worth of positions, and that he'd be a good, hard fuck.

I'm picky about who I fuck, but he's checking off boxes left and right. The main one being that my vagina has taken up begging for a taste of his cock with a ferocity that'd embarrass me if anyone else knew how wet I am beneath these hide-everything coveralls.

I step back, sensing that Reed and Manuel reluctantly go back to work. I change tactics with Cowboy.

"Was that a goat?" I lift my chin toward the parking lot, where that big brown truck just pulled away.

His eyes say that I'm not fooling him and he knows exactly what I'm doing, but he goes along with it. "Vincent van Goat. Sophie's taking him back to his owner."

"Sophie?" Goddamn it. I hate that of everything he just said, the woman's name is what I latch onto. But who names their goat after a depressed, self-mutilating artist from the 19th century?

"She's my sister, I guess?"

The question mark on that statement seems odd. "Well, is she, or isn't she? Like by marriage or something?"

His lips quirk as he scratches at the bottom one with his thumb, the same one that swiped at my cheek. "By force, I guess. Long story. But she's a vet, was taking care of the goat. Now he's going home."

I'd bet my right pinkie finger there's a lot more to that story, but to Cowboy, that's enough. The bare bones.

"She take better care of that goat than you do your truck? Boys usually take care of their toys." If Emily said that, it'd sound flirty. When I say it, I sound like I'm giving him a hard time. I don't know how she does that, not that I particularly care to. Or at least, I haven't ever before.

"Bessie's not my truck, like I told you. Belongs to the ranch I work on, and Mark's taken damn good care of her. She's just had a long two decades of rough ranch work and a lot required of her. And yes, I do take care of my truck. Three-year-old Dodge Ram, silver, a good worker. Belonged to my dad before he passed. Mine now." A shadow passes through his eyes, blacker than the darkness that naturally resides there. Oh, there's a story there, but I don't push.

"You take care of your car?" he asks casually, perching on a stool uninvited. He spreads his legs, like he's giving his dick room to breathe, and crosses his arms over his chest. He's posing, I realize. Maybe not on purpose, but subconsciously, at least. My stone-faced cowboy isn't unaffected by me like he wants me to believe. He's posing for me, which gives me a little buzz of sexual giddiness.

I don't let him know that, though. I glare under one raised brow. "Yes, I take good care of my *truck*. It's the billboard for my business." I point out to the lot to my 2017 Ford F150. It's not fancy. It's meant to work, and it does, but I keep it clean and scratch-free, and it runs like a demon from all the extra guts I've put under the hood.

He's about to say something when the breakroom door opens and Emily comes in like a tornado, as always.

"I'm telling you, Rix, I'm not taking no for an answer. We're going to the resort bar tonight so I can find him." It's her sugar-sweet version of an order.

I hold my hand up, trying to stop her rambling interruption, seeing as I'm with a customer. But there's no stopping Emily. She can't see Cowboy from where she's standing and would honestly probably forget her broody asshole if she did catch sight of him. She thinks she met a bad boy to turn into her golden prince, but Cowboy's another creature entirely. He doesn't wear broody like a personality trait. For him, it's just fuck off o'clock twenty-four seven. Except when he's about to kiss me, then it's just fuck-me time.

Emily's heart is fickle and flighty, but she gives it all, wide open every time. And there's nothing she likes better than turning a bad boy good. She's got a line of guys in her wake, each of whom would swear they're better off for having loved her, even though they lost her. She counts her exes as friends and has even gone to some of their weddings when they've moved on from their post-Emily heartache.

There's a tiny stitch somewhere in my chest as I think about Cowboy seeing Emily, though, how he'd look from her to me and choose her. It's happened more times than I can count. Not her fault. She's just the easier edition of our particular model. I'm like the beta test version, with glitches and bugs and no manual.

"He was so hot, and we had a connection, you know? He might've acted like he was immune to my charms, but I like a challenge."

I can't help but smile at her determination. And as long as she's focused on her mystery guy, she won't be up in my business, which is a good thing.

"What about the woman he left with?" I ask carefully.

"The more I think about it, I think they really were siblings or friends or something. He didn't light up when he looked over and saw her, you know that goofy-cute smile guys do when they see their girl? And they weren't holding hands and didn't kiss hello.

Maybe I jumped to conclusions a little bit?" She holds her finger and thumb up an inch apart, looking sheepish.

"Maybe." I agree because that does sound reasonable, though I'm still not sure. Emily is a bit too trusting sometimes, so it's possible that's wishful thinking on her part?

"Mark my words, Rix. We're going to the resort bar again. I'm going to find my broody asshole and make those dark eyes really see me next time. I think I'll wear my red dress, the strapless man-killer one. What do you think?"

A horrible thought occurs to me. An ugly, awful one that I want to deny, but it's sitting right in front of me.

"Dark eyes?" I glance to my side, where Cowboy is watching my side of the exchange with an amused smirk on his face. I realize he can't see Emily over the truck and is happily eavesdropping.

"Yep, so dark they're almost black. Like hot little charcoal briquets."

"At the resort bar a few nights ago?" Brody's brows climb up his forehead. He's sensing something . . . and I wonder if I'm the first in on a big joke. "Beard or clean-shaven?"

"Neither, it was like somewhere in the middle. One of those five o'clock shadow scruffs you want to feel on your thighs."

Brody's lips quirk, and Reed and Manuel stop working at that, Emily's words painting a picture no one can ignore. But she's long since stopped editing herself for Reed and Manuel. They're basically family, and she spends too much time with my foul mouth as a verbal role model.

"He didn't happen to have on a hat, did he?" I ask slowly, not wanting to hear the answer as we dance closer to the danger line.

"Yes! Oh, God, Rix . . . you're so smart! Maybe I can track down the logo, like it's where he works or something. What was on it?" She closes her eyes and rubs at her temples.

I swear to God if she says he was wearing a black hat with a camouflage silhouette of a cow, I'm going to die. Maybe of laughter, maybe of something more sinister.

"A cow! A camo cow . . . that's it."

Brody's eyes go so wide I can see the whites all the way around. He even pulls the hat off his head, double-checking it himself. He curls the brim, something it looks like he does often, and shoves it back on his head. I can't help but smile at the confused look on his face.

Emily stomps her heeled foot. "Don't laugh at me. I'm gonna find him, claim him, spread my legs, and invite him into my life, if you know what I mean." She teases out the last bit seductively.

Reed raises his hand like we're in elementary school again. "I know what you mean, Emily."

I sigh heavily, knowing what I have to do. I'll step aside for her anytime. It's what you do . . . for family.

A painful knot in my belly whispers that he probably thinks I'm her, anyway. If they met at the resort and flirted, when he saw me here today and almost kissed me . . . he would've naturally assumed I was Emily. Flirty and fun and sexy . . . Emily.

That burns hot and sour through my blood, and I'm glad we didn't kiss. Or at least I tell myself I am.

"Hey, Cowboy. Sounds like my sister's a sure thing if you're interested." I try to sound chill and light. I fail to my ears, but no one else seems to notice.

Emily's nose crinkles in confusion. "What?"

Brody stands up, pulling that hat down low over his eyes.

"Oh, my God! It's you!" Happy excitement sweeps her face, but then horror dawns and Emily whirls on me. "Rix! You let me say all that embarrassing stuff!"

"I tried to stop you. A little." I hold my greasy finger and thumb up an inch apart, the same way she did earlier.

Cowboy is looking left and right, right and left, as the realization sinks in. "Sisters . . . twins . . . identical twins. Fuck, that explains so much! At least now I know I'm not crazy." The words are muttered under his breath, and when he looks at me, I swear there's something deep in the darkness of those eyes.

Hurt, maybe? Betrayal? It's gone too fast for me to get a read on it, but I've seen it before. When some guy is chasing Emily and thinks I'm her. The drop in their smiles when they realize I'm the wrong sister still hurts every time. This time, it's a bit sharper, though. It shouldn't be. I just met Cowboy. Hell, I don't even know his name, but that flash in his eyes as he looked between us hurt all the same.

This is why hearts are stupid. This is why I focus on work. I blink slowly, letting the reality of the situation sink in and forcing my heart to steady. I promise my pussy another round with George tonight, but she whines that it's not the same and that she wants the real thing. *Me too, honey.*

But family first. Always.

"Emily, this is Cowboy. Cowboy, this is Emily. I'll leave you to it, I guess." Even telling her my too-obvious nickname for him seems like revealing too much, and I need to get out of here. I can't watch him fawn all over her. Usually, I get a kick out of seeing her charm melt the coldest hearts. But this time, I can't watch.

I force myself to walk to the breakroom, though my feet want to run, even giving Emily a small encouraging smile as I pass her. Poor guy probably won't know what hit him once Emily starts actually flirting. When she gets her mind stuck on something, she's fierce as a firecracker, and I just stand back and ooh and ahh.

*Fuck, they're going to have pretty babies*, I think out of nowhere. I look at my sister, the mirror image of myself, and Cowboy, the sexy, brooding literal definition of tall, dark, and handsome. But he's not that pretty boy kind of handsome. He's got an edge to him. One I hope Emily can handle. Cowboy's not her usual bad boy, that's for sure, and I hope she hasn't bitten off more than she can chew.

My teeth grit together, wishing they could be the ones biting him. But nope, that's not how this plays out. Never has been, never will be. No matter how much I want it to be.

Fuck it. I've got work to do. I grab a candy bar out of the vending machine, gobbling it in too few bites that I don't even taste but hoping it'll get me through the little bit of time left until I can close for the day.

My couch and a beer sound like a damn good plan right now. I could use some company, but only one face comes to mind. One that's out there smiling at my sister's sweet jokes, falling under the spell of her flirty compliments, and probably dropping to his knees to worship her body, so like mine but also not.

I scrub at my cheek, cursing the smudge of grease I know he didn't fully wipe off.

*Fuck.*

# CHAPTER 5

## BRODY

My conversation with Sophie plays back out in my mind at warp speed. Different . . . same . . . two sides of the same coin.

But they're not.

They're twin sisters. There's two of them, which explains so much. I tease apart the last few days . . . the garage, the resort, the almost kiss.

Minutes ago, I was on the verge of kissing Lil Bit. She'd been all wrong at the resort, but back here in the garage, the connection was undeniable. Confusing then. Perfectly understandable now.

And things start to make the barest bit of sense—why one is so fucking fiery and one is like silk. Lil Bit's ball-busting, wrench-wielding venom comes back to me, and I smile. Emily coming on strong at the resort . . . ice cold.

But Emily is smiling like she just found the grand prize at the end of a scavenger hunt, and I think I'm the gold coin.

I want to chase Lil Bit through that door, and normally, I would. Forget the sister, rudely brush past her, and go after what I want.

But Lil Bit left me here, threw me to her sister like I'm a damn baton she can relay to the next person. And I freeze—analyzing, thinking, and getting pissed the fuck off.

I can't anger Emily because I can read the room well enough to know that if I hurt her, Lil Bit will be mad. But I need to shut this shit down, do some dodging and weaving like my football-loving brother. Then I can go for the sister I want.

Emily steps toward me slowly, the wedge sandals on her feet making her slim hips sway with every inch of covered ground. It looks natural, but I'm guessing it takes a hell of a lot of practice to walk in those things. Her skirt shows off her legs, making them look long even though she's as tiny as Lil Bit. She's wearing a bra this time at least, or at least she seems to be, but her long, dark hair is curling over and around her shoulders, so I can't be 100% sure.

She bites her painted lips, the white of her teeth bright against the berry color, and looks up at me through her lashes.

None of it does a damn thing for me.

"So, that was embarrassing. Sorry about that." She waves her hands around, reminding me of what she said about me, about us.

"No problem," I say flatly.

The wrong sister is virtually pissing on my leg like a territorial dog.

If I can't go after Lil Bit, I need to get out of here.

Deciding that this is as good a time as any to skip manners, I ignore Emily and turn to Reed, who's back to watching the drama play out in front of him like we're a damn live reality show. Cowboy Bachelor or some shit, like the girls are vying for a rose from my grumpy ass. Not that I watch that, but Allyson does and sometimes, I overhear. Fine, I might watch a little too. "Got the keys to Bessie?"

"Uh, yeah. Lemme grab 'em." He's slow to turn around, even slower to grab the keys I can clearly see from here. They're hard to miss with a big metal brand of *The Bennett Ranch* on the keyring.

"Should I just keep calling you Cowboy?" Emily asks, honey drizzled over every slow syllable.

"Brody." I only tell her because I've realized I can use the minimal intel to get some of my own. "So your sister's name is Rix?"

"Well, it's Erica, but she's gone by Rix since she was a kid. Trust me, do not call her Erica if you want to stay topside. Pretty sure the last person who called her Erica is buried in a pasture somewhere." Emily laughs at her own joke, but my lips don't even quirk as I store the information away.

I'm not sure why. I need to just go. This is all too messed up, and even if there was something happening, Lil Bit just bolted as soon as her sister showed up.

No, not Lil Bit. Rix. I chuckle darkly inside, knowing that I'll call her Erica at the first opportunity and every one after that too.

Reed raises his brows at me as he gets closer, holding the keys to Bessie out. I open my palm and he tosses them my way. I catch the set easily, closing my fist around it. "Thanks. Mark handled the money stuff, so we good?"

He nods, looking confused. But not as confused as Emily when I move to turn around and get the hell outta dodge.

"Wait!" Her hand goes to my forearm, stopping me. I look down, seeing her clean hands, and wonder how I could've been so stupid. Sophie called me observant, but I know good and well there's no magical lavender vanilla soap that gets working hands that clean.

The proof that something was different was right there in front of my face, and okay, in my jeans too, but I ignored it. I heard hoof-beats and thought horses, the logical explanation being that one woman had a work side and an off-work side. But it'd been zebras, or rather, twins who look alike, but past that, seem to be very different and have wildly polar opposite responses from me on every level. Especially dick level.

"Let's get a drink. My treat, to make up for the awkwardness."

It's on the tip of my tongue to say not just no, but hell no. I had a drink with Emily a few nights ago, and I'm not looking to repeat it.

Right up until Reed butts in.

"Yeah, that's a great idea. You already invited Rix and me, and now Brody can come too. Sounds like a fun night."

Reed's talking to Emily, but I see his eyes cut back toward the door Erica disappeared through.

Emily claps. "That's a great idea! She'll have to come if you're coming."

I get the feeling there's more there than I know. But Erica was just as close to kissing me as I was to kissing her. In fact, if Reed hadn't blasted that drill, I would know what Erica's lips taste like right now. I'm betting sour cherries, something with a little bite to it, just like her.

I square up to Reed, meeting his eyes. The testosterone in the air between us charges. He's not small, probably only an inch or so shorter than me, and he's lean muscle, built from working hard. I'm the same way, never been to a gym in my life, but ranch life has made me wide and strong. The dozens of fights I've been in over the course of my life have made me a tough motherfucker too. If push came to shove, I'm thinking Reed could make company in that pasture with whoever it was who'd called Erica by her full name.

"Yeah. Let's all get a drink."

Emily smiles at the agreement. Reed hears it for what it is, though.

It's on, asshole.

---

THIRTY MINUTES LATER, WE'RE WALKING INTO A BAR. NOT THE resort, thank fuck. Erica had vetoed that with an 'abso-fucking-lutely not,' which I was glad for. Instead, we're at a rundown, black-painted wooden building with a bunch of faded beer signs nailed to the outside. I swear one is for Zima, and I don't think that's been for sale in decades. I remember my mom drinking it a time or two, though, back when I was a kid.

"Seriously, Rix? Can't we go anywhere else?" Emily seems put out by the venue that is rough and rock-oriented and is drastically different from the resort, which is probably more her speed.

"Two Roses or I'm going home. Take it or leave it." Under her breath, she grumbles to herself. "Not sure how I ended up agreeing to this, anyway."

I know how I got here. I'm here for Erica.

On the surface, I feel like I need to protect her from Reed, even though that doesn't really make sense. Hell, he probably needs protection from her, not that I'd interrupt if she took a wrench to his neck.

It's a good cover, though, even though I know the truth.

I'm here to pick at her rough edges and see where she frays, to make her eyes shoot fireworks as she cusses me out, and maybe to find out if I'm right about the sour cherry taste of her lips.

We find a round table and sit down, fate conspiring with me and putting Erica on one side and Emily on the other, with Reed across from me. Look at us, all boy-girl like it's a damn cotillion. I snort inside at the stupid joke, like there's ever been a cotillion out here in podunk country. I've only ever read about them in old historical stories, but the thought that this rock bar would host one makes my lips twist sardonically.

The waitress comes over, her black-dyed hair the same color as her thick-soled knee boots, torn fishnets, skirt, and tank top. The only color she sports is the slash of red lipstick and the neon-green lip ring.

Toto, I'm not in Kansas anymore.

"Hey, Monica. Can we get a pitcher and four glasses?" Erica orders for the table.

Emily cringes, holding up a finger. "Oh, could I get a red wine instead, please?"

Monica's sharpie-thin brow lifts as she looks from Emily to Erica. "Rix, your sister for real?"

"I wish I could say no, but tell Rob to just make her whatever the college girls are drinking these days. Something fruity."

"You make a Great Falls Flyer?" I deadpan.

Emily beams, delighted that I remembered her drink. Erica cuts her eyes to me, narrowing them as she tries to decide whether I'm joking or not. I am, and eventually, she seems to realize the sarcastic bend of my humor because she blinks and lets me out of her laser beam gaze.

Monica laughs. "Yeah, no. But Rob can do *something*, I'm sure." It sounds like whatever Rob is going to mix up is going to be sweet, sugary, and godawful. But Monica goes to fetch it and the beers.

Silence descends on the table, Reed and Emily looking around easily, but the thread between Erica and me is pulled tight, keeping my full focus on her. It might as well be only her and me for all the attention I'm giving her. She's studiously avoiding looking at me, but I've seen her eyes jump my way five times already and we just sat down. She might've pawned me off, but like selling Grandma's ring for the cash, she's not entirely sure about it.

Emily jumps in to fill the stretching quiet easily.

"So, Brody, I know Rix called you *Cowboy*, but what do you actually do?"

"I'm a cowboy." The 'duh' is heavy on the statement. "Work as a ranch hand at the Bennett Ranch on the other side of the mountain, on the outskirts of Great Falls."

Emily blinks. "Oh, wow! I thought she was just kidding. I don't know that I've ever met a real cowboy. What do you do, like ride horses all day and chase cows?"

The question's not nearly as stupid as it sounds. Most people have no idea what being a rancher is actually about, and I don't fault them for not knowing. Not like I know what other people's jobs entail, either. And Emily at least sounds pleasantly interested and is keeping us from awkward silence or a glaring contest with Reed. Even though I'd win that for damn sure.

"Yeah, ride horses or ATVs, sometimes the Gator. Take care of the herd, move 'em from pasture to pasture for grazing, keep 'em healthy to make it to market, keep the fences mended and secure. It's a sunup to sundown job, with no end in sight. It's hard work, but

I couldn't do anything else. Been doing this since I was a kid." Look at me with whole sentences and small talk. I'm like a regular Chatty Cathy over here.

Emily hangs on every word, but so does Erica, though she's trying hard to hide that fact. Reed's looking for that beer, which Monica sets down in the middle of the table with a thunk.

"Here ya go, Rix's sis." She sets down a pink frozen drink in a beer glass. It's got an orange slice on the rim as decoration, something I bet Rob rarely does. "It don't got a name, but Rob mostly kept track so if you like it, he can probably make another about the same."

Emily smiles at Monica sweetly. "Thank you." She takes a sip through the straw, her lips puckering in a way that should have my dick standing up and taking notice. But nothing's happening south of my belt buckle. She swallows and hums, "Oh, that's good!" She leans back to see the bar, where Rob is looking over uncertainly. But when Emily smiles and lifts her glass, mouthing 'thank you' before taking another apparently heaven-inducing sip, he melts for her. Even from here, you can see him fall under her sway.

I wonder if that's what she's used to. I wonder why it's not working on me.

Monica pours the rest of us our first round. Erica must need a drink to handle this little outing because she taps her glass lightly to the table and upends it, chugging the whole thing in one go. She finishes with a sigh, swiping the foam off her mouth with her fingers.

And my dick is rock fucking hard.

If she can guzzle a beer like that, throat open and swallowing reflexively, I know for damn sure she can do it with my cock stuffed down her throat, her nose buried against my belly. And that is a sight I desperately want to see.

I lift my glass her way. "Impressive." I take a healthy swallow of my own beer. It's not Budweiser, but something light. Might as well be water. I could probably drink this pitcher alone and not feel a damn thing.

Emily gapes at Erica. "Manners." She hisses the admonishment, but it's with a laugh. Shaking her head, she looks at Reed. "I swear our parents taught us manners. Rix has just forgotten how to use them because all she does is hang out with burping and farting boys all the time."

Reed grins at the excuse, like it's an inside joke between the three of them. "I know. She just needs a reason to behave." He winks at Erica flirtily, expecting a smile back.

She burps instead, looking pleased with herself.

I can't help but laugh, which sucks because I'm halfway through a drink and I get a little gagged as the beer-water goes down the wrong pipe. I sputter, and Emily pats me on the back. Pretty sure she's feeling my muscles too. I watch Erica for any sign of jealousy, but she's stone-faced.

"You okay there, Brody? I know she's rough, but don't let her get you choked up."

I keep my eyes on her, but Erica's moved on to ignoring me completely, pouring herself another glass.

"I'm good," I grumble, my voice rougher than usual from the coughing fit. I take another sip to smooth it over.

Reed jumps in this time, taking the conversational softball. "So, a cowboy, two mechanics, and a car salesman walk into a bar . . ." It sounds like he's starting a joke, but I deduce he's talking about us.

"Car sales*woman*," Emily corrects with a giggle, reminding me of Sophie, and Reed smiles. Seems like that's another inside joke. She explains to me as the newcomer, "That's the family deal. If Rix can't fix your car, I'll sell you a new one. Our whole family, basically everyone we know, is all about cars. So please, can we talk about something else—anything else—for a change?" She's begging me to be the subject changer, but I'm fascinated by a whole family that's car-oriented the way mine is cow- and crop-oriented.

"How'd you end up all about cars?" I ask the question to Erica because she hasn't said a word since her friendly chatter with Monica.

"Our dad," Emily answers, not even giving Erica a chance. It doesn't seem rude, though, more like it's their usual MO of conversational flow. I'm betting Emily often takes the focus and responsibility off Erica, in a 'I've got you, Sis' sort of way. It's familiar, like the way Shayanne always chatters away to make up for my selective conversational skills. "He ran the garage for thirty years, brought us up right there in the grease and grime. Reed too." Reed nods agreeably at what seem to be pleasant memories. "They ended up grease monkeys. I got out . . . in a way. But the best salespeople sell what they know. And I know cars."

Erica snorts at that. "You memorize the spec sheets, Em. That's different from knowing what makes them tick."

Emily grins at her sister's dig, and I can see the affection between them. It's like how I tell my brothers that I love them by swapping shots with them . . . just fewer punches and more words.

"You're just jealous because I get employee discounts on a new car every two years. Think I'll get a Mustang next time." She's teasing, dangling an invisible carrot over Erica's head. Or maybe, invisible keys.

Erica sets her beer down, leaning forward with one elbow on the table, her chin resting on her fist. Her excitement pulls me into her orbit. "A Shelby? And so help me, if you say no, I'm gonna tell Dad you're pussing out."

Emily's smile falters at the edges. "No, not a Shelby. Even with a discount, I can't do that. Not even a 350."

"What's the price difference between a 350 and a 500?" Reed asks, but something tells me he already knows. Good for him if he does, because I have no fucking idea.

"Retail? A 500 starts around $73K, a 350 around $60K. Doesn't matter, though, because Dad wouldn't let me drive one. I'd get in too much trouble." She looks to me, trying to involve me again in their car chatter. But unless it runs on diesel and has a John Deere logo on it, I've got almost no idea. "I've got the family lead foot and love for speed, but putting me behind the wheel with enough horsepower to go zero-to-sixty in three seconds is a death sentence. I don't have the technical skills to control that like Rix does."

I'm about to ask a follow-up question on that, but the jukebox roars to life, overtaking any conversation with a loud bass line and a guy screaming from what sounds like the deep, dark, demon-infested depths of his soul. Still, I store the information about Rix's apparent driving skills and the family trait for speed.

"What is this?" Emily says, her shoulders bunching up to her ears. "Sounds like a monster screeching for mercy!"

Erica tilts her head, listening easily. "Mudvayne. *Dig*. 90s metal —no . . . maybe early 2000s. Good stuff." Each bit is punctuated and sharp so we can hear the sound bites over the music.

It's not that loud now that I've adjusted to it, not like the garage music volume, but it is harsh on the ears. Definitely not Johnny Cash, though Erica is tapping out the rhythm on her beer glass like it's her jam.

Engines. Cars. Heavy rock music. Sarcasm. Biting quips. Beer. Wrenches as weapons.

An image is starting to form. But there's more to Erica.

Freckles. Fiery sass. A sense of humor that zings with excitement. Tiny body I want to hold as I bury myself in her. Hair I want to wrap around my fist. A mouth I want to taste.

"I think I'll see if there's anything more . . . well, less screamy. Any requests?" Emily asks me. "Or you could just come see what speaks to you? Maybe we can find something to dance to."

Her nod to the jukebox is an open invitation to more. But it's one I need to close the door on quickly because I'm not interested in door number one with Emily. I'm all about getting behind a closed door with Erica.

"Don't dance. Don't care for rock either, so whatever." I'm intentionally short, my tone flat as I try to let her down easy. Or at least help her see that I'm an asshole she should avoid.

But she just smirks, like I'm playing hard to get, as she gets up from the table and goes toward the jukebox.

"Hey, Reed, go tell Monica that we need to close out." Not a question, an order. He blinks, looking at her with puppy dog eyes that tell me he wants to please her, and then to me, his blue eyes going frosty in warning. I smirk back, knowing my cockiness is needling him like a thorn in his side.

"Be right back." I swear, he virtually runs for the bar.

"What the hell, Cowboy?" She doesn't use my name, though I know she knows it now. It irks me, so I do it back to her, figuring she'll feel just as prickly about it.

"Whatcha talking about, Lil Bit?" My thumb scrapes my lower lip as I smile her way. This smile has dropped panties damn near every time I use its powers for bad, dirty things. Erica is completely unfazed.

"Don't be a dick to my sister. She's into you, and you damn well know it. I'm trying to help you out here, but I won't let her be some notch on your bedpost. *Don't fuck her over.*" The order is punctuated with a pointed finger and a heavy glare of warning.

"That usually work for you?" At her raised brow, I clarify. "Barking orders at people. Get me this . . . and Reed runs off to do it. I'll only go to this bar . . . and here we sit. People usually do what you tell them to?" I'm actually curious, not giving her shit. Okay, maybe I am a little bit, but I do want to know the real answer too.

"It works better when they do. So again, don't fuck her over."

I glance at Emily, who's scanning the listings on the jukebox like something Top 40 is going to magically appear. "I've got no intention of it."

Which is true. I have no plans of fucking Emily over—or fucking her, period. I have about thirty different plans already sorted by priority for Erica, though.

She's shrewd, and her full lips press into a flat, no-nonsense line. "Intending to and not doing it are different. Just don't."

We lock eyes, and the tension between us swirls and morphs, anger and questions turning to heat and lust. She's working hard to hide hers. Mine is all out there and bold.

Reed shows back up with four split checks in hand, intentionally breaking between Erica and me to interrupt the eye-fuck. I reach over, taking the papers from him. "I've got it."

Erica starts to argue, and I'm guessing she usually picks up the tab. But I shoot her a hard look, adding, "My treat for getting Bessie fixed up."

She softens slightly and allows it. I get the sense that's not something she does often, and I want to strut around like a damn peacock. For her letting me buy her a beer. What the hell kind of twisted magic has she worked on me? I don't know, but I want another spell of it.

I hold the check and cash up for Monica, who appears in an instant. "Thanks, Monica. Keep the change."

She glances down quickly, verifying that I haven't shorted her. "Ooh, Rix. This one's a keeper." She winks her heavily black-rimmed eye at me. "Come back anytime, Rix's friend. With or without her."

Reed looks sullen, his arms crossed over his chest and his face thunderous, like he can fight his way into being the alpha here.

He's into Erica, I get that, and it sounds like there's some history there. Maybe. But despite his best puppy dog efforts, Erica's on my hook. So are Emily and Monica, but I only want one woman right now . . . Lil Bit.

Erica hollers out, "Em! We're out!"

Emily's relief is visible from here, and as she gets closer, she huffs. "Thank God. There are barely five songs on that jukebox I even know. And they all make me think of Dad and cleaning tools." She laughs, and I try to imagine her as a snot-nosed kid with greasy hands from wiping down wrenches. The picture doesn't come, though somehow, I can see Erica doing it. Makes no sense, but it's the truth all the same.

# CHAPTER 6

## ERICA

I'm torn. I need to stay, make sure that Emily gets in her car okay and doesn't let her stupid heart lead her into doing something she'll regret. Like Brody. On the other hand, I want to leave because I cannot watch him fall for her, even if it's just for a minute. And especially if he really is her *One*.

Reed heads to his truck, parked down a couple of spots, waving goodbye and keeping a close lookout for anything sketchy. But he heard my dismissal of 'see you tomorrow' and always aims to please, doing as I say, like Brody noticed.

Brody opens Emily's door for her, a gentlemanly gesture that doesn't mesh with the asshole he's been most of the night. Emily's been her usual self, flirty and friendly, able to easily carry the conversational weight. Brody's barely grunted at her, focusing more on me until she's getting in her car, and he's suddenly being nice. Suspicion blooms hot in my belly.

*Don't, Emily. Not yet. You don't even know this guy. Make him work for it, at least.*

He closes her door, slapping the roof of her small SUV, the last vehicle she bought with her discount. He steps out of her way so she can pull out of the spot, but he's standing right in front of my truck so I can't move. He watches her pull out and then turns, and I feel like a deer caught in the headlights, but his eyes aren't bright. No, they're dark and full of filthy promises.

He runs his hand across the hood the way I want it to run over my skin as he comes to my window, and I roll it down. "What?" I bite out.

He shrugs casually. "Just wanted to say goodnight, Erica."

"No one calls me that." I'm continuing with the bitch-fest, apparently.

That cocky grin is full of so much arrogance, I'm surprised he can even stand upright from the weight of his ego. "No one but me."

I saw a video once where a kid was putting rubber bands around a watermelon, one after another, getting tight as a belt around the melon's middle until it burst in a rain of red guts and juice. I can feel those rubber bands surrounding us, pushing us together as it gets tighter and tighter, on the edge of . . . something. A kiss, maybe?

We were close earlier. But I can't—won't—do that to Emily.

"'Bye, Cowboy."

He touches the brim of his filthy ballcap. "Goodnight, Lil Bit."

I can't help but watch him swagger across the row to Bessie. In the light of my headlights, I can trace the wide breadth of his shoulders, the taper down to his waist, the full roundness of his ass in those dirty work jeans, and his long, thick legs. I'll give him this—he looks good coming, but damn, does he look even better going when you can't see that knowing spark in his eyes.

He climbs in the truck, slamming the door with a finality that irritates me for some reason. The window being down is the only reason I hear the click-click-click when he tries to start Bessie.

"Sonofabitch!" I hear him spit out. His window must be down too.

I sigh to myself, looking up at the headliner of my truck and beyond. "You testing me? Because this is so not right." Still, I get out and trace his steps across the parking lot. I lean against his door with my hip, not able to reach the window frame with my forearm like he did, and cross my arms casually.

Not a care in the world, see? Everything's fine, just fucking peachy.

Except it's not.

Because it's just the two of us in this dark lot now, and though my brain is screaming that he's off limits, my body doesn't give a shit. It just wants his, and heat pools low in my belly.

He turns his head to glare at me, but I'm well aware that he watched every step of my approach in the side mirror. Those eyes promise punishment . . . to Bessie? To me? I'm not sure which.

"Pop the hood. I'll take a look."

He reaches down, pulling the lever with a pop, and I push off the truck to walk to the front. After releasing the safety latch, I climb up on the bumper, balancing on my toes to lift the hood into place. A quick check tells me it's probably the battery.

I glance back before I jump down and see Brody right in my landing zone. His eyes are locked on me, tracing along my skin. I can feel it now, from my boots, up the bare backs of my thighs, to my nonexistent ass that's sticking out as I bend over the truck to work. I can't decide whether I'm glad I changed from my coveralls into cutoff shorts and a T-shirt for this little forced outing or wishing I had them back on to hide my skin from the heat of his gaze.

He's not the least bit embarrassed to be caught looking and boldly looks more, daring me to call him out on it.

He reaches for me, big hands wrapping around my waist before I can string together a sentence to refuse. He lifts me off the truck like I weigh nothing, lowering me toward the ground. But he takes his time, letting every inch of me rub along the hard planes of his body. Through the layers of clothes, I feel the tightness of his abs, the bite of his belt buckle against my body, and the bulge beneath it. His hands tighten incrementally as my toes hit terra firma, not letting me go. I'm a little unsteady myself and lean against him, though I'd never admit that. Not even in a court of law under oath. *Nope, I don't recall it that way, Your Honor.*

"I'll have to jump you off . . ." Why has that never sounded so damn sexual before? I rush to finish my thought. "And you can follow me back to the shop. I can drop a new battery under Bessie's hood in a few minutes and have you on your way."

My voice has gone cold and flat, a defensive mechanism I picked up a long time ago.

I've done this dance before. And one of two things is going on here. Option one, he's decided I'll be a good stand-in replacement for Emily, though he doesn't need one because she's just this side of throwing herself at him. Or option two . . . there's a certain subset of guys that has twin fantasies, something about double the pleasure, double the fun. As if we're damn Doublemint gum. No one ever considers that for their twin fantasy to happen, it means me having a sex-moment with my sister, and that's some fucked-up shit. I love Emily, but never do I want to know what sounds she makes or what her O-face looks like. I won't say I've never done it in front of a mirror, but that's actually me, not another person who just looks like me.

Brody hasn't exactly been flirting with us both. He's actually been pretty quiet all evening, but he was being all gentlemanly putting Emily in her car and now he's holding me like he's got plans already formed in his mind . . . and his pants. And he's got that bad boy charm that says he'd be down for just about anything. '*Oh, by the way . . . I saw this thing one time . . .*' and we're back to Doublemint territory.

He lets go of my waist, the evening chill thankfully replacing the warmth of his hands and reminding me of something important. Emily. Not that I forgot, but maybe just a little, for a second.

"Sounds good."

I step around him, shoulder bumping him in that douchebag-dude way that says 'you're so unimportant, I didn't even see you there' and stride to my truck. It starts up easily and I pull up next to Bessie.

I make quick work of the cables and jump Bessie off, her diesel roar loud in the night air.

"Follow me," I order before hopping up in my truck and slamming the door. He can do it or not, his choice. Because I've already made mine.

Brody is Emily's.

And no Doublemint shit.

---

I REMIND MYSELF AGAIN AN HOUR LATER.

Brody is Emily's.

But after we got back to the garage and I did the quick change on the battery, promising I'd only charge for the battery itself and not labor, we're still sitting here. The music is low, a playlist from my dad that's mostly 70s rock, and as the guitar riffs of Kansas's *Carry On My Wayward Son* wash over me, so do Brody's eyes.

Again.

When he looks at me that way, the reminder about Emily gets lost in the static in my head. I'm a good sister. Hell, I'm mostly a great sister, but bad thoughts are taking shape.

Dirty, filthy, sexy thoughts that I should not be having about the guy my sister wants.

I sip at my beer, knowing this one is decidedly stouter than the watered-down piss they serve at Two Roses.

"Don't you need to go?" I shouldn't ask. I should order him to leave. Normally, I would, but apparently, I'm going soft in my old age. I'm only twenty-six, but apparently, that's old enough to be ruining my reputation as a hard-nosed bitch.

"No." Brody doesn't move a muscle, sitting in a duct-tape covered office chair that Reed usually claims. That seems ironic to me, given their pissing match to see who the Alpha at the bar was.

Newsflash: it's me. I'm the Alpha.

And anyone who doesn't think that's possible can check their misogyny at the door. I've had to fight my way through everything that's been thrown at me, not just a woman in a man's world, but a tiny, cute woman. If I had a nickel for every man who's called me 'baby', I'd be a rich bitch, sitting on a pile of silver, taking dead shot aim at the fuckers below who got me there. Every one of them underestimated me, but they'd learned not to.

At Dad's garage, in the Army, and then back again, when it was my turn to take over Cole Automotive.

Now I wonder if Brody's underestimating me too as he watches me carefully. Every once in a while, his left eye squints a bit like he's looking beneath my surface. It's an itchy, uncomfortable sensation, like scrubbing at a rash. You know it's a bad idea, but it feels so good that you do it anyway.

"You always sit like that? Manspread like your dick needs breathing room?" He's sitting in Reed's chair with his thighs wide apart, dick on display again.

"Maybe. You always sit like that? Like you're airing your cunt out?" He lifts his beer my way, pointing with the neck, and I look down at my legs, crisscrossed in front of me in the chair. They're so short my knees still fit between the armrests.

I don't flinch a bit at the crass language, overly used to it. Those same guys who call me 'baby' are the types to try and make me squirm with commentary on my pussy. As if the mere word would make me clutch my nonexistent pearls. Something about Brody's tone is different, though. Like he's not trying to make me uncomfortable but is actually just thinking about my cunt. Maybe the way I'm thinking about his dick.

I go offensive to play the asshole-odds, though. "Yep. Gets hot in the coveralls, working and sweating my balls off all day. A little air feels nice." I use my hand as a fan, flapping air toward my hot (but not because of my coveralls) core.

He chuckles deep in his belly, a grin slashing across his face that flashes his white teeth. He doesn't smile, I realize. He smirks, he grins, and he bares his teeth. But there's something predatory about him even in this relaxed state.

Emily's going to be in over her head with this one. Hell, I might be too. Not that I'm thinking about that . . . because he's Emily's.

"I started riding horses when I was a kid. It probably fucked with my hip sockets because this is just how I sit." He shifts in the chair, the fake leather creaking beneath him, and tries to rearrange his legs. He ends up with one ankle resting on the other knee, taking up exactly zero less space.

I snort derisively at his ridiculousness. It's cute, in a dangerous sort of way. I finish the last dregs of my beer, tossing it toward the empty recycling bin. I don't even follow its arc with my eyes, trusting that the same shot I've made a thousand times will sink this time too. It clatters against the bottom of the rubber bin.

"I am such a dumbass," he says out of nowhere.

"Not arguing that fact," I interrupt, not able to skip the lobbed softball opening. "Any specific reason?"

"I can't believe I thought she was you."

Wait . . . that should be the other way around. People mistake me for Emily. Always. And they're disappointed when I'm the wrong sister, the prickly, bitchy one.

"I even asked Sophie about it because I didn't get how you could be so different here and at the resort." He's talking out loud, but I get the feeling it's really to himself as he puts puzzle pieces together. I've seen this show before so I quietly wait him out. "And now it all makes convoluted sense."

"Yep, we're freaks of nature. Identical twins, eighth wonders of the world. And no, we're not into threesomes." Might as well crush that dream. *Sorry, not sorry, Cowboy.*

He blinks blankly before his eyes go razor-sharp. I'm pinned in place like a bug, but I'm not a butterfly, pretty but helpless. I'm a goddamn hornet, so I stare right back.

"Me neither. I don't share well." He growls the heavy, weighted words, giving them deeper meaning.

The air gets sucked out of the room like a black hole just opened up between us, around us, inside us.

"You thought Emily was me. At the resort?" I need clarity like I need my next breath. Fuck that. I need clarity like I need dick. But I won't be a stand-in for him to pretend that he's fucking my sister.

That's one boundary I've never crossed, and I have zero intention of ever doing so.

"Seems stupid now, but yeah." He licks his lips, and I want to taste his tongue. Hell, I want to ride his tongue.

I stand suddenly. "Leave." I shouldn't soften the order, but for some reason, I add, "Please."

He stands slowly, like he's in no hurry to comply. He drains his beer, and I expect him to toss it to the bin the way I did, an answer to my own skill like he can't let me have one over him. But he sets it down on my desk quietly. A win for me then, but it feels like such a loss.

He stalks toward me, or maybe toward the door. I'm not sure, even though I'm watching his every move closely, looking for meaning and intention in every nuance. He backs me up, two small steps of give. A win for him too as my spine meets the bed of my truck.

I should feel threatened. I should be grabbing for the closest weapon and attacking him. Hell, I should punch out and catch him in the balls to drop him to his knees like I've been trained to do.

I do none of those things.

To my shame and horror, my voice is quiet as a whisper. "What's my name?"

"Erica." He groans the one name no one has ever called me and then covers my mouth with his.

This is not a kiss. This is him shoving his tongue into my mouth to show me how he wants to fuck me.

Me! Not Emily.

Guilt rushes through me, but when he cups my face in his big hands, lifting me to my toes so he doesn't have to bend down so much, all I feel is wild. A scrape along the floor tells me he's grabbed my stepstool, and when he deposits me on it, I battle against the urge to wrap my legs around him. Instead, I use the new height to angle myself up to him, kissing him back as aggressively as he's devouring me.

I don't submit to him. That's not my way. It's not his, either.

Instead, we invade each other with our tongues but only succeed in setting fire to the thin shred of resistance either of us held.

He tastes like beer and bad choices, and when he bites my lip gently, I return the nibble ferociously, leaving the wet heat of his mouth to bite the tanned skin of his neck. I pull at the collar of his T-shirt to expose the thick muscle where his neck joins his shoulder and bite there too.

"Goddamn, Lil Bit." His hissed curse might mean stop, but since he's thrust his fingers into my hair, holding me to his neck, I'm pretty sure it didn't. I suck it sweetly to soothe the sharp nip, but it only creates another type of ache. A deeper one.

His hands mold over my body, learning every angle because there are very few curves to be had. But he doesn't seem to mind at all. He's not gentle, which I appreciate. Sometimes, guys see me as this tiny, fragile thing and touch me like I'll break if they go too rough. Brody has no such hesitation, kneading my skin and muscles hard as he takes my mouth again.

I'm about to fuck him right here against the bed of my truck. It won't be the first time I've had sex in this garage. I lost my virginity in bay three in a Toyota Corolla. And it won't be the last time either, most likely, but I realize one important fact.

I can't do this to Emily.

Shit. Fuck. Damn.

I've already betrayed my sister with this so-much-more than a kiss, but I won't, can't do this to her.

It takes too much work to clear the fogginess in my mind enough to find words, so I push at Brody. He fights it at first, thinking it's part of our battle to consume each other, so I push again. Hard this time.

He steps back, confusion written in the frown lines around his mouth. "What?"

His voice has gone so deep and dark that I can feel it in my core. I clench tightly, feeling empty and knowing damn well that he could fix that. With his fingers, his tongue, and that thick cock I felt against my belly.

"Emily." A reminder for myself and the only word I can find the clarity to say.

"What about her?" He's breathing hard, chest rising and falling as I watch, feeling a sense of pride that I've pushed him to his limits.

"She . . . likes you." I'm well aware it sounds stupid and juvenile, but it's the truth of what's stopping me.

"She can't call dibs on me." It makes me ridiculously pleased that he doesn't take the childish phrase lightly. Sibling relationships are a delicate thing, and I'm known for being more bulldozer than dancer, but I'm trying here. God, I'm trying so hard. "And if we're playing games of who saw whom first—I met *you* first, liked *you* first, wanted *you* first."

Oh, the dirty ideas his words make me think of.

I can feel the heat on my cheeks, which pisses me off. I'm not fair-skinned, but something tells me Brody sees the blush all the same. His nose traces the line of my cheekbone to my ear. "Wanna hear it again?" He pauses, and I don't dare move, desperately wanting to hear whatever he's going to say. "I want you, Erica. Just you. Only you."

I shudder, not realizing until this moment how much that means to me.

I love my sister to the very depths of my soul. I swear I do. And we're not competitive in the least, mostly because I do my own thing and she does hers. We're so different, but she's . . . Emily. Homecoming queen, sweet and pretty, the one guys always go for.

But this time, the guy wants . . . me. Rude, crude, bitchy, sarcastic, aggressive . . . me.

And there's a tiny little sliver that revels in that. But even though it's small, it's there. What to do with that is my choice, though, and I won't be the sister who steals the other one's guy. Even if Brody's not really hers to begin with.

I place a staying hand on his chest, feeling his racing pulse beneath my palm. He's just as affected by this as I am, which heats my blood anew. "I need to talk to Emily first."

He kisses my cheek—and I mourn that it's not my lips—before his forehead lands on the top of my head. "Can you call her now or something? I was hoping to be balls deep in you already."

He's teasing, I think. It's hard to tell, but I laugh anyway as I push him back. "I was planning on being full of cock myself. You can deliver that, right, Cowboy?"

He groans and pushes his hips against me, proving that he can definitely deliver.

"I'll talk to her tomorrow."

His answering sigh is ragged. "Shit."

Yep, that about sums it up.

"You should go. I'll call you after I talk to her, one way or another." I don't think about what I'm going to do if Emily says she's got some claim on Brody. Don't think about that option at all. I'm a fighter, but not against my sister. I won't let anything come between us, sisters before misters and all that rah-rah.

He grabs a pen off my desk and carefully writes his number down on a piece of paper. Mr. Nguyen will just have to understand why there are extra notes on his invoice. "Call me, Erica." The order both bristles and excites me, contrary sensations but there all the same.

Brody looks me up and down once more, and I can feel that magnetic pull yanking us together, but he holds strong and moves toward the door instead of me. He gives in and glances back once, though, and I can see the hungry fire still burning in his eyes.

I'm almost pissed that Bessie starts up easily this time, even though I knew she would because I did the work. But if she'd stalled out again, Brody would've come back in and we could've . . .

*No, it's a good thing*, I think as she roars into the night, taking Brody away from me. But I'm left feeling cold and horny.

Shit.

# CHAPTER 7

## ERICA

I can do this. I'm such a raging bitch of a sister, but I can do this at least. I knock on the door with my free hand and take a fortifying breath as I hear the footsteps on the other side.

The door swings open and I see the surprise on Emily's face a split second before she exclaims, "Rix? What are you doing here?"

Back ramrod straight, I stare her down like she's the firing squad tasked with my execution. "We need to talk. I brought wine and ice cream." I hold up the brown paper bag as proof. And bribery. Not that I have to bribe her to talk to me, but maybe to not kill me.

"*Okaaay*, everything okay?" She shakes her head. "Obviously not, because you're here with wine, which I know you hate with the flames of a thousand suns. So get in here and break it to me."

She ushers me in, taking the bag of goodies. "Em, I—"

"Nope, not yet." She gives me her back to grab two glasses from the cabinet and a wine opener. The pop of the cork on the pinot noir the lady at the liquor store recommended when I told her I hate wine sounds like a gunshot to my jumpy nerves.

Emily takes a healthy swig from her glass and holds mine out to me. I take it but don't drink. I don't deserve for the alcohol to soften the sharp edges of what I'm about to confess. I need to be fully present and feel every bite of the guilt.

"So . . . are Mom and Dad okay?"

I blink. "What? Yeah, they're fine. I mean, they were when I talked to Dad a few days ago. This is something else."

I don't know where to start . . . when Cowboy brought Bessie in? When I introduced him to Emily? Last night when he kissed the shit outta me?

"Did you re-enlist? I'm going to kill you before Uncle Sam gets his hands on you again, girl." Emily growls the threat and I know she means it.

I hate that of the two worst-case scenarios she defaults to, one is that something's wrong with our parents and the other is that I'm leaving again. But I know why.

We'd been so close, always telling each other everything back then. But I hadn't told her I was even considering enlisting and certainly hadn't told her I'd done it until it was almost time for me to go. And that had been the worst betrayal of our sisterhood, putting a wedge between us I still haven't been able to fully repair. But I'm trying now like she'd tried to understand then.

*"What do you mean you're going into the Army?" Emily laughs like I just told her a hilarious joke. When I don't laugh along, she sobers. "Wait, are you serious?"*

*I nod, grabbing her hands in mine as I stare into eyes I know so well, begging her to understand. "Look around, Em. We're on the verge of freedom, and you get to go to school and have all these adventures. You'll probably go to frat parties, meet some popped collar trust-fund bro, and he'll whisk you to his family's summer house in the Hamptons. Or you'll fall for a leather-clad bad boy who spouts poetry and draws Sharpie tattoos on your back after you have dirty sex in a bed he hasn't changed the sheets in for way too long."*

*Her nose scrunches up. "That's gross, Rix."*

*"But the point is . . . you don't know. And that's awesome and amazing, and freeing, and . . ."*

*"Terrifying? I think that's the word you're looking for because I feel like you've got it all together while I'm floundering with zero clue what the hell I'm doing. And now you're just going to shit on it? On Dad? On Reed? By running away to join the Army?" She's mad, which I get, but I'd hoped she'd support me.*

*I try to find a way to explain that I had this moment where I'd looked around and could feel the rest of my life closing in on me. Dad's been talking about me going full-time at the shop, which I want, and making jokes about father-daughter dances at the wedding, which I don't. I think Reed is only waiting for graduation to be done with before he proposes. Hell, I wouldn't put it past him to propose at graduation.*

*And I don't want that life.*

*I want to be young and reckless. I want to drive fast cars and do dangerous shit. I want to decide for myself who I'm going to marry and when.*

*Everyone else is in a rush to get me settled down, especially Dad. I know why, and my enlisting is going to push every one of his panic buttons. That's why I need Emily on my side, a united front.*

*I need him to see that I'm strong, independent, and fierce enough to do whatever it takes to get my way. Even if it means . . . leaving.*

*"It's not forever. Just for a few years . . ."*

It damn near killed everyone but me when I left the first time, and every visit home after that ended with them begging me to stay even though they knew I couldn't. The only person happier than Mom and Dad when I got out was Emily.

And now I'm shitting on our sisterhood again.

"No, not that either." I shake my head, stalling as long as I can. But her eyes narrow as she runs out of guesses. "It's about Brody."

"Oh . . . Cowboy Brody . . ." She sighs out breathily as her hand lays over her heart.

Shit. Fuck. Damn.

I'm the worst sister ever. But I'm ready to take my lumps so I jump in.

"Last night, when we were leaving Two Roses, his truck wouldn't start. I had to jump it off there, and then he followed me back to the garage so I could drop a new battery in. I guess sitting in the lot for a few days was too much for the old battery." I'm adding unnecessary details, but ripping the Band-Aid off slowly seems kinder somehow. Not to Emily, but to myself.

"Anyway, after I did the battery, we got to talking and one thing led to another . . ." I trail off, and Emily's eyes go so wide I can see the whites all the way around.

"Oh, my God! You slut! You slept with him!"

The words and sentiment are exactly what I expected, and shame fizzles in my bloodstream. What I didn't expect was the look on Emily's face. She looks . . . excited? But that can't be right.

"No, no. I didn't sleep with him, but he kissed me. Well, *we* kissed. I think it was a kiss. It seemed more like mouth fucking. Is that a thing? Because if it is, that's what we did. He fucked my mouth."

I'm rambling with nerves. Know what I never do? Ramble.

That kiss-slash-mouth fuck must've scrambled my brains. It's the only logical explanation.

I bury my face in my hands, another thing I don't do. I'm not a hider. I'm a face hard shit head-on girl. Even when I left, it was because I was facing down a future I didn't want and choosing something else. I hadn't hidden then, and I'm not hiding now. I mumble into my hands despite my arguments to the contrary about my nature. "I'm sorry, Em. I didn't mean for it to happen like that. Truly, I'm sorry."

"Why are you apologizing?" I peek through my fingers to see confusion knitting her brows together, and I'm betting she looks a whole lot like me right now, confused as hell.

I lift my head, steeling my back as I lower my shoulders, ready to be brave. Or at least fake it. "Because you like him, and I swear I'm not a shitty sister who goes around poaching, especially not from you." I inject every bit of earnest truth I can into the proclamation, only to have her laugh in my face.

"Rix. Honey. I don't care," she says sweetly, her laugh almost tinkling.

Of course, she's being sweet. That's who Emily is.

"Of course you care. I'm sorry. I won't see him again." Why does that sting a little? I barely know Brody, just met him, honestly, but there's a little puff of smoky sadness like a matchstick getting blown out inside me at the thought of never mouth-fucking him again.

Emily shrugs casually, as if my betrayal of the oath of sisterhood is no big deal. But I know good and well that it is. "Rix, I don't care. He didn't seem that into me at Two Roses anyway, and now I know why. That man likes 'em dirty, just like you." She makes 'dirty' sound like a compliment, right before she slaps her forehead. "Which reminds me that he was trying to figure out how I got my hands clean . . . because he thought I was you!"

She seems delighted at that and laughs like a twin switcheroo is the funniest thing ever. I think Brody would beg to differ. I would too.

"We're good. Go get you some of that cowboy." She shoves at my shoulder with a smile. "Just make sure you tell me *all* the dirty details, each and every inch of them." Her wink is silly and reminds me of those easier days when we were thick as thieves.

"You mean it? I swear, say the word and I'll never talk to him." I sound like I've already made up my mind, but Emily knows me well enough to see right through my front.

Emily freezes, her mouth hanging open before she sets her glass down on the coffee table so hard I'm surprised it doesn't shatter. The glass, not the table, because it's wood. And these glasses must be industrial strength. I'm rambling again, but only in my head now.

"I should beat the ever-loving shit out of you." This is what I expected, but I don't let my hands ball up. Not against her. I'll take the blows, knowing that I deserve them. She throws a sissy shot at my shoulder, more of a tap than a punch, but it's probably all she's got. "You like him! But you set me up with him. What the hell?"

"You said he was *The One*, and I wasn't going to get in the way of that." I'm still apologizing.

She rolls her eyes. "I say that every week, sometimes twice on Sunday if Mr. Saturday Night had particularly good oral skills." She's kidding, I think. She might fall in love all the time, but she's pickier than I am about who she fucks, usually only opening her legs after dating someone for a long while. "But you? You never chase down dick, and the one time you feel like it, you pawn him off on me because I'm mouthing around again?"

Both her hands go to my shoulders, and she shakes me so hard that my teeth clatter together. "Stop it. For the love of fuck, nobody needs you to martyr yourself to make up for years-old shit. If you want your Cowboy, climb on and yee the hell outta his haw. I'll find my own cowboy. Or lawyer. Or poet."

A thought seems to hit her out of nowhere, bringing a big smile to her face. "Or . . . random subject change . . . unrelated to our present conversation." She winks, letting me know that it's right on topic. "Have you met the new doctor in town? He came in to get a new vehicle yesterday, and let me tell you, those scrubs were doing all kinds of good things for his ass. Did I mention he's a doctor? With eyes the color of the sky on a summer day? And a new F-150 in ravish-me-all-night-red? I will definitely be on the lookout for that truck at the grocery store so I can bang his buggy in the produce section. Oops, did I do that?" She places her fingers over her mouth, eyes wide and feigning innocence, and I'm astounded that guys actually fall for that.

I'm stunned, shocked into silence. I was expecting her to damn near kill me, feel betrayed, and filet me with her tears. And she's totally fine with my mouth-fucking Brody, and maybe more. In fact, she's already acquired her next target, a doctor.

"I don't know what to say. This is not at all how I expected this conversation to go." Not thinking, I drain the entirety of my glass in one go and then cringe at the gross taste. "Fuck, how do you drink this stuff?"

Emily smiles and sips hers, eyeing me over the rim of the glass.

"Okay, so now that we have that figured out . . . when are you going out with Brody?"

I reach for her glass, plucking it from her hand and chugging it too because as gross as it is, I could use a little blurriness as I confess. "Em, I'm not you. I'm not looking for the husband, two-point-five kids, and a dog. I've got a husband . . . Cole Automotive. That garage is my husband, baby, and a not-housebroken dog all rolled in one. I don't have a lot of time for anything else. I'm not planning to date him. I just want to fuck him. Maybe a lot if he's as good as I think he'll be. I get the feeling that's Brody's deal, too."

I'm not sure if that's true, but I hope it is. Most guys, even if they have plans for the whole Norman Rockwell painting life at some point, are quite fine with keeping things casual for a while. It's worked for me in the past, and I hope to hell and back that it'll work with Brody.

Her brows jump in surprise. For all her mouthy game, she's a good girl. I'm . . . not.

"Well, when's your dick appointment?" She's trying, bless her heart.

I shrug on the outside, but inside, I'm replaying that kiss, the masterful way he took my mouth but let me take his too. I'm thinking about the hard planes of his belly I felt beneath that T-shirt and the thick bulge I could see in his jeans. I'm hearing that ragged breath as I pushed him back, knowing he wanted to shove me up against the truck and fuck me but was a good man and held tight restraint over those urges.

I must smile or fucking whimper or something, but Emily goes nuts.

"Rix! Oh my God! You're in love! It's about time, girl!" She hops up from the couch and starts dancing around like that girl from *Flashdance*, running in place but with arms flailing as she jumps a bit. Her downstairs neighbors are probably going to call the landlord on her.

Who am I kidding? Emily has the neighbors and the landlord

wrapped around her pretty little finger too. Just like everyone. Except Brody, apparently.

"Whoa, slow down. I didn't say all that. I literally just told you I'm dick-only, no hearts need apply."

She plants one hand on her hip and points at me with the other, the picture of Mom. "Well, any man who makes you all stammery and nervous is someone I want to see you with because *this"* —she gestures her open palm at all of me— "is a riot. No matter who he is —oh, shit!"

Her eyes go wide again as she falls to the couch beside me. "What are you going to tell Reed?"

"Nothing. It's none of his business."

She twists her lips wryly. "You know it is, Rix. Everyone thinks you're gonna end up together, including Reed."

I shrug. "I've made it clear that I don't think that. We haven't dated since high school."

"You know he's waiting on you. He follows you around like a damn labradoodle with sad puppy dog eyes, begging for treats. To be clear, you're the treat." She smirks, looking me up and down like I'm something different from what she sees in the mirror every day.

Damn.

Emily's right, and I do know it, even if it pisses me off that everyone still thinks they get some say-so in how my life plays out. I chose escaping to the Army as a show of creating my own destiny, a fuck-you to everyone who thought they knew best for me, even though I loved them and they only did it out of love for me.

But the Army hadn't played out like I thought it would, since here I am, back home a few short years later, and while I've changed, nobody else has. Neither has the picture in their heads of little Rix and where she's going.

I'm pretty sure Dad thought I'd come home, finally marry Reed, and start popping out grandkids.

But that's his plan, along with Reed and Uncle Smitty.

Know whose plan it's not? Mine.

"I've made it clear to Reed that I'm not interested, regardless of who plotted what when we were kids or what I thought I wanted when we were in high school."

Yeah, losing my virginity in that Toyota Corolla in bay three? That was to Reed at an embarrassingly young age. For me, it'd been a sweet progression of our puppy love, an adventure into something adult-ish. For him, it'd been a declaration that I was onboard with the whole marriage-babies plan that started immediately after high school.

I hadn't wanted that then, don't want it now, and don't know that I ever will. But even if I one day wake up and decide I want that life, it won't be with Reed. I know that much. He's safe, he's easy, and he lets me walk all over him. None of those are things I want, for a right-now guy or a forever guy.

Emily shrugs noncommittally, obviously not convinced. "If you say so. Just don't hurt him too much. But Brody? Go to work on that man and tell me all about it."

A smile teases at my lips. "Are you sure, Em? Really sure?" I don't want to look back on this moment and see that I shouldn't have believed her, that I fucked us up again.

Her hands cover mine and she looks deep into my eyes. I might as well be looking in a mirror because I know every fleck in hers just like my own. "I'm positive. Now tell me everything."

It's like no time has passed between us, like we're back to being teenagers, giggling about boys at school.

I tell her about almost taking Brody's head off with a wrench and cussing him out, and she gasps and proclaims it 'classic Rix.' I don't dispute that she's right.

I tell her about the almost kiss that Reed interrupted, and she raises a knowing brow at me that I pretend not to see.

I tell her about being stingy and bitchy inside about introducing her to Brody, and she smiles as she tells me I'm a good sister. I almost believe her.

And last but not least, I tell her about that mouth-fucking kiss. We both fall back on the couch, swooning. I even drink another glass of wine in one gulp, like I'm swallowing medicine, but instead of a gross bitter flavor, it's just a little bit sweet this time. Not too bad, just like telling Emily wasn't as bad as I thought it would be. And also, I might be a little tipsy.

"I'm no saint, obviously, and have kissed my share of guys. But I swear, Em . . . that was something else entirely."

"So, now what?" she asks, careful to let me fill in the details, an allowance I appreciate more than she could possibly know.

"Now, I'm gonna call him. Obviously." I laugh as I say it, but I mean every word.

# CHAPTER 8

## ERICA

"Remind me again how I let myself get talked into this?" I grumble, holding Em's bags while she browses.

"Because you love your sister, you're a glutton for punishment, and I think you secretly like to be forced to do things that don't involve testosterone and beer." My mom's right, as always.

"And so, here we are," Emily summarizes, stopping to sniff at a candle from one of the vendors' booths.

We've been to the farmer's market on the Great Falls side of the mountain a few times, and despite my current show of fake grumpiness, I always enjoy it. It's just so early, and I have so much work to do at the shop, but Emily's invitation had taken priority and Reed can handle the garage today.

I look at Mom, watching her happily shop with Emily.

We are an interesting family from the outside looking in. Emily and I have tawny skin, freckles, a dark curtain of thick, straight hair, and deep brown eyes, while Mom and Dad are picture-perfect Americana, with blond hair, blue eyes, and an affection for baseball and the 'old days,' which are apparently the 70s. Mom says it's because things were simpler then. Dad says it's because they were high all the time.

But I've never known anything different since Keith and Janice Cole adopted Emily and me when were barely even two. My earliest memories are of Mom and Dad dancing around the kitchen with dinner cooking on the stovetop. I'm glad I only have happy memories, and neither Emily nor I have ever felt called to find out 'where we came from' because we already know. We came from Mom and Dad's heart, just like they always told us when we were kids, and you can tell by the way Mom looks on fondly while Emily flits here and there.

"Are you sure there's no beer here? Seems like they might have some craft brews somewhere . . ." I look around, only half kidding.

Mom pushes her black-framed glasses up her nose so she can glare at me properly. "It's not even noon, Rix."

I wrap my arm around her shoulder, squeezing her tightly. "I know, Mom. I'll take it home for later. Promise."

She lifts one arm, patting my cheek softly. "You'll have to help me pick out a bottle or two for Keith too. But none of that high alcohol content stuff like you got him for Christmas. Good Lord, he was drunker than a sailor on shore leave! I had to put him to bed before he passed out in his recliner." Her pat turns more slap with that informational tidbit, even though it wasn't my fault . . . mostly.

Still makes me laugh. "Well, I didn't mean for Dad to drink it like he does Budweiser. That was Bourbon County Coffee Stout, his two favorite things in one . . . beer and coffee. And fifteen dollars a bottle. It was supposed to be for something special, not to crack open while he watched a rerun of his favorite game."

"Game five, 1956 World Series. Don Larsen pitched a perfect game. Never seen nothing like it." We say it together, Mom and me, having heard Dad say the exact thing more times than can be counted.

"Well, he enjoyed it all right. Maybe a bit too much. I think I'll skip getting him any more beer this time," she says thoughtfully. "Maybe just find him some beef jerky instead."

"I'm gonna grab a coffee. Anybody want one?" I offer, spying an Airstream that's been rehabilitated into a food truck of sorts.

"Please," Emily breathes, and the candle vendor looks on the verge of doing anything Emily asks. I predict that she gets a discount on the candle, so she'll buy two. I've seen it happen time and time again. She doesn't take advantage of people. They just like to be in her orbit, soaking up her radiant positivity and genuine smiles.

Mom shakes her head, pressing a hand to her chest that lets me know her morning pot of coffee is already talking back to her. It gives her heartburn every time, but she never lets that stop her from pouring another cup.

The barista makes quick work of my order, handing me two large cups. One black, one almost the color of milk. Guess whose is whose? I drop a dollar in the pickle jar-turned-tip jar and turn back around to find Emily.

"One for you, one for me," I say, handing her the pale coffee.

"Back atcha. One for you, one for me." She wiggles her bag, and I chuckle that I was right. She bought two candles.

"Thanks." I tell her, meaning it. She smiles back, and while I'd been expecting some weirdness from our conversation yesterday, it's never materialized.

We're just us. Emily and Erica. Sisters, as always.

"All right, let's find some jerky for my jerky," Mom says with a clap of her hands.

Emily and I groan in tandem. "Mom, don't start with the Dad jokes. We're begging you."

"Pretty sure they're Mom jokes if I'm the one telling them." She smiles like that was funny too. "Ooh, let me look at these melons too. I've already got decent ones, but you can't have too many."

Mom shimmies her shoulders in a move I really wish her Zumba teacher hadn't taught her and then scurries off, her sensible sneakers squeaking as she heads toward a fruit stand.

"Did Mom just make a tit joke?" I ask out of the side of my mouth, like saying it full out will make it so.

Emily nods, her face twisted in horror. "She did. She absolutely did."

We meet eyes and simultaneously shudder. "Mom tits. Old lady tits. I can't."

"Promise me we'll get boob jobs before ours go saggy." Emily holds out her pinkie finger for me to shake on the idea, but I recoil.

"Absolutely not. Em, we barely even have any. We're never gonna sag like . . ." I sigh before I say it. "Mom."

"Right. No tits are better than old lady tits." She's trying to convince herself.

"Em? Stop saying tits, 'kay?"

She mimes locking her mouth and throwing away the key, and hesitantly, we follow Mom, scared of what puns and Dad jokes she'll come up with next. God help us if eggplants are in season.

"GIRLS, COME HERE! I FOUND SOME JELLY I WANT TO GET," MOM calls out a few hours later. But now, Emily and I are giggling like pre-teen boys about everything Mom says, finding some degree of sexual innuendo in it, even when there's absolutely none. But jelly is a pretty easy leap to something sordid.

"Sure, be right there."

We come up behind Mom to see her holding a clear cut-glass jar of red jelly and chatting with the vendor. She's a little younger than Em and me, with thick light brown hair that's highlighted all around her face in that way salons always try to duplicate. Hers looks natural, though, like she got the lighter bits the same way she got the tan . . . being outside. She's wearing cutoff shorts and a Kentucky Downs sweatshirt, and I'm pretty sure those boots have some shit mixed in with the dirt on them. She's what a farmer's market is all about, farm to market to table.

"We grow all the fruits and veggies ourselves. My brothers do most of the work there, though." She makes a whipping noise, winking one eye and smiling widely. I instantly decide I like her. "After we harvest, I take over, making seasonal specialties throughout the year. Spring is mostly cherry jubilee jam and lemon curd. Though you can get my carrot cakes by special order or by the slice at the resort."

Mom is enamored, and I predict that we'll be taking home one of everything. "I've had cherries jubilee before, but how do you make it into a jam?"

The vendor smiles like she's got a secret. "After you soak the cherries in the brandy, you light it on fire. Just a little bit, you know. I gotta keep it safe with the kids around these days. *Set a good example, Shay*." She's imitating someone, but I don't know who. Honestly, she sounds wistful and sad about some bare-boned safety measures. "And then I smash it up and add the pectin. It's a lotta fun, one of my favorites all year." She laughs, her smile growing even wider.

I can't help but smile back. Her excitement over jelly is contagious enough that I think I'll buy one too.

"Couldn't stay away from me, could you, Lil Bit?"

Out of nowhere, Brody's voice rumbles right in my ear, making me jump like one of those cats that just spotted a cucumber.

I know I'm blushing from the surprise of his being here, but I calm my features before I turn around, not letting him see how good he got me. "I don't know what you're talking about, Cowboy. I'm just here doing a little shopping." I hold up a jar of lemon curd as proof. "Seems like you're the one stalking me. Should I be worried? I've got a Taser in my purse and my fists are registered weapons."

He runs his hand down from his chest to his abs. "You could hit me if you want to. I'd do just about anything to have your hands on me." The words are low, meant just for me, but Emily, Mom, and the vendor all hear too.

"Brody Michael Tannen! I will wash your mouth out with soap and not let you have any carrot cake tonight if you don't apologize to my customer right the hell now!" I've never actually met someone full of piss and vinegar before, but I can't say that now because the woman is riled up something fierce as she comes to my aid with an actual stomp of her booted foot.

It's sweet. Unnecessary, but sweet.

If Brody wasn't damn near trying to crawl inside my skin right here in front of God and the whole town, it might occur to me to be jealous of this unknown woman who knows his middle name when I didn't even know his last one until just now. Still, I have to smirk. "Brody *Michael* Tannen?"

He chuckles, not at all embarrassed and also not apologizing in the least. "You only have to scream out Brody. If you can get my whole name out, I'm not doing my job." Still talking like it's just me and him, he lifts his chin toward the vendor. "So that's my sister, Shayanne."

"Hi, Shayanne. Nice to meet you." I throw the words over my shoulder, still eye-fucking Brody. "Think I'm gonna need a jar of this lemon curd and a cherry one too."

I notice he doesn't introduce me to her, but that's okay. We're not walking down the aisle or anything, and meeting family is a big deal for most folks.

"Ahem." Mom has no such rule about not needing to meet people, especially not ones who are obviously split seconds away from fucking me against the nearest surface. "Rix, would you like to introduce me to your friend?"

It sounds like I have a choice. I do not.

"Mom, this is Brody. Brody, this is Janice Cole, my mom."

I see his jaw clench like it's hard for him to look away from me, but he does it anyway to offer Mom his hand. He looks a little embarrassed too, like maybe he didn't realize it wasn't only Emily and his sister bearing witness to his heated come-ons. "Good to meet you, Mrs. Cole."

She shakes his hand and smiles, but it's that threatening flash of teeth that Mama Bears do when they try to look perfectly pleasant but are really ready to go to battle for their cubs. Never mind that I don't need Mom's protection.

"Hey, Brod, I sent the family group text a picture just now. Katelyn seems to think you met this one at the resort bar, says she saw you drinking with her. Sophie says she's from the garage. And so help me if you've already been on two dates with this woman and I haven't heard about it, I will gut you and serve you to the goats. Except for Baarbara. She's got a sensitive tummy, you know?"

I try to take in everything she just said, including the clear picture of Brody and me on her phone's screen as she waves it around. A text bubble pops up, then another.

"Oh, the resort was me!" Emily raises her hand like she's telling the teacher she's present for attendance check. "And the garage was Rix, of course. So they're both right."

Emily doesn't realize how that sounds until it's too late.

Shayanne's eyes go skinny and hot as she looks from Emily to me and then focuses sharply on Brody. "Forget the goats. I'm gonna serve you up to Mama Louise on a damn platter like a fat, brown Thanksgiving turkey. What the actual fuck, Brody?"

He holds his hands up, in any man's worst nightmare . . . surrounded by four women.

Mom and Shayanne look ready to tag-team a murder, one of those random 'we don't know each other, so we can't be in on it together' type deals I've seen on late-night crime shows, *Strangers On A Train* style. Emily looks confused at the fuss. And I'm on the verge of busting a gut from holding back laughter.

"Wait, wait, wait a second. I can explain. I met Erica, then saw Emily at the resort and thought they were the same person. Obviously, they're not." He shrugs like none of this is his fault. To be fair, it's not. Just one of those things that happen when there's someone else walking around with your face.

I jump in to save him . . . after I've had a little more fun at Shay texting on her phone and Brody trying to look over her shoulder. "Why aren't I getting those messages?"

"Because I removed you from the group so we could talk about you behind your back. I'll add you again when we're done . . . maybe."

"We're all good here, guys. The important thing is that Emily and I know who we are, and more importantly, Brody knows who we are. And who we're not." I pinch his nipple through his shirt, twisting it hard in teasing punishment for the confusion.

He flinches away. "Shit, Erica. Stop. I said I want your hands on me, but I didn't mean for you to rip my nipples off."

I realize a moment too late that touching him like that implies a level of intimacy I maybe wasn't ready to shout from the rooftops yet because Mom is looking between us as though she's mentally picking out wedding venues. At least she's on board with my never marrying Reed. She understood back in high school why I didn't want that then, even if she hadn't wanted me to enlist to get out of it. But her interest in my future is perking right back up like she got a caffeine injection right to her sentimental heart.

Mom leans in to Emily, a tiny smile on her lips as she stage whispers, "He calls her Erica, did you hear that?"

Emily hums as she concurs. "Yep, and he's still alive and standing. This could be serious."

Mom suddenly yawns, exaggeratedly fake. "Oh, dear, I'm feeling so tired. I'd best be getting home. Emily, dear, do you think you can drive me?"

"Yeah, Mom. No problem," Emily answers as Mom basically drags her away.

"Nice to meet you, Brody!" Mom calls out as they disappear, probably already discussing the whole Rix-met-someone situation.

I turn to Shayanne. "Sorry for messing up your sale with my Mom, but I'll take two of each of the jellies and order a cake too. I love carrot cake. It's my favorite way to eat vegetables, but I promise to share. Or you know, shove it in Mom's mouth so she'll stop asking me questions about the last five minutes of my life."

She somehow glows even brighter. "Wait until you have Mama Louise's zucchini bread with chocolate chips and you'll be singing a different tune. You should come out to the ranch sometime because it's best when it's fresh outta the oven."

Brody stiffens beside me, and not in the good way. He stays quiet and stoic while Shayanne rings up my purchases and puts them in a bag with her business card. "Call or text me anytime . . .

about *anything*." She pauses and adds, "Oh, and for real, let me know if there's a specific date you want the cake. Or if my soonest availability works for you, that'll be about four days from now."

Brody grabs my hand, asking Shayanne, "Think you can handle teardown on your own?"

She raises an eyebrow. "Yeah, asshole. I can fold a folding table and shove it in the back of the truck. I'm almost sold out of everything, anyway."

And before I can tell her goodbye, Brody is dragging me away.

I let him for a few steps, understanding the need to escape family sometimes even though you love them, but quickly, my strides become no match for his and I have to pull at his hand. "Slow down, Cowboy."

He spins in place, pulling me against him. I have to look up and he has to look down, but somehow, he doesn't make me feel less-than or weak.

"Lil Bit, that whole thing was weird as fuck, but the main thing I picked up on is that Emily seemed fine with this. True?" His jaw is clenched, tension woven through his muscles as he waits for me to agree.

"True."

"You didn't call. You still good with this?"

"I thought about you last night. Got a few ideas. Maybe more than a few . . . if you're game?"

Heat flickers across his face as his eyes dart to my lips like he wants to taste those words. I think he's going to do it, kiss me right here to learn all my dirty thoughts, but he growls and starts his speed-walking again.

Now, I can see it for what it really is. He's not escaping his family. He's desperately trying to get us alone to pick up where we left off.

And I am one hundred percent onboard for that plan. "My truck's parked over there."

# CHAPTER 9

## BRODY

"No one's here?" I couldn't care less if there's a garage full of people at Cole Automotive as we pull up. I'll fuck Erica right here in her truck, against any vehicle in one of those bays, and do it with a whole audience of customers if that's who's inside there.

I'm that desperate for her.

I'm not a manwhore, not with all the time, energy, and focus I've put into keeping my family afloat. So I'm used to going a long while between hookups.

But she has me boiling inside, hungry in a way I don't know I've ever felt. I have this bone-deep need to know how she feels under my hands, what sounds she makes, what her face looks like when she's lost to pleasure. And I want her fingertips on my skin, branding me as hers, if only for a moment.

It's been almost thirty-six hours since I last kissed her. Too long by a mile. But it's like we just blinked because all that fire we stoked up has reignited into an inferno, threatening to take us both under. I want to be consumed by her, turned to ash by her, and burn her up too. Fucking someone has never seemed as life or death as it does right now. Stupidly dramatic, but also absolutely true.

"Shop closed at three so everyone's gone home. I live upstairs." She throws the truck in park and is out before I have a chance to bolt around and open her door. But I don't think she cares about the lack of gentlemanly politeness because she's dragging me by my T-shirt toward the garage door.

She makes quick work of the up and down, throwing the latch again so we're secure. And she's mine. Judging by the greedy look in her eyes, I'm hers too.

"Come on," she says as she guides me toward a door across the room, on the other side of the garage.

I can't wait. Alone with her is more than enough for me. I push her against the door, gripping her jaw to lift it as I bend forward to meet her. There's no battle for dominance. It's an acceptance that we're both in charge as we consume each other. Her tongue forces its way into my mouth, and I groan at the invasion, loving how aggressive she is, that she demands that I give as much as she is.

We kiss our way through the door into a breakroom, our hands roving and learning. As we take a split second to gasp for air, I consider the table in the middle of the room. Laminated fake-wood top on metal legs like they used to have at school—definitely sturdy enough for her to lie on, but I'll break it for sure. I'm happy to stand and fuck her laid back on that table, though.

"No. I'm not having sex where my guys eat their lunch."

Shit. When she says it like that, I don't want her pussy anywhere near there, either. She points at another door and I let her lead me that way. A set of stairs is revealed, and she takes them two at a time, even with her short legs. With me a few steps behind her, I have a great view, and I grab her hips, stopping her.

She looks back, a smirk on her pink lips when she sees where my attention is centered. The seductive minx bends forward, her hands going to a step as she presses that tiny ass out toward me.

I spin my hat backward so it's out of the way and lay a kiss to a thigh toned by hard work, thanking the devil himself for these cutoff shorts because only he would be this perverted. I press a matching kiss to the other thigh, tracing the skin from her ankles to her ass with my callused hands. I roughly knead the flesh of her hips and ass in my hands over the denim, now cursing its existence because it's keeping me from the rest of her. Luckily, they're short, especially when she's bent nearly in half. My fingertip teases along the soft skin at the ripped edge, dipping underneath when she dances and sways her hips.

"More. Finger me." There's a breathiness to her voice I've never heard before. Not even when we kissed after the battery exchange. This is a new Erica. Needy, desire-filled, sex goddess Erica.

I love that she's bold and tells me plainly what she wants. No gimmicks, no games, no guessing.

That doesn't mean I do as she says. I'm not one of the people she bosses around, and she needs to know that. I keep tracing along that hem, getting further and further under the denim until I find her panties. Then I run my fingertips along that edge too, and she arches, fucking air as she searches for the 'more' she wants.

Her fingers work the button at her waist and she shoves her shorts down. When my hands get in the way, I move and the denim falls to meet her Converse sneakers, revealing grey cotton bikinis. Plain and sensible, and sexy as fuck on her.

But when she steps her feet as wide as the shorts around her ankles allow, I can see the wet spot on those panties and my cock goes iron-hard as all my blood rushes south. She's wet for me, and fuck, do I want to deserve it. My thumbs graze along the soft skin peeking out at her core as I bury my nose there, inhaling her. I groan against her, and even that slight vibration has her begging for more.

Not.

Any other woman would. But not Erica Cole.

No, she balances herself on one hand and slips the other into her panties, petting herself if I won't do it. "Fuck, that's sexy. But let me." I slide her panties to the side, watching for a moment longer before slowly licking a long line from her fingers over her clit all the way up to the rosebud of her ass. She bucks, her hips as demanding as her mouth.

This time, I give in, not teasing either of us anymore.

I slip my arm around her thighs, locking her against my mouth, and get to work. My tongue tastes every nook and cranny, mapping and memorizing her, learning what she likes and what makes her go wild.

Her moans get higher pitched as she gets closer to coming. I can't wait, want to see her explode, want to taste it on my tongue as she clenches on me. I ease a finger in, finally finger fucking her like she told me to, and she sighs like it's the best thing she's ever felt. My cock throbs, dangerously close to the point of no return.

I will not come in my damn jeans just from the taste of her. I won't. The pep talk isn't helping, so I release her legs to palm myself, figuring if I'm coming like this, I'm going to make it good for me too.

She looks back at me through the window between her elbow and knee. "Let me see you. Jack yourself while you finger fuck me."

My eyes cross as I rasp. "Shit, I'm gonna come just from your talking like that."

"Got a hairpin trigger, Cowboy?"

Her tease is a challenge, one I'm up for. I leave her pussy empty, taking my wet finger to my mouth as she watches with a smirk. "You're fucking delicious, Lil Bit. Pretty pink pussy all wet for me." She nods, watching as my now-clean hand drops to my jeans. I make quick work of the button and shove my jeans and underwear down in the front, freeing my cock and balls. A few slow pumps have her eyes dilating.

"I want *that*." It's the best reaction my cock's ever received. I've gotten the porn-star-mimicked 'oh, my, so big' before, and even a few fearful looks of concern over my size. In three words, the blatant, hungry, honest desire for my thick length from Erica Cole has wiped any other woman's compliment from my mind. "Can you go more than once?"

"I'm thirty, not dead. And have you seen this pussy?" Her eyebrow says I didn't answer the question. "Yeah, Erica. I can go more than once," I answer dryly, unlike her dripping slit and my precum-covered crown.

She sways her hips in reminder of her order. Normally, I'm not one to follow those, but her plan is even better than mine, so I slip one finger back into her wet warmth and the other hand around my cock. "Good fucking thing I'm ambidextrous."

"I'm sure you could make it work even if you weren't." The barb fades at the end, becoming a hiss as I add another finger. "*Yes*."

Her eyes stay locked on my fist, moving up and down my length in tempo with my fingers moving in and out of her slick cunt. In and out, up and down, over and over. And when I brush my thumb over her clit, she comes, crying out my name and making me feel like a fucking god. I slam my fingers into her roughly, curling them against that rough patch along her front wall, milking every bit of pleasure from her I can.

She is fucking glorious, just like I knew she would be. She doesn't do anything halfway, including orgasming. She's wild and loud, barking at me not to stop, and when she tells me to come with her, I couldn't stop it if I tried. Lightning jolts through my spine, going from my balls through my cock, and I spurt all over my hand.

My teeth grit, neck muscles tight as I force her name out. This orgasm is hers. She did this to me even though it's my hand on my cock.

Panting as we recover, I lick lazily over her clit and taste her sweetness on my fingers which are still buried in her and all over her soft outer lips. She makes happy noises that feel like high praise. "Mmm. Let's go upstairs."

She wiggles her ass, which I think is an attempt to dislodge me, so I tease her again. When I don't withdraw, she stands up and moves two steps away.

I whine at the loss and then grin when she runs up the rest of the steps with a deep chuckle that makes me think of smoke and whiskey. She stepped out of her shorts, her T-shirt has dropped down over her panties, which are askew and show me one tantalizing ass cheek, and she's still got her Converse on. In a weird way, it's sexier than lingerie on her.

I follow her, slipping my cock back into my underwear and wiping my hand on my jeans before grabbing her shorts.

My first impression of her apartment is that it's sparse. One big room with a couch and TV area, a small dining table for two in front of a wall of kitchen appliances and cabinets, and a bed pushed up against the side wall. But there are touches here and there that speak to it being her space . . . a photo of a uniformed Erica, a fluffy blanket on the arm of the couch, and a stack of car magazines on the floor like she flips through them regularly.

A habit of ranch life, I toe my boots off by the door, yanking at my socks too. Erica follows suit, setting her tennis shoes neatly by a rack of clothes. Her shirt goes over her head and into a hamper, along with her panties, as I raptly watch her zero-fucks-given, all-efficiency strip show.

Her body is gorgeous, tight muscles and tiny curves. I want to suck the caramel tips of her nipples, trace a line from her belly button to her clit with my tongue, and kiss every freckle that dots her skin. The most beautiful part is her utter comfort in her own body as she stands unabashedly before me.

"Your turn, Cowboy." Her voice has gone husky, sending a buzz through my blood. She might've been casual about taking her clothes off, but as she lies back on the bed, propped on her elbows to watch, she's begging me to give her a little more.

I throw her shorts in the same hamper and then reach behind my head to pull my shirt off. My hat gets tangled up inside it, but for once, I don't care as I let them both drop to the floor. Erica's legs scissor when I reach for the zipper of my jeans, not having bothered with the button. I shed the rest quickly, standing nude and hard again. I give my cock a couple of strokes, making sure he's putting in his best showing for what might be one of the best nights of his life.

Erica bites her lip and smirks. "Goddamn, I am going to fuck the shit outta you."

I can't help but groan at her words—not telling me to fuck her but bluntly telling me that she's going to do the fucking. I don't know why that's so sexy, but it is. Like she's in this as much as I am, as affected as I am, and not shy about expressing it. Her boldness is enticing as hell.

In three strides, I'm at the bed's edge. She's sat up, watching my approach, and when she opens her mouth, her desire obvious, I'm leveled. "You want a taste?"

She kisses my crown sweetly and then lays little laps all along my length, teasing and torturing me deliciously. I don't expect it when she takes me all at once, letting me in her mouth and to the edge of her throat. I spasm, pushing deeper before I can wrestle back control of myself. "Fuck, Erica."

"Say it again."

"Erica." I grab a handful of her hair, stopping her mouth from taking me, and she looks up at me. "Erica."

Her shudder is my undoing. I pick her up beneath her arms, throwing her toward the soft pillows and mussing up her perfectly made bed as I follow her. She opens her arms and knees, welcoming me. "Condom. In the nightstand."

She points to the small table, and I pull the drawer open to grab a foil packet. We both watch as I roll it over my cock and notch at her entrance. "You sure?" One more time, I have to ask, need her to tell me.

"Hell yeah, Cowboy." Her smile is bright until her mouth falls open as I inch inside her. "*Yes*."

She wraps around me with everything she has—short nails scoring my back, heels digging into my thighs, and tight as a vice pussy slickly clenching my cock in waves. We move, slowly at first but rapidly gaining speed.

Her moans are buried against the skin of my chest, and I swear I feel the sharp edge of her teeth. We're wild, our hips banging into one another and the headboard banging into the wall in a staccato rhythm, chasing this thing building between us.

Sex. Orgasms. Maybe more?

Right now, all I know is pleasure.

I lift up to my knees, fighting the tight grip she has keeping us locked together. It changes the angle and lets me see my cock disappearing inside her, coming back out covered in her honey.

"Fucking beautiful."

So is the flush on her cheeks and the flutter of her lashes as her eyes roll back in her head. Maybe I say that aloud because she nods, agreeing with me or asking for more?

I strum at her clit with one hand and pluck a nipple with the other. "Get there, Lil Bit. Come for me." A few more sharp thrusts later, which she matches stroke for stroke, she detonates, bucking her hips fast and hard as she destroys me with her orgasm.

"Fuck . . . Erica . . ." I bite out as I follow her over, jerking violently as I come.

I hold myself deep inside her, not wanting to lose this connection yet. A soft and hazy-eyed Erica is a sight to behold, and I take a mental snapshot of the moment, knowing I'll replay it just as much as the amazing sex we just had.

Too soon, she moves, and I get up to take care of the condom.

I don't know why, but I mostly expect her to kick me out when I return from the bathroom. Like she got what she needed from me and now, I'm free to go. But she smiles and pulls back the covers, patting the bed beside her in invitation. "Do you need to go?"

I climb into bed, finding my space next to her. "Nope, there's nowhere I need to be."

That's not true at all.

Shayanne will have told the whole family about Erica and me leaving the market together, and my phone is probably blowing up in my jeans pocket. I don't give a shit and don't have any interest in answering their intrusive questions.

And chores will need to be done dark and early in the morning. But if I'm not there, the guys can handle it. I've done the same for them. Though they'll have just as many questions as the women. Gossipy old assholes, with their knowing looks and smirks.

Regardless of what's at home, I do exactly what I want to do.

Maybe for the first time ever. I simply lie down in bed with a beautiful woman and don't give a second thought to anything but what I want and what she wants.

In her bed, in her arms, I feel that little bit of freedom welling up.

---

"Wake up, sleepyhead."

Erica moans in her sleep. For a former soldier, judging by the picture I saw in the living room, she's shit for waking up for reveille. Is that even a thing still? I've got no idea beyond what I've seen on television.

Admittedly, as a rancher, I'm always up with the sun. But it's a bit hard to rise and shine for me too this morning.

Mostly because we last fell asleep about two hours ago. We spent the night dozing and then waking up to fuck again.

Last night was like Olympic-level sport fucking.

Erica is amazing, insatiable, a revelation.

I need carbs and Gatorade this morning to refuel and recover. And probably some of the udder balm we use on the cows for my dick. Not that I'm complaining in the least. Hell, I'd go again right now if only she'd wake up.

I press a kiss to her forehead, letting her drift off one more time as I get up, pull on my underwear, and hit the kitchen. I'm a shit cook for the most part, but there's one thing I know how to make from scratch. A quick rustle through her cabinets and fridge provides all the supplies.

"What's that smell?" a sleep-roughened voice says from the pile of blankets in the middle of the bed. For a tiny thing, she takes up the whole bed herself, damn near lying diagonal and spread-eagle. I didn't mind at all because she was half draped over me that way.

"Pancakes. Coffee."

"Shit. If this is a dream, don't wake me up. It's too good to end yet." One eye peeks over the covers, and she looks at me skeptically, as though I'm going to disappear before her very eyes. Well, eye because just the one has opened.

"Not a dream. But if you don't move your ass, I'm going to eat your pancakes."

"Nightmare" is the mumbled reply, which makes me chuckle. But she does get up, making a pit stop in the bathroom. She comes back out in fresh cotton panties and nothing else to sit down at the table. "Looks good." A blink follows. "Scratch that, looks great. I don't remember the last time someone cooked me breakfast."

My chest puffs up at that. Either there hasn't been anyone warming her bed in a while or they were assholes who bailed. Or she kicked them out, more likely. But I'm here, still here, which feels like a damn accomplishment with this woman.

"Haven't cooked for anyone in a while. Shayanne and Mama Louise do the cooking at the ranch, mostly."

It just slips out. Normal conversation, sharing tidbits with a stranger. Okay, definitely not a stranger if I know how hard she likes her hair pulled and what she sounds like when she's ready to come. But I'm not usually one to share . . . anything.

Erica takes it in stride, having no idea that my walls just cracked a little bit. "I met Shayanne, and she mentioned Mama Louise. Is that your mom?" A big bite of pancakes goes into her mouth and she moans obscenely. "Ohmigod, these are so good."

I smile at the compliment before answering her question. "No, Mama Louise is a Bennett. They own the ranch I work for." I don't tell her half of it used to be my ranch but I had no way of saving it from the debt Dad put us in when he died. It doesn't matter now anyway, since that's all water under the bridge. Murky water for sure, but done and over with. And we're all good now working with the Bennetts. Working *for* them.

And I'm patching over that wall crack with a few dabs of hope and shut-the-fuck-up.

"I figured you would be more of a morning person being military, or is this lazing about a rebellion against those sunrise mornings?"

She freezes, suspicion on her face.

I point with my fork. "Picture over there. Emily doesn't strike me as the guns and boots type." A small tease and she relaxes again.

"I went into the Army shortly after high school. Those boot camp mornings were hell, but that was the easy part." She shrugs and adds, "After basic, I went to Virginia for advanced training. I was lucky, posted stateside the whole time, with pretty regular hours. I came home a couple of years ago to run the shop when Dad retired."

"And now you get lazy Sunday morning brunches specially made for you," I conclude with a smirk.

She finishes her pancakes, putting away as many as I do and using more syrup than a sugar-starved toddler. She takes our empty plates, washing them in the sink. "What are you doing today? Need me to drive you home?"

And so it ends. She's kicking me out now. But she offered a ride, and I'll take those extra minutes with her. "That'd be great. Thanks. What do you usually do on Sundays?"

Her eyes tick to the microwave clock. "There's a car show over at the high school today. I figured I'd hit that up, but it's fine. I'll skip it to take you over the mountain."

I move to tug at my hat but find it's missing since I'm sitting here in my underwear. I run my hand through my hair instead. "Or I could go with you?"

My head is literally on the chopping block here. Either one, or hell, maybe both, as I hold my breath.

"You don't have to do that." She sounds uncertain, nothing like the badass who swung a wrench at my head.

"I want to," I decide. "Though before you agree to this, you should know that I will have to wear yesterday's clothes. It will be the longest walk of shame in the history of mankind." I get up and strut my way over to her, feeling no shame at all, to back her against the counter.

I kiss her passionately, tasting the pancake syrup still on her lips and tongue. Holding her cheek, I look into her eyes. "I want to go with you, Erica. If you want me to go with you. It doesn't have to be a thing. We can just hang out."

I'm testing her here and I damn well know it. I figured she'd kick me out, but she hasn't. The opposite side of that coin is that she's deemed us a thing now, one dick insertion somehow committing us to more. But maybe there are more than the two sides of a coin? Maybe it's a multi-sided dice instead, with lots of options—like going to a car show.

Her eyes clear, brightening with a comeback a moment before her mouth lets it loose. "We can dab some motor oil behind your ears. It's the only smell those guys would recognize and respect, anyway. We'll even make it some of the special synthetic stuff so you're fancy."

Her playful wink is flirty.

Seriously. This ball-busting, wrench-attacking she-devil just winked at me after fucking me all night and declaring my pancakes the best ever. Or almost . . . okay, she ate them all, but that's almost the same thing.

I feel like I just fell down the rabbit hole with Alice, but I'll drink that damn rabbit's tea everyday if it makes Erica smile like this and my dick this happily sore.

# CHAPTER 10

## BRODY

Walking around the 'car show', as Erica called it, is basically like entering another world. There are gorgeously flashy cars lined up every few spaces with the doors, trunks, and hoods open. Some are old, some are new, but they're all spit-polished and shined for the display. A few have owners perched in folding camping chairs by the hoods, ready to talk shop with anyone who happens by.

Which Erica does. A lot.

"What'd you do to this thing now, Ernesto?" Erica leans over a classic Chevrolet that I'd guess is '50s-era. It's only different to me than the other four old cars we've looked at because it's bright turquoise with a white leather interior, complete with matching turquoise stitching in the seats and doors.

That's me . . . there's a red one, a white one, a black one, the other black one, and now a blue. Erica knows everything about them, though, bumper to bumper and inside and out. You can tell by the way she talks to the owners and appreciates every detail.

"Nothing too much, Rix. You know me, keeping it all original. My girl's just for show." The dark-haired man chats Erica up about the differences in engine blocks and I get lost again. But they are in their element, bantering back and forth with one another as I stand by, hearing a version of Charlie Brown's teacher from their conversation . . . *wah, wah-wah-wah-wah-wah.*

Ordinarily, I might be bored by a topic I know next to nothing about, but watching Erica shine like this is far from boring. She's magnificent, drawing a crowd of three other old guys as she and Ernesto discuss something called an 'SS'.

"Hell, Ernesto, don't be too cocky. Not like that old thing's got a 409." Judging by the 'ooh' that goes through the guys, that's a big insult. Ernesto flips the newcomer, a silver-haired guy in a Ford T-shirt, his middle finger. I decide I like Ernesto just fine.

"Screw you, Wilson. At least mine's OEM, not a Franken-car of shit you found at the scrapyard."

Even I snort at that, which draws the guys' eyes all to me.

"Who're you?" the no-409 guy scoffs. Ernesto called him 'Wilson.' He's at least three, if not four, decades older than me, a good six inches shorter and fifty pounds lighter. None of those things matter to him in the slightest as he stands up tall to face me head on.

Ballsy old fucker. I can see where Erica gets it from if this is the crowd she hangs out with.

I stand up tall myself, out of respect to the old guy because the last thing a man like this wants is to be seen as too old to be a threat. And hell, for all I know, he's a damn Clint Eastwood clone with dead shot aim and a gun in his back pocket. "Brody."

I don't offer any more than that, letting my one-word, people-suck attitude shine through, dark and ominous. Wilson grunts, his eyes locked on me as he talks to Erica. "Hey, Rix, where's Reed? Usually see him car shopping around here with you. You two are always locked at the hip. 'Least he knows shit about cars."

I let my lips spread slowly, danger in my eyes that a man like Wilson can see a mile away, even though I wouldn't really hurt the old guy. Reed ain't here, but I sure as shit am. Even if I don't know about cars, I know a hell of a lot about Erica and am learning more every second.

I cross my arms over my chest, glaring at Wilson, who to his credit, glares right back pretty well himself. Erica smacks us both on the arms with dual fists. "Enough, assholes. Wilson, you know Reed might be around here somewhere, so if you want him to work on Sally, then keep running that trap. If you want me under her hood, shut the fuck up. And Cowboy, seriously? Don't make me send you to the truck while I do business."

My lips quirk as she scolds me like an errant kid, something that would have me bailing if it weren't for the shit-eating grin I see in her eyes. But I also hear the reminder. This is her work, her livelihood, her passion, and I don't want to fuck that up by pissing off Wilson, who sounds like a good customer.

Like a good little boy, I take her order this time. "Yes, ma'am." She's gonna pay for that later, but I think we'll both like the punishment.

Wilson grumbles but agrees too. "I'm just fucking around with you, Rix. Sally's got an appointment for new whitewall shoes this week still, yeah?"

Rix beams, having set us both in place without breaking a sweat. "Yep, tires should be in on Wednesday. I'll let you know if that changes."

That handled, she tells the guys to 'fuck off,' which seems to be their version of goodbye because they all answer in kind and throw her two-fingered waves.

It feels natural to take her hand in mine as we move down the row of cars, but I can feel those guys' eyes on me as we walk away.

We look for a while, and she educates me on car culture, telling me details about every vehicle we approach like a fucking *Wikipedia* page. We get closer to the end of the row, doubling back to where the newer vehicles are. Seems the classics guys and the hot rod guys are two very different crowds, and never the two shall mix. Odd, seems like a car guy is a car guy to me, but what do I know?

Not enough, that's what.

"So, what's the deal with you and Reed?" I venture, well aware that she might rightfully tell me to mind my own business.

She looks around like Reed might actually be here, so I automatically do the same but don't see him anywhere. Erica must not either because she sighs.

"We grew up together at the garage because our dads are friends. We dated in high school and Dad thought . . . hell, *everyone* thought . . . that Reed and I were going to get married." She pauses, and I pray there's a big 'but' coming. "I didn't want that, not then, and not with him. So I bailed, took the easy way out and ran away to the Army. It wasn't the only reason, but it was a big one."

"And now that you're back, he thinks you're going to pick right back up where you left off?" I guess, which is a pretty easy leap given his alternating possessive and forlorn puppy dog behavior toward her.

Her nod is clipped. "There's a lot of history there. We were each other's first relationship, first everything. And I love him, but not like *that*, never like that. He's a great friend, always was, and now, he's a good coworker too, but that's it. No matter what Reed, Dad, or Uncle Smitty think."

"Or Wilson," I add, glad that I'm not stepping on anyone's toes here. Well, I'm sure Reed thinks I am, but Erica hasn't been his in quite some time, by the sound of it.

She laughs and agrees. "Or Wilson." Her face goes a bit blank in a blink, and I can see a guard dropping over her. "Listen, Brody. Last night was amazing . . ."

"Motherfucker, are you dumping me at the damn car show?" I interrupt, somehow both horrified and amused. And maybe a little turned on. Girls don't dump me, not because I'm the dumper and not the dumpee, but because it's always been a casual thing, nothing serious since I've been way too busy being a family man for brothers and sisters. Failing spectacularly at it, too, but that's not really the point of her ditching me.

And damned if her trying to put a bit of distance between us doesn't make me want to chase her. Shit, maybe I'm no better than Reed after all. One little taste and I'm addicted to Erica's sour-sweet combo.

She doesn't smile. "I want to be clear. I don't have a lot of time in my schedule for this." She moves a hand from her chest to mine. "I've got the garage and it keeps me busy. Like ridiculously fucking busy. So if you're looking for someone to call and show up, be available for dates, and hell, take showers, shave, and put on dresses, I'm not that girl."

I look her up and down slowly and methodically, letting her know I'm not missing an inch of her. Her hair's back up in that knot on top of her head, the one I've realized keeps her long locks from getting tangled when she's dipping in and out from underneath hoods, and her bare face puts her freckles on display. She's wearing a Beartooth band T-shirt, a group I've definitely never heard of but judging by the shirt is apparently something to do with acid-tripping alien UFOs and snakes, a fresh pair of cutoffs, this time black with a bit of white paint spattered on them, and those steel-toed boots she already pushed me away with once before on her feet.

"I see you, Erica. Badass, beautiful, and way out of my league. If you're looking to get married, sounds like you've already got an offer on that. But if you want to just hang out when we have time and see what comes up, I'm good with that." I shrug, hoping it reads as casual. "Like I said, it doesn't have to be a thing."

I mean it. I really do. I'm not looking to get married either and am quite busy myself, actually, since we've got to get the cows to market soon. But I definitely wouldn't object to spending what free time we do have together, preferably in bed, but at car shows if we have to.

Hell, maybe I'll take her to the market auction when we sell the cattle. A bit of tit for tat. I listen to her talk cars with the guys and she can listen to me drone on about the price of cattle with the other ranchers. Something tells me she won't find my cow knowledge nearly as sexy as I find her car knowledge, though.

She squints like she's looking beneath my hood too, figuring out all my parts and pieces the way she does a broken-down car. "All right. If you say so. Just don't come crying to me when you get your heart broken because I'm up to my eyeballs in transmission repairs and can't suck your dick for a while."

My eyes cross. Holy hell, this woman.

I growl, throwing my arm over her shoulder and pulling her to my side. "Show me some cars or something, Erica, or I'm gonna find the nearest deserted corner of this lot and let you do that now."

She flutters her lashes before smirking. "What? Suck your dick?"

Goddamn it. I adjust myself in my jeans, looking for more room as they get too tight. Her dirty talk is brazen, like some curse-laden version of a weird love spell, but fuck, does it work for me. Or maybe it's not the words. It's just her.

Having won this round, she licks her finger and makes a tally mark in the air. "Oh, by the way, no fucking on school property. That's probably a felony, don't ya think? And wrong and gross even if it's not."

"Is a felony a deal breaker for you?" I tease back, an oh-shit look on my face.

"Seriously?" she hisses.

"Nah." I laugh. "Got a misdemeanor charge for fighting once, spent a couple of nights sobering up in the drunk tank when I was younger, and definitely had some black eyes, but nothing felonious." I don't tell her that Dad was the primary giver of those black eyes. It's not like it sounds, anyway. He was just raging. Hell, we all were raging. He took out his shit on me. I took out my shit on him. And now it's done. "You?"

She knocks on her head like it's a piece of wood. "Nope, not planning on getting caught, either."

*She doesn't say she's not planning on committing any felonies*, I think with a smirk, wondering just where she's thinking about fucking. She's right, the school's probably a bad idea, but there are some old dirt roads on the mountain, federal reserve land that no one goes on except the occasional ranger. We could definitely get up to something there . . . and most likely, not get caught.

I put a pin in that idea as she starts walking again. We look at some newer model cars, ones I can mostly identify. Mustang, Camaro, and a few Corvettes.

A mullet-haired blond kid in baggy jeans, probably no more than twenty, judging by his smooth jawline, waves at Erica, and she gives him a friendly smile. I'm already directing her that way, knowing she'll want to talk to the guy, but she puts a hand on my chest. "Hey, would you mind grabbing me a Coke?" She points at a vendor on the far side of the line of cars. "I'll meet you right here, by Todd's Challenger. That's the *purple* one." She winks as she says it, teasing me.

I look from her to Todd, trying to get a read. "Yeah, sure . . . be right back."

I use the full breadth of my strides to get to the drink vendor, not shortening them for Lil Bit's stride the way I've been doing the rest of the day, and get back with a cold can of Coke in record time. Not that there's a record for that, but if there were, I'd have just beaten it because I was damn fast.

Erica and Todd are deep in conversation. I try to judge if it's personal. Hell, I don't know, maybe she dated him too? Or he's Reed's little brother? I don't know, but I'm standing here like a chump with her drink, feeling a little too much like Reed, I reckon.

But when Erica points Todd to the driver seat and dips under the hood, I can see there's something more professional going on. Or at least I hope there is. She leans over the engine and he revs it loudly. Erica doesn't even flinch, listening closely.

*She's like the Engine Whisperer*, I think proudly. I have no reason to be proud of that. It's definitely not my doing, but I like that she's someone other people seek out for her brain. That she's got this whole thing going on that she's in control of.

I had that once with the farm. Ran it and myself to the ground, but she's thriving with it. That much is obvious from today.

Todd gets out from behind the wheel, feet spread wide and hands crossed over his chest, a stance I know well. He's pissed. He frowns as he says something I can't hear, and Erica shakes her head. Todd kicks the tire of his fancy car, saying something again. Erica shrugs and shakes her head. I can see the no on her lips as I approach with her Coke.

"Here you go, Erica."

Todd's brows jump together. "Who's Erica?"

She elbows me in the gut, not hard, but I wince anyway. "Me. You don't get to call me that," she tells the kid.

"Whatever, Rix. You sure you can't do it? Just a little more." He's needling her, though I haven't the foggiest idea what about.

"Nah, I'll do a little research to confirm. But I think you're maxed." She takes my hand this time, pulling me away. "'Bye, Todd."

The kid looks even more pissed as we walk away.

"What's that about?" I ask, curious and not the least bit jealous. That's my story and I'm sticking to it. And really, the kid wasn't even looking at Erica that way. Dumbass doesn't see what's right in front of him, but I do.

"Nothing. Just car shit." I hear the 'drop it.' "I think I'm good. You ready to head to the other side of the mountain?"

I nod. "Yeah, take me home, Lil Bit. Maybe if you're lucky, I'll feed you dinner too. Fair warning, though. All I can make are pancakes, so I hope you want them again." She laughs, shoving at my chest.

I think she's feeling me up again, so I flex a little for her. She grabs my nipple again, twisting and laughing. "Come on, Cowboy."

At the same time, she's nearly brought me to my knees. "Shit . . . stop. You want me to do that to you? And I don't mean in sexy way." The threat holds no heat since I'm rubbing my chest soothingly.

"Go ahead," she dares, pushing her tits up at me. I know she doesn't have a bra on because I watched her get dressed earlier. But when she does that, I don't want to give her a purple nurple. I want to cup and suck those nipples until she begs me to give her more.

And with that evil thought, I promise her, "Later."

# CHAPTER 11

## ERICA

The drive out to the ranch is never-ending, but scenic, at least. I'll admit to staying in my little corner most of the time, rarely even venturing to the mountain, much less the other side. But we drive through Great Falls and Brody points out things of interest . . . the corner where he had his first fight—he was nine, he says, and of course it was about a girl. The feed store, 'Buy supplies for the critters there, other than hay, of course,' like I would know that, and his favorite restaurant, a honkytonk named Hank's that has meatloaf to kill for.

"Meatloaf? Worth a life? I doubt that," I say skeptically. "Meatloaf is pretty much the fuck-it-all of dinners. Oops, not enough meat? Throw some breadcrumbs in it. Taste like shit? Cover it in ketchup. I'm not buying it."

"You'll see. It'll change your life," he says with a smile. An actual one, with light in his dark eyes and his white teeth showing between those full, kissable lips.

Not too long ago, I'd thought he simply never smiled. There'd always been something behind it, a little bit of mischief or challenge, something at least. But now, he looks happy. Pretty sure I did that with my pussy. Okay, maybe my personality a tiny bit too. The thought is exciting. Somehow, so is eating dinner at some future date with him, even if it's meatloaf.

We leave the small town that honestly looks quite picturesque with its rural, comfy vibe. I can imagine tourists who come to the resort taking a quaint getaway day trip to Great Falls when they need a break from skiing. But for the locals, it's home, with a cute downtown Brody says is where they have festivals, playgrounds teeming with kids, and an old-style movie theater with only two screens. It's different from Morristown on the other side of the mountain for sure, which is mostly commercial in contrast. We have a downtown and locals, and it's home to me, but it feels more businesslike all the time. Not the same welcoming warmth Great Falls has.

I should've come over here more often. Not just the occasional farmer's market trips with Emily.

*Maybe I will come over more often with Brody here*, I think. I meant it when I said I don't have time for anything serious, but a little part of me isn't ready to drop him off and drive away. Not today, at least, when the garage is closed and the day is mine to do with as I please.

The road becomes more deserted, only an occasional truck passing us, and Brody directs me well beyond the outskirts of town. "There'll be a break in the fence on the right." I see it and turn in carefully, feeling the bumps of metal beneath the truck. "Cattle guard," he explains. "Keeps them from just waltzing out the front gate."

"You leave it open?" I ask. I don't know why, but that worries me. Like I know shit about taking care of cows, but that doesn't sound safe. Is cattle theft still a thing? If so, a thief would just need to back up to the front door and rob 'em blind. Okay, maybe that's an overreach, but I'm a total city slicker and proud of it.

Brody shakes his head. "No, I texted that I'm incoming so someone rode out to open it because I don't have an opener with me. I'll close it after you leave so we're secure for the night."

Relief washes through me. That the cattle are safe or that he is?

As if he needs protection. I internally roll my eyes at my protective streak. It's just habit. Protect Emily, the garage, Mom and Dad, the whole damn country.

We pull up to a two-story country house, white with black trim that matches the barn set off to the right. There are several trucks parked outside, and I can't help but mentally take their measure. Mechanic's habit.

"Shit." Brody's murmur is under his breath.

"What's wrong?" I look around, looking for . . . something?

Two men appear in the doorway of the barn. I can see the grin on one from here, it's that bright. The other guy looks thunderous, murderous.

"Who's that?" I ask, on edge as I switch out my feet to put my left on the brake and right hovering over the gas. Old habits die hard, and if we need to move quickly, I'm fucking ready.

"My boss, Mark. His brother, Luke." Brody's voice has a tinge of affection to it, but I suspect he doesn't realize it. "Come on, I'll introduce you."

The adrenaline coursing through my blood evaporates to be replaced with fizzy nerves as I throw the truck in park. I hop down and meet Brody at the back gate. Neither of the Barn Door Boys moves. That's what I'm calling them because in my head, they're a boy band and therefore the least intimidating guys ever, not that I'm scared of anyone, ever. Usually. Mostly.

You know how mirrors have that warning, 'objects are closer than they appear'? Perspective is like that as we walk closer to the Barn Door Boys too. Only as we get closer, they get even larger.

Dear God, what the hell do they feed these guys out here? I know I'm small, have dealt with that disadvantage my whole life, and Brody's big. No doubt about that. But I'd figured he was a one-off. Nope, there are at least two more just like him—tall, broad, muscled, with a healthy dose of asshole. Different versions of it—one cocky, one mean—but different sides of the same coin. Been there, done that with a veritable buffet of options when I got my uniform. Military guys all have a good streak of asshole-itis. Me included. You have to if you want to handle even a single enlisted day. And that thought makes me stand a little taller and face the Barn Door Boys head on with my own five-foot-nothing version of a swagger.

Brody makes introductions. The mean one is Mark and the cocky one is Luke. "Good to meet you, Rix." Luke holds out his hand.

It definitely did not escape my notice that Brody introduced me as Rix, though he's never called me the name everyone else does. I know it started as an easy way to irk me, but I like that he calls me Erica. A little. Fine, a lot.

"Mama Louise set an extra plate at dinner." Mark's simple statement is heavy with meaning.

Brody turns to me. "You are absolutely welcome to stay, but don't feel like you have to. She'll understand if you want to run. I sure as fuck did when she first got her claws into me."

Luke snorts. "We were stuck with her from birth. You could've run. You *chose* to stay around." Mark clears his throat, which could mean nothing, but I'm pretty sure he just subtly told Luke to 'shut the fuck up.'

Brody's eyes flash something dark and pained, but it's gone quick as a blink so maybe I'm wrong because his answer is light and teasing. "Don't let him fool you. Mama Louise is the scariest thing on this ranch and no one stands a chance against her."

All three guys nod like that's the God's honest truth, and I'm curious as can be about a woman who has these monsters damn near quaking in their boots. "I could eat before my drive back, I guess. Though I'm a vegetarian. That gonna be a problem?"

Mark and Luke lose their foreheads to their eyebrows. Brody's lips quirk in amusement without giving away that I'm fucking with them. He knows I'm full of shit since he saw me pack away a huge corndog at the car show today.

"Just kidding. Take me to the beef show."

The Barn Door Boys breathe a sigh of relief as Brody chuckles. But they quickly set him right, Mark telling Brody, "Shay made a pot roast today." Again, such simple words, but everything Mark says seems to have three more meanings, each deeper than the last.

"Shiiiit." Brody's horror doesn't equate with the dinner menu, and that confuses me until he asks the guys, "What's she been up to?" Mostly, he's giving a hairy eyeball to Luke, and I remember Brody said that he's married to Shayanne.

"Little bit of this, little bit of that. Ranting about you quite a bit. But don't worry, I distracted her for you." Luke's grin is back in full force as he offers a wink to go along with the day's report.

I elbow Brody, sensing his torture and piling on the way only friends can. "Cowboy, I think that means he was dicking your sister to shut her up."

*Blink. Blink. Blink.*

Three cowboys look at me blankly for a long, slow heartbeat as they process whether I actually said what I said.

Brody, used to me already, unfreezes first. "Damn it, Erica. Don't say shit like that about my sister."

Mark snorts and Luke points at me. "I like her, Brody."

As we head into the house, the Barn Door Boys stomping their boots to get the dirt off, Brody whispers in my ear. "I like you, too." The sweetness is tempered when he nibbles my earlobe a little hard, a nip for my own biting words.

I take a steadying breath as we walk in the back door, ready to face down the monster inside if the guys' description of Mama Louise is accurate.

From behind the wall of the Barn Door Boys, I'm invisible because I hear a woman's voice say, "Well, where is she?"

Mark and Luke step apart like curtains opening for a great reveal, but it's just me. I swear a record scratches in the air as I get a glimpse of Brody's family and they get a first look at me. Shayanne is doing some fist-punching, boot-kicking air fight thing from her chair that looks to be a celebration at my arrival. There's a blonde woman holding a big bowl of mashed potatoes, another blonde at the sink, and a brunette holding a baby with crazy pigtails. A child that small should not have enough hair for pigtails, but this one does. A young boy is making faces at the baby, who laughs in delight. There's also another edition of a blonde Barn Door Boy, a threesome then, and two more tall, dark, and handsomes who must be Brody's brothers. Each and every one of them looks from me to a petite blonde woman standing by the stove with a spoon in her hand.

Mama Louise.

That has to be her. I know who the commanding officer is in any room. It's not by size. It's not by age. It's purely by presence. And she's the fucking Commander in Chief here.

"Nice to meet you, Rix. Come on in and have a seat. First-timers don't have to help." The implication is that next time, because she's already deemed there will be one, I'll be expected to help with dinner. I'm not sure how I feel about that yet.

Brody guides me to a chair and sits down beside me. Everyone else falls into what seems to be their usual places. Brody goes around the table, giving me everyone's names, and I make a joke that there'd better not be a pop quiz later, but really, I learned them all. Barn Door Boys plus one are Mark, Luke, and James. Their wives are Katelyn, Shayanne, and Sophie, who is holding Cindy Lou. The other kid is Cooper, and his mom, Allyson. Brody's brothers are Bobby and Brutal. I don't ask about the nickname, but Shayanne has no such filter.

As soon as grace is said and food starts passing, she asks, "Why Rix? I'd get Ric or Ricki from Erica, but Rix? What's the story?" She's plopping mashed potatoes on her plate, never missing a beat as she passes the bowl to Luke and takes the plate of pork chops from Sophie.

I swallow a bite of cinnamon apple chutney, testing it alone before adding it to my pork chop because I don't even know what a chutney is. Cooking is definitely not my strong suit. It's pretty good, though, so I spoon it over the meat. "It actually was Ric when I was a kid, but I went through a grabby mine-mine-mine phase when me and my sister were around four. Anything Emily got her grubby little hands on, I wanted it and would rip it from her, saying 'Ric's.' Apparently, toddlers tend to talk about themselves in the third person?" I shrug at the memory and the story I've told several times before. "Before long, 'Ric's' became 'Rix' and here I am."

"Cute," Shay decides. "I like it. But I'm *pretty sure* I like that Brody calls you Erica even better if everyone else calls you Rix."

She's looking from Brody to me and back again like we're going to declare our undying love for one another at any given moment and she doesn't want to miss a thing.

Suddenly, this whole thing feels ridiculously awkward. I mean, Brody and I explicitly said that we're not doing serious. Just hanging out and okay, fucking. And yet, here we are, doing family introductions after one night of crazy-awesome sex and one spontaneous date.

Is a car show a date?

I think yes. I think Brody thinks yes too.

So yeah, one night and one date.

And now, family dinner.

What the hell have I gotten myself into?

As much as my brain is thinking this whole thing through and trying to sound the alarm, my body is warm and fizzy thanks to Brody's fingers tracing soothing circles on my thigh. He's not even high, closer to my knee than anything naughty, but any skin on skin contact between us feels intimate. His touch is purposeful, like he knows I'm about to bail and is telling me it'll be fine.

Luckily, the not-quite interrogation ends as conversation turns to cattle, something I know zilch about. But their worries are clear—cattle prices are falling and it's almost market time. That's straightforward enough.

"You gonna be good without me here?" Luke asks Mark. Shayanne's face goes anxious, a new expression for the seemingly always bubbly and biting woman.

Mark grunts and lifts his chin toward Brody. I take it to mean he'll be fine with Brody's help. A movie plays out in my head, Mark and Brody astride horses, working the cattle one way and then another. I'm not sure that's even what they do since Brody said they use ATVs and a Gator too. But it's my mental movie fantasy, so I can choose anything I want.

Like a shirtless Brody, with the sun reflecting off his bare chest. And oh, yeah, he's pouring water over his head, the droplets running in rivulets I want to chase with my tongue.

Errrk. Definitely a mental movie I need to save for later. Not at Mama Louise's dinner table.

"We'll have to get in a night out before we go. Celebrate the start of market season with fried food, good music, and friends."

Oh, shit. Shayanne's looking at me as she says that. Normally, I'd throw up a middle finger and tell her to fuck off. I don't do things I don't want to do. Or at least I like to think that's true. But with every eye at the table on me, including Brody's, I'm finding it hard to be that crass. Mom would be proud that some of her manners and politeness did wear off on me. She's had serious doubts over my mouthy nature.

"Oh, uh . . . maybe." It's all I'll promise now. And that's mostly because I felt Brody's hand squeeze my thigh supportively. Or encouragingly? Or in warning? I don't know, but it'd felt nice there.

Shayanne doesn't take no for an answer. She doesn't take maybe for one, either. "Next Saturday night. Hank's. Brody'll pick you up. Wear boots if you got 'em for the dancing."

I cut my eyes to Brody. "You said you don't dance."

The smirk he gives me says 'oh, I dance', and I realize he only said that to get out of dancing with Emily. Well, maybe that and the fact that the music wasn't exactly danceable at Two Roses. Mosh pit bouncing off one another like pissed-off pinballs, sure. Dancing, no.

Oh, the music.

"What kind of music?" I grin widely. "Please don't say country." I'm kidding, mostly, but not a single smile cracks.

Bobby beats everyone else to the punch. "No carrot cake for you if you talk smack about country music. It's the best genre known to man. And I don't just say that because I contribute to the industry."

He places his hand over his heart, and I swear he's serious, but there's such a current of humor through the Barn Door Boys that I can't be sure how straight he's being with me. "What do you listen to if not the best music ever created?"

"Rock. Seventies, from my dad. Eighties and nineties, from my sergeant. And everything since just because I like it. The louder, the better."

"Loud is right," Brody deadpans. "It's more screaming than music too."

Everyone cringes as if I pulled out my phone to start my latest Spotify playlist.

Brody sighs heavily and confesses, "You don't have to come, but I'd like for you to. Unless you don't want to hang out with these guys . . ." He mouths *assholes* behind his hand, hiding the curse.

I should run through town, over the mountain, and back to my garage. Work all night alone with whatever decade of rock music I want playing loud enough to shut up the chatter in my head.

What I shouldn't do is sit here and get to know these people. What I shouldn't do is agree to a night out with them. What I shouldn't do is look forward to seeing Cowboy in his country element, busting out his moves to impress me.

But that's what I do, anyway, knowing it's a piss-poor decision that's got the potential to get someone hurt. Mostly, me. Maybe Brody. He said he's fine with casual, and I have to take him at his word, but tonight doesn't seem casual, doesn't feel like no big deal. And that worries me.

"Sounds like a plan. Saturday night. Twirl me around the dance floor, Cowboy."

What the fuck did I just agree to?

Quiet and low enough that no one should be able to hear, Brody whispers out of the side of his mouth, "Fuck yeah, I will, Lil Bit."

Mama Louise, who's been silently watching the whole dinner and a show before her, finally interjects. "Language."

I almost laugh. The air actually bubbles up from my belly and the sound catches in my throat when I realize that she's serious. A table full of big, growly alpha guys and their wives, who all seem to be pretty awesome themselves, but they all bow down to a single word from Mama Louise. She doesn't even have to try. Her power here is absolute.

I want to be her one day.

# CHAPTER 12

## BRODY

"Fuck you doing?" Some people can be described as their bark being worse than their bite. Mark isn't one of them. His bark is bad. His bite is worse. I'm pretty much the same, but we've found some degree of respect in our similarities. For the most part, we try not to piss each other off. It'd be too easy to bury the body on the thousands of acres out here where no one would ever find it.

Not that I've considered that. Recently.

Today might challenge that, though.

"Texting." Translation: what the fuck does it look like I'm doing, dumbass?

"Erica?"

I give him a dark look that threatens imminent violence even though I know he's pushing my buttons on purpose. "Yep. How's Princess this morning?"

No one gets to have that degree of familiarity with Katelyn but him. Mark and Katelyn are wound up in each other tight and are possessive as fuck of one another. So using her pet name is damn near like waving a red cape in front of a bull.

He returns the glare, dips his chin, and the battle ends. Hell, it was probably his version of fun. Or more likely, he's testing out the situation to get a read on me.

"How's Rix?" The change to the name everyone else uses is as much of an apology as I'm going to get because he's damn sure not sorry. But my reaction at his using Erica's given name wasn't lost on either of us. He's got reason to be possessive, and the sentiment is returned with his wife. I've got no reason to be greedy about being the only one to use her name, and she's made it crystal clear that we're casual. Exactly what I want too.

Except . . .

We've been texting every day. Pictures of cars and pictures of cattle. Pictures of her short, muscled legs wound up in her sheets. Pictures of my chest with the sheets puddled a bit low.

I haven't read a single page of a book all week because we sit in bed at night talking, the phone bridging the distance across town. Sometimes, it's just her voice in my ear. Sometimes, we FaceTime, and I love to see her in thin tank tops with sleepy eyes. We have conversations about our day—work, people, random tidbits of life.

I've heard stories about her time in the military and how she had to work twice as hard to prove herself because, according to Erica,

*"Apparently, engines are these magical, mystical things that can't be understood if you have a vagina instead of a dick. The guys hadn't liked it much when I told them that if I could find a G-spot, I sure as fuck could find a carburetor, but I doubted they could say the same thing. About either of those."*

I'd laughed my ass off so loudly that Brutal had knocked on the door to check on me. When I said I was fine, he'd told me to shut the fuck up because Cooper had school in the morning. Like I wouldn't be up two hours before Cooper, anyway. But I'd quieted down because I like the kid. And we have plans for a rematch at cornhole tonight so I can redeem myself after getting skunked during our last match.

Erica and I have talked about her coming back to run the garage for her Dad, who retired a bit earlier than she expected. He's fine and healthy, apparently, which is good, and wants to spend time traveling the US with Janice, which is great. But there's a hitch in Erica's voice there, something between her and her dad she's not sharing.

I don't push because I don't like talking about my dad, either. Which is why I tell her all the great things about ranch life, focusing on the hard work and pride in a job well done. I show her the goat herd and tell her how I raised them from newborn babies to adults that prance around mischievously, kicking me in the shin every chance they get. I explain raising calves and selling cattle every year so we can do it all again in a never-ending cycle. With close to fatherly pride, I tell her how Shayanne became an entrepreneur on her own terms, Brutal is becoming the almost-husband and father he was always meant to be, and Bobby is getting deeper into his music every day.

It's only been a week's worth of conversations, but I feel like I'm getting to know Erica a little more in those few minutes of conversations before we both crash, knowing we have early mornings ahead. Last night, the looming alarm hadn't seemed to matter and we'd talked for almost two hours. And I'm feeling it today.

"She's all right." I answer Mark on delay because I'm glancing at my phone again, smiling at the picture Erica just sent. Black tires with white stripes along the side walls.

*Me: Putting shoes on Sally?*

*Erica: Good memory. Wilson says hi.*

Wilson did nothing of the sort.

*Me: <middle finger emoji> Tell him I said hello too.*

I look up to find Mark looking at me, his face carefully blank. I don't ask, don't say a word, knowing if he has something to say, he will.

"I like her for you. She's brash, keeps you on your toes. A bit wild, but smart too." He nods, having said his piece.

I shake my head. "You met her for the grand total of like one hour, and it ain't like that. We're keeping it casual."

He laughs, deeply and violently. A rarity from the stoic man, which is probably why it sounds like rusty metal in his chest. I swear to God, he even wipes his eyes, tears leaking out from laughing so hard. At me? At the idea of Erica and me being casual? Fuck if I know.

He sobers, and it's like the laughter never happened. "You weren't around back then, or well, not around like you are now . . . but James and Sophie? They were a *summer fling*." He spits out 'summer fling' like it's the stupidest thing he's ever heard. "They seem casual?"

He already knows the answer as well as I do.

"Me and Katelyn? Supposed to just be friends." He actually does finger quotes with his thick, muddy hands. "Till she stomped out here in the middle of the night and forcibly yanked my head outta my ass for me."

My brows jump together. "Katelyn?" She's the sweetest woman I think I've ever met, literally nice as can be, with the patience of a saint. I try to picture her giving Mark what for and can't even imagine it.

He snorts. "She's tougher than she lets on." His eyes go distant, and I know he's thinking about his bride because he's got that stupid-in-love look on his face. The look I never want to have.

"Yeah, well . . . Erica and I are on the same page. Casual only. She's busy, I'm busy, and we ain't got the time nor the inclination for anything serious."

My phone dings in my hand. I'd like to say it's a saved by the bell situation, but it feels more like it's calling me out on my shit.

"Time's a fickle bitch. Don't let her fuck you over." He narrows his eyes like he's imparting great wisdom. "I ain't never regretted a single moment I've spent with Katelyn. Hard to say I regret the part when I was fighting us because we got where we needed to be in the end, but I'm a greedy fucker and I'll take every second I can get with her, so I wish I'd had a head-out-of-my-ass-ectomy a little sooner."

Mark is not a share your feelings type. So he might as well have just opened his chest and fileted his heart to tell me how much his wife means to him, all the while implying that the woman I've spent one night with plus a week of texting looks like a pretty damn similar situation to him.

Fuck this. "Are we going to hold hands, sing *Kumbaya*, and talk about our periods, or work?"

These cows need to move over to the next fenced pasture, and we need to spread some hay and do a wellness check on as many as we can before the sun sets. James is riding fence on an ATV today, far on the back pasture where we're eventually headed with the herd. It's never-ending, it's what I know, and it's even what I love.

And I'm gonna win that damn cornhole match tonight if it's the last thing I do. My buddy Cooper is going down. I like that a simple game with my nephew is the biggest thing on my plate right now, and I plan to keep it that way.

---

*Me: I'm here.*

*Erica: On my way down.*

At Cole Automotive, Erica's upstairs apartment doesn't exactly have a front porch for me to climb up and knock on the door like a proper date. But the text does the trick. Because this is a date. An official one, preplanned with me picking her up and nervous excitement in my gut. I don't know why I'm nervous. Hell, we talked earlier today, for fuck's sake, but while I stand outside the door waiting for Erica to come down, my belly feels like I ate a gas station burrito.

I peek through the single row of windows when I hear a door inside close. Erica's not visible over the truck she's got in bay one, but then I see her as she rolls the overhead door up like she's revealing a prize on a game show. And she's the fucking grand prize.

Black suede boots reach just below her knees, fishnet hose disappear beneath a grey denim skirt that looks touchably soft and worn, all topped with a black tank top. Her hair is down, a shiny curtain of dark brown silk that nearly reaches her waist, and her eyes are smudged with black stuff, making them look hypnotic and smoky.

"Fuck, woman."

I'm not known for being eloquent, and she's taken what few words I do have. But her smile says it's enough.

"Looking pretty good yourself, Cowboy." She lets her eyes lick up my body, and I hold still, not just letting her but wanting her to. I can tell she took her time getting ready for tonight, and so did I.

I detailed my truck, well aware that Erica will be judging me on it, left my dirty hat at home, and wore my best jeans, nicest boots, and a grey plaid button-up shirt. Without even meaning to, we sorta match. And doesn't noticing that make me feel like a thirteen-year-old girl?

"Thanks. You ready?" I ask instead of pushing her back inside and going straight upstairs like I'm tempted to do.

"Almost. Just one thing." She beckons me with a crook of her finger, and I bend down as she tilts her chin up, the intent obvious.

There's no shy reacquaintance with us. We both dive into the kiss in equal measure, fighting to taste each other. When she falls back to her flat feet, taking those lips away from me, I growl at the loss. She pats my chest, knowing damn well that she's driving me crazy.

"Okay, now I'm ready. Let's go."

"I kinda hate you right now," I tell her without any heat as I adjust my dick in my jeans.

"Then my plan's working," she says as she goes around to the passenger side of my truck. I open the door for her, but she rejects my hand in favor of using the oh-shit handle and rails to climb up into the cab by herself. It's not graceful, and I get a shot up her skirt. Her look back says that was intentional too.

I get in behind the wheel and ask, even though I know it's a softball lob she's pitched on purpose. "Plan?"

"To tease you mercilessly all night. I'll decide later if I'm going to do anything about it or just leave you with blue balls." She taps her lips, which are fighting a smile, as she contemplates.

"What if I work you up all night too?" I ask lightly, finding a flaw in her plan. Well, maybe not so much a flaw as another angle she hasn't considered.

"You'd damn well better. That's my intention. Otherwise, I wouldn't have told you about the plan."

Oh, she's considered the angles, all right. Every last one of them, and I'm rushing to keep up with her when my brain is fogged over so quickly around her.

Two hours later, she's agreed that maybe Hank's is the singular exception to meatloaf being disgusting, which he accepted graciously from behind the bar by sending over the beers we ordered with a lime wedge garnish. They're not Coronas, so maybe a nice gesture, but also maybe a *fuck you.* But the meatloaf was good, and Lil Bit admitted it. That much I know for sure.

Using the full space of the booth, I lean in close, putting my head on her shoulder and licking my index finger to make a tally mark in the air. I won that one. She laughs and shoves at me. "Get off me, asshole."

"That ain't what you said last weekend," I tease back quietly, mostly not caring that everyone's listening to every flirty word between us.

But they are, and I can see those wheels turning in each of their minds. When I look at Erica, I don't care because she's holding true to her word and I'm holding to mine. And that's what matters.

We've had fun all night—dancing, laughing, talking, and touching. And it's just what I need. She's what I need, like this and nothing more.

Katelyn hops up, and by some invisible signal, the other women do too. Erica leans down, close to my ear so only I hear her. "Bathroom break so they can interrogate me. No worries, I'll talk shit about you so they know I'm only after your dick," Erica promises and then winks as she struts off behind Katelyn, Shayanne, Sophie, and Allyson.

I can't help but track her across the room as she goes. She stands out in Hank's, her rocker look and spitfire attitude different from the mostly rural ranching types who frequent this bar. But fuck, if that isn't what draws me to her. I realize that Mark's right. She keeps me on my toes and I like it. Not that I'll tell him that, and not that it has some greater, deeper meaning the way he suggested.

"Well?" Brutal asks when the girls turn the corner into the hallway and we can all focus on something besides their asses again.

"Well, what?" Playing dumb seems prudent.

He pops me on the back of my head, knocking me forward. I'm a big motherfucker, but next to my brother, I look like an average-sized Joe. And he sometimes forgets his strength, but sometimes, he sure as hell uses it on purpose.

"What the fuck, Brutal?"

He leans forward, elbows on the table and eyes narrowed. "Get on with it before they get back."

Bunch of gossipy assholes.

"Nothing to tell. I like her, like fucking her. She likes me, likes fucking me. The end." How many times am I going to have to say this? Guys don't usually do this, do they? Five pairs of eyes are laser-locked on me. Three blue, two brown, all telling me I'm a dumbass, but I'm not. "I swear it. She's as much about casual as I am. We're good."

One laughs, I'm not even sure who starts it, but then they're all chuckling. At me. "Fuck y'all."

I sit back, arms crossed over my chest, knees spread wide beneath the table, a menacing glare on my face. They laugh harder.

Thank fuck the girls come back, all atwitter. Each of us stands, letting them sit back down, but I hold out my hand to Erica. "Let's dance."

"Fuck yes, Cowboy." She sounds as relieved as I am to get away from the table for a minute.

As we take to the dance floor, Morgan Wallen's *Chasing You* pours out of the jukebox and over the swaying couples. We start to move, nothing fancy now, though I showed her how to two-step earlier and she can follow a lead for some simple turns and switches. But we need to talk, so I just sway her back and forth. "How bad was it in there? You running on me?"

A grin stretches her lips, but there's a tinge of fear deep in her eyes. "You have a great family and they obviously love you . . . a lot. They were singing your praises, how you're so good with animals which means you'll be a great dad one day, how you look after everyone so you'll be a good husband, how you're smarter than you let on so don't let the dumb redneck act fool me, and that once you're in, you stay in, hell or high water."

"*Shit.*"

It's nice that they said those things, really, it is. But I can feel the foundation rumbling beneath Erica and me from their assumptions. She's quiet for a second, our eyes locked. It hurts my neck a little to look down when she's this close, and her fiery eyes make it hard to say this. I pull her in even closer, and she lets me, laying her cheek to my chest.

"You know how you said everyone thought you were gonna marry Reed?" I feel her nod. "My family wants me to get married. It's sweet, and mostly because they're all so happy that they want everyone to be in love, but it doesn't have anything to do with what I want. Nothing's changed from what we said."

The tension dissolves and she melts in my arms. "You sure?"

"Hell, you don't have to be so excited that I'm not dropping to a knee." I sound harsh, but I'm fighting back a laugh and she knows it.

She smacks my chest. Feels like a butterfly landing on me—okay, not really, because she can pack a punch I'm sure, but she's taking it easy on me. "We met a fucking week ago. I've already tried to kill you with a wrench, almost sucked your soul out of your dick, damn near killed you with marathon sex, done the meet-the-family deals for the most part, been on two dates, and texted like teenagers who got their first phones yesterday. I think we're good."

By the end, she's laughing too.

"What?" I grab my ear with two fingers, wiggling it. "I didn't hear a thing you said after 'suck my dick.' Was it anything important?"

Her head shake, smile, and the light in her eyes tells me our foundation just steadied. We're back to where we were, thankfully. Or mostly, at least, but my family damn near fucked this up for me with their expectations. Haven't they figured out that I'm not good at meeting those by now?

I glance over and they're watching us on the dance floor. I sway Erica around so her back is to them and flip them my middle finger, eyeballing each and every one of the nosy, gossipy, intrusive, meddling family members at the table. They smile as if I just told them all 'thank you.'

"Give it a little extra 'fuck you' from me too." Erica knows exactly what I'm doing, and why. I think she wishes she could tell her family the same thing, probably the same way, knowing her.

Instead, we dance. That moment fades to be replaced by the simple pleasure of holding her in my arms and moving around the floor. I add back in the turns I taught her, catching her and pulling her in tight every once in a while, building a fire between us each time our bodies press together. I pick her up and tilt her back for a dip, which makes her hoot with surprise, and when I stand back upright, she's high enough on my body that I can kiss her lips easily.

It's a sweet, quick kiss, but damned if I'm not rock-hard for her. She doesn't taste like sour cherries the way I thought she would. No, it's something deeper and more layered, uniquely Erica. And I want more of it, already addicted to her. I let her slide down slowly, enjoying every inch of her against me. When I'm sure her feet are on the floor, I spin her out again, teasing us both, and that fire lights up in her eyes again. "Brody."

Just my name, but so much in the two syllables. Lust, need, desire, challenge, an order.

I pull her back in, aligning our bodies. I know she can feel that she's not alone in her current predicament, being in the middle of a dance floor instead of in her bed, my bed, or shit, my truck in the parking lot, for all I care. But I don't move toward the door. I just keep shifting right and left, and she follows me, damn near trying to melt into each other's skin through our clothes.

I hear a throat clear behind me, and I open my eyes, already pissed that someone's interrupting my moment with Erica.

"I hate to do this . . . you have no idea how much . . . but Rix, your phone is laying on the table and it's blowing up. Somebody named Reed called several times in a row and texted too." There's a big question mark in Shay's tone, asking who the fuck Reed is.

Sweet sister looking out for me when it's always been the other way around.

"Shit. Fuck. Damn. Something must be wrong at the garage." Erica's eyes meet mine. "I need to see what's up."

I let her go and she struts to the table, grabbing her phone before heading to the bathroom hallway for a little bit of quiet to make her call.

Shay hisses, "Who's Reed?"

Slowly and lazily, I cut my eyes back to her. "Her employee at the garage." Shay relaxes. "And her ex."

Jaw tight, she hisses again. "Well . . . don't just stand there, do something." She flaps her hands around, gesturing me toward the hallway.

What does she expect me to do? Charge back there, take Erica's phone, and tell Reed not to contact her again? That'd work out pretty shitty when he needed to show up to work on Monday morning. More importantly, that's not my place. Even if we were something else and I was dropping to my knee—*which I'm not*—it would be a bitch move to tell your partner who they can and can't be friends and work with.

"Shayanne, calm your tits. They're not like that because Erica doesn't want them to be. And we're not like that either. Just chill." She looks at me like I'm stupid, and also, like she's about to go ten ways of beatdown on me. I bend down, getting in her face so she hears this loud and clear. "Y'all need to slow your roll, because whatever shit show you pulled in the bathroom damn near ran her off. *Back off. I'm good*."

She obviously has her doubts but doesn't get the chance to tell me so because Erica walks up. "I gotta go. Reed's broke down and I need to get the tow truck so I can get his car to the garage. I'm sorry."

"It's fine," I say, daring Shayanne to say otherwise. "I'll drive you home so you can go get him. I'm happy to help if you want a spare set of hands too."

She shakes her head. "I already called an Uber to pick me up. No sense in us both leaving. Stay and have fun with your family. But can you walk me out?"

I'm disappointed, but I escort her out front. I walk her over to my truck, away from the door at least, and drop the tailgate. I lift her under her arms to set her down.

"I could've hopped up here myself, you know." Stinging words meant to hurt a little.

"I know, but we don't have much time and I was in a hurry to do this . . ." I step between her knees and cup her jaw, my lips hitting hers a breath later. Under the cover of night, I can do what I've wanted to do all night on the dance floor. I trace a hand down her neck, across her collarbone, to palm her breast. No bra. Fuck, does she even own one? I hope not.

She arches into my touch and I take the kiss deeper. Her legs wrap around mine, locking me in place as if I have anywhere else to be, and her hands grip my shirt, pulling me in closer. She kisses me back ferociously, our teeth clacking together and tongues invading, and that's before she nips my bottom lip, pulling it sharply.

"Fuck, Erica." I'm contemplating just how out of sight we are in this dark corner of the parking lot when her phone buzzes.

Her posture changes instantly, going from straining toward me to straight-backed. "That's my ride. Go back in and have fun with your family. Don't let me ruin a fun night before Shay and Luke leave town."

"Yeah," I say, though I know I'm not going back inside to listen to everyone's opinions on what I should and shouldn't do. "Is it a bitch move if I say that I'm really pissed at Reed right now? I was hoping to be balls deep in you again tonight."

Erica tilts her head, teasing laughter in her words. "Aw, Cowboy. You say the sweetest things."

"You sure Reed's a good mechanic? Seems like a good one wouldn't have his car break down." Fine, so I'm a bit pouty.

"He's good. Just bad luck, probably."

"Yeah, ours," I say darkly, pressing one more kiss to her lips.

I let her push me back and hop down from the tailgate. "Goodnight, Brody." She rights her skirt and walks the few steps toward the silver sedan that's picking her up before turning back. "Oh, and you were right . . . the meatloaf was good and the music didn't suck too badly."

I grin at her parting words, waving as she climbs in and disappears into the night. I look at the door to Hank's, knowing my family expects me to come back inside. Instead, I send the family chat group—yes, Shay added me back in—a middle finger emoji and get in my truck.

Fuck those fuckers. I'm going home, maybe reading a book before bed, and waiting to see if Erica texts me tonight when she's done with Reed's shit.

# CHAPTER 13

## ERICA

I should change. I knew it before the Uber driver dropped me off at the garage. But I don't. I'm mad that Reed interrupted the fun I was having with Brody and pissed at the cock block. So a small piece of me wants to irritate the fuck out of Reed in return.

Petty? Yes, admittedly so. Am I doing it anyway? Also, yes.

So I climb up in the tow truck, knowing that Reed will have to do all the work of hooking up his car while I stay in the relative comfort of the driver's seat. Serves him right. I'm not a monster. I don't typically blame folks when their vehicles break down. Like I told Brody, sometimes it's just bad luck, or maybe maintenance snuck up on them and they couldn't afford it, or a laundry list of reasons a piece of machinery might stop working unexpectedly. But Brody is right . . . a mechanic shouldn't break down. It's bad for business.

I pull up to the lot where Reed told me he was parked to find him sitting on the hood of the Camaro he overhauled himself, leaning back against the windshield and staring at the stars. He looks lost in thought, small against the big blackness of the night surrounding him.

My petty anger dissolves. If it were me, he'd rescue me without a second thought. I should afford him the same, especially since we're friends. Also, maybe partially because we have so much history. I know I hurt him when I left, more than I thought I would. But I shouldn't have to keep apologizing for wanting to actually live my life according to my own dreams and wishes. Stupid, eighteen-year-old me hadn't had words for that and had immaturely bolted, but I've tried to man up and explain since then. Reed doesn't want to hear it. But at the minimum, I should pick him up in his time of need without being a bitch about it.

"Find anything new up there?" I ask, pointing to the sky.

A smile blooms on Reed's face. When I was too young to know any better, I used to love that smile, but now it makes my stomach turn to stone with sorrow. In a way, I wish I could just change, want what Dad and Reed want too. It'd make everything so much easier if I simply settled into the life they designed for me. It wouldn't even be a bad life. Reed's a great guy, after all. He just isn't *The One*.

Shit, I sound like Emily.

But as much as I goad her about finding Mr. Right on every corner, I know there really is someone out there for everyone. I've seen it with Mom and Dad. And I won't settle for less than that. And less-than is what Reed and I had.

I'm not looking for more-than, though, not right now, except with the garage.

"Nah, just searching for shooting stars and contemplating life."

I nod, not wanting to open that door to deeper conversations. "Let me get in position so you can hook it up." I let off the brake, pulling forward and shifting in front of the Camaro. I back up, quick and efficient, getting aligned, and then I can hear the chains rattling as Reed gets everything set. It's a rule that you don't tow something you don't check yourself, but I'm breaking that rule tonight because I'm not getting out until we're back at the garage.

The passenger door opens, the overhead light coming on and illuminating me. Reed stops halfway into the truck, one leg in and one leg out as he scans me from head to toe. I see his nostrils flare and his jaw clench. "Shit. Didn't mean to interrupt a date, Rix. Sorry."

He's not sorry. He's pissed as fuck.

"Didn't mean to rub your nose in it. Sorry."

I'm not sorry either. Not really.

It hurts him, I know it does, and I am sorry for that. But maybe seeing me dating and fucking other people will help him to finally move on. I know he hasn't been just waiting on me either. He's dated and fucked around, even bringing one girl to the garage a few times. But it'd seemed more like an attempt at making me jealous than a show of being over me. He deserves more. He should have a woman who wants him the way he wants her. And that's not me.

"Tannen?" he asks, climbing in and buckling up. His voice is tight, strangled in his throat.

I level him with a stare. "You wanna do this?"

That shuts him up, and the rest of the trip to the garage is silent. We get the Camaro into bay two and park the tow truck.

"Take my truck home if you want. You can work on the Camaro tomorrow or Monday, whatever you want." The dismissal is a kindness because I know he wants to get away from me right now.

"Yeah, I'll come by tomorrow so I can see what's wrong. Think I popped a belt, but it was too dark to tell out there." He grabs the keys to the garage truck out of the desk drawer and is gone without a look back.

Until he gets in the truck. He watches to make sure I lock up, mostly because he's a good guy and wants to be sure I'm safe. But deep inside, I know he's checking to see if I'm going back out, going back to Brody.

I don't answer the question in his eyes one way or the other, but I lower the overhead door, lock up, and turn off the light. I don't need it to get across the garage I know like the back of my hand.

THREE DAYS.

Reed is giving me the silent treatment. Manuel is walking around on eggshells because of the tension at the garage. And Brody is ass-deep in work, splitting time between cattle care with Mark and crop work with Brutal and Bobby.

I'm not even entirely sure what all that entails, even though he told me. But dirt quality and growing seasons, calf weights and contracts? It's like he's speaking a different language, but the final result is that he's so tired at the end of the day, he keeps falling asleep on me.

And I don't mean literally *on me*, unfortunately, but rather after a few texts, he apologizes for being boring company and zonks out. At this point, I'm eating cheeseburgers with layers of tomatoes and lettuce in protest for the cows and crops getting all the attention from Brody that I want myself.

It shouldn't be like this. That's part of the deal of keeping things casual. I shouldn't miss him after a few days.

But I do.

I miss that intense way he looks at me, like he's thinking of filthy things to do with me. I miss the peek at his humor that he's stingy about sharing with most people but not with me. I miss the rumble in his chest when he says my name. I miss feeling like I'm enough when I'm in his arms and the sole owner of his attention.

Not that I'm sitting around pining like some sappy-sentimental bitch, though. That's definitely not my style. I've been working after hours on a special project of my own.

The roar of the engine doesn't purr as it breaks the quiet of the garage. It growls, blub-blub-blubbing as it fights to idle because it was designed for speed.

My 1984 Ford Mustang GT.

Once upon a time, it was probably some douchebag's version of a gas-guzzling, poor man's sportscar to get to and from work. But it ended up in the junkyard, where it was waiting patiently for me to rescue it. I found it a couple of months after getting home.

I've worked on every bolt and bit of it now, customizing it for myself. That's not to say it's pretty. No, it's not a trailer queen hot rod that never touches actual asphalt. But it doesn't have to look pretty to go fast.

It's got some of its original navy paint, but mostly, it's washed out to gray and rust since I'm saving paint for last. The original seats have been replaced with five-point harness racing seats, and under the hood has been gutted and replaced with a custom Frankenstein of my own design.

And *fast* is putting it mildly.

My baby is a screaming demon that begs to be let loose even when I put the pedal down, and I'm not shy about pushing it to the metal floorboard. I can hit 120 by the time I hit third gear on a straightaway.

I yank the cover off Foxy and pop the hood, tinkering here and there. But I'm restless, have been all day.

That's probably why I called Emily earlier and invited her over for a sister night, with ideas about ice cream and popcorn—yes, in the same bowl. Don't knock it. Vanilla ice cream with the crunch of salty, buttered popcorn on top like sprinkles is divinity in a bowl. But you gotta eat it fast so the popcorn doesn't freeze. It's like racing but with food—who'll win, you or the popcorn? Only the dentist bill will tell.

But she'd had plans with her friends. Oh, she'd invited me along, promising me a great time, and while I love my sister dearly, her friends are all just a bit much. So I opted out of it, even though it was my idea to hang out, with a 'remembered' engine checkup I needed to finish.

I look over the shiny chrome monster of an engine concealed by the rusty hood. Yep, engine check done. I already know I'm going out tonight so I might as well get gone.

I slam the hood, giving Foxy a pat. "In rust and Rix, we trust." It's my motto, a play on a common saying that probably needs work, not that it matters since it's only between me and Foxy. A quick opening of the bay door lets me get the car out, and while I should probably turn her off while I lock up, I don't. I love listening to the rumble, letting it wash over my skin and pull goosebumps to the surface. The neighbors? Not so much. But it's barely past seven, so I'm not breaking any laws. Yet.

I pull out of the lot, and as soon as my tires touch city road, technically, I'm illegal. Foxy hasn't seen the right side of an inspection in this century. We won't be confessing to the legalities of what's under the hood, either. Nothing's hot—I'm always meticulously careful about that—but some of the imports under her hood do things the DMV doesn't exactly approve of.

I keep it slow and safe through town, knowing exactly where I'm going. The track's closed, but there's a spot outside town where people drag race and that's where I head at a respectful, responsible speed, using my blinkers and everything. I can't get pulled over if I'm using my fucking signals to change lanes on a nearly empty road.

Once I get to The Mile, I drive it extra slow to check for any hazards. The stretch of road is long, straight, and flat, lit with street lights even though the sun hasn't fully set yet. I swear whoever designed this road for the Department of Transportation had to be a racer him or herself because it's damn near a perfect drag strip. It's all clear, and I line up at the north end.

I complete my own mental checklist—seatbelt clicked into place, black-faced gauges reading correctly, pedals unobstructed for quick presses, road clear as a bell as far as I can see.

Three, two, one . . .

I slam the clutch in and hit the gas at the same time, the engine jumping at the demand and meeting it joyfully. A blink later, I switch to second, and as the engine whines, third. I hold, contemplating fourth . . . fifth. But I know I don't have road space to hit those speeds and recover before the slight curve far ahead. So I do the responsible thing and slow back down.

It might not seem responsible. Dad certainly doesn't think so, or at least he doesn't anymore. But I'm doing what I love in a way that considers all the risk factors and mitigates them as much as possible.

But tonight's just for fun.

I pull a U-turn at the south end, lining back up and counting myself down again. And I'm off.

I listen to every nuance, feel every thrust of horsepower, knowing Foxy better than I know myself. Power at my fingertips, rumbling under my ass, all controlled by the press of a pedal. It's everything.

I must make six or seven runs before I realize I've pressed my luck.

Shit. Fuck. Damn. Those cherries coming from the south side have got to be for me.

I'll admit that I have one little moment of thinking 'fuck it' and seriously contemplate hitting the gas and getting out of here. I know Foxy can outrun a police cruiser. I'm wild enough to do it, too, but I'm not that stupid.

But still . . .

*Shit.* I am so busted.

Majorly busted.

Dad's going to be so fucking pissed at me. I'm not even supposed to be racing anymore, but here I am, racing the sunset, racing my past, even racing myself.

# CHAPTER 14

## BRODY

Some metal song I don't even know screams out of my phone. It's whatever Erica chose as her personalized ring tone while we debated musical genius at Hank's. Her current favorite is something called Five Finger Death Punch, which is a band, apparently. One I already can't stand. Mine is Tyler Childers, one she said sounded like a dog dancing on a banjo. Two tastes that couldn't be more different, which is why she took such delight in picking whatever that racket is that's coming out of my phone. Every time it sounds out, I damn near jump out of my skin. She thinks it's hilarious. Fine, I do too. Not that I'll tell her that because then I'll have to confess that it only makes me smile because of her.

"Well hello, Lil Bit." I drawl out the greeting, glad to begin our nightly chat.

"Brody, I have sixty seconds so listen up. I'm in Morristown county jail and I need you to come bail me out and not tell anyone. Please."

The words are one long jumble, each word tumbling over the one before it.

Jail. Bail. Don't tell.

All important details, but what guts me is the 'please' with a hint of desperation. Erica is not someone who begs . . . ever. But she is now, and that's more than enough for me to click into handle-shit mode.

"How much?"

I hate to say I've done this before, but I've done this before. With Dad. A few drunk and disorderly charges that never stuck, but I'd have to go pick him up at the police station after he sobered up. I'd bring money we didn't have to pay the fine, he'd bitch about me nagging him, and then rinse and repeat when he lost big at the tables again. But that was better than when the alcohol would make him sad and weepy because he'd tell stories about Mom, about how much he missed her, about how nothing was the same without her by his side. Pissed off Dad was better than miserable Dad for sure.

"A couple of hundred for tonight."

"On my way, Erica. Be safe."

"Bro—" She's cut off by an officer in the background telling her time's up. And the phone goes silent in my hand.

Motherfucker. What the hell happened? What was she doing that got her arrested? I search my brain but come up empty. Erica doesn't drink too much, which is my first thought, of course. She has a mouth on her, but not enough to go around getting in fights, and her military background probably helps her stay cool and collected if someone else is fucking off. Wrong place, wrong time?

Or maybe . . . wrong person? What if Emily did something and Erica's taking the fall? I could see that because Erica would do anything for her sister. But if that were the case, why wouldn't Emily be the one bailing her out?

Erica told me not to tell anyone, and that really can only mean Emily and Reed since I've only met her mom the one time.

Confusion whirls though my mind, but my body's in action. I grab my wallet and keys, step over Brutal's old dog, Murphy, who's lying by the front door, and fly down the grassy drive in my truck going a bit too fast. As I wait for the automatic gate to open, my phone buzzes.

*Brutal: Where you going so damned fast?*

*Me: Erica's.*

*Brutal: Guess I'll plan to feed the goats in the morning. <winky face>*

*Me: <middle finger emoji>*

I want to say thanks, but that'd be suspicious, and he already knows I appreciate it. Plus, it's not like I can tell him where I'm going or what I'm doing since Erica asked me not to, so letting him think I'm just running out hellbent for pussy is the right thing to do. Better he thinks I'm a manwhore than that Erica's in trouble.

The drive over the mountain is quick this time of evening with zero traffic, so I get to the police station before I've come up with any reasonable answer to what in the hell Erica might've done. But I pray to fuck-all that she's okay and safe. Jail isn't exactly an easy place to be.

I tell the desk cop, a thick-chested man with a huge gray handlebar mustache, "Erica Cole."

He lazily looks up from the paperwork on his desk, giving me a once-over. "Nice to meet you, Erica."

I swallow the growl, knowing that it won't do Erica any good for me to piss off the people holding her. "I'm here to bail out Erica Cole."

His eyes drift back to his paperwork, seemingly dismissing me, but after a moment, he sighs. "Three fifty. Cash or charge?"

"Cash," I say, glad I went ahead and grabbed everything I had at home. Three fifty is a lot more than a couple of hundred, but I can float it and I trust Erica to pay me back.

Maybe I shouldn't, but I do.

"What are the charges?"

He shrugs, not giving me any information, but he sure takes my money damn fast. I sign a bunch of paperwork and then the guy directs me to a bank of waiting room chairs. I can't sit, but I move to the far side of the room to pace worriedly.

After a few minutes, he calls out. "Son, you're a big guy, and pacing around like a caged tiger is making me nervous." He fidgets with his mustache, the perfect picture of calm no matter what he says. "Sit down and wait. We'll get your girl out lickity split."

My girl.

She's not. But I'm the one she called.

Does that mean something? Other than that she didn't want her family to find out about whatever this is? More questions and still no answers.

A door opens with a creak and Erica walks through. She's got on those baggy navy coveralls, her steel-toed boots, and her hands are dirty. She's been working, so how did that go from the garage to jail?

"Let's go." Her voice is clipped, her stride purposeful, and her posture military precise. I open the front door of the police station for her and she struts right through without a word.

I glance back, and Mustache Man raises one brow. I don't have time for him and his judgements when Erica's little steps are eating up the ground.

She climbs into my truck, not letting me help her as usual, but I close the door with a slam. I do the same with my own door and then look at her.

The sun has set, and it's dark, but I can see the hard set of her jaw.

"You okay?" I ask. I have so many questions, but that's the most important one.

It breaks something in her though. "*Fuuuuck*!" Her shout is full of anger and tinged with regret. When she runs out of air and tapers off, she inhales forcefully and turns her head to look at me. "I'm fine. Fucked, but fine."

That's enough for now, so I leave her be and start up the truck. She disappears behind a tough, hard shell, silence wrapped around her protectively as she stares out the window.

At the garage, I park and don't wait for an invitation but rather follow her toward the door. She'll tell me to fuck off if she doesn't want me to come up, I have no doubt about that, and when she stays quiet, allowing me inside before locking up, I know she's okay with my presence. Once in her apartment, she pulls two beers from the fridge and holds one out to me.

I take it, popping the tab. Before I swallow a sip, Erica has chugged the whole can. "Ahh . . . shit, I needed that after tonight."

My sip is small in comparison, and I look at her openly, no judgement and no demands.

"Aren't you gonna ask what I was arrested for?"

"Nope."

Her eyes go wide as saucers and then narrow suspiciously. "No?"

I take another sip, feeling the minefield all around me and wanting to tread carefully. "Erica, I like you. A lot. And I want to spend time with you. But we've already established . . . you've got shit, I've got shit. If you want to talk about what happened, I'll sit here all night and let you rage, cry, whine, or whatever you need to do. If you want to pretend it never happened, we can do that too. Your call. I'm not here to make things hard for you." I mean that honestly, even though I'm curious as fuck about what happened tonight. But it's not my place unless she wants it to be. That's the agreement we made.

She thinks on that for a long moment while I await my fate. Finally, a small smile takes her face. "You want something to eat?"

I knew she wouldn't get rid of me. Well, I hoped she wouldn't.

"I think you've had a rougher night than me. If it's all right, let me feed you?"

Her smirk grows. "Let me guess . . . pancakes?"

"Fuck yeah, Lil Bit."

Pancakes and beer are a weird combination, but carbs and alcohol are probably exactly what she needs.

She sits down at the small table, leaving me to have at her kitchen. I can feel her eyes following me to the fridge and back to the counter. I know where the mixing bowls and skillet are, so I make myself at home. Within minutes, I'm setting a plate down in front of her.

After a few bites and with an eye roll, she gives in. "Fine, twist my arm already, Cowboy. I got arrested for excessive speed. Officer Miles probably would've let me off with a warning, but he was training a new rookie tonight so he had to go by the books."

I swallow the last bite I took, giving myself a moment to process, because her confessing to me is a big trust. Even more than the fact that she called *me*, not Emily, her parents, or Reed. That was a necessity for some reason, but this? Her openly and willingly sharing is something I think Erica Cole doesn't do easily or often, and I'm gonna wallow like a happy pig in slop that she chose to do it with me.

Even after getting the pancakes to my belly, all I manage to do is repeat what she said. "You got arrested for excessive speed?" Erica nods affirmatively. I remember Emily saying there's a Cole family trait to have a lead foot. "Not a ticket, but arrested? Shit, woman, how much over were you going?" The question comes out reflexively, even though I'm trying damn hard not to pry.

"More than double." She sounds casual as hell about it, the shrug in her tone even if her shoulder doesn't move.

Breadcrumbs, breadcrumbs, all she's giving me are breadcrumbs. But I want every one of them, following along her trail to see where it leads.

"So what, you hit a hundred and they went hardcore on you?"

She levels me with a withering look, but I don't know what I said wrong. "Miles said he clocked me at one thirty-four. Though I disagree. Speedometer said one thirty-eight."

My beer goes down the wrong pipe when I inhale sharply. I cough and sputter, swiping at the small spray that covers my lips. "Holy. Fuck. You were going a hundred and thirty-four miles an hour down an open road?"

She shakes her head and smiles. "No, Cowboy. Listen carefully. One. Thirty. Eight. If you knew what I had to do to that engine to get those four more miles per hour, you wouldn't be discounting them so easily, but I wasn't even topped out."

I try to wrap my brain around that type of speed. I'm no granny out for Sunday drives when I hit the highway, but I've never driven that fast. Not even close. I can't imagine that much power at the touch of a toe.

"Wait, what were you driving? Your truck won't do that."

Mischief blossoms in her eyes, her excitement palpable. "My rat rod. Eighty-four Ford Mustang."

I get the feeling she just mic-dropped me. I have no idea why.

"What's a rat rod?" I'm still trying to make some semblance of sense here.

Her face looks like I just asked her what that big ball of fire in the sky is. "Like a hot rod under the hood, but the outside isn't all fancy like the cars we saw at the show. My rod's navy and rust, loud as hell—should've gotten a ticket for that too." She puts a finger to her lips, telling me to keep quiet about that. "But it's all about what's under the hood. She's totally custom, gutted and rebuilt with my own two hands. She's got a 426 Hemi that I've tweaked. I'd have stayed Ford loyal and put a 385 in there, but I couldn't find one."

I blink, and she rambles on. "She's not the usual ratter, way too new for that. But I like it because it's what my dad had when he married my mom. It was their honeymoon getaway car, beer cans rattling behind them and everything. Foxy reminds me of those pictures and their smiling faces."

Even though I barely understand what she's saying, I'm starting to get a picture here, something bigger and deeper than her fixing up Bessie's transmission.

"You're like one of those car guys on TV, aren't you? Making something from nothing."

She buffs her dirty nails on her coveralls, not even feigning modesty. "Something like that. Except those shows are staged, edited, and dramatized. I make good cars great and fast cars faster."

It's not even a humble brag. It sounds like it's the God's honest truth, straight from her lips. Maybe her most important truth, and she gave it to me, trusted me with it.

"You're amazing." I lean over the table and kiss those lips. She tastes like syrup and secrets, ones she's sharing with me.

Her blink is slow and suspicious. "You're not gonna tell me I'm being reckless and stupid? That I have no business doing something so dangerous? That I should leave the racing to the big boys?"

That those questions are on the tip of her tongue tells me she's heard them all before. This is a test, sure as shit.

I take another bite, letting her stew for a moment. "Reckless and stupid? That's my idea of a fun Saturday night." My grin grows and she smacks my shoulder.

"Asshole." But she's smiling, and I know that whatever she expected from me, that wasn't it. "And it's Tuesday."

"Yeah, Saturdays are for reckless and stupid. Tuesdays are for crazy and illegal. And watch out for Thursdays . . ." I pause dramatically, and Erica's smile tells me she's on board with me. "That's for secrets and sneaking around."

"What about Monday, Wednesday, Friday, and Sunday?" Laughter is dancing in her eyes.

I break first, my laughter rough and rusty. "Shit, I don't know. I'm making this stuff up as I go."

She gets up, coming around the table to kiss me. "You surprise me, Brody Michael Tannen."

I could say the same thing to her, but while it feels like a compliment to me, I think she'd take it as an insult. As much as she's shared tonight, and as wild and outrageous as it sounds, I feel like she thinks it's no big deal. Just another day, another engine, another hundred and thirty-*eight* mile an hour drive through the city.

So I keep my big, fat mouth shut tight as she grabs our plates and takes them to the sink.

"I'm gonna take a quick shower and wash the jail off me. Can you stay?"

"Yeah, I can stay." I see her smile, though she turns quickly to hide it from me. It's cute, and that's not a word I'd ever use to describe Erica. It feels like another layer of hard-edged fierceness cracked away. I don't know that she's soft and sweet underneath all that armor, but I damn sure want to find out.

As soon as she's gone to the bathroom, I text Mark.

*Me: Late in the morning. Brutal's handling goats.*

*Mark: This is Katelyn. Are you at Rix's?*

*Me: <middle finger emoji>*

*Mark: I'll let him know not to expect you. I like her. Do you like her?*

I turn my phone to silent and do some Googling on *rat rods*. I've never heard the term before. I mean, NASCAR? Of course. Hot rods? Yeah. Drag racing? Yep. But if this is Erica's hobby and I don't want to look like a total dumbass, a little research seems in order. *It's not a thing*, I tell myself. Just being friendly, that's all.

I don't believe me, either.

The bathroom door opens and Erica walks out, naked and soft-skinned. My eyes trace her body, loving the peaks of her brown nipples, the map of freckles I'm still memorizing, and the puffy pink lips peeking out between her thighs. She opens a drawer and puts on a pair of bikini panties.

That's when I realize I'm about to get kicked out.

"I'm sorry, but I'm really tired. I'm probably gonna fall asleep before my head hits the pillow, Brody." She yawns as she says it, and I can see the wear and tear tonight took on her. There are slight smudges under her eyes and a sense of weariness in the set of her shoulders.

"You're in luck. It's after midnight, so officially Wednesday, and I just decided that's snuggles and cuddles day." I smirk at my brilliance, and after a too-long pause where my heart doesn't beat and I don't breathe, she smiles back. It's small, but I'm counting it.

"That shit usually work?"

I shrug noncommittally, even though my brow says 'every damn time'.

She shakes her head and laughs but then says, "Come on, then."

# CHAPTER 15

## ERICA

Though I'm the one who claimed exhaustion, Brody falls asleep long before I do. I close my eyes, listening to the white noise of his breathing. It's almost meditative in its consistent predictability, relaxing me even as my mind processes everything.

He really came through for me tonight. Surprisingly so.

It could've been a fucking shitshow if I'd had to call someone else. Emily would keep her mouth shut for me, or she'd try, at least. But she lacks one important feature . . . a filter. She's unapologetically herself, and that includes being shit for secrets because she just doesn't see the point.

But I do. I know better.

Emily doesn't have secrets because she's never gone against Dad the way I have. *The way I am.* And that's why I couldn't have called her or Mom or Reed. Or anyone else. Because they'd all tell Dad.

He didn't have to do it, but Brody Tannen rescued me tonight. And I fucking hate being rescued.

He'd been chill about it, though, not asking too many questions and trying to keep a straight face when I told him what I'd done. *Unsuccessfully*, I add with a smirk in the darkness. He was shocked down to his core, and I get a little thrill out of that the same way I always do.

I might be little and female, but I'm fierce as fuck behind the wheel of a tricked-out car. Still, I'm mad at myself for the rookie move of getting caught tonight. I know better, am better, and I'm definitely smarter than that.

Eventually, the sound of Brody's breathing and his warm presence lull me closer to sleep. I relax into him, my head on his chest and my legs wrapped around his. Unconsciously, he pulls me closer. I'm glad he's here tonight, not just because of the bail but because he feels right in my bed, beneath my cheek, under my palm.

I STIR BEFORE THE SUN'S EVEN UP, A SLOW STROKING OF FINGERS along my arm bringing me from the call of sleep.

"Mmm, that feels good, but stop it so I can sleep for five more minutes." In my head, that's what I say. What actually comes out of my mouth is a growled, mumbled version of that, which makes Brody chuckle.

The vibration and rise and fall of his chest wake me up even more. Damn it.

"Want me to make you breakfast while you sleep in, lazy girl?" I can hear the smile in his voice.

"Not lazy. Be nice to me. I went to jail last night." I'm kidding . . . mostly. And also, maybe a bit bitchy from lack of sleep.

But I did manage to process through a few things, the most important being that when the chips were down, I turned to Brody and he came through for me. I didn't mean to test him, was just desperate, but even so, he passed with flying colors. Good to know, but not something I want to ever repeat again.

I want to be the badass in his eyes again, wash away the weak girl from last night who needed a rescue from a dark knight in a shining truck.

"No more pancakes. Let me cook this time."

Brody's hand popping me on the ass surprises the fuck out of me. "What the—"

"Hell yeah, Lil Bit. Show me what you got, though we both know whatever you whip up ain't gonna top my mom's pancakes." Challenge extended.

"I'll admit those are some damn good pancakes, but wait till you see what I can do." Challenge accepted.

He wiggles us around, shoving me to my feet even though my eyes are still closed. I stretch, arching my back, trying to work out the kinks from sleeping curled up against Brody's hard body instead of stretched out across my cushy mattress.

"Son of a bitch, Lil Bit."

I peek open one eye to find him propped up on one elbow and watching me hungrily, his gaze tracing along my body appreciatively. I pose a bit as I contemplate skipping breakfast entirely in favor of sucking him, because behind the black cotton of his briefs, he's sporting some serious morning wood I could put to good use. But it's going to be a long day, so I really should start right. With bacon and eggs, not dick. And no, there's not time for both. I already considered that too.

"Nuh-uh, no time for that." I move out of his way, feeling his eyes follow me across the room to the bathroom.

He groans and falls flat on the bed. "You're killing me, woman!"

I laugh and continue on my merry way. When I come out of the bathroom, I've yanked my hair into a bun, brushed my teeth, and washed my face. Brody's managed to pull on his jeans and start the coffee pot, which he's now watching as hungrily as he was me just a few minutes ago. Somehow, I don't feel any less special because while he is a vision of raw masculinity filling my tiny kitchen space, I want that coffee too.

But since it's not ready yet, I let my eyes trace over him. There's something about a big, barrel-chested man with no shirt on, a messy bedhead, and a bit too much scruff that does it for me. The barely-on jeans and bare feet help too.

"You changing your mind on priorities? Because I can grab breakfast later. You? Now's my chance." His eyes stay on the coffee pot, though I know I could have them with a single agreeable sound.

"Eggs." I swear I mean the chicken kind that I'm going to scramble for breakfast and not my ovaries bursting at his offer.

He shrugs, but I catch the smirk tilting his lips. I hurry to the refrigerator and the stove before I second—no, fifth—guess my choice of how to spend the few precious minutes I have this morning. Brody pours two cups of coffee, setting one next to the stove for me to sip as I cook before sitting down at the table with his own.

"I looked up rat rods." He's telling me a lot with that simple statement, and I hear everything he's not saying . . .

An admission to a lack of knowledge on something I know all about, which is surprisingly difficult for some men to say.

An acknowledgement that cars are important to me, and he respects that.

And ultimately, that I mean something to him. I mean enough that he saw fit to educate himself on something solely because of me.

Brody might not say much, but damn if he isn't saying a lot.

"What'd you think?" I peek over my shoulder, still stirring eggs.

His shrug is casual. His reaction is not, his eyes watching my every move, measuring and assessing. "Seemed cool. I can see how you'd make the jump from the garage to racing pretty fast. No pun intended."

I'm quiet, not filling in the blanks he's not asking about, and the moment stretches uncomfortably.

From the corner of my eye, I see Brody set his coffee cup down and interlace his fingers on the table. "Can I ask one question?"

Ah, here we go. I knew this was coming, have been waiting on it, in fact. The judgement, the 'why don't you just—', the condescending mansplaining about safety, the *talk*.

I turn, my back against the counter, and cross my arms, spoon still in hand. "What?"

Brody chuckles. "No need to threaten me with a spoon this time,

Lil Bit. It ain't that serious. I just wondered why the secrecy? I was happy to come getcha, but I bet Emily" —his voice tightens— "or Reed would've too." He shakes off whatever jealous bullshit he's feeling to finish. "Just wanted to see what I've stepped into here."

I sag, confused beyond measure because that is not at all what I thought he was going to say.

"I . . . uh, I wasn't expecting that," I tell him honestly. I go back to stirring the eggs because they're in danger of burning and I promised him a better-than-pancakes breakfast. I toss in some shredded cheese to make up for the bacon it's too late to fry up now.

"It's kind of a long story, but the shorthand version is that once upon a time, my dad ran the garage and did racing engines on the side. I spent many a night at races with too-big earmuffs covering my ears from the racket. When I was about sixteen, Dad had a friend who died in a crash. It wasn't even at a race, but he was showboating his hot rod—the one he built with Dad. It damn near killed my dad too, even though he wasn't there. It just hurt him." I absently rub at my chest, remembering Big John, Dad's friend who had been larger than life until the tree he wrapped his car around had taken his. "Anyway, Dad went totally strict after that. He wanted everyone to live in this safe little bubble, for our own protection, you know? From then on, Cole Automotive only did maintenance and repairs for regular cars. Dad never even touched a racecar after that. Won't so much as watch NASCAR these days."

Brody puts some puzzle pieces together. "And if you called Emily or Reed to bail you out on excessive speed charges, they'd tell your dad and he'd be pissed that you stepped out of the bubble of safety. So you're trying to protect him while doing whatever the fuck you want?"

I nod, plating our breakfast. He understands. The only question now is if he'll *understand.*

He chews thoughtfully. "This is good. Not as good as my pancakes, but damn good."

I growl at the topic change, and he smirks that grin that kills me. Or makes me want to kill him. Maybe both.

"Okay."

"Okay, what?" I demand.

"Okay, I won't say anything. I just want to make sure I'm not getting in the middle of something major, like you're the getaway driver for your family's bank robbing side hustle or something. You drive fast? Okay."

"Stop saying okay." I shake my head, not sure I heard him right.

That shrug again, the one that's driving me crazy with its casualness when I'm letting him in on something huge to me. But he's just . . . accepting it?

"I keep stuff from my family too, for their protection. My dad . . . we grew up good, but after Mom died, he didn't . . . well, I guess you could say he didn't handle it well. I bailed him out of the drunk tank a few times, kept my brothers and sister from the worst of it, and took the brunt of it. It was better that way."

I tease all that apart, the information between the words he actually said. Maybe he does understand me and what I'm doing. A tenuous thread weaves its way between us, something more than sex and flirting, dangerously closer to friendship. Or maybe even more.

"Thank you." It shouldn't be hard to say that, but it is.

"No problem, Lil Bit." Our plates are empty, and he stands to pick mine up, planting a kiss to my lips before hitting the sink.

I have no idea what just happened. I expected something dire, feared a harsh judgment, but none of that materialized and I'm not sure what to make of it. Brody is different from most, and I don't think I gave him enough credit, making some pre-judgments of my own.

He washes our dishes quickly and lays the towel out to dry. "I'm guessing you've got work today?" I nod, enjoying the show of him at my sink. "I should probably get to the ranch too."

He lets that hang in the air, giving me a chance to disagree.

I make a spontaneous decision, praying it doesn't kick me in the ass. "Do you want to come with me tonight?"

"Yeah, I'd love to." His answer is instant.

"I didn't tell you where or to do what yet," I tease.

"Bank robbery?" he asks, narrowing his eyes.

I roll my eyes. "No, the track. I'm not racing, but some of my engines are. I never get to share that with anyone . . . well, the guys I build the cars for, but that's not the same."

Smug satisfaction swipes over his face as he steps in and pulls our bodies together, looking down at me. "Not the same as me?"

"Don't get cocky, Cowboy."

He drops down, closer to my ear. "Well, I tried that, but you said we didn't have time."

I push him away, laughing lightly. "Let's get dressed. We've got shit to do today."

It's a damn tragedy to watch Brody put his T-shirt and hat on, but I distract myself by pulling on a tank top and clean coveralls. We pause at the door so we can both put our boots on, smiling stupidly at the symmetry, though mine are covered with grease and oil and his are covered with dirt.

Downstairs, Reed and Manuel both look up when the breakroom door opens, framing me. I can feel Brody's presence looming behind me, but just as heavy is the look in Reed's eyes.

I walk with a purpose across the garage, not looking back once. Brody follows me, and though I can't see, I imagine him and Reed are mean-mugging at each other in some dick-measuring, territory-pissing contest. A useless one because nothing they do will determine this situation. That's all up to me.

Outside, I pause by Brody's truck. "You don't need to do that. It only makes it harder on him."

Brody backs me up against the door, weaving his fingers into the hair at my nape and tracing his thumb over the freckles along my cheekbone. "That's where you're wrong. It pisses him off because it hurts, but it's a kindness in a way. Unless you're trying to string him along and keep him on the back burner?"

My brows knit together. "What? No, I'm just trying not to be a bitch about it when I know he still has hope."

"You're pulling the Band-Aid off too slow, ripping out each hair and every bit of skin, prolonging the agony. You need to tell him, show him that it's not happening. I can't believe I'm saying this, but you're gonna have to be a bitch to be nice. Does that make any sense?" He says it softly, as if encouraging me to be mean is somehow a caring thing. I'll have to think about that.

"Just kiss me goodbye and shut up, Cowboy."

He smiles at that. "Yes, ma'am." He steps back to lean down to meet me as I lift to my toes. Our lips press together, and though we don't get too involved for a quick goodbye in the middle of the garage parking lot during business hours, it feels important. A seal on everything that happened last night, a vow to keep it between us, a promise to trust one another.

Brody pops me on the ass as I start to walk away, and I turn back, flipping him off, which only makes his eyes darken. But he climbs in his truck and I watch as he pulls away, surprisingly not second-guessing myself on sharing my secret with him. In fact, I'm looking forward to showing off my engines to him a bit tonight.

Inside, Reed is standing stock-still, arms crossed and feet spread wide. "This what we're doing now, Rix? Sleepovers and coming in whenever we want?"

He doesn't care that I'm late for work. He cares that I just paraded Brody through the garage after obviously spending the night with him. Brody's words replay in my mind as I see the betrayal in Reed's eyes. *Rip the Band-Aid off?*

"That's what I'm doing, Reed. Fucking who I want and working when I want. You know, since it's *my* garage."

My belly revolts at the vitriol. Reed's been my friend for so long, and I don't want to be mean, but maybe it is a twisted sort of compassion?

"Fuck you, Rix." He turns away, throwing a wrench at the ground before stomping off.

Manuel looks after him with dark eyes and then back at me before nodding solemnly. Guess he thinks Brody's right too.

But if Reed and I both feel like shit and are pissed, can it be a kindness?

# CHAPTER 16

## BRODY

Erica is a mystical, magical witch.

It's the only explanation.

Somehow, she managed to talk me into riding in her Mustang to the races. Yes, the one she got arrested for driving too fast just last night and the one she got out of the impound lot this afternoon. Also, the one that was not made for guys my size, which means I rode bitch, with my knees damn near tucked up under my chin like a toddler. And now, she's holding court over a whole racetrack full of swinging dicks.

Somehow, not a one of them seems to give her any attention, though, which I totally don't get. Oh, they talk to her, laugh with her, and when we arrived, several of the older guys gave her hugs that left her feet dangling a foot off the ground. But it all seems very platonic and community-like. She's one of their own, and they're protective of her, which is where the swinging dicks come in. They're all competitive against each other, smack talking about car stuff that means jack shit to me but also eyeballing me like I'm trying to steal away with their girl.

Their Rix.

"What do you drive?" Jerry asks. The pot-bellied man introduced himself a second ago and instantly made me think of Papa Smurf because of his white beard and round face. The white ballcap on his bald head adds to the image.

"Ram dually," I answer, knowing it's not what he wants to hear. Or at least not all that he wants to hear.

"Shut your piehole, Jerry. He's not a car guy, I'm giving ya that. So you and the lot of you can let that go now." Erica starts out talking directly to Jerry, who looks slightly chagrined, but ends by addressing the whole crowd.

Another guy, this one a twenty-something guy with an honest-to-God mullet, calls out, "Never thought I'd see the day the great Rix Cole would settle down with a regular Joe. If he can't talk engines, what do you even talk about?"

"His dick, Mike."

I choke on my tongue. She didn't just . . . but oh, yeah, she did.

A snicker goes through the crowd, but they seem to take her outburst in stride, like it's a normal thing for her to say. Hell, maybe it is, I don't know.

Erica's eyes stay on Mike, but she talks over her shoulder. "Hey, Jerry, what'd Marlene say when you were trying to decide between the 305 and the 350?"

Jerry's brows lock together. "Not a thing. She don't care what I'm running. She only cares if we've got enough money to go on our summer cruise. Alaska this year." Pride and excitement tinge his voice.

"Regular Joe, huh?" Erica's conclusion works its way through the crowd slowly, each of them seeming to realize that their significant others don't always share their enthusiasm for their hobby. Is it a hobby or an obsession? Both?

Erica claps. "Now that that's settled, let's do some racing. Who's up first, Ed?"

And just like that, she's the queen of the racetrack again and everyone moves toward their cars to do her bidding.

The racetrack isn't what I was expecting, though I don't know what I thought it would be like. It's a straight quarter-mile track with black streaks covering the length of the asphalt, a lighting rig at the starting line, and an official with a clipboard. That'd be Ed, and this is his racetrack.

"Mike versus Clint," Ed calls out.

Mullet-haired Mike holds out his hand to a dark-haired guy with a beard that reaches down to his belly. That must be Clint. They shake and then turn toward their cars. The quiet hum of talk is drowned out by a loud car starting and then another with zero harmony. It's all growl.

Mike and Clint line up. Mike's driving a large older-style car from the '50s in flame red. Past that, I can't tell much about it. Clint's car looks more like a '70s sportscar, something I can imagine Burt Reynolds driving. My money's on Clint, partly because his car looks fast and partly because he just seems like a guy who won't back down from a challenge. In contrast, Mike seems like a bit of a punk ass kid with more mouth than brains.

As Ed goes to each man's window, Erica fills me in.

"Ed runs a tight ship here. First and foremost, cars have to meet safety requirements. Drivers too. He does a track check at the start of the night and again if there's a crash." Erica says 'crash' like she might say 'hello', zero inflection or concern.

Slowly but surely, over Mike and Clint's race and then several more (Mike wins, surprising me), I get to see a different side of this woman. She's a roller coaster of emotions, from still and almost prayer-like when they line up to excited and yelling when she's rooting for her guy to win. Or more precisely, her engine.

She's worked on a large number of these machines.

"If so many people know that you're doing all this custom work, how does your family not find out?" I ask in her ear at one point of not-deafening noise.

"I trust them. They trust me. They all know my dad, and a lot of them knew Big John too. When Dad pulled his one-eighty and stopped working on their engines, it left this void that needed to be filled. Who better than his daughter, the one who learned at his elbow?" She smiles at the memories, letting me know that despite the secrets, she has positive feelings about her dad.

"The first few I did for the cost of parts only, no labor charges at all. Had to prove myself as more than a tool bitch to these guys. The first time my engine got the win was one of the happiest moments of my life. I started charging that night, and now, I've got a sweet side gig with a lineup of work to do. The guys keep it quiet out of respect for my dad, who they loved and miss seeing around here, and for more practical reasons, a.k.a. if my cover gets blown, there's a real shot that they'll lose their best customizer and mechanic." Zero modesty or brag, merely all truth.

"You're amazing," I tell her honestly and then plant a smacking kiss on her lips.

I don't hear her answer because another race takes off and the loud squeal of tires drowns her out. But I see her smile. I feel it in my bones.

As Erica watches a few more races, I watch her. This whole thing is a big share, something she chose to tell me. She could've asked me to bail her out, then told me to fuck off. Honestly, I probably would've and not given it a second thought.

Okay, that part's a lie. I would've thought about Erica again. At least once or twice, maybe a couple of dozen times. But the secret part I wouldn't have pressed about.

They say the best way to keep a secret is to tell no one. If you keep your own mouth shut, there's never any risk of discovery. Erica, though, has a secret an entire group of people knows but have managed to keep quiet. Plus me now, but I won't let her down.

At one point, Jerry calls over. "Hey, Rix, you wanna show your boy toy what you can do?"

Boy? Toy? He's obviously talking about me, but I can't say I've been called a boy in a long while, and never a toy.

Erica grins but doesn't move from my side. "Nah, Foxy needs a full check. Damn Officer Miles had her towed and I won't race her till I know they didn't fuck anything up. Can you believe they wouldn't even let me oversee the hookup?" Her eyes hold fire, like it would be a common thing for a handcuffed prisoner to be in charge of handling the car they were just arrested for speeding in. "I told them if they so much as chipped her rust, I'd know it and make them pay."

The threat seems pretty damn valid, though I don't think anyone would pay for rust chipping. But something tells me Erica would make them pay, one way or another.

"Drive mine. She ain't got a bottle like the newfangled ones you're doing, but test out that 350 you put in her," Jerry offers.

Erica's smile is brighter than the spotlights lining the track. "Wanna see something cool?"

Test, test, test. Oh, she's prodding and pushing me, testing to see how much it takes for me to tell her no. But this is her show, her expertise, not mine.

"Fuck yes, woman. Show me what you got." I smile, honestly excited to see. And yes, a little terrified, but mostly excited.

She blinks slowly, eyes locked on me like a lie detector, and I stand there and take it. She needs to know I'm not stopping her, won't stop her.

"Fuck it, Jerry. Let me grab my gear while you tell Ed." Erica smacks me on the butt, making my grin grow, before she takes off at a jog toward her car.

I've never felt like such a sideline bitch before. But right this moment, I don't mind it a bit. It's a give and take. Like at Hank's when I was teaching Erica some moves, she followed me easily. Now, when this is her thing, I'll follow her. Hopefully, later, we can fuck each other stupid. See? All things in balance, as they should be.

Erica reappears a moment later with a helmet tucked under her arm. She smiles at me and then gets down to business, chatting with Ed and some other guy, who I guess she'll be racing.

"She's a pretty special gal, our Rix," Jerry says from beside me.

"Yep." I don't offer more, letting him say his piece.

"If she told you about this, brought you here, she must think you're pretty special too." I cut my eyes his way. "Are you?"

"Nah, just a guy." I shrug and he chuckles.

"Just a guy? If you say so, Son." He claps me on the shoulder, and I flinch involuntarily at the combination of the term of endearment and motion. If Jerry notices, he doesn't say anything, and we both focus on watching Erica race.

Jerry chatters about his car, an old Camaro that Erica's dad first fixed up and that Erica overhauled more recently. I don't hear much of what he says because my eyes are tracking Erica's every move.

She's comfortable, walking a loop around the car and checking under the hood. She sends Jerry a thumbs-up which he returns, and then she climbs behind the wheel. Her and the other car, another classic that sounds like it runs on grit and gravel, line up.

That's when my heart stops beating and I quit breathing.

Oh, fuck. She's racing. Like, speeding down the track going one-fifty with just metal surrounding her and no airbag in sight. "Uhm, Jerry . . . ?"

He chuckles. "Wait till you see her, Just a Guy. You're gonna be floored by what she can do."

His hand is gentle on my shoulder this time, letting me know he definitely saw my earlier flinch. He holds me steady, encouraging me to stay in place. I cross my arms over my chest, my feet wide and my eyes laser locked on Erica. Not the cars, not the race, not the lights changing from yellow to green.

Erica.

She's there one second and gone the next, a blur speeding away from me.

And damn is she going fast. It's like time simultaneously slows and speeds up, which makes no sense but is the God's honest truth. The straight line down the track that seemed fun and wild when the other racers were doing it now seems like seriously risky business. Not because Erica's a woman but because she's . . .

Nope, I stop that thought, not giving it space in my mind because it's not remotely true. Casual, nothing more. That's the deal. My dick and my heart snort at my assessment of the situation, knowing I'm full of shit. I care about Erica, not anything serious but enough to not want her to risk her life and limb doing stupid shit.

But the way she's handling Jerry's car makes it seem like it's not craziness personified. She might as well be out for a Sunday stroll in that beast of a car, never wavering on her straight shot to the finish.

The other car is easily two car lengths behind when she crosses the line. I release my breath and clap, loud and proud, for her. "Hell yeah!"

The brake lights glow red for a minute and then Jerry's car spins a one-eighty that makes my heart leap a little before I realize she's just celebrating before heading off the track toward the parking lot.

"Whoo-hoo, she just won me three hundred bucks! Thank you, Rix!" Though he's thanking the woman in the parking area, he looks skyward, like she's a goddess. Hell, she damn near is.

Badass, fierce, racing, engine whispering, dick owning . . . goddess.

I shake hands with Jerry and excuse myself, beelining for Erica. She's parked and is pulling her helmet off her head, her hair an absolute sweaty, beautiful fucking mess. She's never looked happier. That probably says something about my fucking skills, but I get the feeling it's more about how important racing is to her.

Her eyes are bright and dancing before clouding with worry when she sees me. "Hey," she says hesitantly.

I don't pause at all, stalking toward her like a man possessed—by her. I pull her to me, cupping her cheeks and lifting her to her toes as I bend down and our lips connect. It's sweet and appropriate, though the hooting crowd thinks differently, but damn if I'm not trying to tell her just how awesome that was.

As she falls back to her flat feet, I copy her greeting. "Hey." She smiles. "You're amazing."

Her eyes roll hard. "You already said that."

"Thought it again, so I said it again." I pull my hat off, curl it, and pull it back on. "You ready to get out of here yet?"

*Say yes. Say you're ready to go back to your place, because that was one of the sexiest things I've ever seen in my life and I want to be buried inside you as soon as possible.*

My telepathic plea seems to work because she pulls at my T-shirt. "Let's go, Cowboy." Louder, she calls out, "She drives like a dream, Jerry. The 350 was definitely the right choice."

He waves but answers, "I'm gonna tell Marlene you said that."

Erica smiles, and we keep moving toward her car. If we were in my truck, I'd find the nearest dark road and pull her into my lap. In her car, there's definitely no room for that, though my mind doesn't stop trying to figure out a way.

The drive to the garage is slower than Erica's race pace, but we're definitely well over the speed limit. I don't give a shit because I'm in just as much of a hurry as she is.

# CHAPTER 17

## ERICA

There's something no one ever talks about with racing—how sexual it all is. The purr of the engine, the vibration of the seats beneath you, the barely controlled power, it's all such a turn-on. Or at least it is for me.

When Brody asked me if I was ready to go, a tiny whisper of doubt had tried to worm its way into my heart. *He doesn't want you here, doesn't want you racing.* But then I saw the sexy promises in the dark depths of his eyes, felt the fire licking along his skin, and realized I was so wrong. He didn't want me to leave. He just wanted *me*. As in, if I'd said no to leaving, he'd have happily turned me around, bent me over the nearest front bumper, and fucked me right there until we both screamed.

In an instant, my doubts evaporated like smoke, leaving only hope and hunger.

I'm driving as fast as I dare back to the garage, and almost before I can turn Foxy off, Brody and I are out of our seats and leaping toward each other. We meet in front of the hood, his hands going to my ass and lifting me easily. My legs wrap around his waist as our lips smash together, devouring one another.

"Goddamn, you're a fucking beast behind the wheel. So sexy, Erica." The words are stilted and murmured against my lips.

"It doesn't scare you that I do that?" I whisper, throwing my head back and closing my eyes as he kisses a line of heat along my neck. Even now, I'm challenging him, testing his reactions, and expecting him to bail or go into lecture mode.

"Terrified me, but it was worth it to see that smile on your face when you climbed out. Gonna make you smile like that for me."

I'll have to remember to revel in the sweetness of that later because he lays me back on the hood of Foxy and I forget everything but how I feel as Brody leans over me, looming and large. The car's warm beneath me, keeping me from chilling as Brody shoves my shirt up and runs his callused hands along my sides.

"Do you even own a bra?" he growls.

"You complaining?" Arching my back, I silently demand for him to touch my breasts. Finger, tongue, mouth, any of them will do.

"Never. Complimenting."

The explanation is enough as he gives me what I need, his finger and thumb rolling one nipple while his mouth suckles the other. I weave my hands into his hair, scratching at his scalp before holding him to me, not letting him go as I demand more. He nibbles lightly, and I cry out and arch harder. He works my breasts back and forth, sucking one and then the other, never letting one feel neglected though his hands work their way to my waistband, undoing my jeans and shoving them down along with my panties. I manage to kick them both over my boots, leaving me in a rather oddly incomplete outfit, but I don't give a shit.

Brody pulls off my breast with a pop and stands tall. He looks me over and I let him, not shy in the least. I know I'm not for everyone. I don't have big tits or an ass they write songs about, but my body is strong and I'm confident in my own skin. And that's sexy.

"Beautiful, Lil Bit."

The soft and honest confession unexpectedly pierces my armor, reaching dangerously close to my heart. I'm bitchy and prickly, mean and hard, and so defensive my picture's probably beside the definition in the dictionary. But Brody finding me not just sexy, not just a hot fuck while we're riding on endorphins, but *beautiful*? "Thank you."

There's a burning in my eyes I don't like, so I blink and reach for him.

Brody gathers a handful of T-shirt behind his head, pulling it over in one swoop, like my own private magician. I expect him to drop the shirt to the floor, maybe to the hood if it's a favorite, but he wads it into a ball and lifts my head to slip it underneath like a pillow. Sweet, sexy, romantic . . . and not the rough fucking on the hood of my car that I want. "Condom?"

"I want to taste you first," Brody says, his eyes locked on my core as he spreads my knees. I let him, enjoying the cool air on my overheated pussy, knowing he's getting off on the slickness I can already feel gathered there.

"Later. Racing always makes me horny, and right now, I'm on edge and I want to come with your cock buried inside me."

"Shiiiiit." Brody's groan is lazy and drawled out, but his hands reach for his wallet and he holds up a condom packet. He unbuttons his jeans, pushing them and his underwear to his knees before rolling the condom down his hard length. I watch the whole show, my hips curling up and my pussy pulsing. I feel a droplet of my juices run down toward my ass, and Brody's eyes trace its path. He dips down and licks one long line, savoring it. He grins that 'gotcha' smile, so cocky that he got a taste, and then lines up with my opening. "Need you, Erica."

My heart is damn glad he doesn't give my brain time to pick that apart, because those words seem dangerous and deep. Instead, he thrusts into me with one stroke, bottoming out. I spasm and clench tight on his cock and somehow feel both invaded and complete at the same time. I didn't know I was empty without him. *Wait, what?*

My brain starts to dip into that, knowing that sharing my secret with him, taking him to the track tonight, and how he reacted so well are important. Not just for me, but for us. But there's not supposed to be an us.

Except when he's buried inside me, it feels like maybe I'm wrong about that.

"Hey, where'd you go?" Brody pauses, his fingers brushing the hair out of my face before tracing the dots along my cheekbone. He cups my jaw, eyes looking deep into mine, almost as deep as he is inside me. And I'm not sure I only mean his cock.

I shake my head, not wanting to do this now. For now, I just want to fuck and enjoy him. "I'm here. Fuck me."

That makes his eyes narrow suspiciously for some reason I don't understand.

"Show me what you do. When you come home from a race, turned on by the vibrations underneath you, the power you wield . . . show me what you do." He takes my hand, kissing each fingertip, pinky . . .ring . . . middle . . . and swirling his tongue over my index finger, and then guides my hand to my clit. "Show me while *we* fuck."

There's an emphasis to his words that brings me back to this moment between us. Not the future, not somewhere deeper, but right here, right now, taking pleasure in each other.

I spread my lips open, knowing that it probably looks obscene and sexy to him to see the place where he disappears inside me. I tease a circle around my clit, heat gathering there from my own touch and his eyes. I find a rhythm, speeding up slightly, and then a pattern, circling a few times before tapping my clit. Brody watches each movement, adding slow and shallow thrusts to the building momentum of my orgasm.

"That's it . . . fuck, that's sexy." I'll never admit, not even to myself, that his words turn me on even more. I've never been with a dirty talker, but I swear, Brody's more verbose when he's having sex than when he's not. "Want more?"

I don't trust my voice not to waver so I nod, and before I know it, Brody's got my ankles on his shoulders, dirty boots and all, and his hands locked over my thighs for leverage. He pounds into me, hips slapping and slamming against my ass as I struggle to keep up. He's going at me so hard my breath escapes with every thrust, leaving me lightheaded and on edge.

My fingers blur over my clit, and though my voice is strangled, I manage to get out, "Don't. Stop. Fuck, don't stop." Beg? Order? Both, most likely.

I hover on the edge, feeling the flight right at my fingertips in a moment of anticipation, and then I explode. My vision blacks out as I squeeze my eyes shut, lost to the overwhelming pleasure coursing through me, and my hearing goes fuzzy as my blood roars. I'm probably glad I can't hear myself very well because I know I'm being loud, but I'm too far gone to care what the neighbors think. Not that I even have any neighbors this time of night. The garage is the only building around with an apartment upstairs, and we're blessedly alone.

Brody growls and falls over me, damn near folding me in half as I quickly pull my hands out of the way and try to find purchase on the smooth car hood. I resort to pressing my flat palms down to stay in place. Distantly, I'm thankful for the yoga stretches Emily's talked me into to prevent back problems because otherwise, I'd probably have just pulled a hamstring from this position. Brody grabs my shoulders, curling my body into his and covering me, his abs to the backs of my thighs.

And then he *really* starts fucking me.

Except his eyes are wide open, looking right at me as though he can see to my soul. I think for a moment that I can see into his, too. Dark and lonely, good and sweet, misunderstood and honorable.

His thrusts are steady and powerful, just like the man he is. He's watchful and caring, making sure he's hitting that sweet spot inside me just right. And I can tell from the tension around his eyes that he's getting close.

"Come, Brody. Please." I wish I could feel the heat of his cum when he does, but we're way too new, way too casual to go without the condom. Even still, I fantasize that it's just us, bare and raw, with nothing separating us physically, even though there's so much separating us emotionally.

He groans, deep and guttural, and grits out, "Err- Ca!" That he can't get out my full name but tries anyway is sexy as fuck. I love that he's so lost to pleasure—in me, with me—that he can't speak.

I can't feel his cum, but I feel him grow harder and pulse, and it's enough to satisfy that greedy bitch inside me who wants more. As Brody comes down from his orgasm, he tilts his head, leaning it against my leg. A smile stretches his lips. Not the cocky one or even a flirty one but just pure, unadulterated bliss. Exhaustion tinges the edges, but I can tell he's happy. I don't need to see my matching smile to know how I feel.

Tonight was big. Majorly so. And though I keep throwing landmines in his way, Brody is dodging each and every one of them, not ignoring them or denying their power but giving them the respect they deserve. The respect I deserve. As a woman, as a racer, as . . . me.

My armor cracks a little, a small piece of hope worming its way inside. Maybe he won't try to make me small or make me fit into whatever box he deems appropriate. I don't have time for him, but if he's willing to wait while I figure some shit out, a guy who likes me for *me* is who I would want by my side when I'm ready for more.

Brody flexes and his cock jumps inside me. "Where'd you go again, Lil Bit?"

I focus my eyes on his, and the smile that had melted under the weight of my thoughts returns. "Just thinking that you surprise me, Cowboy."

Oh, now I get that cocky grin and full-fledged arrogance. It should piss me off, but it's sexy for some reason. "Well, let's get upstairs and I'll surprise you again."

I wiggle, trying to get up but still impaled on him, and he groans as he puts fierce hands on my hips, stilling me. "Nope, not like that." He lets my legs fall from his shoulders and slowly tortures us both as he pulls out. He takes off the condom and throws it in the trash can by the wall of toolboxes.

"Two points," I offer generously, which gets me a sardonic brow in response.

He adjusts his clothes, zipping his jeans, and then reaches for me. He picks me up like I'm light as a feather, my legs wrapping around his waist even as I argue. "Put me down," I say with no heat, smacking his shoulder like a butterfly. I don't know why I feel the need to fight this even though I'm enjoying it, but I do. Fighting it feels like something I should want to do.

"You maybe weigh a buck ten, Lil Bit. I could carry you all damn day, so I can sure as shit carry you up the stairs to your apartment."

That sounds like a challenge to my ornery ears, so I decide to make this a little extra hard for him. Seeing as I can't eat a dozen cupcakes and weigh more, I go with the distraction method. "Mmmkay, if you say so." I'm certain those words have never passed my lips, in seriousness or sarcasm.

I kiss and nibble along his stubbled jaw and he groans. Victory tastes sweet. His skin tastes salty. I nuzzle into his neck, smelling the fumes of the racetrack on him, another thing I never knew would turn me on so much. I sniff him and swear to God I don't know who I'm becoming around this man. When I suck at the skin of his neck a bit, he groans and pauses on the stairs. "Damn it, Erica. You wanna get fucked on the stairs again?" He's being stern, like that's some grave punishment.

I laugh, and he takes two more steps, slow and easy. I'm sure he wants me to think he's doing it so he doesn't drop me. I'm almost certain he's doing it so I'll keep kissing his neck. I think I found a new erogenous zone on my Cowboy. His hands grip my ass hard, encouraging me. I'm pretty sure I just got ten fingertip-sized bruises on my nonexistent butt, but fuck if I don't like the idea of that. In response, I find that sweet spot over his pulse and suck it, delighting in the way I can feel it race under my mouth. I murmur against his skin, "Keep going upstairs or I'll stop."

My threat holds no weight because as soon as I say the words, I go back to kissing down his neck to where it joins his shoulder. A good bite in the muscle there has him taking steps double-time as I bounce and laugh in his arms. "Brody!"

I fly through the air and bounce as I land on my bed. He follows, and we get down to round two.

---

BOTH OF US ARE EARLY RISERS, EVEN WITH THE NIGHT'S ACTIVITIES. So I wake to find Brody curled around as the big spoon to my little spoon. I can feel his hardness, and I wiggle my hips a bit, encouraging him. "Good morning," I whisper in the darkness of the predawn.

"Mmm, good morning." His voice is gravelly with sleep, but he grinds against me.

I arch, and he moves his hips, slipping between my legs. I buck my hips, sliding along his length and coating him with my arousal. I swear, I'm always wet when he's around, but especially when he's in my bed, all soft and sleepy.

"Condom."

His hands tighten on me. "Can we just do this? I won't go in bare, but just slide on me, use me."

I look over my shoulder, meeting his eyes. There's no deceit, no doubt there, just pure need and hope. The thought of feeling him skin on skin is too tempting to say no to. I slip my pussy along his cock, over and over, liking the idea of leaving my juices all over him. Marking him with my essence the way I marked his neck last night. I'm not a possessive woman, but fuck if that idea doesn't turn me on, and I buck faster, searching for my orgasm. Not for my own pleasure but to coat him with it.

He reaches over my hip, finding my clit easily and helping me get there. He rubs me, mimicking what he watched me do last night perfectly, tapping and petting me as he growls in my ear.

"Fuck, Lil Bit. I'm gonna come. Can I come on you like this?"

His cum on my skin is equally filthy and also arousing as hell. "God, yes, come on me, Brody."

My words are enough to send him over, and he jerks behind me. I feel the heat of his cum this time, feel him rubbing it onto my clit and using it to slide his fingers against me faster and harder. "Come on me too. I want to feel you come with nothing between us. Please."

Brody Tannen does not beg. In the bedroom or anywhere else. I know this as well as I know I don't beg, either. But damn if that order with the request at the end doesn't send me spiraling. I come hard, feeling every inch of him behind me and between my legs. He encourages me, whispering in my ear how beautiful I look when I let go and telling me to keep going and give him more. I take delight in the sweetness of his words as I filthily cover him with my cream.

Who knew I'd be into that? Certainly not me. Guess I'm learning things every day, about Brody and even about myself.

We sag, sweaty and messy, and I make a note to wash my sheets today. Brody lays a kiss to my shoulder, his morning scruff a bit scratchy in a good way, and disappears for the bathroom. A minute later, he's back with a wet washrag which I use to wipe up as he looks on, proud as a peacock at the mess we made.

"We've got another hour to rest before we have to get going for the day. Wanna move to the couch?" he offers. He holds out a hand, taking the corner of the cloth and tossing it to the hamper in the corner.

"You're pretty good at adulting. I think most folks would just fall back into bed, fighting over who had to lie in the wet spot and leave the cleanup rag on the floor."

I mean it as a joke, but as we walk to the couch and settle in, my back to his chest between his spread legs, he doesn't laugh. In fact, he's gone quiet. "Been adulting for a long time. After my mom died, I was it. I was technically grown, but not really, you know what I mean? Overnight, though, I grew up real fast. I took care of my family the best way I knew how. I kept the animals working, did both dad's and my share around the farm, kept them all safe and protected. And yeah, I did laundry too."

I remember his words of understanding about my keeping my secret from Dad. This is Brody letting me into his past, his secrets. I'm quiet, listening and taking each of them into my heart, holding them more delicately than I thought I'd be capable of.

"What happened?" Nothing in his words leads me to believe he's doing anything but still keeping everything running smoothly, and he's talked about the cattle and harvests, even showing me pictures when we text. But the tension through his body tells a much different story.

"Everything went to shit, and no matter how hard I tried to keep it, I lost everything. It all washed through my fingers like sand I couldn't hold onto." He holds his hand up, making a fist to catch the invisible grains. I weave my fingers through his, kissing his knuckles. I feel the thick swallow he makes and wonder what part of the story he's forcing down. I know his Dad died so maybe that's what he's understandably not ready to talk about? "Actually, that's not true. I have near everything now, just not in the way I thought I would. Mama Louise and the Bennetts are real good to us, better than we ever deserved, especially from them. I'm grateful for them."

I think back to the oddly comfortable dinner I'd had with the Bennetts and how it'd seemed like they were one big, happy family. But maybe that's not always been the case? I don't voice the question, letting Brody share what he wants the way he let me do the same.

"One day, I'll have a ranch and own and work my land, not someone else's. It'll be somewhere safe for my brothers and sisters, a place to be Tannens, no matter what else is going on. It won't be the same as it was before, I know that. Shayanne and Luke are always jetting off here and there, and they've got a place of their own. Brutal and Allyson's house will be done soon enough, and they'll be gone. Bobby'll find his way—maybe fall in love, maybe just run off to Nashville. But one day, I'll have a ranch where the cattle's mine, the choices are mine, the good times and bad times are all mine." It sounds like a prophecy, like he's putting that out into the universe and expecting it to deliver any moment.

I realize with a start that he wants what I have, in a way. My dad's garage, a legacy from him to me, is exactly what Brody wants. A place of his own, for his brothers and sister, like he said, but I think it's more than that. Brody wants a future and roots. His is just grass and dirt, while mine is grease and oil. He thinks he's a casual, fly by the seat of his pants type, but he's not. He's just playing at it.

He rests his chin on the top of my head, a move that feels like a connection. A string. We said no strings when this started, but damned if they're not stitching themselves to us with each and every share. Right now, I don't examine that too closely. I just snuggle into him and will the tick of the clock on the wall to slow down, wishing for the sun to sleep just a little longer so I can stay in Brody's arms.

# CHAPTER 18

## BRODY

"Last load, I promise!"

Shay's sing-songing voice tells me there are at least three more crates that's she's 'forgetting' about in her twisted way of motivating me to do her bidding. I set the no-way-it's-the-last-one in the back of the truck but make zero moves to close the tailgate.

In three, two, one . . .

"Oh, I forgot . . . there's still a couple more in the kitchen. On the counter by the fridge."

"Called it," I announce victoriously as I boop her nose. She scrunches it and swipes at it like I rubbed dirt on her. To be fair, I have before but didn't this time. Helps to keep her on her toes if I make it where she doesn't know for sure.

In the kitchen, I stack two crates to carry and she grabs the last one. "You sure? This everything? Nothing in the fridge or on the porch or in one of the other trucks or in Mama Louise's kitchen?"

Shay instantly shakes her head, but I can see her mentally double-checking herself so I wait while she actually confirms. When she sticks her tongue out at me, I know we're golden. "All right then, let's roll."

Finally in the truck, we start the trip down the grassy drive toward the gate. "This is the official last run of spring jams to the resort. And I'm hoarding carrots like a bunny for the Easter carrot cakes they ordered." She holds two fingers up behind her head, scrunches her nose again, and sticks her top front teeth out over her lip. She does look remarkably like a rabbit when she starts twitching.

"Never do that again, Shay. I don't want Luke figuring out what a weirdo you are and bailing on you. We have a no take-backsies policy. You're his problem, and it's a done deal." I'm teasing and she knows it, but she huffs in annoyance and punches me in the shoulder anyway. It's okay. I deserve it and had already flexed in preparation because I knew it was coming. Shay can throw a mean right jab, and the sharp bite of a little pain is bright. The pride in my heart is brighter. I taught her how to fight like that and then made damn sure she never needed to.

"Luke likes me weird, so don't you worry, brother o' mine. We're happy as two pigs in slop. Speaking of pigs, did I tell you that Bacon Seed is learning tricks now?" Bacon Seed is her savagely named miniature pig, which was a Christmas gift from Luke, so maybe he does know and appreciate her 'uniqueness'. That spoiled rotten mini-monster is their pseudo-baby in every way, sleeping in their room and almost always in Shay's arms with her cooing and singing to the pink squealer. Mama Louise even has to pig-sit when Shay travels with Luke. And apparently, he's sitting on command, according to the long-winded story with several sidetracks that Shay just completed.

She looks out the window, smiling at the antics of the goats in the penned yard by the house. "Look how cute they are! Maybe we should take a few over to the pens by our house. Ooh, and get a full-sized pig too!" She makes it sound completely reasonable and exciting. It's absolutely not.

"Shay, for the love of fuck, give your man a break. We got cattle, goats, dogs, cats, a pig, and kids running around now. You don't need a full-sized pig. Besides, what're you gonna do when it's ready to go to market?"

"Shh." Her hiss is accompanied by her hand slapping over my mouth. "Don't you say that where the animals can hear you."

My brow rises, snark in the small movement, and she takes her hand away slowly. "They can't hear me. We're in the truck." Still, she looks out the window like a pissed off cow might knock on her window. They won't . . . one, because they're cows, and two, because they're in the back pasture where we finally got them moved to after some fence repair work that took Mark, James, and me two days to complete.

"Fine." She pouts, her arms crossing over her chest and her left boot tapping the floorboard. "How is market prep going?"

I give it a fifty-fifty chance of whether we're adding a pig to our menagerie of animals. Poor Luke, such a sucker for my sister. I only hope she appreciates how lucky she has it while she does.

"We're making good strides. Mark's decided on how many he's gonna sell, which ones he wants to keep, and he'll probably look for a few more to add to the herd. Prices are looking good now, which means he'll be selling high but buying high too. He's got a couple of quality bulls, so the herd should be good for next mating season. Prospects are solid overall."

Shay nods along with my assessment but ends on a head tilt with her eyes laser-locked on me. "You say 'he' like he's the only one out there working the herd day in and day out."

I shrug. "They are his—his cattle, his decisions. I'm okay with that." I don't tell her that I want our family farm back so much I can taste it and that I still curse Dad every chance I get for causing us to lose it. I'd been able to save us from his stunts for years, but he'd gotten the last laugh when he died and I'd had to sell it to settle his debts. I'm just thankful it was to the Bennetts. If not for them, we'd have likely split up to work ranches and farms wherever we could get hired on. Maybe Bobby would've gone on to Nashville, because that's where he belongs, and Shay was already dating Luke so she would've been okay, but Brutal and me would've been fucked if the Bennetts hadn't saved us.

But I don't tell her that. She doesn't need my regrets on her shoulders, not when she's happy. And she is—with Luke, with our new family, with her business, and even with her pig. The miniature one she's already got, and hopefully *not* a full-grown sow.

I'm happy too, but there's a constant gnawing in my gut that something's wrong. It's the land, the Tannen farm. I might still live in my childhood home, on the same land I grew up on, but it doesn't feel the same. Thankful and grateful as I might be for the Bennetts, the sunrises and sunsets over land that I lost are still a daily reminder of my shortcomings.

"They're yours too, Bro. It's a good thing to be invested in the herd—it makes you a hard worker, a responsible cowboy, and mostly, a good man."

"Mmm-hmm." I scratch at my lip as I try to believe her sweet compliments, and maybe I even do . . . a little. Still, the sound is more one of 'let it go' than agreement because even if I'm good, I'm not good enough, obviously.

"Speaking of . . ." Shay pauses, and though I think she intends this to feel like a segue, I can sense the *errrk* of a change in direction, but Shay always does and says what she wants. We all just try to keep up. "We've missed you at dinner here lately. Is it safe to say another one bites the dust?" She doesn't so much as blink as she scans my face for any small tell, but I can see the excited smile she's holding back. I force myself to stay still, my hands light on the wheel and eyes on the road.

"Not sure I know what you're talking about." I absolutely know she's referring to my forgoing family dinners in the evenings in favor of seeing Erica damn near every night for the last two weeks.

At this point, I'm battling exhaustion, working myself to the bone with the cattle and driving back and forth to Morristown. We went to the races again, just to watch, and have spent just as much time curled up in one another talking as we do fucking. I can tell something's changed between us, the connection getting deeper and filled with more than orgasms, but Erica has made it a point to repeat her early mission statement of casual-only, and though I'm nervous the lady doth protest too much, I'm following her lead.

"Brody, don't lie to me with your lying mouth. Tell me the good stuff." The order is emphasized with another stomp of her foot against my floorboard.

"Quit kicking my truck or you'll be walking home." The growled threat would shrivel most people to goo, and the fire in my eyes would singe their soul. Shayanne suffers no such weakness and merely scowls at me in return. I'm not even really mad about the truck. It's a truck, after all, not some prissy import, but getting on to her about the truck is safer than admitting she's getting too close to something I don't want to talk about. She's like a bloodhound and won't let that go for anything until she gets what she wants.

"Fine. Then I'll tell you what we all think and you can grunt along and tell me if we're right or wrong." She smiles that sassy grin that says she already knows how this is going to play out.

"What the fuck? Y'all talking about me behind my back? That's some fucked-up 'family' shit there." I spit out the word 'family' as if it's a curse, which makes Shay's eyes narrow. I realize a breath too late that I just gave her the first bullet to kill me with.

"We are family, Brody. The four of us Tannens and the Bennetts. Blended Brady Bunch family with a spoonful of redneck and a cup of country thrown in."

*Grunt.* Agreement or disagreement, I'm not sure, but I really don't want to go into analyzing our family dynamics. Now or ever.

"Moving on. Are you going to Rix's at night when you're not at home?"

Silence. I'm not playing this game, am most definitely not talking about my sex life with my baby sister.

"So that's a yes." I cut my eyes in her direction, knowing I didn't give away anything that would confirm or deny her question. "We figured, just making sure you hadn't started going to a fight club or something."

I give her a rumble of disapproval this time. It's not much, but I basically just agreed to her game.

"I like Rix, not that it matters." It does and she knows it.

"You barely know her." And now I've gone and done it. She knows she's got my ear, knows that despite my protestations, I care about what she thinks of Erica.

Shayanne and I have always been close, just like Bobby and Brutal. We're a family of four, but the connections between us all are squiggly lines of twisted knots. And as the oldest, I took care of Shay, even when she was literally taking care of all of us, cooking and cleaning while we all worked in the fields.

"Pshaw, I know more than you think I do. I know that Rix caught your interest enough that you talked about her with Sophie before even going out with her. I know that she didn't freak out when confronted with all of us unexpectedly, and that speaks volumes about her courage. We're an intimidating bunch." That's an understatement and a half. Tannens are known for being one step shy of hooligans, though it's more because memories are long in this town than because we've gotten up to anything rowdy in recent years.

She's not wrong, and now I'm curious what else she thinks she knows, so I let her go on without interrupting her with an argument we both know would be a lie.

"I know that you smiled the entire time at Hank's when you were giving each other shit and when you were teaching her to dance. I know she was smiling the whole time too. I know you two look like Tom and Jerry, this big grump of a cat and this tiny mouse, but damned if she's not leading you around by your tail." Her smile is smug. "And by tail, I mean your dick. Whatever magic her vajay-jay is rocking has got you running off to get another dose every chance you get."

"Shayanne!" I growl, but my warning tone is met with a palm.

"Don't want to know. I just mean that she makes you happy. You're smiling even though you have purple circles under your eyes that are worse than back when we had more month than money."

I didn't figure anyone but me had noticed the smudges of color beneath my eyes, and I wipe at them even though they won't disappear.

"So . . . another one bites the dust?" Shay hedges, asking a question again instead of telling me things.

"Nah, this isn't some big love story, but I'm enjoying it while it lasts." My thumbnail scrapes along my lip, and though I won't say it to Shayanne, I know that the last few times I've been with Erica, it has felt different. Less casual, more intense, and . . . real. Our conversations are deeper, our sex is more intimate, and feelings are developing whether I want them to or not. But I can handle it. I know how this goes.

But fuck, am I gonna miss her when she's done with me. I'll miss the way her cheeks flush when she's turned on, highlighting the sprinkles of freckles. I'll miss her passion for cars and her intellect, because the woman knows everything about engines and has the drive and ambition to do so much with her brilliance. I'll miss the sharp wit she uses to flay me wide open, verbally sparring with me like no one ever has. I'll miss the soft and sleepy rasp of her voice when she first wakes up, says good morning, and then snuggles into my side for 'five more minutes'. I'll miss the sight of her not giving a single solitary fuck as she walks around naked. I'll miss . . . her. I'll miss . . . us.

*Fuck.*

"While it lasts? Just don't screw it up and then it can last forever." Her voice goes soft and breathy at the end, like a little girl talking about a princess finding her prince.

But that's not my story, not anyone's, really. Disney just never showed the truth after the happily ever after-fade to black ending, the part where Cinderella bitches that Prince Charming left his socks on the floor, or where Beauty missed dinner again because her nose was buried in a book. Or most importantly, where Snow White dies and leaves behind her prince and a whole rag-tag group of pseudo-children who fucking need her.

"It's not that simple, Shay." Even I hear the bitterness and cynicism.

She taps her nose knowingly. "Except it is."

She sounds so certain, so sure. I wish I could still have that naïve belief in forever, but I'll take it as a job well done that I managed to get Shay to adulthood as a woman who still believes in fairy tales. Maybe I at least did that right.

"Let's get this jam delivered. I've got shit to do."

As far as conversation enders go, it's weak, but Shayanne allows it. Though she gives me a glance that says she's still thinking about this topic. I turn the radio up to circumvent her.

"Good song," I tell her as I sing along to Josh Turner's *Your Man.*

"Did you know Chris Stapleton wrote this song?" Shay asks, feet tapping along as she dances in her seat.

"No shit?" She shakes her head. "Huh, had no idea."

We sing along, and for now, I can live in the moment where everything is fine enough.

THE DELIVERY TO THE RESORT IS HANDLED QUICKLY BECAUSE THE kitchen workers hustle to help unload the truck. I leave Shayanne with Katelyn to hitch a ride home and take off like a demon to see Erica.

I know I'm treading into dangerous territory here, but I meant what I told Shay. I'm going to enjoy this while I can. Because Erica is someone special.

At the garage, music is playing again. Greta van Fleet, I think? They're the new guys that sound old school, and that I know that much speaks volumes to my musical education at Erica's side.

I find her standing on her stool, head buried in a truck again. I wave silently to Manuel and Reed then put a finger to my lips. Manuel grins back, curious. Reed glares, still mad at my existence. I sneak right up behind Erica, bending down low to stay out of range of those fists, and pinch her on the butt.

She whirls, already cussing. "What the fuck, asshole!" She sees my smirk and her fury stalls. "Oh, hey." It's like the anger never existed, evaporating on a nonexistent wind, then her lips spread into a slow smile as her eyes meet mine.

"Hey yourself," I answer, crowding into her. She leans back against the truck and licks her lips, inviting my kiss. We've got an audience, one I know Erica is still trying to be sensitive to, so I make the kiss a polite greeting, not a face-devouring precursor to something more. But still, I'm helping to yank at that Band-Aid on Reed's sensitive little heart a bit too, so I weave my hands into her hair and whisper in her ear, "I missed you."

I swear to fuck, I'm not lying, but this woman actually laughs a sound that is almost a giggle. It's got to be the most foreign sound to ever pass her lips. I would be less shocked if she started speaking a foreign language. But that sweet sound, throaty and deep, will be one I remember for the rest of my days, however many I get.

"I missed you too." She ends her answering whisper in my ear with a sharp bite to my earlobe. And there's my Erica, grinning as she pulls away. "I thought you were gonna come by later?" Her eyes glance at the truck behind her.

"I know, but I got done early and couldn't wait to see you. Do what you need to. I can entertain myself." She looks dubious but spins around and gets back to work. "See, I'm already entertained." My eyes are locked on her ass, which is basically invisible in the baggy coveralls, but the middle finger she throws over her shoulder is can't-miss.

We spend a couple of hours in companionable chatter while I sit at the shop desk. She works on that truck, Manuel is working on one of those dancing gerbil cube cars, and Reed alternates between glaring at me and puppy dog eyeing Erica. Oh, he works on another couple of cars too, but his eyeballs are getting more of a workout than anything, ping-ponging between Erica and me.

Erica's head pops out from under the hood, and she goes to the door, leaning in to start the truck. It's loud and growly, which seems to be what she's looking for because she closes the hood and moves the truck out to the lot. When she comes back in, she leans over me to get an invoice. After a quick message to the truck's owner, she gives me her full attention. "Lunch break?"

"Fuck, yes." I don't mean it to sound like I'm taking Erica upstairs for a lunchtime quickie, but I also don't not-mean for it to sound like that.

*Riiip*. Sorry, not sorry, Reed.

The immature shithead in me wants to give him a little wave as we go through the door into the breakroom, but I'm mature enough to keep my hands in my pockets and only throw a cocky smirk his way. As the door behind me closes, I hear his hissed, "Motherfucker."

"What did you do?" Erica asks over her shoulder, not even bothering to pretend I didn't earn that curse.

"Just smiling at watching your ass, that's all." Her *harrumph* says she doesn't believe that at all, but it's the set of her shoulders that I notice the most because they're drawing up tight. I pull at her hand. "Hey, really . . . I'm not trying to make this harder on him for shits and giggles, but I still think it's gonna be worse before it's better. Maybe for both of you?"

She sighs, leaning back against the wall and crossing her arms. Only weeks ago, I was tasting her here for the first time. It seems like ages ago. I could draw that map of her freckles blindfolded, can tell you where the gold flecks in her eyes appear when she sits in her favorite chair by the window at sunrise, and know her heart is pure goodness, which means it hurts her to hurt Reed. "You're right, and I've been trying to talk you up so he knows I've moved on and that he should too. He's just not getting it. Or he doesn't want to get it, I guess."

I step up to the stair she's on, caging her in. "He will. In the meantime, he doesn't matter. Let's eat some lunch, Lil Bit."

She nods and lets me lead her the rest of the way upstairs to her apartment. I wish we had time for that nooner I was teasing Reed with, but really, we need to eat so she can get back to work. It matters that she sets a good example and doesn't take two-hour lunches she would never allow her employees to take.

We make sandwiches, dancing around each other in the tiny kitchen space like pros. They're nothing fancy but good and filling, and we sit down at the two-seater table to eat.

"Did you get that part for Todd's Challenger?" I ask her around a mouthful of food. Most girls would probably be disgusted. But Erica's doing the same thing.

She shakes her head. "No, he texted me and said never mind. I don't know what he's doing instead—probably saw something on a forum of armchair mechanics." Her eyes roll, and she huffs around the sandwich she's chewing.

"Is that like an armchair quarterback? Guys who think they know their stuff but are just yelling from their recliners with their sixth beer in their Cheeto-crusted fingers?"

Erica points at me. "Just like that."

"You are so much better than that. I don't know a damn thing about cars or engines, but even a dumbass like me can see that when you go to the track, they're all looking to you for guidance and to make their cars be the best they can be. You're good, Erica."

"Thank you."

Later, looking back, I'll hear the hesitancy, but right now, it blows right over me and all I hear is an answer on automatic when I want her to see herself the way I do. Magical, powerful, fierce.

"No, really. I know you're protecting your dad by staying quiet on the whole racing thing, and believe me, I get that secrets are sometimes in everyone's best interests. But you have a real gift. It's a shame you can't share it with him when he's the one who inspires you. He's probably the one person who could most understand the miracles of engineering you're working."

I smile, hoping she hears just how amazing I believe she is. I've never met anyone like her before, so skilled at something that seems pretty straightforward, but for her, it's pure artistry.

I've watched her tinker with parts downstairs and in a corner of the apartment where there are chunks of metal I can't even identify strewn about the floor. But not only can Erica ID them, she redesigns them, reworks them, creates something from nothing. It's amazing to behold, and I know enough about parenting from raising my sister to know that Erica's dad would be proud as fuck to see what his little girl can do with her hands and her mind. Only the sheer force of physics holds her back.

Erica drops her sandwich to her plate, wiping her hands on her coveralls. "I told you why I can't tell him."

"I know. But that doesn't mean it's not sad that you don't get to share that together anymore." I can tell something's wrong, but I don't know what. Even so, I'm backpedaling, realizing too late that I've stepped into something I didn't intend to. "But at least you have the garage, right?"

"This garage is everything to my dad, to me. It's supported us my whole life, brought us together as a family." The temperature in the room has dropped by degrees. Erica's stony expression and crisp biting tone hit me like blades. She's acting like I dissed the garage or its importance to her, which I definitely didn't do.

"As it should be. You've created something special here." Generic platitudes and walking on eggshells are what I'm reduced to?

No, fuck that. I'm not that guy, not gonna simper around every time she gets her feathers ruffled.

"I don't know what I said, but I'm sorry." I don't sound apologetic in the least. I sound as pissed as I am. "I didn't mean to upset you, was actually trying to give you a compliment. But I guess I fucked that up."

Erica blinks at me, silent for the first time ever. Not threatening me, not joking around, not . . . anything. She's completely blank and I can't get a read on her at all.

"Maybe I should just go." I get up, leaving my lunch on the table. I'm halfway down the stairs when she pulls on my arm, short nails digging into my overheated skin.

"You don't get it. He forbade me. Racing is the one thing" —she holds up one finger and then swipes at the air, correcting herself—"the *only* thing he ever asked me not to do. Dad didn't even argue about my going into the military as hard as he did about racing. He made me promise."

"But you do it anyway because it's what you love. It's who you are."

Fire flashes in her eyes. She's angry that I see her, know her truth. I thought that sharing that secret with me meant something, but right now, I can see that it's the opposite. She shared it with me because I'm not important . . . not like her parents, her sister, not like Reed.

All those guys at the track know and she calls them *friends* or *buddies* or even *dumb fucks*. I guess that's what we've been all along, friends who fuck. And I'm the idiot who managed to catch feelings for her and think something deeper was going on.

Right as always, Dad. *Love just means it'll hurt worse eventually.*

I can't love Erica, but I do feel something for her. Obviously, or it wouldn't hurt to have her dismiss me this way.

I shove through the door, stomping through the breakroom, and then shove the door to the garage open too. Reed and Manuel jump as the door swings back and hits the wall behind it.

Manuel reaches for the music, turning it down even though it's already quieter than when Erica and I went upstairs because she's the one who likes the blaring tunes. "You okay, man?" Manuel asks.

Before I can answer, Erica catches up to me.

"You don't understand. This is enough. It has to be." The doubt in her heart paints her cheeks pink, her eyes gold.

Gobsmacked, I look around the garage. "Understand this? Understand why the shop is so important to you?" I laugh, incredulous. "Fuck, I'm probably the only person who does, Erica."

She scoffs, her eyes rolling as she waves her grease-covered hand. Guess she didn't wash up for lunch as well as she thought, and something about that is adorable, which only makes me madder. The mannerism is dismissive, almost that of a bratty spoiled princess, something she's damn well not. She's also not correct in the least.

"Go ahead. Play the martyr no one is asking you to be. You gave up on me for Emily. You'll give up on . . ." I have the foresight to stop myself before I say racing, though it pisses me off that even as she's killing me, I'm still protecting her. "Give up on everything else even when it's all you want. Wanna know where that gets you?"

I hold my hands out wide, letting her look her fill at me. Broken, angry, distrustful, with nothing but should-have-beens to my name.

Fire flashes in her eyes as they narrow down to slits. "What am I looking at? A grown man with nothing to show for it? You don't know what it means to give everything to your family's legacy. You work someone else's land, no skin in the game, with pie-in-the-sky dreams of something bigger one day. Tell me, what're you doing to make that happen? Because I am making shit happen." She points at herself, her fingertip denting the delicate skin of her chest, which is rising and falling rapidly with anger as she fights dirtier than she realizes.

*Sonofabitch, that hurts.*

Mostly, because she's right. I talk about owning my farm again, dream of the land being Tannens' again, but I haven't done a damn thing toward making that happen other than wish for it and want it. It's been a relief to be free of that responsibility, but it's like a vacation, nice while you're gone, but you know you'll have to get back to work eventually. I've been putting that part off, though, pretending that it'll happen on its own somehow. It won't.

Erica senses that she gained a foothold, digging deeper into that wound that I thought had scarred over. Her barbs are sharp as nails, though, freshly opening up my battered heart.

"My family depends on this garage, on me, to survive. I need to make sure that's my focus."

I think she's telling me to leave the racing stuff alone, though I'm still not sure how this fight even really started. But now that we're in it, I can feel the accelerant catching fire at every corner.

And that's when I realize, she's not telling me it's the garage over racing. She's saying it's the garage over me. She told me she didn't have time for anything serious, and I guess she's making good on that right now.

All the fight goes out of my blood as it runs cold. I'm losing something I didn't even realize I had. It snuck up on me, drip by drip like honey, and filled that gaping void in my center with warmth. But the warmth dissipates too fast, unexpectedly leveling me. I curl my hat in my hands and shove it back on my head.

I sigh, blinking hard as I try to focus. Feet wide, hands on my hips, and voice steady, I tell her the truth she hasn't quite caught up to yet. I learned the hard way, and she will too, but there's nothing to be done for it now. "One day, when you're all alone and wishing for someone to take care of you the way you take care of everyone else, I want you to remember this second. The moment you shit on the one person who truly sees all of you and wants you for *you*, Erica Cole. No restrictions, no expectations, no cages. You are amazing, brilliant, beautiful . . . but none of that matters if you stay in other peoples' bubbles. The worst part is that you . . . you let them keep you there. And that is a damn tragedy. Goodbye, Erica."

I turn on my heel, eating the ground between her and my truck with fast strides. I slam the door shut with finality and pull out of the parking lot. I tell myself not to look back, but I do.

Erica is standing in the shop, right where I left her, arms crossed over her chest and jaw dropped in shock.

I feel the same way, Lil Bit.

I don't know how we went from having lunch to a devastating blow-up fight, but some things are inevitable. I've always known that.

I guess I just hoped I was wrong.

# CHAPTER 19

## ERICA

"Wow, you're a real bitch, you know that? I never would've thought that, but damn, Rix . . . way to kick a man when he's down."

I whirl on Reed, who looks as shocked as I feel. "Excuse the fuck out of me, but what did you just say?" I'm hurt and confused, which translates to full-blown armor mode with spikes and verbal bombs at the ready.

Reed shakes his head disbelievingly. "I said, you're a real bitch. I can't believe you're making me feel sorry for that asshole, but fuck, Rix."

I blink, surprised at the venom in Reed's voice. He never talks to me like this. "Stay out of it, Reed. Figured you'd be happy to see him go." Shit, that sounds like there's an opening for him now, and there most definitely is not.

"I asked around about him, you know. Figured if he was going to be hanging out with you, I wanted to check up on him, see if he's the asshole I thought." He laughs mirthlessly. "He works on the Bennett Ranch, right? That's the job you're giving him shit for? Ever heard of the Tannen Farm next door? Or maybe you didn't talk about that before you fucked? Well, before you go climbing higher on that pedestal, Princess, you should know he's right. If anyone would understand your obsession with this place, it'd be him."

I have no idea what Reed is talking about. Brody said his Mom died, which is why he helped take care of Shayanne, and he's talked about growing up around animals and ranching. But I've never heard him say one word about a Tannen Farm.

Reed flashes his teeth, victory in his feral grin. "Seems I know more about your boyfriend than you do. Of course, I was actually looking into his story, not just fucking him. Guess that's the difference."

Reed turns and stomps out, his car pulling out of the lot a hell of a lot faster than Brody's truck did.

Has everyone lost their minds? What the hell just happened?

Manuel looks at me patiently and kindly asks, "What do you need me to do, Boss?" At least he's rock steady. One of us has to be, and it's certainly not me.

---

"I THINK I MIGHT'VE FUCKED UP, EM." I HOLD UP A BIG BAG FROM the grocery store, hearing the bottle of wine clank against the six-pack of beer. "Bad."

"Oh, shit, get in here." She heads straight for the kitchen to pull glasses down. I offer her the wine bottle before twisting off the cap on my first beer. I have a feeling I'm going to need all of them tonight.

I chug it down, starting the process of numbing myself from the pain. Because fuck, this hurts. A lot.

And it's my own doing.

Emily shoves me toward the couch, and I flop to it in a heap, my legs crossing in front of me and my back curved inward around a pillow I hug tightly. But I can't protect myself from this because it's inside me.

"What the fuck did Brody do? Or should I just go kick his ass now?" Emily sounds like she might be willing to try it on my behalf.

"Nothing . . . well, something . . . but it was mostly me." I grab for another beer but she holds it a few inches further than I can reach, and I'm too frustrated to lean forward and get it.

"Rix, I need something to go on here. Speak and then you'll get the yummy treat." She waves the bottle around by its stubby neck, taunting me with it.

I growl and lurch forward, snatching it from her. But I don't open it, I just hold it. The label seems inordinately interesting all of a sudden, and I pick at the corner, wondering how I can put all of this.

"The long and short of it? I'm a bitch, apparently." Beer number two opens and I toss the cap to the coffee table.

"Agreed. What else you got, because everyone knows that." Emily sounds like that's no big deal whatsoever, agreeing readily and easily.

I shove at her shoulder, careful not to spill on her couch. I might not deserve it, but I'm sure gonna drink this thing, not waste it by sacrificing it to her fluffy cushions. "Fuck you, you're supposed to be on my side."

"Does it help if I say that your bitchiness is one of the things we love most about you?" Her smile is placating, and I'm ashamed to say it works a little bit. "Get on with it. You came here for a reason, not just for me to stroke your ego, so tell me what happened."

I sigh and swallow half of the second beer. "You asked for it, Em." I look her in the eye, the anger still right beneath my surface. "He told me I'm a great mechanic, talented and brilliant."

"That asshole! How dare he!" She couldn't be more sarcastic if she tried, and she clearly thinks I've lost it. She's basically right. I have.

I realize that I can't tell her this story, not the truth of it, without telling her about racing. And I can't do that. That's the foundation of the whole problem to begin with. I thought Brody understood that, really got why I had to keep that secret.

*You should tell your dad.*

In the end, he thought he knew better than I did. Just like everyone else.

I've gone quiet, and Emily is searching my face for some kind of clue. She must find it because she quietly whispers, like someone other than the two of us might hear, "Does he not want you to race anymore?"

The room spins, and it has absolutely nothing to do with the beer and a half I've had. "What did you say?"

Emily shrugs. "I know you race, Rix. I figure Brody knows too. Did he ask you to stop? Or God forbid, *tell* you to stop?"

Laughter bursts past my lips, and I hope it sounds real, covering the horror bubbling up inside. "I don't race anymore, you know that. Dad told us we couldn't even go to the track anymore. I haven't been there in years."

Lies, lies, lies. I hate lying to her, but it's for her own good. Okay, if I'm being completely honest, it's selfish too. I do want to keep doing whatever the fuck I want to, but I don't want to put that on Emily's shoulders. She shouldn't have to lie for me, especially not to Dad, and I don't know if she would, anyway.

One of Emily's brows quirks, and she sets her wine glass down on the coffee table. She takes my beer from my hand despite my protests and sets it down too. Then she grabs my shoulders and shakes me . . . hard.

"Talk to me, dammit. I know you race, have known you raced through high school and picked it back up the same week you came back home from the Army. So quit lying and talk to me." She's loud, and now her whole building is more than aware that I'm racing. I'll probably have to swear them all to secrecy with promises of free oil changes.

Something about my brain bouncing around in the beer bath in my head makes her words click together like a puzzle. "You know. *You know?*" My eyes and mouth pop open wide at the same time. "Why didn't you ever say anything? Oh, my God, Emily!"

So many things take shape . . . her occasionally stopping by to bring me dinner on random afternoons that always made me nervous because I had to leave to make the first race, her talking about the horsepower of every new model on the sales floor at the dealership, her never inviting me to Wine Wednesdays with her girlfriends, and when she told me about the new salvage yard a few towns over that was a treasure trove of goodies for my automotive heart.

Emily has the good graces to look sheepish, but she's cut from the same cloth I am and that doesn't last long before she bows back up. Finger in my face, she bites out, "*You should've told me.* I've given you every chance in the world to tell me, but you never did. And I'm mad about it, have been for a while, in fact, and finally, I get to tell you . . . I'm mad at you."

"Take a fucking number!"

I get up, pacing around the living room to deal with the shocks of electricity rushing through me. Emily knows.

Shit. Fuck. Damn.

"Does Dad know?"

Emily is still sitting on the couch, looking perfectly comfortable. If anything, she looks more casual, as if getting that off her chest helped her. Well, it sure doesn't help me.

*Ugh, I am a selfish bitch, aren't I?*

She rolls her eyes. "Of course he doesn't know. Did you think I'd narc on you?" I'm silent, not answering because yes, I absolutely assumed that she would. "You did!"

Emily's repetition is quieter, filled with hurt. "You really thought I'd tell Dad?"

I throw my hands wide. "I didn't know, and I didn't want to put you in that position. I don't want to hurt Dad, but yeah, I basically never quit. I just let him think I did."

Emily shakes her head and pats the couch beside her. "Okay, one problem at a time. We'll come back to Dad. And how mad I am at you for not telling me, because I've been holding on to that for quite some time, so you'd best buckle up for that shitshow because it's coming." I sit, pulling the pillow back to my lap as she rants on.

"For now, tell me if I need to kill Brody. The broody, grunty asshole probably deserves it. He told you not to race too, didn't he? Don't listen to him, Rix. He's a Neanderthal, probably thinks you need a dick to push the gas pedal and only supports Danica Patrick when she's in a bikini, lying on a car hood."

My brows knit together because that sounds especially personal and specific. "Uh, Em . . . what the hell are you talking about?"

She closes her eyes and breathes deeply, her fingertips and thumb pulling together in a yoga-esque motion. "Sorry. That part was my issue, not yours. There's a new guy at the dealership who's pushing all my buttons. He seems to think that because I have a vagina, I'm unqualified to sell sports cars and trucks. Despite the fact that I put up the best numbers in the state last quarter." She waves her hand, refocusing on me, and though I'd love to go with the distraction she's offering, I do need her help. Especially if I can be honest and tell her what really happened, racing and all.

"He told me I'm a good mechanic. He actually said I do miracles of engineering, and he used the words 'brilliant' and 'amazing' about *me*."

"And . . . I'm not seeing how that leads to a Beerfest Bonanza on my couch."

"He said I should tell Dad about the racing. That it would be a nice thing for him to know that he inspired me, that he'd be proud." It feels uncomfortable to talk about myself like this, but I'm trying to give Emily the full picture.

"He's right." At my horrified expression, Emily adds, "Dad made this sweeping decree when he was hurting after Big John's accident. Oh, he meant it, every word of it, but he loves you, and if he knew you'd been keeping this from him, he'd be devastated. What is your big plan there, anyway? To just keep hiding it forever?"

"Uh . . . yeah, abso-fucking-lutely." Duh, that's obvious.

"Continue. Get to the bad part, where he says something mean or does something stupid because so far, I'm not getting it."

My face turns hot and fiery. "He didn't. I did. I think." I talk into the pillow. "I don't know. Reed said I was a bitch."

At that, Emily's eyes jump wide. "Holy shit, what did you say? Reed is like the quintessential sweetheart who would never . . . but he did. What did you say?"

She's on the verge of shaking me again so I spill it all. How Brody's kind words had made me feel warm and fuzzy, and that had scared the shit out of me. How his encouragement to tell Dad everything had felt like another decree from someone else who thought they knew better than I do about my own life. How in my anger, I'd lashed out in the one way I'd known would hurt him the most.

Emily stays quiet, letting me get it all out. When I reach the end, she shakes her head. "So, let me get this straight. You, a known secret-keeper, let him in on your secret, which he's kept. And he, an apparently quiet and non-sharing sort, showed you his soft belly about his family and his big hopes and dreams. And at the first sign of his not letting you walk all over him, which let's be honest here . . . you like to test people that way . . . you went straight for his jugular and threw it all back in his face. That about sum it up?"

I nod sullenly. "Reed said I don't know the half of it, though, said something about a Tannen Farm, but Brody's never mentioned it. I don't know . . . I feel like I don't know anything."

"Do you know that you have feelings for him?" Emily asks bluntly.

"We said casual. I've got the garage and racing and . . . I don't have time. I can't—"

Emily snaps her fingers in my face, cutting me off. "Excuses. You'll notice that I didn't ask *if* you have feelings for Brody. I asked if you *know*, because everyone else does. You're the one sitting on the starting line well after the checkered flag dropped." She grins. "That was good, yeah?"

I groan at the analogy that sounds like something Dad would say once upon a time. "It's not NASCAR. It's drag racing and you know it."

"You know what you need to do?" Emily asks, leading me where she wants me. I'm so messed up that I even let her.

"Apologize?"

She laughs . . . hard. "Apologize? Oh, God, Rix, you are so clueless sometimes. I swear all the time with bros has done you no favors at all. Think . . . *what do you need to do*?" I blink, not following this time. With a sigh, she tells me. "Grovel. Girl, you need to apologize, grovel, and tell him that you freaked out because you have big, scary feelings for him that make you want to spend forever in his arms, have his beautiful babies, and watch sunsets on the porch when you're both old and gray."

Cringe. Massively uncomfortable cringe that makes my whole body shiver from head to toe.

"That's maybe more than where I'm at right now? And telling him even a bit of that sounds awful. And Brody's not really that kind of guy either. I don't think that's . . ."

At Emily's harsh glare, I taper off. Not many people can shut me up with a look. She's one of them.

"I'm gonna be honest here, so listen up and let Girly Ol' Emily tell you something you don't know about guys. Their masculinity is fragile sometimes, especially a guy like Brody who's probably used to being the biggest swinging dick in the room. Not literally, but figuratively . . . oh, except maybe literally?" Her brow quirks, her hands moving through the air, measuring big to small, asking about his dick, apparently. I do not answer. "Later for that convo, then . . . where was I?"

"Something I don't know about guys?" I prompt dryly. Because I'm so ignorant about men.

"Right. A guy like Brody is tough, with this hard exterior and stoic façade. And you, you're like a sledgehammer, coming in and banging away . . . see what I did there?" She looks pleased with herself but shakes her head, hopefully focusing. "He let himself be vulnerable with you, which is probably a big fucking deal to him, and you punished him for it because of issues you have, ones that have *nothing* to do with him." She holds up one finger. "You need to let him know it's okay to share with you and that you want to share with him." A second finger comes up. "You need to tell him that you have feelings that are scaring the shit out of you and that you overreacted because you're a lucky bitch who doesn't know what she's got when it's right in front of her."

"Harsh much?" She's right, I know she is, but each of her words is another painful reminder of how badly I fucked this up.

"Holding someone's heart is a big responsibility, one you just showed him you can't be trusted with. So yeah, apologize, but more importantly, be worthy and hope he gives you another shot."

Shit. Fuck. Damn.

"So, how do I do that?"

"That part's up to you, Rix. You'll figure it out. Might I suggest a ballpeen hammer style rather than another sledgehammer approach, though? And also, I just said peen and somehow was not talking about penises . . . penis-i? I would like karmic good girl credit for that."

"Penises," I correct.

She nods, grabbing her wine. "Okay, so now tell me all about racing . . . *finally*."

I pick up my beer and tell her about everything I'm doing, from racing my Mustang to designing entire systems for the other racers at the track. Somewhere around nitrous oxide percentage ratios, I lose her, but she still nods along, and I realize how much I wanted to share this with her all along.

And maybe how I should share it with Dad too.

# CHAPTER 20

## ERICA

This might be the craziest thing I've ever done, but I'm doing it. I'm not giving in to my own fears and insecurities this easily.

At least that's what I tell myself right until I pull up to the gate at the Bennett ranch. Well, the closed gate of the ranch, at least. Shit, I hadn't thought of that. I only planned on coming out here, saying all the things I've been practicing in my head to Brody's face, and hoping for the best. I didn't have a plan B for what to do if that didn't work out.

Hopefully, this isn't a sign of bad things to come.

I stare at it blankly for a moment before I remember that Shayanne insisted that we trade numbers at Hank's, and I'm suddenly really grateful for their overbearing behavior that night.

*Me: Hey, it's Rix. I'm at the ranch. Can you let me in?*

*Shayanne: Brody's being an asshole. That your fault?*

*Me: . . .*

*Shayanne: Are you here to fix it?*

*Me: Yes.*

*Shayanne: On my way then. <smiley face>*

That was easier than I expected. Or maybe she's just setting the trap and I'm waiting here like a dumb fuck for her to come kill me in person? But I've got to try with Brody, even if it means his sister trying her damnedest to hurt me for hurting him.

I see a small ATV coming toward the gate, a plume of brown dust billowing behind it. When it gets close, Shayanne brakes hard, almost drifting it to a stop by the fence.

"Thanks for letting me in."

"Not happening." Her eyes are narrow slits of accusation. "I'm not sure what you did, but Brody damn near tore the house apart last night, slamming cabinets and bitching about the back door that hasn't closed right in ten years. The boys resorted to getting him drunk as a method of controlling his hissy fit. He's sleeping it off at home."

She's watching me carefully, scanning for my reaction, and I stand tall, almost at attention. "Okay . . . well, will you tell him I came by then? When he wakes up . . . he can call me if he wants."

Plan B . . . Plan C . . . I didn't have any plan at all. And now it's biting me in the ass. Another failure on my part.

Shayanne groans, shaking her head, and hooks a thumb over her shoulder. "Go on to the house. He'd skin me alive if I got between whatever this is." She swirls her finger at me. "Not to mention, I can't wait to get a front-row seat. I knew it."

She starts humming under her breath, and I look at the still-closed gate. "So, are you going to let me in then?"

Her head tilts, her right eyebrow raising. "He's at home. At *his* house?" At my confused look, she laughs. "Oh, my cheesus and crackers, that's too funny. You don't know anything, do you? This is gonna be fun."

"So are we gonna keep doing this or are you going to fill me in here?" I'm losing patience, and nerve, and the barely-there sweetness in my voice.

A few minutes later, I'm following her directions—getting back in my truck, following the white fence down the road to the next gate marked *Tannen Farm*. I guess Reed was right about that, which definitely doesn't bode well for me because I'm afraid he's right about my being a complete bitch too.

Just like Shayanne said, the gate opens automatically, and I drive up to a red and white farmhouse. It's worn and faded but cute with simple lines and a small porch along part of the front. The wood shutters on either side of several of the windows make it look warm and cozy, as does the dog lying lazily on the front porch.

I get out, calling out gently, "Hey there, big guy. Who's a good boy?" The dog's head lifts, and he sniffs the air before letting out a baleful howl.

"Shut up, Murphy!"

Brody's rough-voiced shout comes from inside the house, telling me I'm in the right place, at least. *It's showtime*, as Emily says. Time to put it all out there, pick my guts apart, lay my fears bare, and hope that it's enough for Brody to forgive me and take another chance on us.

He doesn't have to. We said casual from the get-go. Well, I did and he agreed. I'm not sure when that changed for me, but it did.

I pet Murphy on the head. "Good boy," I whisper, knowing he had every reason to bark at a stranger. I knock on the door, calling out, "Brody?"

There's a crash from inside, like Brody is stumbling and falling toward the door, so I open it and peek my head inside. It's darker, but the sunlight is shining through the windows, throwing lines of light through a wood-paneled living room. Brody looks like hell . . . hair a mess, beard scruffy, eyes sunken and purple-smudged. But he also looks like heaven . . . his chest bare and a hopeful spark as he looks at me. "You okay?"

"Depends. Are you real or not?" He pulls his hat off, runs his fingers through his hair, then shoves the hat back on. I think he's nervous at my sudden arrival to a place he never invited me to. Come to think of it, he might still be mad as fuck. That's a distinct possibility too, unfortunately.

I hold an arm out. "You wanna pinch me and find out?"

Brody squints a little and reaches behind me, pinching my ass. I yelp and smack at him, but it does help break some of the awkward tension. "You want something to drink? I'm sure the guys left coffee for me." He doesn't wait for me to answer, turning and heading through a doorway into what seems to be the kitchen. I follow to find him pouring two cups and take one with a smile of thanks.

"I'm sorry."

I almost spit my coffee out, shocked. "What? Why are you apologizing?"

"I'm not sure, but I obviously did something to piss you off and apologizing seems like a safe bet. Rule one-oh-three in the guidebook." Distance. He's putting so much between us again with sarcasm and asshole-itis.

I sigh and set the coffee on the counter. "I've been practicing this, so I'm just gonna do it in one go. Don't interrupt me, okay?"

He blinks and holds a hand out, giving me the floor, where I pace back and forth while he looks on.

"I overreacted, that's the short of it." He takes a sip of his coffee, not telling me anything with his expression. "You were trying to be supportive, I know that, but it felt like you were telling me what to do. Like everyone else has done. In case you haven't noticed, I have a bit of a hair trigger with that. I quite literally ran away from home and joined the military the last time someone tried to do that."

His lip twitches, almost a smirk, giving me the balls to keep going.

"I didn't run away this time. I went nuclear, slashing and burning everything. Slashing and burning *you*. I think there's a lot I don't know about you." I look around the house we're standing in, feeling like shit for never even questioning where he lived beyond 'the ranch'. We've spent many nights together, but they've all been at my apartment, something that didn't occur to me until it was too late. "But I want to know. I want to share things with you and be here for you to share with. Whenever you're ready. If you're ever willing to do that with me again."

He's quiet for a moment, just watching me coolly, and I feel like I'm awaiting his verdict.

"You asked for casual, but I think we both know we left that behind a while ago." His eyes dare me to disagree or argue, but I stay utterly silent.

My hope cracks under the weight of the moment. This is him letting me down easy, ripping off the Band-Aid slowly. *Hypocrite*, I think, knowing he said it was kinder to Reed in the long run to do it in one yank. Yet, here he is, pulling at my edges one tiny tear at a time. Maybe I don't deserve the kinder, gentler version of Brody. I didn't give him one of me.

"I'm not a fairy tale kind of guy," he says carefully, his eyes not wavering, "not looking for some Disney happily ever after shit. But."

I look up, not even realizing that my eyes had fallen to the floor. "But?"

"You're the first person I think of when I wake up. You're who I want to call at the end of the day to talk about the crazy shit that happens out here. You're this whirlwind of epic power that I want to stand back and watch as you make your own path to wherever you're going." He lets that sink in, for both of us, I think, because when he speaks again, his voice is gruffer, like he's choking the words out. "I want to tell you things and spend time with you—*not casually,* which is hard for me too. But only if you want that." His brow lifts, and I realize he's letting me set ground rules too. Because he sees me as an equal and doesn't want to sway me. It means more than he'll ever know, but all I can do is nod in agreement and smile as hope blooms inside me.

"Okay then. Let's try this again. How about we start here? This is my house." He spreads his arms out wide, his wingspan nearly touching the cabinets on either side of the kitchen. "I grew up here, learned how to make those pancakes you love so much right there at that stove," he says, pointing to a white appliance that's seen better days, "from my Mom. She was amazing, and I miss her every fucking day. Losing her changed everything."

Shadows pass through his eyes, and I know there's more there, and the urge to ask hits me so hard. But I have to let him tell me when he's ready. He will. I have to trust that.

"Can we get out of here? Will you walk with me, let me show you the farm?"

I'm rocked, my heart leaping as I realize the enormity of his question. That he would even consider sharing this with me now is a sign of how forgiving he is, how invested in us he is. I'm equally and simultaneously scared shitless and excited beyond my wildest expectations.

"I would love to see it." It's the plain truth. I want to know what made this man who he is. My armor is thick. Reaching deep into my core and finding softness is a difficult and treacherous dig. For Brody, I think his hard exterior and cocky arrogance are only surface deep. The true core of him is something much softer. No, *stickier*. He's a nurturer, a put-others-firster. But I doubt anyone ever gets that far, only seeing the asshole he portrays so well.

He steps over the dog, who's gone back to sleep by the front door. "That's Murphy, Brutal's dog. 'Bout the only thing he's good for is cleaning up under the kitchen table when Cooper doesn't like his vegetables." He chuckles a little at that, and I remember his telling me about their cornhole tournament championship, which Cooper won, as expected.

I tell the soundly sleeping dog hello as we walk outside. In my mind, I promise him my vegetables too.

"Come on. Goats first. They're always everyone's favorite."

We walk across the yard-slash-driveway area toward a metal barn. Brody pulls the door open and leads me through to a fenced-in pen. I almost immediately have to plant my feet so I'm not knocked down by the herd of animals swarming me. "Hi!" My voice is high-pitched, tight with excitement. "Holy shit! Cowboy, look!"

A black and brown spotted goat is trying to climb my leg, jump into my arms, and otherwise love me unconditionally. Or at least only conditional on petting her. I bend down a little, scratching behind her ears.

"That's Baarbara. She's mostly friendly, most of the time. Well, occasionally—NO! Don't let her get your ponytail! She'll chew the ends right off!"

I shake my head and feel a little tug as Baarbara loses her tasty snack. A twist of my ponytail puts my hair up into a bun at my nape and out of nibbling range. I hope. Brody moves close, fingering the ends of my hair in a move that feels ridiculously intimate. The air charges between us, and for a moment, I'm certain he's going to kiss me.

"These are Shay's goats. She uses their milk to make her soaps," Brody says, cracking the tension and stepping away as another wave of attack-goats approaches. He goes on to tell me how she started small, selling at the farmers market where I met her the first time, and later, expanding into the operation she has now with a website, international shipping, resort orders, and specialty holiday scents. "She did the same thing with her canning and baking stuff. Started out with just smashed pumpkin puree in the fall, but now she has a rotation of items she makes each season. She's always looking for new recipes and her, Brutal, and Bobby figure out what they can plant and when it'll be ready so she can start advertising. She's turned into quite the entrepreneur."

The pride he feels at his sister's success is obvious and vaguely parental. "I haven't tried her soaps, but if they're anything like the jelly or the cake I had, they're amazing. I'll definitely have to stock up at the next farmers market."

Brody nods, humming under his breath. He does this sometimes when he's thinking or figuring out how to say something. Every word out of his mouth is deliberate and intentional, nearly the opposite of my tendency to pop off. I breathe and let him speak when he's ready without jumping in to start the conversation, whatever it is.

He picks up a small baby goat and my ovaries nearly explode. I have no desire for kids, not yet, anyway, but a hungover-vulnerable Brody gently holding a tiny animal, spindly legs dangling over his forearm, is about the cutest-slash-sexiest thing I've ever seen and instantly makes me think of Brody as a father. He'd be an excellent one—by all reports, he raised Shayanne pretty damn well.

Finally, he speaks low and slow, like he's scared I'm going to go nuclear again. "Can I explain?" I nod, still not sure where he's going but readying myself for just about anything. "Shay is why I said you should talk to your dad about racing."

I open my mouth to argue, and he lifts one brow to glare at me from under his hat. Slowly, I shut my mouth for once. It's harder than it should be.

"Thank you." He acknowledges how hard that was for me. "We grew up happy, and Mom and Dad were good together. But when she died, Dad was gutted and never right again. I picked up the slack and took as much of his anger as I could, but he was . . ." He pauses, looking for the word. "Stuck, I guess? After that, Dad would never let Shay grow. He kept her small, though I don't think he meant to. She was just a kid to him, to me, to all of us. She still is sometimes, though these days, she won't let us forget that she's not. But she's just so damn good. I wish Dad had seen her succeed, not for his sake because fuck him, but for hers. For the longest time, she had a soft spot for Dad, and it would've meant the world to her to prove herself to him." He's quiet, scratching behind the goat's ears and seemingly lost in the past.

"That's why I said what I said. I think it would mean something to you to show your dad what an amazing mechanic you are, especially with all the custom shit you're doing. It's your art, and I can see how it's wearing on you to hold back a part of yourself from everyone. That's all I meant, but it's your call. Always." He sets the goat down, dark eyes focused on me, imploring me to understand that his heart was in the right place.

Words fail me, so I strut right up to him and grab a handful of his shirt, pulling him down to me. He comes willingly, our lips crashing together. I apologize again without words, make promises across our shared breath, and taste his good intentions upon his tongue.

When we need to stop for air, and so that we can assume a more natural posture, with me not on my tippy toes and Brody bent and hunched over, I ask him for more even though he's given so much. "Reed said this was Tannen Farm, and that's what the sign said too, but you work for the Bennetts. How does that happen?"

He sighs deeply, and I know this isn't going to be a happy story. My heart is already cracking for him because however it happened, he lost the one thing he told me he wanted. A ranch of his own. "I said Dad didn't take losing Mom well, but it was more than that. I don't think he ever had a happy day without her. That was when I took over around here—the house, the farm, the kids. Well, technically, Shayanne was the only kid, but really, we all were young fuckers who grew up fast. And I was doing it, handling it all until Dad died too. He owed money to some unforgiving people and we had to sell the farm to pay them off. We didn't have many, or any, options, and the Bennetts saved us by buying the farm and promising us a chance to buy it back if they ever sell. We basically do what we always did, but Mark gets all the profits and credit." A smile as he says that part lets me know that while it's not his dream, he's mostly good with how things are.

That's important to me. Not whether he owns his own ranch or has a five, ten, and fifteen-year plan. I do, but not everyone thinks the way I do. And that's okay.

Besides, my plan is sort of weird. Like don't get arrested—again—and don't tell Dad about racing and building racecars. Not exactly mature, exacting, progressive-thinking standards. And maybe not the best plan anyway, if I listen to Brody.

So maybe his version of being grateful for where you are at the moment is something I can learn from.

"I'm sorry. If I could fix it for you, I would." I've never meant it more. I would do just about anything for Brody to get this back, and one of the things I do best is fix things. But this isn't something I can fix with a torque wrench. Mechanics don't have magic wands in our toolkits, and I don't have a way to just wave my hand and make Brody happier.

Brody shrugs as though he's already made his peace with the

shitty situation. "I lived a lifetime of stress in under a decade. It's nice to not worry for a bit, like a working vacation. I do what I know, what I love, without worrying if the bank is gonna foreclose or whether we'll have enough money to keep the heat on through the winter. I want the responsibility back, and yes, I'm going to work my ass off to get it." He looks at me from beneath the brim of his cap, reminding me of the painful words I threw at him. "And when I do have it all back, it'll be because I earned it . . . each and every inch of dirt."

"Would it make you mad if I said your dad sucks? I mean, I know I've got some pretty significant Daddy issues happening over here, but . . ." I'm teasing, a little. But hearing Brody talk about his dad's relationship with Shay and Brody's struggles to be an adult at a time when he should've still had a soft place to land makes me sad for him.

Brody huffs a laugh, a small smile cracking. "Nah, he was all right, just broken. I don't forgive him for everything, but I'm not casting stones too much anymore. Just on occasion, when it feels warranted." He takes a deep breath, seeming more settled than a moment ago.

"Will you show me some more?" I'll take whatever he wants to show me—his heart, his body, his soul, his farm. Though I suspect those last two are one and the same.

"Come on, Lil Bit." He guides me back into the barn, leaving the ovary-popping adorableness of the goats behind, and to a golf cart on steroids. "Get in," he says, climbing into the driver's seat and turning the machine on. It's more of a diesel *putt-putt-putt* than the growling engines I'm used to.

He looks over at me, and a fizzy sensation washes through me. This is something I only feel when I'm the one sitting behind the wheel of a car on the line, with the light about to change.

I feel like I'm right where I should be. Like I'm on the edge of possibility, a moment where anything can happen from one blink to the next.

And then it does.

Brody takes his dirty, ever-present, camo-cow hat off his head and places it on mine backward. His thumb runs over my cheek, and this feels like a huge gift for a country boy like Brody.

"You look good in my hat, Erica."

He slowly leans over and places a sweet, soft kiss to my lips. This is the first time we've kissed this particular kiss. Not sexy, not as a stepping stone to more, not even as a greeting, but just because we like each other and can't stand to not tell the other person how much that means. His lips press against mine, and I breathe in his scent—sunshine, dirt, sweat, a little alcohol . . . and *mine*.

He's right. Casual left a long time ago, and I'm glad to finally acknowledge that because I want more of these kisses, more days with Brody where I can tease that hard-to-get full smile to his lips, more nights making him lose his words, and more of a life making him trust me to have his back. Always, no matter what. I want him to know that I'm here for him and trust him to be there for me, because I choose him.

Shit. Fuck. Damn.

I do. I choose him. For the first time, I'm choosing something for me, not as an escape from something else like I did with the military, not like racing for my dad, even if I can't tell him that now. But Brody? I'm choosing him . . . for myself, which makes us feel that much more important.

He leans back, and I feel the loss of his closeness until I see the shine in his dark eyes. He might be in his seat a few inches away, but he's with me in this all the way.

"You ready for this, Lil Bit?" he asks, that cocky arrogant smile turning his lips up. He's not talking about a farm tour.

"Might be the other way around, Cowboy. I can handle damn near anything, so what you should be asking is if you're ready for me." I can do cocky too.

"Fucking badass ball-buster. Let's go." He doesn't give me a chance to respond, putting the vehicle in gear and pulling out of the barn. As soon as we're clear, he gives the pedal a good push and shows me what he can do. He might not be a racer, but he's a wild and reckless cowboy through and through, speeding across the grass as I hang on for dear life. This isn't smooth and sleek engineering careening straight down a track. We're bouncing and rambling over hills and ruts, my ass only meeting the seat every few seconds and my hands bracing on the oh-shit handle and the dash. I'm not embarrassed to say I scream out like a damn girly girl a few times. Okay, I take that back . . . I am embarrassed, but only because Brody is sitting in his seat like a damn steady rock, leaning into every donut like he's done this a thousand times and laughing his fool head off.

"I'm gonna get you back for this," I threaten, knowing that I'm gonna push the limits if I ever get him to ride bitch in Foxy when I race. We'll see if he likes that. On second thought, he probably would.

The camo-cow hat flies off my head when he does a quick turn, and I yell out. He glances at me and lifts a sardonic brow before turning around. He doesn't stop, only slows to a crawl as I lean out to pick up the hat from the dirt. I feel a pinch to my ass and jump, only to hear him laugh. Still on a mission, I grab the hat, bonus dirt and all, but this time, I pull it on facing forward with my hair through the hole at the back, hoping that'll help it stay secure.

Brody nods his approval, and at a more reasonable pace, he drives me out to see the farming operation—the 'home garden' that grows for Tannen and Bennett usage and the 'business plots' that are reserved for Shay's products and the crops they sell at the farmer's market. After explaining the differences, he shows me the cattle, who come ambling toward the Gator as we approach.

"They think it's feeding time," he explains. "Which it's not," he tells the cows, though they probably can't hear him from here. Actually, I don't know . . . do cows have super hearing?

We get out and walk over to the barbed wire fence, which seems like nothing to get through if they decided to mosey on wherever they want. "Can I touch them?"

"Yeah," he says over the animals who are mooing in anticipation of his paying them a little loving attention. *I feel ya, ladies . . . he'd get a moo from me too. Except that's weird, so maybe not a moo, exactly?*

I can see why he loves this life—a bit of wild, a heap of responsibility, some peace and quiet, and a family that feels the same way about the dirt that you do. I've learned more about Brody today than in all our weeks before. Or maybe now, in addition to knowing what makes him laugh and where his favorite place for me to nibble is, I also know his heart and soul. I think he's known mine all along, but I'm finally catching up. And yeah, I get the irony that the race car driver is the last one to get anywhere, but I'm here now and that's what matters.

He shows me how to approach them carefully and scratch behind their ears, and after a few minutes of easy, comfortable silence, it feels like we've been reset. Not like I didn't fuck everything up, but maybe that because I did, things are actually better than before.

"Can I show you one more thing?" Brody asks, his voice deep and rough and his fingers playing with the end of my ponytail.

"Anything," I answer. The scariest part of all is that I absolutely mean it.

# CHAPTER 21

## BRODY

"Third door on the right," I tell the fabulous view as Erica goes up the stairs. That my mind is distracted is a testament to how important today has been because her ass is begging for my tongue and her thighs are pleading for my fingertips.

She whispers, "Why does it feel like I'm not supposed to be here? Like we're doing something wrong?" She sounds more than a little intrigued at the idea, which doesn't surprise me about her in the least.

"Because you're going into my childhood bedroom to fuck. Luckily for you, I just took down my WWE posters last week." She glances back, brows raised in question. I smack her ass in pseudo-punishment. "Kidding. I seem like a fake wrestling sort to you?"

She smirks. "Abso-fucking-lutely, you do, Cowboy." She drawls out the 'cowboy' in a fake accent that'd make John Wayne cringe.

I asked for that one, so I go ahead and give her the grin she earned and the grunt she's expecting.

She opens the door, and I watch her, knowing exactly what she's seeing. A full-sized bed in the corner, unmade, of course, because I don't see the point when I'm getting back in it tonight, a nightstand with the latest John Grisham book laid open to save my place, a basket of clean clothes sitting right next to a pile of dirty ones, and a chest of drawers where all the clean clothes should be.

"Very bachelor pad-ish," she says. I can tell the unmade bed is driving her nuts. She basically makes hers the second she gets out of it, a military habit holdover, she's told me. Suddenly, she gasps. "You are a fucking monster!" She picks up the book from my nightstand, waving it around in offense. "Use a bookmark, for fuck's sake!"

I shrug, not caring in the slightest. "It's my book. I'll crease the spine if I want to."

She looks horrified, so I make a show of grabbing a condom packet out of the top drawer, placing it inside the book, and closing it with a sarcastically affectionate pat. I set it back on the nightstand, hugely implying 'you happy?' She smirks and wanders over to the chest of drawers, looking at a picture of my family, all six of us.

"I think I was around fifteen then, in high school for sure. Brutal must've been around thirteen, because that was one of the last times I was taller than him. He shot up that summer, passed us all, even Dad."

"You look happy. You all look happy." She touches the easy smile on my teenage face in the picture. There are flashes of this boy inside me still, but the man is more hardened and cynical from what I've gone through between that camera flash and now.

"We were. We are. It was just the in-between that was hard, but we're all good now. Truly. And one day, we'll be even better. I didn't show you today, but over the hill to the west, Brutal is building a house for him and Allyson and Cooper. And Bobby lets us all come listen to him perform at Hank's now, something he never did before. He's gonna be on the radio one day, I just know it. And Shay is happy with someone who wants her to live the life that she wants and deserves."

"You said everyone but you. What about Brody Tannen? Is he happy?" she asks softly, setting the picture back down and turning to face me fully.

"Yeah, Erica. I am happy. And I'm gonna carpe the shit out of this diem like it's all we get." I pick her up, and her legs go around my waist naturally.

I mean that. I still think relationships are a ticking time bomb, waiting to destroy you when they inevitably end, but I get why everyone risks it now. Why, even if you know it'll gut you eventually, it's worth it to be with the one person who can make every minute mean something. Without them, there's no risk, but it's merely an existence, not life.

If I can have one happy day with Erica, I'll handle any days of pain later. I put off any worries and just focus on the now, a gift I've rarely gotten to truly appreciate.

I sit down on my bed, her tiny ass in my lap and her sweet pussy against my thickening cock. "I've never had a woman in here before."

She looks at me skeptically. "I don't believe that for one second. Teenage Brody Tannen was a bad boy who snuck girls into his room every chance he got, I'd bet money on it."

I laugh. "You'd lose then. I live in the middle of nowhere. Ain't nobody coming out here." The important jump that she came out here to track me down whispers in the air between us, and her smile falls as something deeper takes root.

She runs her fingers through my hair, which is getting a little long, but it feels good when she scratches my scalp and tugs on the strands to get my attention so I've let it go longer than usual. "You're worth chasing, Brody. Worth caring for. Worth sharing with. Worth living every day to the fullest with."

I swear I hear more, hear things with my heart that her lips aren't saying because I feel them too. We might both be hesitant to speak the words out loud, but today has changed everything.

Something breaks inside me, something I didn't even know existed. Or maybe it's not breaking—it's healing? Scabbing and scarring over, stronger and better than before. I rise up, throwing her on the bed. "I need you."

It's not so much that I need to fuck her but that I need to be inside her the way she's inside me. She's in my skin, in my blood, in my . . . heart. And I don't know what to do with that other than fuck my way into hers too and hope she understands me.

She's already scrambling, pulling her shirt over her head as I undo her shorts and pull them down her legs. Her hands yank at my shirt, and I duck out of it, then both of us are shoving my jeans down. I reach for the book, grabbing the condom out of its pages, not caring at all that I lost my place because I've found one . . . with Erica.

Sheathed, I lean over her, one hand on either side of her head, and slam into her. She instantly spasms below me. "Too much?" I growl, praying she says no.

Her short nails claw at my arms. "More. More. Fuck." Her eyes pop open, and I can see the pleasure there, the hungry need, and also the absolute pure connection we've forged, no matter how hard both of us were fighting it.

It's there. It's deep, wide, and powerful. It's everything I never knew existed. Other people aren't crazy for feeling like this. I'm just a dumbass who thought they were exaggerating. Now I know they weren't.

Whatever rollercoaster this woman has me on has already taken me to the highest highs and the lowest lows, but right here, this moment feels like pulling into the safety of home.

Her calves lock around my hips, and she pulls my chest to hers. I don't want to suffocate her and hold some of my weight back, but she twines in and over me like a vine, taking it all. Her hands lock onto my back, and I freeze to make sure she's okay. But she's got other plans.

She uses the bounce of the bed to fuck me from below with shallow thrusts, keeping me inside her slick cunt as she works me. "Fuck, Erica. Keep doing that. You're gonna make me come. That what you want?"

My face is buried in her hair, surrounded by the scent of her, a combination of oil, hand cleaner, and her shampoo. I rumble words of encouragement in her ear. "You are amazing . . . feels so good . . ." I don't even know what I say after that because I'm one big ball of sensation and pleasure and my brain can't form words, only grunting sounds.

I hover right on the edge as long as I can, and then when I can't take it anymore, I jerk back from her. She cries out at the loss of my cock, but I grab her legs and fold her in half, putting her pretty pussy on display for me. I turn slightly so that I can support her legs with one hand and use the other to finger fuck her. At the same time, I tease her clit with my tongue, and she thrashes, both trying to get more and trying to get away from the onslaught.

"Oh, my God, *yes*," she hisses. She flies apart beneath me. I feel her pussy start to clamp down as she gushes for me, and I rise up, quickly thrusting back inside her with her calves resting on my shoulders.

I find a punishing rhythm, fast and hard, giving zero fucks to the racket we're making with the headboard banging against the wall and both of us damn near grunting like animals. Through it all, we never lose eye contact.

We're fucking, make no mistake that this is a rough, aggressive, nearly violent taking of each other's body, but there's more beneath the surface of the pleasure. Her eyes are deep and full of a future I let myself dream of, and I tell her with my own that I accept her, just as she is.

We find our climax together, her second pulling mine from my body as my spine jolts, my balls tense up, and my cock swells. The condom is between us physically, but there's nothing between us emotionally as I hold her tight, coming down from the haze with panting breaths.

I lower her legs, turning us slightly so that my weight is on the bed, but stay inside her a little longer. Pushing her hair back from her face, I trace over the freckles on her cheek with a fingertip. "You are so fucking gorgeous, Erica. Outside" —I sweep the swoop of her nose— "and inside." I press my lips to hers, willing her to taste the depth of what I'm feeling but unable to say it.

Her mouth opens to speak back, but a door closing downstairs makes both of us freeze in place.

"Who was that?" she whispers.

I look at her, telling her silently that's a dumbass question because how would I know? I've been in here with her.

A moment later, my phone buzzes in my pants on the floor. I hate to do it, but I pull out of Erica, tossing the condom in the trash. I dig my phone out and see that I've got a text.

*Mark: Sorry. Mama says she'll set Erica a place for dinner.*

My eyebrows must rise or I must grit my teeth. Something must give me away because Erica asks, "What's it say? What's wrong?"

I scratch at my lip, downplaying the awkwardness. "No big deal. Mama Louise says you're expected at dinner."

Erica blinks once, twice, three times before she sits bolt upright. "Are you serious? Mama Louise heard us fucking like rabbits and is all 'golly gee, perhaps they'd like some dinner'?" She falls back to the bed, arms spread wide like an angel with a halo of messy, dark hair splayed out beneath her.

"Not exactly. The text is from Mark, so it seems like it was both of them."

Her hands go over her face, but I hear the mumbled reply. "Of course it was." A slow beat later, she clarifies, "Only the two of them?"

I shrug even though she's not looking at me. When she peeks one eye open, I smirk. "Silver lining? Mark knows I'm not working today. This morning, because I was hungover. Now, because you're here."

I approach the bed with every filthy idea I've ever had about having a woman in my bed written all over my face. Erica's embarrassment morphs before my very eyes, her blush turning into a flush and her hands falling to the bed as her legs writhe. "Well, if they already know, guess there's no harm in hiding out a little longer."

"Woman after my own heart." I quote the expression without thinking, but the truth of it is, she's already got it.

She stalls my prowling with a single finger held up. "Go lock the damn door or I'll be nervous the whole time."

I huff like I'm annoyed by her request, but it's a good idea.

None of us are in the habit of having guests over so there's no real family protocol for that. Not that I want to think about it, but I wonder how in the hell I've never noticed Brutal and Allyson fucking. They live in this house with me, Bobby, and Cooper, yet I've never heard a peep. I should probably pick his brain for some tricks on *Mission: Impossible, Quiet Sex Edition.*

"Fine. You stay there, though. Hand, hand, foot, foot." I point at each corner of my bed, knowing she can't reach the bed edges, teasing her to spread eagle while I'm gone.

Naked as the day I was born, I make a run for the front door and then the back door, locking them both. Hustling back up the stairs, I take them two at a time, honestly curious whether Erica will be laid out the way I said to. Hell, knowing her, she'll be sitting cross-legged in the middle of the bed just to be ornery and noncompliant and keep me guessing.

*She really hates being told what to do*, I think with a smile. *I love that about her.*

As I open the door, the breath I didn't know I was holding escapes in a hushed, "*Fuck.*" She's laid out just like I told her to, but never one to follow orders—how was this woman ever in the military?—she's face down with that tiny ass in the air.

She smirks, her cheek against my sheet as she wiggles her hips, knowing exactly what she's doing to me. "Like this, Cowboy?"

"Yep, Lil Bit. Just like that." Hell, I'm not gonna argue when her plan for round two is better than mine.

---

"So lovely to see you again, Rix," Mama Louise says as we pile ham steaks, bourbon glazed carrots, and fried okra onto our plates.

It's probably just my hearing, but I swear there's a tease in there. A slight emphasis on the 'see you'?

I should've known better. Big-mouthed men, clucking women,

and hot gossip are the worst combination for polite dinner conversation.

Erica chokes a little on the swallow of her tea. "Uhm, yeah . . . good to see you too." She looks to me, eyes asking 'what the fuck?' loud and clear.

Shayanne is next. "I *heard* you've been *real* busy lately." After a dramatic pause, she finishes, "At the shop."

Erica blinks. I blink. I take Erica's hand beneath the table for moral support. Hers? Mine? I'm not entirely sure.

"Guess you're feeling better after staying in bed all day," Brutal grunts my way. He's probably the one who made the coffee for me this morning and left the aspirin on the coffee table for me when I passed out drunk last night.

I look around the table, every pair of eyes looking from me to Erica with giddy humor. I'm glad Allyson and Cooper are in town tonight at a school thing because I wouldn't want to scar the kid with what I'm about to do. I'm not a shy, oh-no-don't-make-fun sort. So I do what I always do. Go hard.

"Elephant in the room. Erica and I had sex. Enjoyed it. Mark and Mama Louise heard us today. It's basic human functionality. We good here? Any questions?"

Ah, shit. I was doing so well. They all looked slightly chastised by my facing their teasing head-on, but now Shayanne raises her hand with a shit-eating grin. "Oh, I've got a question or twenty."

I hang my head, talking out the side of my mouth to Erica. "I am so sorry."

Somehow, the already disastrous situation devolves even further, though I'm not sure how.

"Don't act like you didn't give me hell when Shay and I started dating," Luke throws out.

"Language," Mama Louise says quickly.

James jumps in. "You still give Sophie and me a hard time!"

Mark growls, "Because you two are so loud the neighbors threatened to call the cops."

Sophie points at me. "Brody was the neighbor, so guess the

table's turned there, huh?" She shovels a tiny bite of pureed, non-bourbon-glazed carrot into Cindy Lou's mouth, who is completely oblivious to the rantings of the adults around the table. Thank goodness the only words she knows are *mama*, *dada*, and *baba*. The last one is what she calls Bacon Seed.

My turn again. "And we all know what you and Katelyn get up to, so don't even start with me," I tell Mark.

"You don't know anything, and don't you forget it." Cold ice has entered his voice and it becomes an actual threat.

"That doesn't even make sense," I snap back. "I can't forget what I don't know."

"Exactly," Mark says. I love the guy like a brother, and yeah, we're more alike than different, but fuck, he's weird sometimes. And that's saying something coming from me.

"You know what I hear?" Mama Louise interrupts us all, and we turn our attention to her dutifully. "That my kids, all my kids, have grown up to be loving people who show their love with their chosen partners in a beautiful, pleasurable way."

"*Blech* . . . Mama is talking about s-e-x. All stop. Abort conversation. Over." Luke acts like he's talking into a CB radio.

We all cringe a little. It's one thing to give each other shit. It's quite another to think of Mama Louise and sex in the same conversation, much less sentence.

"Hush up, Son. Your father and I had a *very loving* relationship. Not like we only did it three times with the lights out to get you boys. Why, this one time . . ." She trails off, smiling an evil grin. She knows exactly what she's doing, that she's killing a little thread of innocent denial in her boys' hearts and diverting the conversation. Luckily, in this moment, she's not my actual mother, so I don't have to be too weirded out by her proclamation.

We're quietly thanking the good Lord that we didn't have to hear about Mama Louise and John's nonprocreative activities.

Erica squeezes my hand. "Uh, Shayanne. Before we go sidetracked." That's putting it mildly. "Did you have an actual question?" Erica's like me, a face-shit-head-on-er, and I don't feel so alone.

No, that's not it. I don't feel . . . protective. I always protect everyone, from Dad, from the stress of the farm, from themselves. But Erica doesn't need my protection. She's willing to let me step in front sometimes, willing to step in front herself, and mostly, willing to stand by my side against the storm of my family. And she doesn't need my protection to do it. She's strong in her own right. Tiny, fierce, badass, mouthy Lil Bit.

If she's going into this, I'm going with her.

Shay looks from me to Erica, but her question is all mine. "Another one bites the dust?"

She's bragging about being right. I grunt, knowing she'll take it as an affirmative.

Bobby intones solemnly, "And then there was one."

# CHAPTER 22

## ERICA

"It's weird that we've never been on a date." My proclamation probably would've served me better in my head, but of course, I said it out loud.

Brody is lounging on the couch, watching me get dressed. It's warming and sexy to know that's all he's doing—not watching television while he waits, not playing on his phone, not trying to hurry me up. He's just watching as I pull on panties, brush out my hair, slick on a tinted lip balm—my only makeup—and hold up T-shirt after T-shirt in the mirror.

In the mirror's reflection, I see one of Brody's dark eyebrows raise. "Two Roses. Hank's. The races, twice. Your place dozens of times. My place a few times."

His list is pretty succinct and accurate. But tonight feels different. It's the first time we're going out after the fight. And more importantly, after we made up and faced some hard facts.

Like I am so fucking over the moon for this man that I don't even care if that makes me sound like lovestruck Emily because it's the damn truth.

After that awkward dinner, I'd spent the night at Brody's, a first apparently that had required rules about bathroom usage and knocking on doors. Allyson had assured me that they were mostly kidding and teasing Brody.

Still, though we've stayed at the farm house a few times like Brody said, we mostly choose my place, with its privacy and a bathroom we don't have to share.

"The black one," he suggests.

I hold the black shirt up, turning around to face him. "Why?" I'm honestly curious because I was about to put on the red shirt I bought while shopping with Emily. She'd said it looked 'more approachable,' which is mostly code for 'not bitchy like usual.'

"The lacing at the shoulders makes me think of unwrapping you like a present and it makes your tits look good."

Sweet and sexy. This man is my damn undoing, making me want things I don't have time for but am making time to do with him. Like go on a double date with my sister and her doctor guy.

"You don't need to undo the laces. You could just pull the shirt over my head. Or . . . we could just stay here and not even put it on." I throw the shirt to the bed, standing in front of him in just my bikini panties, my nipples already hardening.

"Tempting." His hat comes off, curls in his hands, and goes back on his head, letting me know he's thinking about that plan of action really hard. "You and the laces. It's the tease of it." His voice has gone dark and deep, hitting every button I've got and he damn well knows it. He smirks. "Clothes. Date. Then we'll fuck later."

He's good. The ordering me around, grunting like he's telling me what to do is a surefire way to get shut down even now, but promising me exactly what I want? He's playing dirty, and he's good at it.

---

"HOW DID YOU TWO MEET?" DOCTOR DAN ASKS BRODY. DAN IS A tall, slim blonde and blue-eyed dreamboat, and I can absolutely understand what Emily sees in him. He seems friendly and kind, easily a Prince Charming type from Emily's romanticized fantasies come to life.

"Funny story. She almost killed me with a wrench. I knew she was it for me right then." Brody looks at me, his face perfectly impassive and not giving anything away.

Dan chokes on his whiskey and water at Brody's dry delivery of the truth, sputtering. "You're kidding, right?"

Emily places her hand on Dan's arm. "Unfortunately, no. I told you my sister is a bit . . . interesting." She winks at me, the smile letting me know she means it as a compliment.

"How about you?" Brody redirects.

"She sold me a truck and gave me her card. I took the chance that it wasn't purely for warranty issues and was right, fortunately." He chuckles like that's funny, and Emily laughs along too. Brody and I look at each other, finding exactly zero humor in his lame joke. But I smile anyway because Brody looks hot tonight.

He's got on black jeans, ones I know he's never worked in because they're completely free of any stains or rips and fit like a second skin over his ass, loosening up over his muscled thighs. His button-down shirt is black and so are his boots. He's like a dark knight, with a gunmetal belt buckle, a camo-cow hat, and a thick leather strap bracelet.

That bracelet had been a surprise tonight. I've never seen Brody wear a single bit of jewelry, and I would've said he'd find it as unnecessary and useless as I usually do. But for some reason, all I've been able to think about are his fingers on and in my pussy with that leather bracelet on . . . and nothing else.

He licks his lips, likely knowing exactly what I'm thinking, and takes a sip of his beer.

The waitress comes by to take our orders, doing the double-take that Emily and I are used to. Luckily, this time, there's no stupid twin-ology question. *Can you read each other's minds? Do you get confused over who you are? If one of you is hurt, does the other feel it? Do you ever switch places?*

We've heard them all, but our waitress seems much more taken with Dan and Brody than Emily and me having matching faces, and the guys are who she's staring at.

"Chicken sandwich, plain and dry, sweet potato fries," Brody says, pointing at me, then he continues with, "cheeseburger, medium rare, A1 sauce on the side, and onion rings." He glances at me, giving me an opportunity to make any corrections, but he got it perfect. The best part is that I know he ordered that way so we can split everything, having the best of both worlds on every front because that's what we always do.

We have a 'usual order', and the idea of that makes my heart jump into my throat. In a good way. It means history, of the evening where I could not make up my mind so Brody came up with the amazing idea to share everything, and it means understanding that we are an 'us.'

And also . . . we might need to add some veggies to our diet. Maybe a salad night? I laugh a little at the image of Brody digging into a big dinner of salad. His dark eyes search me questioningly.

"Salad," I say, with no context or frame of reference at all.

"Pass," he answers as if we're having a normal conversation. "That's what we feed the hamburgers."

Emily is watching the Erica and Brody show with rapt attention, like we're fascinating creatures to study. I glare at her, ordering her not to make a big deal of nothing. Except I know that double negatives aside, it's *not* nothing.

It's something . . . when Brody casually lays his hand over the back of my chair and I snuggle into his side.

It's something . . . when he tells me his Tree House stout is delicious and I take a sip from his glass, agreeing that it's pretty good, but not as good as the lager he brought over last week.

It's something . . . when my hand naturally lands in his lap, cupping his thigh and tracing small lines along the denim but imagining it's his bare skin beneath my palm.

It's something . . . when he talks about his animals, and I remind him to be nice to Baarbara because she's my favorite badass goat. And that's something I never thought I'd have.

It's something . . . when Brody kindly proclaims me to be an artist with engines again, like he's decided that's the best way to describe my dirty, work-with-my-hands-all-day job.

"Emily tells me that you do a little more than run a repair shop. Is that right?" Dan asks politely.

I scowl at Emily, but she shrugs like sharing my secret is no big deal.

It is.

Brody knows. Emily knows. And fine, all the guys at the track know. But the more people who know, the higher the risk becomes of Dad finding out. I do the mental calculations of how likely Dad and Dan are to run into each other. Dan already said he spends most of his days, nights, and weekends at the hospital, though I suspect what free time he does have is spent with Emily. Dad avoids doctors as if they're death peddlers, so unless he happens to pop into Emily's at the same time as Dan, statistically, their crossover rate is pretty low.

"I don't advertise it." It should sound playful and coy, but it sounds like a threat, which is honestly more my intention. "In fact, don't tell many people at all . . . but I do custom car work on the side for a select group of car enthusiasts. Under the hood stuff, mostly, though I can outsource. I work on classics, newer models, nitrous add-ons, and specialize in getting the most horsepower out of every single engine."

"Racecars?" Dan asks as a follow-up.

"Yes."

I blink, realizing how good it feels to say all that out loud, to claim it semi-publicly. I'm not looking to shout it from rooftops or anything, but even the small step of speaking it to an outsider is powerful. Brody squeezes my shoulder, and I glance over to find him looking at me proudly. He knows what a big step this is for me too. His joy feels warm, like honey smoothing over the fizzy nerves and excitement of my own pride.

"Cool," Dan says, not understanding the foundational shift that just occurred.

The waitress brings our dinners, which look and smell delicious. The burgers and chicken are fresh off the grill, steam still rising from them. Emily's salad, because of course she eats vegetables, looks bright and lush. Brody cuts our sandwiches, re-plating them so that we each have a burger half and a chicken half. I grab an onion ring from his plate to munch while he does the work.

And dinner is relaxed and comfortable, chatting about this and that.

Emily tells the story of how we switched places for a test one time in middle school, which would've gone well except while I was covering her math test, she had to do a surprise pop quiz in my history class. She got an A and I got a D, which warranted further questions and staredowns from Mom and Dad until we confessed. In the end, we both got Fs for cheating. I've heard the story dozens of times, told it myself half of those, and still, I smile at Emily, remembering those days when everything was so easy. I find myself missing that straight-forward effortlessness of youth that we all lose as we grow up.

Emily pulls her napkin from her lap, laying it beside her bowl of rabbit food. "Excuse me for a moment." She stands, and both guys lift out of their seats like gentlemen. I shove another fry into my mouth. "Ahem." Emily clears her throat, and I look up from my internal debate of fry versus onion ring. Emily tilts her head toward the bathroom, the universal sign of 'come with me.'

I know the female code of always going to the bathroom in packs. Hell, of going everywhere in packs for safety. But in the middle of dinner, in the middle of the restaurant, when there are onion rings to be had? Because I've decided they're the better option of the two, for tonight, at least.

She blinks slowly at my lack of hop-to-it-ness. "Rix."

"Excuse me, apparently," I tell Dan and Brody. Okay, and maybe the onion rings too.

Emily locks our arms at the elbows, already gushing as we walk into the bathroom. "Oh, my gosh, Rix . . . I love him! And so do you! I never thought you'd beat me down the aisle, but there are like bluebirds of fucking happiness singing all around you two." She's dancing around the bathroom, nearly banging her swinging hands into the paper towel dispenser as her fingers flit around like . . . birds, I think they're supposed to be?

"Uh, slow that roll. We're dating, not getting married."

Hands on my shoulders, her nose is suddenly inches from mine. "*Yet*. Mark my words . . . he's *The One* for you."

I blink, the argument on the tip of my tongue, but I can't voice it. I won't lie to her again. I place my hands on her shoulders, copying her pose and intertwining our arms in a knot. "Don't freak out. I need you to stay calm, okay?"

She nods, biting her lip with bright eyes.

"He might be *The One* . . ."

Her squeal is loud for a split second before her hands slap over her mouth, her eyes going so wide I can see the whites.

"For later," I finish. "I'm not ready for that, still have the shop and the custom work, and he's got his family and the animals. We've got *stuff*, Em. And literally just admitted to giving a shit about more than bumpin' uglies a week ago. Slow down."

Her light dims, but I can see that spark of romantic hope still burning inside her. "But one day?"

"Maybe." It's all I can give. All I know for sure is that when I wake up, I reach for him. When something good or bad or funny happens at the shop, he's the person I want to tell. When the workday is over, I want to collapse into him and be the place for him to fall into too. And when I go to sleep, I want to do it in his arms, preferably with his dick still inside me after we fuck each other stupid.

That's romantic, right? The sum total is, I'm sure of that much, at least.

Emily claps a few times, ridiculously overexcited compared to what I just admitted to. "Okay, let's go back to dinner."

I look around us. "Don't you need to pee?"

She rolls her eyes. "Well, now I do. Why'd you have to ask?

You know I'm *suggestible*." She walks toward one of the stalls, disappearing behind the door.

"You brought me to the bathroom. What else would I think you planned to do in here?"

"Gossip, obviously," she huffs.

After washing and drying our hands, we make our way back to the table. Dan and Brody are talking comfortably, but I realize disappointedly that his plate is missing.

They stand as Emily and I sit, and then Brody's arm goes around the back of my chair once again. His inky brow lifts as he points at my plate with his chin.

Two small, crunchy onion rings sit on top of my fries, the almost-overdone ones I love. He saved them for me.

Shit. Fuck. Damn.

This man is everything I never knew I wanted, everything I never knew I needed.

# CHAPTER 23

## BRODY

"Does it make me sound like a pussy if I say I'm gonna miss you?" Even as I admit it, I don't really care about the answer. Okay, maybe a little, so I shove half a drowned-in-hot-sauce taco in my mouth in one go as if that'll prove my manhood.

Erica grins, sucking queso off her index finger. Tacos for our last lunch before I leave for the market auction seems like one of my more brilliant ideas right about now. "Nah, I'm definitely missable." My eyes track her tongue, which has snaked out to lick off any last bits of cheesy goodness. "Besides, pussies are inherently tough as a mother, hence the expression, and designed to take a pounding. You might be balls . . . all sensitive and fragile." Her voice has gone soft and sad as she teases me.

"I'll show you sensitive and fragile," I growl, grabbing at her. She laughs riotously, acting like she's going to move around the breakroom table to dodge my hands, but I know she doesn't move far enough away on purpose. She lets me catch her and pull her into my lap sideways. My cock, which is resting against her hip, decides to take notice and thicken in my work jeans.

A naughty smile plays at the corners of Erica's lips before she leans in, kissing along my neck. "I'd rather you show me a pounding," she murmurs against my skin.

"Fuck, Lil Bit. What are you doing to me?" I groan, not really complaining as she readjusts so that she's straddling me. Unable to rip her coveralls off, my fingers dig into the flesh of her hips as hers pull at the strands of hair at the nape of my neck.

"Anything I want," she moans back between nibbles. She takes my hat off, putting it on her own head backward the way I do when I eat her pussy out.

"You are so fucking beautiful," I tell her, meaning every word. Her hair is in haphazard low braids, like she couldn't be bothered to do more than a couple of twists on each side, and now it's topped with my dirty hat. Her face is bare of makeup, as always, but it's also free of any façade. She's wide open—no walls, no distance, no shutters to keep me at bay from her true self. Her dark eyes are full of heated lust, but also sweetness and hope. And these coveralls are so loose, I could just slip inside to cup her breast. I know she's got a tank top on underneath, but I can make quick work of that.

I grab the braids with one hand, pulling gently as I use my other hand to push her chin up. The exposed length of her neck begs for a mark, and I kiss and suck, testing her. "Can I?"

Her moan of agreement turns my cock to steel against her pussy. She pulls at the collar of her coveralls, sliding her tank top over too. "Not visible. It's unprofessional."

"Fuck professional," I snarl, already licking my way down to where her neck meets her shoulder.

I kiss and nibble and suck, swallowing the taste of her skin. Her hips grind against me, her hands grabbing at my chest for leverage. Her short nails dig into my skin, marking me too, and I know that tonight, when I'm sharing a hotel room with Mark before the biggest day of our ranching year, I'll appreciate the half-moons of her claim.

Suddenly, the door opens. "Hey Rix, Mr. Turner wants—*Shit.*" Reed freezes in the doorway of the breakroom, the horror on his face quickly morphing to fury.

Erica's back goes straight and stiff, her walls erecting from one instant to the next as she climbs out of my lap. Standing tall, she glares at Reed, who's moved on to grinding his teeth, not saying a word.

Erica snaps her fingers, prompting, "Mr. Turner wants . . ."

Reed drags his gaze from mine to Erica's. "You, to talk to you."

She adjusts her coveralls, but not quick enough to hide the bruising mark from Reed's eagle eyes. I see it hit him like a punch to the gut, but Erica's beelining for the door, focused on work. She tosses over her shoulder, "Play nice. Don't get blood on the lunch table."

With that, she's gone, leaving Reed and me alone in the breakroom.

He glares at me, any pretense of politeness evaporating. He'd beat the shit out of me if he could, but we both know he won't. One, because he can't. I'm a big fucker, and even if he wanted to, he can't take me. Two, he won't hurt Erica that way. And that tells me more about him than anything.

He's hurting and that Band-Aid needs to get ripped off like I told Erica ages ago. She's been doing it, but not fast enough, not with enough yank. For all her blustering, she's kind at heart. I am too, but I have no softness for Reed. Not when softness is cruelty.

"Guess I'll have to play nice and not fuck you up for hurting her like that." He's spouting off about the hickey, knowing full well that it didn't hurt her. But it hurt him. The too-fast rise and fall of his chest and the pain deep in his eyes tell me that much.

I lace my fingers together, putting them behind my head with my elbows and legs spread. It's a show of force, that I'm totally at ease in what should be his environment, with him throwing threats.

"She was telling *me* to play nice. You" —I lift my chin his way — "are actually nice. Me, not so much." I smirk and tilt my head, knowing the cocky arrogance will irritate him.

"Asshole," he snarls.

"Meant it as a compliment." Truthfully, it is. Reed is a good guy.

He's just a mouse caught in a wheel, and he doesn't know how to get out. I'm gonna show him, though.

Band-Aid removal in three, two, one . . .

"I get it, Reed. You've had a vision your whole life. Whether it was yours or someone else's doesn't even matter anymore because it plays in your head like a favorite movie. Problem is? She ain't watching the same one. She cares about you, she loves you, but not like you want. If it wasn't me, it'd be someone else. But it's not you, won't ever be. You need to move on from her."

He flinches, probably because she's told me so much and also because it's all true, and though he won't admit it, not even to himself, he knows it. "Fuck you. You think you're special? Nah, you ain't nothing. And when she needs a shoulder to cry on, a hand to hold, I'm who she comes to."

Time to hit the jugular. "Maybe so, because that's what *friends* do for each other. But what about when she wants dick? It ain't yours she's going for, hasn't been in a long time." What Erica and I have is a lot more than dick, but it's what he needs to hear to get it through that thick skull of his.

His hands curl into fists, but he holds his ground, booted feet rooted to the floor. I stand slowly, making no sudden movements, cross my arms over my chest, and look him in the eye.

"She loves you, but not like that. I swear to fuck, I'm not being an asshole here. I really am trying to play nice. Because you're important to her, but so am I." The weight of that is heavy, but it's a responsibility I welcome. A reminder that I can handle so much more than what I've been shouldering recently. That I'm good at it, even if seems like I'm stumbling around aimlessly.

"What the fuck ever, man. Just don't fucking hurt her or I will fucking kill you." He points a finger at me threateningly. He might be tied with Erica and me on the record number of curse words in one sentence.

"Let's be honest. I'm not going to hurt her. When and if this ever implodes, it'll be me left broken and hurting." The similarity to how Reed feels right now is painfully obvious to us both. "Luckily,

I've got brothers with the balls to tell me to tape my shit together, build a bridge, and get over it."

It's silent for a long second, the tension thick, and I realize that I might have to actually fight this fucker. It'll break my longest streak of not punching someone since elementary school. Not that I take particular pride in the number of fights I've been in. It's nice not having swollen, bruised knuckles, but if that's what it takes, I've never backed down. And I won't start today.

Reed kicks out, shoving a chair my way. It screeches along the floor but I don't react. My arms stay crossed. My feet stay still. But the growl in my throat won't be stopped.

Luckily, Reed spins and stomps back out the door to the garage. I shake my head as I watch him go, sadly wishing that he would listen. But he can't hear the truth yet. He's not ready to give up and chase a new dream. I get that, having been forced into that situation myself, but it really is for his own good. He deserves to be happy . . . with someone other than Erica.

Alone, I clean up our lunch mess and throw the leftover tacos in the refrigerator for Manuel and Reed. He might be mad, but no one turns down free food. Especially not tacos this delicious.

Once I get it all picked up, the door opens again. "Seems that went well." Erica's sarcasm is sharp, her lack of surprise dry.

I shrug. "No bloodshed. Winning."

She shakes her head, a smile playing on her lips. "Fuck, I'm gonna miss you."

I sweep her up in my arms, our bodies pressed together with her on her steel-toed tippy toes. "I'm gonna miss you too. Two days, Lil Bit."

Two. Whole. Fucking. Days. Without her.

I don't know how it happened, but I don't know if I can handle being apart from her. And yeah, I'm well aware that makes me as sensitive and fragile as . . . fucking balls. Whatever.

The goodbye kiss is almost worth it, though, with her trying to climb into my skin with me and our tongues tangling together. I swear I can taste her soul, sour and sweet and prickly and kind, all at the same time.

I hope that I'm wrong, that my fears are just ghosts. I'd be broken if Erica's ever done with me. If that ever happens, I might make Dad's decline after Mom seem like a positive coping mechanism because I would destroy the world for her. And like Reed, some fucker telling me to move on would be like pissing into the wind. Ill-advised and messy as fuck.

"I'll be back as soon as I can," I promise her. But really, I'm promising myself.

# CHAPTER 24

## ERICA

"Let's get to racing, boys!" Ed calls out. He dropped the 'and Rix' years ago because I'm simply one of the guys.

There's a rousing round of hollering, which Ed allows for long enough to flip to the correct page on his clipboard. "Up first, we've got Jerry versus Wilson. Good matchup . . . Chevy versus Ford. You two knuckleheads ready?"

They're already bowing up, good-naturedly mouthing about how good they are and how the other one is craptastic behind the wheel. I know which is going to win because I built both engines and know exactly what they can do. The driver makes the most difference, of course, but the guts under the hood matter, all things otherwise equal.

So though Ed officially forbids betting, my money's on Wilson because his car's got a little more horsepower and he's willing to push the boundaries to coax every single bit of power out of that engine. He's basically crazier than Jerry with the engine to back it up. I flash two fingers at Ryan, our secret bookie, and he nods. He manages to keep it all straight, who bids what and on whom. I don't know how, but he's never been wrong, not a single time.

They line up, and with a quick, light progression on the tree, the race is on. Tires squeal, engines growl, and they roar down the quarter-mile.

As expected, Wilson gets the win and a round of applause goes through the small crowd. Everyone's watching closely, either for entertainment or because it'll be their turn on the line soon enough, and it's always an advantage to know what and who you're up against.

The races continue on for the evening, pairing after pairing. I bet on a couple more, but mostly, I watch and wait.

Jerry wanders up while Mike and Clint chat up a possible rematch. They run pretty close, trading wins depending on the night. "Good run," I tell Jerry, knowing that he's probably a bit grumpy about losing to Wilson.

His lips twist wryly. "Next time. Where's Just a Guy?"

"Who?" I ask, my brows knitting together.

"Brody," Jerry says with a smile. "First time you brought him, I told him he must be special for you to bring him here considering the whole situation with Keith. He said he was 'just a guy'." Jerry does air quotes, but his fingers are straight, not curved like most folks do it, which makes me smile. As does his story. I didn't know Brody told him that. "He ain't just a guy, is he, Rix?"

My smile grows. "Nah, he ain't 'just a' anything."

Jerry throws a fatherly arm over my shoulder, side hugging me. "Aw, our little Rix is growing up, falling in love."

I cringe, knowing he means well, but *shit*. He's going overboard here, and I don't want anyone to overhear him and swipe away my hard-earned reputation with some softie Emily-style romance fluff. I shrug his arm off as kindly as I can. "I'm not that girl, Jerry. Brody and I are good, though."

He doesn't take offense at my moving a step away. "He met Keith yet?"

"Abso-fucking-lutely not," I snort. "And don't go saying his name again. You'll conjure him like Beetlejuice."

"Beetle-who?" Jerry asks, turning his head like he misheard me. I almost repeat myself and explain the say-his-name deal, but Jerry laughs. "Just messing with you. I saw that movie with the kids when they were little."

I push at his shoulder, teasingly glaring as he looks mighty pleased with himself. "Really, though, you're gonna have to introduce him to Keith." Jerry looks around like Dad is going to magically appear. If he does, I'm totally fucked. Luckily, that's just a movie, not real life. Still, I look around too, smiling at Jerry when there's no one but the two of us around.

"I know. I will when the time is right." Or never, which is preferable.

I care deeply for them both and don't want to hurt either of them. Their paths never crossing seems like the most surefire way to be kind. Dad won't get upset over the reality that I'm never going to marry Reed, Brody won't have to lie to my dad's face about the racing, and I can keep on doing exactly whatever the fuck I want. Win all the way around.

I'm saved from any further fatherly advice by Ed calling my name. "Rix versus Mike Senior." I nod toward the middle-aged guy standing across the crowd from me. He's a good driver, with a great car—a tweaked-out NISMO Skyline GT-R. But I'm a great driver with a great car . . . Foxy.

"Let me go kick this guy's ass real quick, then we can talk more," I tell Jerry as I strut away. Half of racing is mental, and if Mike Senior thinks I'm better than him, I will be.

We all know each other's strengths and weaknesses well, but posturing is always a factor. Especially when you're a tiny woman in a male-dominated field. I'm more than happy to let him think I've got some advantage, maybe a recent tweak to my engine that he doesn't know about yet.

Oh, I haven't done anything major to Foxy in ages, but that doesn't mean Mike Senior knows that.

I do my walk around Foxy, verifying that she's ready, and then climb in. I shut the door, but really, I'm shutting out everything but me and Foxy. The rest is unimportant white noise.

I pull up to the staging area, and Ed leans in, his voice loud to be heard over the engines. "You good? You ready?"

What might seem like casual questions are anything but. He's asking if I'm ready mentally and physically to drive ridiculously fast while maintaining control and responsibility. He's asking if I'm comfortable with my car as she sits. Man and machine is a powerful relationship, and he's asking if I'm ready to test its limits.

"Yes and yes. Let's go," I yell, nodding my head to be clear.

"Track rules," he states as always before going over to Mike Senior to do the same pre-race check.

Track rules are simple. Be honest, responsible, and safe. You have to know your own skills and limits, and your car's, and not push either too far. Good sportsmanship is an expectation. We give each other shit, but at the end of the day, we're a community of racers that backs each other up, so all 'fights' are on the track only.

I pull up to the burnout box and heat my tires. Some people love the smell of Christmas trees or warm cookies out of the oven. I love the smell of burning rubber, acrid and pungent and a reminder of so many happy memories. I pull up, triggering the pre-stage light and then the stage light, and wait for Mike Senior to do the same.

I'm poised, my entire focus on the shades of yellow in the three lights on the tree. I see the third start to darken and floor it, letting off the clutch simultaneously. Right as the green illuminates, Foxy crosses the line and we're off.

The car glides down the lane accompanied by a deafening roar. The vibration of the seat beneath me spurs me on, the engine screaming at me to shift, shift, shift.

I have no idea where Mike Senior is. Somewhere behind me would be my guess. I cross the yellow line and slow down to turn onto the return track, stopping to get my time slip from Patricia, Ed's wife. She mostly stays in the booth with her fan these days, claiming heat exhaustion if she has to help in the staging area.

"Good run, Rix. You hit one forty easy and early." She actually sounds excited for me, and considering it's probably one of the faster runs of the non-juiced cars, that's understandable. Mostly, I think she likes having another woman around who likes cars because other than her and me, we only see the occasional bored girlfriend or wannabe car magazine model.

"Thanks, Patricia. How're the kids?" She and Ed have two kids, a son who's almost thirty and a daughter who's twenty-three and lives in a group home an hour away.

She tells me about her son and daughter-in-law who have decided to become electric car-driving vegans. "Ed about had a heart attack, but I held him back. Those kids are gonna give me grandbabies one day, and I'm not letting a diet or a car get between me and those chubby cheeks." She pinches the air as though there's already a sweet baby in front of her. "And Jennifer got herself a job! She's working at a warehouse doing inventory. It's perfect for her. She gets to count and make spreadsheets and track discrepancies. Right up her alley."

"Good for her, glad to hear that."

Our conversation is drowned out by the roar of engines running. I smile and wave at Patricia, knowing our time has been cut short because those two racers will want their time slips to analyze. She waves back as I pull on around and park Foxy.

I walk up to the crowd of spectators, who offer me high-fives and congratulations.

"Thanks. Another day, another run." I'm happy with my performance and Foxy's, but bragging after a win is unsportsmanlike and asshole-ish. I try to follow a mantra I heard once, 'humble in victory, gracious in defeat', and so far, it's served me well.

"Gassers are done. Ed's doing bottle-feds now," Jerry tells me. "Todd's up against a new guy with an import." Foxy is a pure gasoline engine, along with Jerry, both Mikes, and a handful of other cars. Todd's part of the more heavily modified group that runs nitrous.

"What'd Todd put for his dial-in?"

Dial-in is what a racer estimates his car will do and is an important part of deciding who races whom. If you fudge your numbers, you can be disqualified, so honesty is key.

"Nine flat," Jerry says disbelievingly. I eye him, not reacting in the slightest, but he reads me anyway. I make a mental note to never play poker with Jerry. "That's what we all thought too. What'd you do to his Challenger?"

"Nothing," I say carefully. "I ordered some stuff for him, but he canceled. Said he figured something else out."

A million thoughts run through my head at once. Mostly, I try to figure out how in the hell Todd thinks he'll pull numbers like that. His car is fast, and he's a good driver, but that's nearly half a second off his best time. There's no way.

Todd and a blue Toyota Supra do their burnouts and hit the line, both revving their engines and purging their nitrous.

The tree lights switch from the first yellow to the second, to the third, and then the green illuminates, and both cars rear up before lurching forward. Right off the line, Todd doesn't seem like himself. The tires spin slightly and the front end lifts off the ground. Even once he gets all four tires connected with the asphalt, he's barely in control, not holding his line the way he usually does.

"What the fuck?" I say.

At the same time, Jerry hisses, "*Shit.*" I can count on one hand the number of times I've heard him cuss and not even need all my fingers.

In slow motion, there's a deafening *pop*, and flames rise from under the Challenger's hood. Instantly, people are on their feet and running toward Todd.

That's what family does for one another.

"Get out! Get out!" I yell as the flames rise higher. I'm close enough that he should be able to hear me, but another burst of flames ignites loudly. I'm the first one to approach the flaming car, so I automatically flip the kill switch on the back to shut off the ignition and pull the driver side door open.

Todd is banging on the steering wheel. "Fuck! Fuck! Fuck!" Or I assume that's what he's saying, but it's muffled by his helmet and overwhelmed by the hiss of extinguishers as several people aim the hoses under the hood to put out the fire.

I grab a fistful of his shirt and pull. "Get the fuck out now, Todd!" He turns, and his eyes are glassy with shock, not focusing on me. But he sticks a leg out and then the other, letting me yank him out of the car. "You okay?" I yell.

There's another *pop*, and flames leap out from underneath the car, catching both Todd and me by surprise.

*Hot. Hot. Hot.*

My legs are on fire, actual flames licking along my calves, reaching for my knees.

I cry out, but it's lost in the sound of everyone else cussing and yelling. Todd tackles me to the ground, and my head hits the asphalt hard, ringing my bell. I blink, trying to focus and trying to breathe beneath Todd's weight.

"Be still!" someone yells.

"Close your eyes and hold your breath!" someone else yells at the same time.

It's so quick, but it's in slow motion too, like every second has been teased apart for maximum carnage. I feel the cool foam of the fire extinguisher hit my legs where there should be jeans and moan at the stinging sensation even though it's better than the burn.

"Patricia called 9-1-1. Ambulance is on its way," Ed says. "Hang in there, Todd. You okay, Rix?"

I realize that Todd is no longer smooshing me and thrash my head around to find him. "Todd?"

"You okay, Rix?" he says from my other side, his voice rough and tight. I turn to see him lying on the ground next to me. Someone has taken his helmet off, and he looks pale and clammy, his eyes getting shinier and more vacant by the second. My legs hurt, and I can't see what's wrong with Todd, but I can tell he's a lot worse off than I am.

"I'm good, Todd. We're gonna get you some help, 'kay?" I look back up to Ed and dig deep for my balls. "Get that fucking ambulance here now, Ed!" I bark.

He tries to chuckle, a watery smile trying to come through, but he fails and instead his lips just quiver. "Even down for the count, she's a bossy one, our Rix."

Jerry pats my head, something that would normally piss me off royally. Right now, it's just what I need. But not who I need it from.

"Hey, Ed?" He leans over, coming into my field of vision, his brows raised. "Call my dad to meet us at the hospital."

He nods, looking grim. I think we all know the shit just hit the fan in a spectacularly fucked up manner, and we're all going to pay the Keith Cole price for keeping this from him.

# CHAPTER 25

## BRODY

Motel rooms used to be so exciting. Once or twice a year, Dad would take me to the market auction to buy and sell for our herd, and it'd seemed like such an adventure. Fancy towels, folded toilet paper, fresh sheets, pizza delivery, and just the boys. We'd sit around with no shirts on, not shower, and once I was in high school, Dad would even let me have a beer or two.

Those are some of my best memories of my dad, actually, because back then, he really was amazing. I looked up to him, admired him, and respected him. He was worthy of it, earned it by giving us his time, attention, and lessons about his years of ranching.

Only now, as an adult, do I realize how hard staying in a motel can be. Everyone you care about is back at home, carrying on without you. You worry about germs in the towels and sheets, which aren't fancy at all and are actually cheap and scratchy, and a pizza and beer diet makes you feel like shit.

I send a silent thank you to Dad for making it seem like fun when I realize how hard it must've been for him. But only for that. Not for the later shit when he was angry, miserable, and spreading his poison around like fertilizer. I forgive him, mostly, but I still blame him for being weak when we most needed him to be strong.

"Good picks today," Mark says from his double bed. He's leaning back against the headboard, long jeans-covered legs crossed at the ankles, his chin dipped low and eyes closed even though he started the conversation.

I grunt, knowing he'll hear the agreement about the few cows and calves we bought.

"What'd you think of the buyer?" His sock-covered toes wiggle as he scratches one foot with the other.

"He's all right. Fair price." I sit on the other bed, elbows on my knees and rolling my neck to stretch out the tension through my shoulders.

Market day is hard on both of us, the high-pressure culmination of a year's worth of work, blood, and sweat. *No tears because we're fucking cowboys*, I think with an internal cocky smirk. It requires chatting up other ranchers about everything from hay prices to cattle weights, and being personable isn't either of our strong suits.

Even so, we sold every head we brought to the same buyer, making it a convenient exchange. The cattle have already left the sale barn with their new owners, and we'll load our purchased ones up tomorrow for the drive home. All in all, it's left us in a good position for the next year of ranching.

Mark grunts.

A full-blown conversation for the two of us.

"I'm gonna walk across the street to the 7-11 for a beer. You want one?" I offer. I don't give a fuck about the beer, but I know Mark will want some privacy to call Katelyn and I don't want to be here for whatever they're getting up to, anyway.

"No thanks. I'll take a big water bottle, though." He looks more alert now, eyes open and his phone in his hand.

By the door, I pull my boots back on and lift one brow at Mark. Unspoken code of 'you've got thirty minutes,' which he answers with a slow blink. This is why we get along so well. We understand each other's subtle nuances.

I slow walk my way to the store, in no hurry and enjoying the cool night air after sitting on bleacher stands in a warm barn all day. The stars aren't as visible against the inky sky here, even though we're not exactly in a busy city, and I realize how comforted I am by the expanse of nothingness around me at home. Here, the buildings, cars, and people feel suffocating. At home, the world feels almost limitless when you stand outside, blanketed by the dark of night.

The convenience store is empty, and I grab a can of Bud and a bottle of water. The cashier seems bored, half looking at his phone while he rings me out. "Have a good night," he finally says as I walk out the door. I don't acknowledge the last-ditch attempt at customer service.

At the motel, I lower the tailgate on Mark's truck and have a seat. My feet dangle, and I kick them a few times, wishing I'd brought my book with me. It's sitting in my duffel bag in the room, and I've still got a good fifteen minutes before I can go back in.

I look at my phone and consider calling Erica. I know she's at the races tonight and probably busy, but it'd be nice to hear her voice even if it's on her voicemail.

But I don't do that.

I crack open my beer and take a long swallow. How in the hell did I get here?

Things I knew—I would die before I lost the farm. I would never settle down. I would fall asleep and wake up every day on the land I grew up on.

Things I know now—I lost the farm, and it's mostly okay. Damn better than I ever thought it'd be, but I'm sitting down with spreadsheets again to figure out how to get it back. I'm not settled, exactly, but Mark's insight that this thing with Erica is reminiscent of him and Katelyn has been coming up in my mind more and more. I'd be a lucky fucker to one day have a marriage like his. And I wake up at Erica's apartment more often than not these last couple of months. There might not be a sunrise over the pasture to greet me there, but the sun shines in through the window over her bed, touching the curve of her hip and highlighting each freckle while I watch each morning. She jokes that it's creepy to wake up to me eyeballing her, but she always says it with a smile teasing her lips as she stretches and poses, tempting me with wandering fingers along her skin and mine.

My life is nothing like what I thought it'd be, and it's heading in a different direction than I ever would've plotted, but I feel like I'm getting where I'm supposed to be despite the fuck-ups along the way.

My phone rings beside me, rattling on the tailgate. I glance down, but it's an unknown number so I decline the call, sending it to voicemail. The home screen shows a picture of Erica leaning up against Foxy, her black boots and bare legs the first thing to grab my eye, but then it's the pissed off look of 'take the picture already' that really does me in. Damn, that woman.

The phone rings with the same number, interrupting my view of Erica and irritating me. Damn sales calls, probably a robot dialer. I decline it again.

When it rings immediately, I decide to fuck with the sales guy a little. "What?" I bark into the phone, sounding more pit bull than man.

"Brody?" a soft voice says.

"Who's this?" I say, sitting up straight. I know the voice, but it's muffled like they're not really talking into the phone.

"It's Emily. Brody . . ." She sniffles and my gut turns to stone. Something's wrong, I can feel it in my bones. "It's Rix . . . the races . . . there was a fire."

My first instinct is always to fight, so I stand like there's an imminent threat, as if there's something I can do right here, right now, from hundreds of miles away. "Is she okay?"

"We don't know. Ed called Dad, said it got her legs, but they won't let us see her. I thought . . ." A sniffle and a sob this time. "I thought you'd want to know."

"I'm on my way. Text me the hospital address." She makes a

sound of agreement, and I can hear her dissolve into tears, but I can't comfort her right now. I have to get to Erica.

I bang on the motel door, three hard raps, and the two short seconds it takes Mark to answer are two seconds too long. "Fuck, man." Mark's confused irritation at my aggressiveness with the door changes instantly when he sees my face. "What's wrong?"

"I need the truck keys." I don't wait for him to give them to me, grabbing them off the dresser myself. That's all I need, keys in my hand and my wallet in my back pocket.

Mark blocks my way at the door. "What's wrong?"

"Erica. There was a fire at the races. She's at the hospital. That's all I know. I gotta go." He shows no emotion, but he's gritting his teeth like they did something wrong. I push past him, throwing over my shoulder, "Sorry."

I hear Katelyn answer, so he must've still been on the phone with her when I barged in. "We're on it, Brody!"

---

I DON'T REMEMBER THE DRIVE. I GOT IN THE TRUCK, AND A MOMENT later, I'm pulling into the hospital lot and parking like one of those assholes who thinks the lines don't apply to them.

I don't need to glance at my phone to know where to go. Emily's text is burned into my mind.

*Burned.*

Fuck.

The doors open automatically as I stomp my way toward them, and the smell of antiseptic hits me full-force.

In the back corner, what looks to be the entirety of the racing community is pacing around like there's a track on the floor that only they can see, I see Ed, Jerry, Mike, and Clint, along with a few other familiar faces.

The crowd parts, and I see her . . . flip flops and shorts, long, dark hair down her back. For a brief moment, I think it's all a mistake. Some misunderstanding or trick. And then she turns.

Emily.

I can tell them apart easily, but my heart had hoped for a moment that Erica was okay. *Fuck, let her be okay.*

"Brody." Emily's cry is accented by the *thwack-thwack* of her flip-flops as she runs to me. "You're here." She hugs me solidly, her tears starting fresh though the dried tracks down her face say this isn't her first or second time to break down.

"What do we know?" My throat is tight, the words clipped.

"Nothing. Dan came in to help since it's Rix and said he'd let us know." I pat her back, looking at the doors leading into the treatment area. I want to get through them, need to get through them to Erica.

"Who are you?" a deep voice asks.

Emily jerks and pulls back, clearing her throat. "Uh . . . Dad, this is Brody. Brody, this is Keith."

He's sizing me up, and I know there's no way I measure up. Even on my best days, I'm a dirty, rough cowboy who smells like cow shit. Today, I've been sweating my balls off in a barn with cowboys who smoke like chimneys, cows that shit where they please, and I think I spilled some of my beer on my shirt when Emily first called. Keith Cole is a little over six feet tall, but beneath his Carhartt T-shirt and pants, he's lean muscle. His hair is dirty blond shot through with gray at the temples, and he's got a matching blond-gray goatee and mustache. His eyes are bright blue and laser-locked on me. I can see the resemblance with Erica in those eyes—not the color, of course, but in that fiery spark. He might not be her *nature*, but he's her *nurture* through and through.

I hold my hand out. "Brody Tannen."

He shakes my hand, squeezing a little too hard. "Keith Cole. And again, who are you?"

"So good of you to come," Janice interrupts, also making a move to hug me.

"You know him?" Keith asks Janice, who shrugs and doesn't look the least bit sorry.

"We met at the farmer's market."

That seems like a lifetime ago, even though only a couple of months have passed.

Jerry comes over, offering me a hand and interrupting the third-degree interrogation Keith is ready to launch. "Hey, Brody. Our girl's gonna be just fine, you hear? She's a tough one, that Rix."

Keith's back goes ramrod straight, and I try to imagine what he's going through right now. I knew Erica was racing, knew that there were inherent dangers, but I trusted that she would do everything to mitigate those. But sometimes, shit still happens.

Sometimes, the good ones, the ones who deserve to stay around the longest, leave too soon, and there's not a damn thing you can do about it.

Keith didn't know Erica's been racing. He got side-swiped with a double-whammy tonight—that his daughter's been hiding something from him and that she got hurt doing it. And then I here come, strutting in like I belong here, and he's never even heard my name.

"What happened?" I ask Jerry.

He tells me about Todd's nitro going wrong and fire shooting out from under the hood. He tells me about Erica pulling Todd out of the car, and I shake my head at her brave stupidity. It's not that I want to hold her back, but I can't help but think she wouldn't be hurt if she'd let someone else do the dangerous part. But that's not who she is. And then he tells me about one last explosion and how Todd shoved Erica to the ground and took the brunt of the flames himself.

The whole racing crew plus Erica's family listens in, though I suspect this is a repeat of what they've already heard.

"Good guy," I say about Todd, which doesn't begin to describe how thankful I am for his sacrifice to save Erica from anything worse. Jerry is stone-faced but nods, agreeing. "He okay?"

"Don't know anything yet, about either of them. Emily's doctor friend . . ." He trails off, looking toward the door like I did.

As if he conjured it, the doors open and the first thing I see is Dan smiling. He's pushing a wheelchair . . .

Erica!

"Erica!" I shout as my mouth catches up with my brain. My strides eat the space between us.

She looks like . . . everything. She looks like . . . home. And also, a bit pale and dirty. Her legs are sticking out of scrub pants that have been chopped at the knee, leaving a frayed hem. Her calves and bare feet are wrapped in white gauze.

"Brody, what are you doing here?" she says, and my heart stutters. She doesn't want me here? But then her eyes flick behind me to Keith, and I realize her hesitation isn't about me.

"We met. He's got questions. Later."

Her arms open, and I hunch over to hug her. "Scared the shit outta me, Lil Bit," I whisper in her ear.

She smiles big and bold, putting on a front for her audience. "Just another day of racing."

I see her throat swallow as she looks to Keith. "Dad?"

Janice and Emily are bookending Keith, who's breathing heavily and turning red. I think seeing that Erica is okay has relieved his initial fears, freeing him up to be angry at the situation he's been thrust into.

"What the hell is going on? Do I even know you at all, Rix?" Hurt and betrayal thread through the words painfully.

"Of course you do," Erica says, but she doesn't sound certain. "I'm a racer, just like you taught me to be." Better, stronger, and with pride.

Janice jumps in. "What did the doctor say?"

Erica looks to Dan. "Dr. Dan here says I have to keep the burns clean and dressed, and he gave me an antibiotic ointment prescription. I'm on concussion watch, but they don't think anything's wrong with my brain that wasn't already a little bit wrong to begin with."

Jokes? The woman's got jokes after something like this? But I see the fear flashing in her eyes. More bricks, more walls, more façade. I don't know why everyone thinks she's this wild, devil-may-care creature. On the surface, maybe that's true. But the truth is, she does everything for everyone else. Even now, comforting them with humor when we should be comforting her.

"It's all on my discharge paperwork." She points at the stack of papers tucked beside her in the wheelchair.

"It's a little more complicated than that, but Rix has assured me that she'll be a compliant patient. Right?" Dan prompts, and Erica nods, only a little sarcastically.

"Well, let's get you home then. I'll set up your old bed so that you're comfortable," Janice says, already mentally making plans to have Erica recover under her motherly care.

"Mom, I want to go home. To *my* home."

Janice balks and Keith steps in. "Rix, don't be silly. We'll go home, and you can heal while you tell me what the hell's been going on." Keith eyes me again, still not having an answer he's satisfied with. Though I think the greeting and hug between Erica and me made things pretty clear.

Erica looks at me, a question in her eyes. I blink, answering her easily. Seeing her, touching her, soothes something deep inside, and I'm not ready to drop her off at her parents' and go to the farm alone. I thought I'd failed again when I got that call, that she'd left me too. And I feel like I'm getting a second chance, one I won't fuck up.

She turns back to her parents. "I'm going home. Brody can take care of me and you can come over in the morning so we can talk everything through." The no-nonsense, take-no-shit version of Erica is back in full force, leaving no room for compromise.

"*Brody* is going to take you *home*?" Keith parrots. "Who is he?" Blunt and straightforward, just like his daughter. "And where the hell is Reed?"

"I'm her boyfriend," I answer. It's the closest word I've got to describe this thing between Erica and me, even though it feels woefully inadequate.

"Boyfriend." Not a question, but Keith shakes his head in denial.

Erica's eyes plead with him. "I want to talk to you about everything, if you'll listen."

Janice steps up to Keith's side, laying a hand on his arm and providing a calming voice of reason. "That's fine, honey. Brody, if you two need anything at all, you call me right away. Otherwise, we'll call in the morning to see how you're feeling before we come over."

Keith wants to argue, but he stays quiet and stone-faced.

Ed steps forward, addressing Dan. "What about Todd?" I don't miss the frosty look Keith gives Ed. I figured they'd be friends, but there is no love lost between the two right now, that's for sure.

Dan looks over his shoulder. "Family only for updates, I'm afraid." But he winks and gives a thumbs-up, and you can feel the relief work through the crowd. "His family should be here any minute."

Ed holds up a fist and Erica pounds it. "Damn near scared the speed demon outta me, girl. You'd best get home, and we'll hold court for Todd until his family gets here."

"Thanks, Ed. See you Wednesday?" she says, and the answering silence is deafening. "Too soon?" she says, laughing. But the laugh turns into a cough.

Janice holds out a bottle of water and Erica takes it gratefully. I nod my appreciation her way too.

"Let me pull the truck up and we'll get you loaded up." I almost hate to leave her alone with them, sure they'll get her to change her mind about going home with me. And then I crack the smallest sliver of a smile. Someone change Erica's mind? I'm not sure that's even humanly possible.

I pull up to the exit door where Erica, Emily, Dan, Janice, and Keith are waiting. Surprisingly, none of them, not even Erica herself, stops me from picking Erica up and placing her in the passenger seat. I buckle her in and close the door as she calls out to them, "Call me in the morning?"

Janice nods, then makes pointed eye contact with me as she puts her hand on my shoulder. With a weighted breath, she tells me, "That's my baby."

"Understood." Erica is important to her, and with one word, I let her know that I will respect that and do my best to take care of Erica the way she would. It's a vow, a promise, and I'm a man of my word, so I take that shit seriously.

I offer my hand to Keith, who shakes it too tightly again, but I can forgive that under the circumstances. Honestly, I'm surprised he hasn't punched me. My Dad would've if some strange, dirty, rough guy had shown up for Shayanne. "This isn't over."

"Wish we'd met under better circumstances. I've heard a lot of good things about you." He doesn't soften in the slightest at the sweet nothings I'm saying.

Emily hugs me. "Do you want me to come sleep on the couch and help? I don't know if I can *not* be with her when she's hurt. Oh, God, how come I didn't feel it when it happened?" She's getting hysterical.

I whisper, hoping Erica can't read lips. It'd be just like her to forget to tell me she can do that and use the skill for maximum impact at the right time. "If you come over, you know she'll put on a front." Emily nods, her eyes glassy with tears again. "Tomorrow. I have her for now."

I circle the truck, getting in the driver's side, and Erica waves at her family. We pull off, and as soon as we're out of the lot, she sags in her seat.

"Letting you know now . . . that took everything I've got out of me. I'm fucking toast . . . get it?" I lift a wry brow her way. "Still too soon?"

"Too soon," I agree dryly.

She sighs. "No racing jokes, but I need to crash and sleep for a few weeks. Can you or can you not make that happen?"

She's still got some walls up, but they're crumbling fast. Exhaustion laces her voice, and her eyelids are getting heavy.

"I can make that happen."

Sleep for weeks? No, because her parents are coming with some hard questions in a few hours, but I can make it seem like weeks if that's what she needs. I'll get her in bed, comfy and cozy, give her some tea with her pain meds, and make her pancakes in the morning.

I've got experience taking care of people, maybe not from injury, but from illness. Mom's cancer, Dad's broken heart. And one thing I know for sure . . . my mom's pancakes can heal whatever ails you.

# CHAPTER 26

## ERICA

I direct Brody to pull into bay one when we get to the garage. It looks empty in here with Foxy still parked at the track. I'll have to get her tomorrow.

Shit. Fuck. Damn.

I can't even drive her home with my legs like this. Dan, I mean Dr. Deardon, told me not to drive on the pain meds, and I'm definitely going to want some of those. But I'm sure I can get one of the track guys to bring her home. They're good like that, and we take care of our own.

I get a flash of Todd's face, really just his eyes, going wide and white as the flames reached him. It's the last thing I saw before I hit the ground and my eyes closed. I didn't pass out, but I'd kept them closed protectively—from the heat, from the dirt, from the pain in Todd's scream.

I inhale, willing my heartbeat to slow as Brody gets out and comes around to the passenger door. He helps me out, and I step gingerly, testing the pain. My legs hold, and though it feels like being poked with hot needles, I take the few slow steps through the breakroom as he props me up, ready to catch me at any second.

At the stairs, I pause and look up. They have never seemed as daunting as they do now. Thirteen stairs of hell, but heaven is waiting up there . . . covered in cotton sheets, a fluffy blanket, and a feather pillow. And Brody wrapping his arms around me.

It's a great incentive, and I lift my right foot for the first step.

"Let me carry you." Brody's voice has gone rough and deep, more of a rumble, as if seeing me in pain hurts him too.

"I can do it," I argue, stubbornly moving my left foot to the first step too. Two feet per stair. That's how I'm going to do this.

But I sway and lean more heavily on Brody. "You don't have to do everything on your own. You don't have to be strong now. It's okay to admit that you need help."

"I don't." What should sound strong and powerful sounds weak and ridiculous when I'm still standing on the first step.

Brody could just do it, sweep me into his arms and carry me upstairs, and I wouldn't be able to do a damn thing about it but bitch him out. But he doesn't. No, he stands beside me, supporting and steadying me, letting me call the shots. As if we've got all the time in the world, he starts talking, his voice calm and soothing as he gives me another piece of himself.

"One of the strongest women I've ever known was my mom, and when she got sick, I didn't think it was going to be bad. She was invincible. But her treatments got harder, she got sicker, and Mama Louise started coming over more. They were friends back then, and she'd say she was just visiting, that she'd baked too much dinner or too many cookies, or even that she'd found a new cleaner that was supposed to make the glass shine like diamonds. All so that she could help us without it seeming like she was cooking and cleaning because Mom couldn't. I never thought Mom was weak, not when she needed help and not even when the cancer won. She went out fighting every last step of the way, and that wasn't changed by her letting someone carry her stubborn ass up the stairs."

Love, pure and bright, shines through, and I wish I'd gotten a chance to know his mother. She raised a good man, and I'd like to tell her that. I won't ever have that opportunity. But I have one now with Brody, if I'm willing to be real.

"Okay, take me upstairs." My walls are crumbling, breaking down, and it feels like a gush of relief to not have to perform for everyone. To not give, but to take, if only for a minute. To not be hard but to be okay with being weak, knowing Brody won't judge me for it.

I want to cry and scream and admit how scared I was to someone. And he's that someone.

"Thought you'd never ask, Lil Bit." He gives me that cocky smirk of victory before picking me up carefully. He carries me up each of those thirteen steps and to the bed, where he sets me on the edge. He pulls my shirt off, tossing it to the hamper, and plucks a ponytailer from the nightstand, holding it out for me. I do a quick twist of my hair, getting it off my neck as Brody kneels in front of me.

"Can you lift your hips?" I press my palms to the bed, and he slips the cut-off scrubs to the floor, taking care over the bandages. He guides me to lie back, and I sink into the pillow as he tucks me in. "Tea?"

I don't remember the last time I felt this small. I mean, I'm a short woman, but I'm like one of those chihuahuas that doesn't let their size hold them back, barking at the biggest pit bull in the park. Right now, I feel small and vulnerable and only want one thing.

"No. Will you just lie with me?" A question, not an order, but Brody reacts the same either way.

"Of course." He strips down to his underwear, laying everything out neatly over a chair. He climbs into bed with me, curling around me to spoon me from behind. And finally, I can let that last shred of wall crumble.

The tears come slowly at first, Brody's breath by my ear whispering that it's okay and to let it out. He hugs me tighter when they start to rack my body, shakes and shivers from the stress finally working their way to the surface. He traces the freckles on my shoulder, kissing them every so often while I fall apart.

And he loves me through it.

The words come eventually, spilling over my lips. "I don't know what happened. I keep playing it over in my head—he purged, he was shifting, it was fine. And then it wasn't, and he wouldn't get out of the car. It was so hot . . . his face, I can't get that look out of my mind. I need to know that he's okay."

I'm rambling, eyes closed as I see the scene at the track again and again.

"He's fine, Dan said so. And we'll find out more soon. And honestly, I don't give a fuck about Todd right now. I only care about you." His voice cracks as he spits the words out and buries his nose in the hair at the nape of my neck. "I thought I was going to lose you before I could tell you that I love you. I wanted you to know that and was so afraid I'd missed my chance."

I roll to my other side carefully, the sheet brushing over my legs but the gauze preventing it from hurting too much as I face Brody. I need to see his eyes for this, need to see the dark depths he hides with a front of cocky asshole-itis the same way I disguise my heart with bitchiness.

"I know you love me. Words or not, it's in everything you do. Making me those pancakes, encouraging me to follow my dreams, and accepting me just as I am. I know you love me. I love you too."

He inhales sharply. "Fuck, that sounds good."

"You didn't know?" I ask, surprised. I guess even I was fooled by his arrogance to some degree, thinking he would assume that every woman in the Tri-State area would fall for him, given the chance. Because I sure as fuck have.

"I'm not exactly known for my emotional development. I'm a simple guy." He says it like he actually believes that to be true.

I snort. "You are *so* not simple by any standards, Brody Tannen." But my words are getting slurry as the pain meds kick in.

"Neither are you, Erica Cole. Get some sleep."

I nod, and he guides me to turn back over, snuggling up behind me and wrapping me in his arms. I'm almost asleep, or maybe I dream it, but I think I hear him whisper, 'I love you' again one more time. I think I smile as I drift off.

---

MORNING SUNLIGHT BEAMS IN THROUGH THE WINDOW, ROUSING ME from a deep sleep. For a second, I forget everything and have a moment of panic that I'm late for work. I scramble in the bed and am instantly reminded of last night when pain shoots through my legs.

"*Shit*," I hiss.

"Good morning, sunshine. Coffee's on the nightstand." Brody's watching me carefully from the kitchen. He's wearing his jeans again, which is a shame. Not that I'm in any state to take advantage, but I can at least enjoy the look.

He's standing at the stove and makes no move to come over and hand me the coffee. He's letting me get it myself. It's the smallest, littlest, nothing of a thing, except it's not to me and he knows it. I let myself break down with him last night, and I think deep inside, I worried he would use it against me or it'd change how he sees me.

But that's not who he is.

I reach for the coffee, struggling a little, and he simply turns around, letting me work it out. That first sip tastes amazing, maybe partially because I got it myself.

"Enough about me," I start, knowing that it's all going to be about me for a bit. "What about the auction you're supposed to be at?"

Brody delicately plates a pancake, adding it to the stack he's already made. "Talked to Mark last night after you fell asleep to let him know I'd be out for a bit. James went up this morning with his truck to help finish things up." He glances at the microwave clock. "They should be on their way back already. Fair warning, the girls will come by later today too, led by Mama Louise who's bringing fixin's for her famous fried chicken."

People coming to my apartment? I never have company, except

for Brody and Emily. Actually, I usually go to Emily's apartment because she has a more comfortable couch. So just Brody and me here, our own little pocket of space that's going to be invaded soon.

"What about Reed and Manuel? And my parents?"

"The guys are working downstairs. I gave them the short version. Reed's fit to be tied, and I almost got into it with him so that he wouldn't disturb you while you were still sleeping. You need to talk to him today, though, so he doesn't break down the door or force me to set him straight." Brody scratches at his lip, though I don't think he even knows he's doing it. I've figured out that's his tell. When he's lying or exaggerating, he'll scratch his lip like the words tickle as they come out. I don't think him and Reed are ever going to be best buds, but Reed cares about me and Brody can respect that. As long as he doesn't cross the line.

"My parents?"

His answer is more hesitating this time. "They called a bit ago, should be here in about ten minutes, actually."

He walks a plate of pancakes over to me, already cut up like I'm a child. It's on the edge of my tongue to bitch about it, but then I realize that I don't really care and probably couldn't cut them while lying in bed anyway. "Thank you," I say, truly grateful.

"Your dad is angry—he was cussing and hissing things for Janice to say when she called. But I think he's covering up how hurt he is. I can see where you get it from now." One brow raises, daring me to argue, but he's right.

"One of the best things he taught me," I say, though I'm realizing that's not necessarily true. If I'd just been honest a long time ago, we wouldn't be in this position, but I covered up my true desires and am going to pay the price in a painful way with Dad.

Brody grunts his opinion.

I eat the pancakes, which taste like fluffy, carb-y bites of heaven, while he gets me a T-shirt and pair of shorts. He helps me dress and then carries me to the couch, neither of which I argue about in the slightest. What would be the point? We both know I'm not doing it on my own.

The best part of the morning might be when he turns right back around and goes to make my bed. I can't help but laugh because I know he's doing it for me and couldn't care less about it.

"Thank you," I say honestly.

I hear footsteps coming up the stairs and my eyes jump to Brody. All of a sudden, I feel like a teenager who's about to get busted with a half-naked boy in her room. "Put a shirt on!" I whisper.

Brody shoots me that cocky smirk, and in no rush at all grabs his shirt off the back of the dining chair.

I hear Dad snap in the hallway, "I ain't knocking on my own damn door. I own this place and I'll come and go when and where I please."

Shit. Fuck. Damn.

I make a mental note to be better about locking that door. The last thing I need is Dad walking in on me and Brody fucking.

"Hey, Dad," I say as the door swings open. "Mom."

Dad's eyes flick from me on the couch to Brody standing barefoot and right at home in the kitchen. Mom's do the same, but she looks pleased as punch while Dad looks murderous.

"Mr. and Mrs. Cole." Brody greets them like this is a perfectly normal social visit. "Coffee, tea, beer?"

"It's eleven o'clock in the morning," Dad barks judgmentally.

Brody shrugs. "Long night. You earned it."

Mom breaks the staredown between the two men. "I'd love a coffee, and you can call us Keith and Janice."

Dad snorts. "No."

Brody pours a cup of coffee and grabs two beers from the fridge. He sets it all on the coffee table and then drags the two dining chairs over. Mom sits down gingerly beside me on the couch. "How are you feeling?"

Dad eyes Brody again, stubbornly refusing to sit until Brody does first. Finally, I speak up. "Guys, sit the fuck down or pull your dicks out and start measuring."

Mom gasps. Brody and Dad look at me with matching raised brows that say 'really?' but at least they sit down.

"Finally. I'm fine, Mom. The burns aren't that bad, and I'll be good as new in no time." That's not exactly true. Dan said that I'd have to be careful about infection and probably won't be able to work or drive for at least a couple of weeks. Maybe more. I'm going to go stark raving mad sitting on my ass, but now is not the time to tell Mom that or she'll plan out an entire schedule of people to come sit with me and play cards. No, thank you.

Brody clears his throat, and I glare at him, telling him to keep his big, fat mouth shut. He opens his beer and takes a swallow.

Dad watches, still judging until Brody sighs in satisfaction. That gets Dad, and he leans forward to grab his beer. He cracks his open and takes an even longer drink. Apparently, we're still measuring dicks.

"Okay, let's do this," I say, clapping my hands, and three sets of eyes land on me. Support—that's Brody, betrayal—that's Dad, and hope—that's Mom, all surround me at once. I focus on the most important issue at hand. "Dad, I should have told you I was racing and I'm sorry I didn't. Well, not really sorry because you would've tried to stop me, but I'm sorry you found out like you did."

He narrows his eyes and leans forward, elbows on his knees and beer dangling dangerously. "Just so we're clear—you're not sorry you did it. You're sorry you got caught."

"Basically." I shrug like that should be obvious.

"What the hell, Rix?" Dad says, standing up. "I said no more! You know why. I can't believe you'd go behind my back, that everyone would go behind my back . . ." His voice strangles off.

"We didn't mean to hurt you, Dad. Big John was important to all of us. But do you think he'd want you to give up something you love over him? He wasn't even racing when it happened." Dad flinches when I say Big John's name. "We're careful, you know that. The nitrous thing with Todd's car was a fluke that could've happened to anyone."

"But it happened to you!"

Brody is watching carefully, and I hate that he's meeting my Dad at his worst. He's such a great guy, they both are, and I think they'll like each other eventually. But right now, Brody's got a front-row seat to a moment I've been dreading for years.

"I'm okay, though," I say calmly, hoping Dad will see reason.

"You're not going back." He issues the decree as if he has a single say-so in what I do and where I go.

So, that's a no to being reasonable, then.

"Yes," I tell him in a clear, determined voice, "I am. That's my business, my hobby, my passion. One you taught me, and I'm not giving it up. I'll be back out there next week" —I gesture to my legs — "not driving, but watching the races, tuning my engines, and doing what I love."

"Business? Your engines?" Dad's interest piques despite his anger.

"Yeah, custom work," I say, pointing to the parts on the floor in the corner.

He walks over, examining the parts on a padded moving blanket and picking up a carburetor I've been working on.

"It's a bored out Edelbrock for Clint's '72 Nova." His eyes jump to me, a question in the quirk of his brow, and I give him everything. "I've been doing custom design work for almost everyone at the track and the car shows. Gassers and nitros, trailer queens and daily drivers, and everywhere in between. I mostly work downstairs, but I store it up here when I can so no one would get suspicious."

"Reed?" Dad asks, already knowing the answer.

I don't dare look at Brody, keeping my attention focused solely on Dad. "He didn't know. He would've told you." I frustratingly fight down the urge to stand up, wanting to be on even footing. "It's not going to happen with him, Dad. It never was."

Dad looks from me to Brody, his eyes going hard and cold. "I want you to be happy, honey. You and Reed have always been two peas in a pod, cast from the same die." He makes it sound like an inevitable pairing.

"He doesn't want me anymore than I want him. He's just too brainwashed to know it yet. We fight like cats and dogs, or like . . . brother and sister." Ew . . . I think I just grossed myself out. I've never thought of Reed as a brother, mostly because we've had sex, but over the years, as whatever heat we had when we were younger has cooled, we are more like siblings.

I shudder, and in my peripheral vision, I see Brody cover his smirk with a sip of beer. Cocky bastard. Fuck, I love him.

"Dad, I love Brody."

*Showtime, Cowboy.*

Brody's echo is firm, even, and full of love. "I love Erica too."

His dark gaze turns to me, talking to me even though he's talking to my dad. "I love when she's bitchy and brash, putting everyone in their place because she knows best. I love when she's soft and sweet, but only when she feels safe. I love when she talks about cars and her eyes light up with excitement over five more horsepower. I love how she sacrifices everything for the people she loves, even if it hurts her to do it. I love her heart, her soul, and even that mouth when she's cussing worse than I do."

Mom, who had been tearing up with her hands over her mouth, laughs as Brody finishes his speech. "Oh, Rix, honey . . . that's all we want for you. For you to be happy with whoever you want, doing whatever you want."

At least she has words because for the first time in my life, I think I'm stunned quiet. My eyes burn with unshed tears, ones I refuse to let fall right now, but I have never felt so understood. Brody gets me, all of me—the good, bad, and ugly parts, and he still loves me. Or maybe he even loves me because of the bad parts?

I would go to him if I could get off this damn couch, but he simply dips his chin. He knows. He understands. And we're not finished with that conversation, but right now . . .

Dad grunts, not agreeing but not disagreeing with Mom either.

"Keith!" Mom scolds.

"She coulda died, Janice. You get that?" he yells, pointing at me. I won't say my parents are perfect. They've fought over the years here and there, but never about me. Or at least if they did fight about me, it wasn't in front of me.

Mom points at me too. "But she didn't, did she? She could get hit by a bus walking to the store tomorrow." She turns to me. "Sorry, honey. Just saying." Back to my dad, she continues, "But you're not locking her up in a bubble to keep her from getting groceries."

He softens slightly at her words, and I wonder if Mom is going to do all my fighting for me. I hate to say it, but she's doing a better job than I was, so maybe I'll let her take the lead for a minute.

"How many smashed fingers did you have? How many close calls when something didn't go right with the jack or the lift? It's a physical job, Keith. And she can handle it because you taught her well, just like you taught her about racing. You think I was excited every time you roared down the track? No, I wasn't, but I never once tried to stop you. It would've been pointless, and worse, it would've killed you to stop. It almost did."

I jump in. "Everyone at the track misses you. They ask about you and talk about you like you're this mythical god and I'm special because I'm your daughter. Well, it used to be because of that, but I've made a bit of a name for myself," I brag boldly. "Because of what you taught me, RIX Customs are in high demand."

Dad runs his hands through his hair several times and looks at the carburetor on the floor where he set it down and the other projects too. Slowly, his eyes drag up to mine and he sighs heavily, resigned to what's right in front of him. I'm expecting more arguments, more orders, more . . . him. But somehow, we've reached his tipping point. "This is nothing like what I can do, honey. You're . . . talented."

He goes silent, lost in his memories . . . of his own work, of Big John, of teaching me? Those are all the thoughts running through my mind. And a compliment from Dad about my work soothes an uncertainty inside me that's been aching for a long time.

"Thank you, Dad. I can't tell you how many times I've wanted to share this with you." I glance at Brody, who has the good graces to not look smug about being right.

Dad follows my gaze, looking at Brody with new eyes too. He blinks several times before looking at the ceiling and then stands tall and straight. "I think I owe you an apology."

Brody frowns. "Not necessary. You were protecting what's most important to you. I can understand that." Brody looks back at me, heavy meaning in his eyes. He would do anything for me. I know that as clearly as I know I'd do anything for him too.

We might not have been looking for each other, not looking for anything serious, but fuck, did we find it in each other.

The moment is broken by a herd of elephants coming up the stairs and then a quiet knock. A too-loud whisper follows, "Shh, she might still be asleep."

Brody looks up at the ceiling as if praying for patience and unintentionally copying Dad's move of a moment ago. I think they'll get along fine once all the shit settles. "That'll be my family coming to check on Erica." He gets up to open the door, greeting our new guests.

Finally catching on to Brody's habit, Dad mouths at me, "Erica?"

I smile, blushing, though I'll deny that to the day I die . . . many happy years from now, God willing.

Sophie, Katelyn, Allyson, and Mama Louise come in like women on a mission, leaving no doubt that their mission is me. They shake hands with Mom and Dad, introductions all around, and say that Shayanne will be madder than a hornet that she was out of town for this. I didn't know hornets got especially mad, but I'm not going to ask.

They ooh and ahh over my nothing-special apartment before Mama Louise helps herself to the kitchen, setting up to make fried chicken and mashed potatoes with a cast-iron skillet she apparently brought from home. She claims that comfort food will help me heal faster, and Mom hops up to help like she was waiting on a mission and the healing properties of fried foods are completely plausible.

Shit. Fuck. Damn.

Both moms conspiring together could be bad, really bad. But at this point, what harm could they really do? Brody and I have already admitted our feelings and there are no more secrets.

Sophie and Katelyn whisper something about the fried chicken recipe and its importance, but I miss the details because Dad stands and says he and Brody are going downstairs.

"I think you're in good hands here, honey." He scans the group of women taking up residence in the tiny space and kisses my forehead before walking out the door.

Brody has the sense to look from me to the girls to the moms in the kitchen, almost like he's checking to make sure I'm okay with the situation, but then he throws me that arrogant smirk and follows my dad. "Pussy!" I call out to him.

Mama Louise sing-songs, "Language!"

Mom shakes her head. "I swear I taught her manners, but that girl is her father's daughter through and through."

"And proud of it," I say with zero humbleness.

For a hot second, I worry. Is Dad playing nice and then taking him downstairs to kill him? Reed would definitely help. But Brody can handle himself, and honestly, I think Dad is truly seeing reason. He's had all these plans for me for so long, and I've been skirting some and latching onto others. I think he's finally on board with my having my own plans too, or he's at least considering the idea.

Once that's settled in my mind, I look around me. Normally, I'd be irritated to be left with the womenfolk in the kitchen while the guys go talk shop just because I have a vagina, but these women make me feel like one of them, even though we're all so different. And I find myself enjoying their camaraderie and feeling a part of it myself. Even from my couch confinement.

I've missed this. I have it with Emily, of course, but I don't have female friends other than her. I have nothing in common with them, but somehow, that doesn't matter with this group. The only thing they have in common is that they love each other and will do anything for one another. That I can support.

Mama Louise and Mom chat away about stubborn husbands, and Sophie, Katelyn, and Allyson chime in here and there. I mostly doze, feeling the pain meds kick in again.

But when I fall asleep this time, it's with a clean slate and a full heart.

# CHAPTER 27

## BRODY

Downstairs, Reed and Manuel stop what they're doing and intercept us, Reed with his feet wide and his arms crossed while Manuel just looks worried.

"She okay?" Reed asks Keith.

He hums, nodding. "She will be. Just gonna take some time. I'll come back and help at the shop while she's recovering."

That's the first I've heard of that, and though it makes perfect sense, I'm a smart enough man to know that Erica's gonna feel like Keith is stepping on her toes. But I have to trust that they'll work it out. Fuck knows, she won't sit idly by and make it easy on him though the man successfully ran the shop for thirty years.

Reed's hands drop to his sides, fists curling before he points a greasy finger my way. "This is your fault," he snarls.

"Mine? I wasn't even here and sure don't know a damn thing about cars for it to be my fault."

"You knew what she was doing, and any idiot knows how dangerous it is! And still, you let her go out there and get hurt!" He points out the open garage door, like he means Erica could be hurt anywhere in the great, big world. He cares about her, and the fear Reed must've felt when he heard what happened is starting to worm its way into his voice, though he's fighting valiantly to stay hard and cold.

I chuckle, shaking my head. "Let her? *Let her*? Have you even met her, man?" I'm trying to keep it light because Reed is on the edge and I really don't want to finish my first introduction to Keith Cole by beating the shit out of the guy he considers a son. But I will if I have to.

He growls, turning to Keith. "You told her no more racing, right?"

*Errk*, all stop. What the actual fuck? Does Reed think Keith would actually do that? Hell, would he? I feel like he understood where Erica was coming from upstairs, but he forbade her once and it nearly destroyed her, taking away something she loved. Now that it's even more important to her, and all out on the table, I think it'd destroy both of them.

Slowly and carefully, Keith tells Reed, "I think it's time to see what she can do if she can live her wildest dreams. I think it's time for her to fly."

Reed looks pissed, but he deflates while Manuel just continues on his stoic way. Keith therefore turns to me. "Come on, Brody. You're taking me to the track to pick up Rix's car. What's she driving, anyway? I can't wait to get behind the wheel of a racecar my little girl built."

He sounds genuinely excited, and I know that I was right. Erica should've shared this with him a long time ago so that they could have this thing together. But I'll never tell her that. It happened when it did, how it did, for a reason, even if Todd would probably beg to differ.

"I think I'll leave that a surprise, mostly because I know I'll fuck up all the horse-this and throttle-that she told me, and I don't want to look like a dumbass in front of you. In my world, horses have four legs and help me herd cattle."

Keith laughs even though I'm not kidding. But I'm taking the win.

We get in the truck, and Keith immediately runs a hand over the dash, then opens the console, rooting around inside. "What the fuck, man? That's private," I snap, glad that Mark didn't have anything weird in there since I commandeered his truck to get to the hospital.

"No such thing now, Brody. Tell me everything I need to know about you, and don't leave out the shitty stuff. I'm playing catch up here, and it pisses me off, especially when it's about one of my girls." He leans back sullenly in the cushioned comfort of the seat, waiting for me to spill my guts.

Shit, his daughter is a total mini-me version of his stubborn bluster. But I decide to use that to my advantage. What works on Erica will probably work on Keith.

"Cowboy. Oldest of four. Mostly raised my youngest sister but did a shitty job of it so she raised herself to spite me. Not as dumb as I look."

Keith grins at that. "Didn't think Rix would have you if you're stupid." It's as close to a compliment as I can expect from him. "A cowboy, you say? You got land?"

Damn, he goes right for blood. The knife cuts through my heart, and I wish to hell I could say yes. "Neighbors bought it and now we work for them. They're like family, though. That's who invaded back there. Technically, Mama Louise is my boss. Mostly, she's a pain in my ass." I scratch at my lip, grinning. There's no heat in the insult and I don't mean a word of it. "I've got a plan to get it back, though, just gonna take some time and a lot of hard work."

"You up for that?" Keith eyes me from the passenger seat, and I keep my eyes fixed on the road.

"Been working every day my whole life. Ain't scared of it or anything."

He chuckles. "You scared of Rix? Because you should be. She probably knows three different ways to slit your throat and hide the body."

He's joking, but she's already told me this one. "It's five different ways. And I'm not scared of her because of that. I'm scared because she's got my heart in her hands and that's a scary position for a man to be in." It's a big confession and a gamble, but

I'm laying it all out there because I don't think there's anything to be gained from holding back at this point when it's blazingly apparent that Erica has me by the short hairs. "Reckon you know what that's like with Janice?" I hedge, side-eyeing him.

From what Erica has told me, her parents are happily married and have given her and Emily a great example of what lifelong love should look like. The test is whether Keith will admit that he's a big old softie for his wife.

"I guess I do," he says.

I think we both just passed a test.

---

AT THE TRACK, THERE'S A GOOD-LOOKING SILVER MUSCLE CAR sitting by the gate. "I'll be damned, he's still got it," Keith says incredulously.

"What?" I ask, not getting why he's excited.

"Ed. I texted him that we were coming for Rix's car. That's his 1969 Chevy Camaro. It's a top-notch drag car, and he's got it modded up like nothing I've ever seen."

"You still have his number?"

Keith's eyes never leave the car. "Friends are friends even when they don't talk for a while."

I hum in agreement. "You didn't do the work on his Camaro?"

Keith looks at me in confusion. "Nah, I'm good but not that good. He bought it already overhauled years ago and kept it pristine. Can't officially race on your own track, but I've seen him run it. Thing of beauty."

He goes quiet, and I imagine he's thinking of his time at the track with his friends, and mostly, about walking away from it all.

I stop by the gate, and the three of us get out. Keith and Ed's greeting is stilted and uncertain until Ed admits, "We missed you, and I wanted to tell you about Rix, but I wanted to respect her wishes and yours too."

Keith takes a deep breath, his jaw clenched, and I wonder if we've come out here for Keith to lay into Ed. The thought had crossed my mind, but Keith seemed pretty resigned to Erica racing. But maybe not?

Finally, he offers Ed a hand. "Never should've let it go this long. John would be mad as hell at me."

Ed takes Keith's hand, shaking before pulling him into a hug. He pats him on the back hard and then pushes him away like it never happened. "John was one of the good ones. Your girl tell you what she did to my Camaro?"

Keith's eyes nearly bug out of his head. "You let Rix work on your Camaro?"

Ed laughs. "You have no idea what she can do, do you? She's amazing, Keith, really something. I let her loose with a blank check and she got me running in the 8s."

"You're full of shit!"

"Listen to her growl," Ed says, already popping the hood.

I have no idea what they're saying or what they're talking about, but they point to various things under the hood and I can tell that this more than anything has made Keith a true believer in Erica's talents. Seeing it up close and personal, knowing exactly what she's done to creatively pull as much out of the car as possible, is enough to put Keith solidly in Erica's corner.

I knew he would be . . . eventually. I'm glad it's not taking that long for him to support her.

After they've walked the whole car twice, with me standing by like a bump on a log, Ed says, "Come on, I'll take you to Rix's car."

We get back in the truck and Keith is smiling like a kid in a candy store with instructions to buy anything he wants. "Damn, she's good. I knew, but I didn't know like *that*."

There's a new respect in his voice, one I hope Erica gets to hear for herself soon.

I stop the truck by Foxy and Keith blinks. "This is what she's driving? It's not the usual, but I guess I shouldn't be surprised. I used to have one of these." He already sounds nostalgic, and I wonder how many memories he's got in his old Mustang.

"You fell in love with Janice in it. I know. Erica told me." He pries his eyes away to look at me. "She wanted to share this with you in the only way she thought she could." I look back at the car, seeing Erica's hard work, passion, and heart. "That's why she has this model. Her whole life is built around you."

"And you?" he asks directly.

"I fucking hope so, but who knows with that woman?" I can't help the bark of laughter that comes out, but he doesn't seem offended by me smack talking about his daughter. In fact, he laughs too. "She might kick me out tomorrow, but I think that's part of the challenge."

Keith wipes his eyes, which have teared up from seeing Foxy and from the laughter. "You're not quite right, are you?

"You have no idea," I say honestly. "But I love your daughter and that's what matters."

He nods, and I know I just passed another test. I might not know shit about engines, but I know people, and Keith Cole is a good man who wants to keep his family safe and happy.

It's a good thing I want the same thing.

"Let me see what my girl's car can do. I'll meet you back at the shop?" He's got the door open, one foot on the ground, ready to roll.

"You think you're gonna beat me there?" I tease, knowing full well that this truck won't beat Foxy, nor will I drive that fast. I'm not trained for those speeds the way Erica and Keith are.

"I damn well better or I'm gonna be disappointed in Rix." We both know that'll never happen.

"First one there has to hang out with all the women."

He grins back. "Nah, first one there gets the first beer and first pick at that fried chicken your *boss* was promising when we left. Janice don't let me have fried foods, says it's bad for my cholesterol and feeds me grilled salmon. Do you know what I would do for a meal that consists of fried batter, greasy chicken, and potatoes?" He holds his chest dramatically.

"Then you go on and get first dibs. I eat like that every day."

Keith's smile, which had started to spread, falls. "I don't think I like you."

I hear the truth though.

He likes me a lot.

I like him too.

# CHAPTER 28

## ERICA

"Pull that thing onto the lift so I can see what the hell went wrong," I tell Reed. He backs the tow truck up, dropping the Challenger in the garage, then he and Manuel push it into place. I sit in my chair and direct them around, supervisory duty only for the sixth day in a row.

They think I'm enjoying this. Truthfully, I'm going stark-raving mad. And bossing Dad around is weird even though he's letting me run the shop my way and acting as my errand boy. Honestly, I think he's a bit relieved to see how well we're doing here without him. He built this shop from the ground up, and I know it was hard for him to retire, but I think going back to the track this week is going to help with that void.

I'm happy he's involved with cars again. It's like the light has turned back on inside him. He went for a beer with Ed last weekend, and one night this week, he pulled out a photo album of Big John, telling Mom, Emily, Brody, and me stories about him over dinner. It was the first time in years he'd even said John's name.

And as much as I hate to admit it, and fuck, do I ever, I need his help right now because nothing is going to stop me from checking out Todd's car. There's always a risk with racing, and that's amplified by using nitrous. But Todd's a solid racer. I know the ins and outs of his car, and what happened should not have.

Once they get the Challenger locked in place and lifted, I roll my chair under it. Head craned back, I use Dad as my hands. "Pull that line."

Dad preemptively knows what to do for the next thirty minutes as we look at various things that could've gone wrong. It's when we pull the tank that I see the problem.

Shit. Fuck. Damn.

"What the hell, Todd?" I ask, even though he's not here. "That's it, Dad. Thanks." I roll out from under the car, carefully setting the bottle on my desk. Staring at it, I try to think of any good reason it wouldn't be what I put on the Challenger, but there's only one. And it's not a good one.

Dad perches on the edge of the desk, arms and ankles crossed the same way he has countless times before. Usually, it was because he was watching over me or Reed in the shop. Now, it's because he's watching to see how I'm going to handle this.

I grab my phone and push Todd's contact number. While it rings, I breathe, attempting to settle my rage.

"Hello." Todd sounds groggy, probably on pain meds. His burns were significantly worse than mine, but he's recovering at home now after being discharged from the burn unit four days after the accident. We've already done the 'are you okay . . . thank you' phone call that was more than awkward for us both, but that'll be nothing compared to this call.

"Todd." One more breath.

"Rix?" He sounds more awake now, and nervous.

"Got your Challenger over here. Ed let me tow it so I could get the tank out of it and see what went wrong since I built it." My voice is steady and calm, nothing like my pulse, which is racing so fast I'm feeling it in my legs where the burns are still healing.

"You do?" Todd says slowly. "Rix, I can explain—"

I cut him off, growling. "Who did your install? Because this isn't my work."

He sighs, the sound heavy even through the phone. "I did it. I talked to a couple of guys on a forum, and they told me what to get and how to install it to get a few more horses out of it. It was running perfectly. I don't know what happened."

He's running from self-righteous to confused. I'm running from mad to fucking furious.

"Guys on a forum? Holy shit, man, you could've been seriously injured!" His burns aren't anything to sneeze at, literally because it's an infection risk according to my discharge paperwork, but people have died from their nitro going wrong. "Todd, you are a great racer. But that's different from getting under the hood and you fucking know it. You don't know shit about installing high-performance nitrous systems."

There are some racers who can wrench, and some wrenchers who can race, but more often than not, the two don't cross, especially not with the specs Todd runs. I'm an abnormality, and to be fair, I'm more of a mechanic who happens to be decent behind the wheel. I'm not even half as good of a driver as Todd is. But he's shit for a mechanic.

"I'm sorry, Rix. Do you know what happened?"

He sounds genuinely apologetic and worried, though probably more about his Challenger than either of our injuries. That car is his baby the same way Foxy is mine. "Your safety disk burst because it was a cheap piece of shit and you were demanding too much of it. I told you that you were maxed."

"Can you fix it?"

I roll my eyes even though he can't see me and follow it up with a haughty sigh. "Of course I can. It's gonna cost you, though, because I'll have to pull the whole system and check everything for fire damage. And send it out for paint work."

"Of course. Blank check, just fix it. Please." I swear he sounds on the verge of tears, and I wonder what kind of pain pills he's on. Good stuff, apparently.

"I'll be in touch when it's done." I hang up, glaring balefully at the Challenger like it betrayed me.

Dad looks at me, lips curled in a smile. "You are something else, honey."

The pride in the pat he gives my shoulder says that we're okay. I'm so glad.

I thought that he would be mad and would be disappointed in me, and he was. But he's getting over it quicker than I expected. Maybe we didn't give each other enough credit? All I know is that I have my dad back, closer than ever before, and I still have racing, the garage, and Brody.

It couldn't be more perfect.

"Where do you want to start?" Dad asks, excitement shining in his eyes.

Boys and their toys. Well, and me and my toys. We'll do anything for them.

# CHAPTER 29

## BRODY

"Mark, will you say grace?" Mama Louise says. Everyone bows their head and he repeats the same thing he does every night. But tonight, he adds to the end . . .

" . . .and thank you for bringing more good people to the table. Amen."

We lift our heads, and Mark doesn't so much as look at Erica, but I know he was giving his stamp of approval. Not that I need it, and not that he hasn't already given it and warned me not to fuck this up because she's way out of my league, but it's a kind gesture. Erica smiles his way, only to finally be greeted by his blank stare. Fucker.

We pass the platters around, serving ourselves meatloaf, green beans, new potatoes, and cornbread. "Do you have any Tabasco?" Erica asks Mama Louise.

Blink. Blink. Blink.

All around the table, brows knit together.

"Of course, dear." Mama Louise grabs the Tabasco sauce from the pantry and hands it to Erica.

She starts shaking the bottle over her meatloaf, and I can't bite my tongue any more as horror settles in my stomach. "What in the world are you doing?" I ask, editing myself for Mama Louise.

Erica looks at me, attitude and challenge in her expression. "You put ketchup on yours. I put Tabasco on mine."

"That's disgusting," Cooper announces. "Ketchup and Tabasco."

Brutal jumps in. "This coming from a kid who puts ranch on literally everything."

Erica cuts off a too-big bite with her fork and moans loudly as she eats. "Mmm, delicious as always, Mama Louise. I think this is even better than Hank's. Especially with the little extra kick added." She's proud of herself, her smile so big I can nearly see the food in her mouth.

"Thank you, Rix."

As she cuts another bite, she adds, "Know what else is good, Cooper?" She's got his attention now. "Ice cream with popcorn sprinkles."

"Can we try that, Mom?" he instantly begs Allyson.

There is zero shame or regret on her face until Allyson says yes. "Of course, Cooper. Rix can make you some tonight after we play cornhole. Bruce and I need to go over and check the progress on the house, so that'd be perfect."

Well, shit. Erica just walked us into getting cockblocked by a kid. And I know damn well that Brutal and Allyson aren't checking the progress of their house in the dark. I guess that's how they avoid being heard fucking . . . they get someone else to watch Cooper and take off in the truck. More than I need to know about my brother, but I'm damn sure storing that trick away for Erica and me. And also, I'm never getting in Brutal's truck again.

"Sounds like a plan." Erica fist-bumps Cooper from across the table.

Shayanne starts humming under her breath, and I instantly recognize the tune. *Another One Bites The Dust.*

I grin, not fighting it anymore. I'm all in with Erica, for as long as she'll have me. She's it for me.

And I know I'm it for her. Because I love her just as she is and accept all of her, even the prickly parts that made her a badass on the day we met and a badass every day since then.

Bobby shakes his head mournfully. "Last man standing." He points his fork at each of the women at the table. "And that is *not* a challenge. If anything, I challenge you to let me live in peace. Me and my guitar."

Rookie mistake. He just painted a big ol' target on his back.

Over dinner, we talk about the new cattle, who are doing well and blended with the main herd, the rising price of hay, and Cooper's latest building project, a birdhouse for the tree in Mama Louise's yard. Then the conversation turns to Brutal and Allyson's wedding, and all hope for any other topic is lost as they discuss their plan to turn the foundation of their new home into a wedding venue with the addition of some rugs. I don't get it at all, but Katelyn and Allyson say they have a 'vision' and I don't doubt that they'll come up with something beautiful.

After dinner and the dishes are done, we head outside for a cornhole tournament. "The first bracket is Erica versus Cooper," Shayanne announces. "Watch out for that one, girl. He's little but he's got good aim."

Erica looks Cooper, who is only a couple of inches shorter than she is, up and down and grins. "Me too."

Their game is the upset of the night when Erica wins, but Cooper quickly forgives her when she loses to Bobby on the next bracket. Bobby takes on Shayanne, and most everyone gathers in the yard to cheer on the close game. Except Erica and Cooper, who take off to catch fireflies.

I sit on the porch, sipping at a Budweiser and watching the two of them run around. Erica's good with kids. I don't know why that surprises me, but it does. Or maybe she's just good with Cooper because he's bit of a spitfire himself. Her soul probably recognizes a kindred spirit.

Mama Louise drops into the chair next to me. "Pretty evening, huh?"

I grunt and take another sip, avoiding the conversation she's trying to start because I'm still me, even if I have grown a bit.

"You don't have to talk. I know how you boys are, but I've spent a lot of years reading people, especially stubborn, grumpy old men, and I'm perfectly happy to carry the conversation myself and say what I want to say."

'Old?' Hardly. The rest I won't argue with.

"You're almost there, Brody. I can see it for you, the future you've been quietly dreaming of."

She looks at me, and though I fight it, my head turns and I meet her eyes. Once upon a time, I thought she'd been a godsend, helping Mom and helping us through a rough spot, and then she was gone from my life. Another of Dad's doings with his piss-poor decisions.

But the joke's on him in the end, because Mama Louise has a heart bigger than the sun when it fills the whole horizon, and when we needed her like never before, she came through. I will never be able to repay her for what she's done for my family. For me.

"Thank you. For everything," I say quietly, my voice rough and scratchy like I haven't used it in too long.

She nods, not needing the thanks but appreciating it all the same. "Keep at it. You've got your family to a good place, and now you're finally letting yourself live too." She puts her hand on my arm, squeezing tight. "Your parents would be proud of the man you've become. You took the best of both of them—"

I open my mouth to contradict her.

"Don't argue with me about your Dad. Paul had his demons, but don't we all?" She lifts a brow, telling me to shut my mouth, and I oblige this time, not sure what to say. "You took the best of both of them and grew into a man with a good heart, a strong work ethic, and a mouth fouler than the Devil himself." For once, she says it like it's a compliment instead of her typical reminder to watch our language, something I've never quite understood.

I smile, hiding it with a sip of Bud, and she goes back to watching Erica and Cooper run around and Bobby and Shayanne play cornhole. But after a second, I give her more.

"When I lost the farm . . ." I clear my throat, not used to opening myself like this. "It could've gone . . . *I* could've gone wrong, turned into Dad. He lost the most important thing to him, and so did I, in a way. I'm not diminishing how important Mom was or how much losing her hurt, but that farm became a barometer of sorts. And I lost it. I felt like a failure. Hell, I still do sometimes. But I won't always be. I'm going to buy it back from you one day."

It's both a promise and a notice of my intentions. I don't want her, or the rest of the Bennetts, to get too comfortable with the Tannen farm on their books. It's temporary. I have to believe that.

She nods agreeably. "I don't know many things that would make me happier than signing your farm back over to you. Trust me, Brody . . . I'm just holding it for you. Safekeeping it for when you're ready for those roots again." She points at Erica, who's managed to catch a firefly, but before it can get injured in her gently cupped hands, she sets it free. Her arms are spread wide, her smile is bright in the dim porchlight, and her dark hair blows wildly in the soft breeze. "I think you've got some more flying to do first, though. Enjoy it. Enjoy each other. Let us do the heavy lifting for a bit while you take care of you the way you've been taking care of everyone else. Take the time you need to just *be*."

My throat is too tight to respond this time, so I grunt. She chuckles and pats my arm again. "I'll do the popcorn and ice cream deal with Cooper tonight. I like trying new things. Keeps me young. Though I do think he's right. Tabasco on meatloaf sounds disgusting."

"Thanks," I manage to say.

Both of us having said what we needed to, we companionably go back to watching the cornhole tournament. It's gotten heated, with Mark and Katelyn somehow playing against each other.

"Katelyn's gonna win," Mama Louise asserts confidently.

I raise a brow. "You think? Mark's good, and competitive as . . . heck."

She smiles at my stilted correction. "He is both of those things.

But I didn't raise him to be a stupid man, and he will make sure Katelyn wins that match because it'll give her something to hold over him. Mark my words."

In the end, she's right. As always.

"COME ON, LET'S GO TO BED." I STEP OVER MURPHY, WHO'S 'guarding' the front room and waiting for Brutal to come home.

"So romantic," Erica teases, but she slips her hand into mine. "Is that what passes for a pickup line these days?"

She's baiting me on purpose and we both know it.

"You wanna get picked up?" I smirk at her for a split second before taking her by the waist and flipping her over my shoulder, heading to the stairs.

"Brody Tannen! Put me down!" she yells, pinching my butt, but it doesn't hurt through my jeans, so I laugh and smack her ass. She squeals, kicking her feet. Luckily, I make it to my room before she kicks anything important, and I toss her to the center of the bed, enjoying the way she bounces and the fire in her eyes. "You're gonna pay for that," she warns.

"Bring it," I counter, yanking my shirt over my head and throwing it in the general vicinity of the dirty clothes pile.

Her eyes dilate when she sees my bare chest before grinning dark and dirty, rising to stand in the middle of the bed in her bare feet. She gives zero warning before she launches herself at me, latching onto my front with her legs wrapped around my waist and her arms around my shoulders. Her teeth nip at my neck, her tongue soothing the nibbles, and she whispers hotly in my ear, "Remember, you asked for this."

She licks down my shoulder, leaning back to blanket my chest with open-mouthed kisses. Her legs untwine, and she kneels on the bed, still working her way down my abdomen. Her tongue traces the skin at the waist of my jeans while her hands work the button and zipper down. I help shove them to the floor, stepping out and standing before her naked and rock-hard while she's still in her shorts and a Ford T-shirt that's seen better days.

She takes my cock in her hand, roughly stroking me as she lowers her mouth to taste the precum on the head. No hesitation, no easing into it, she's full-throttle as always, jacking and sucking me hard right from the get-go. "Fuck, Erica."

The words are half-formed grunts as I bury my hands in her hair and thrust with her strokes to get as much cock in her mouth as she can take.

She slurps and swallows around me, moaning against my skin. When she pauses to breathe, using only her hand for a moment, I grin down at her, knowing that I look smug as shit. "If this is how I pay, I think I'll have to throw you over my shoulder more often."

"Keep thinking that, Cowboy. But you're not coming until I let you." The words are soft and sweet as can be, my cock cradled against her cheek, but there's an evil glint in her eyes when she looks up at me.

Oh, fuck. My eyes shutter closed as I groan, knowing deep inside that she's going to destroy me. I can't fucking wait.

"Do your worst."

Her mouth engulfs me again, torturous heaven surrounding me. Her head bobbing, she teases at my balls with her free hand. When she feels them draw up, she stops everything with me right on the edge. "Uh-uh."

Her fingertips dance along my thighs, which feels good but is nowhere near where I need them to be.

She takes me to the edge again, pulling back when I get too close. My legs start to buckle at the demand to stand upright when she's bringing me to my knees.

"Lie down," she tells me, climbing off the bed to stand.

I do as I'm told, putty in her callused hands. "Yes, ma'am," I say with a little fire left in me too.

She pulls her T-shirt over her head, caramel nipples my instant reward, and then drops her shorts and panties. “Come here,” I tell her, hands reaching out for her.

She shakes her head and does whatever the fuck she wants, like always. She straddles me backward, on her knees with her head toward my cock. I’d absolutely be down for sixty-nine, but she’s so damn short, she can’t suck my cock if her pussy’s in my face. “Enjoying the view?” she says, her hips swaying and her pussy just beyond my reach, even if I lift my head.

She giggles. Well, not really because it’s Erica, but her belly jumps a little like she is. She puts her mouth back on my cock, and I decide to ride this trip to wherever she’s going. I put my hands behind my head to prop up and maximize the view so I can watch her pussy get wetter and wetter as she sucks me.

“You like sucking me? Your cunt’s damn near dripping on my chest, Lil Bit.” She moans in agreement. “Let me have a taste of you.”

She lifts off my cock, dropping her hips back toward me. I lick and taste as much of her as I can while she grinds against my mouth. Her hands grip my hips for leverage, and I spread her lips wide to dip my tongue inside her. Too soon, she takes her pussy away, going back to suck me.

I never thought I’d whine about getting a blow job, but damned if she isn’t making me feel like a petulant child who just lost their favorite lollipop.

I can’t lie back and just watch any longer. My hands trace and knead along her skin, from her thighs to her ass and waist, and my hips thrust up to meet her open mouth. “Enough, I need inside you.” My voice is more animalistic than human, demanding and forceful and at the absolute edge of sanity. She’s done this to me, driven me completely wild.

Erica lifts off with a pop of finality this time and scoots her knees down the bed to kneel over my cock with her hands on my shins. I stand it up at the right angle, and with a lift of her hips, she impales herself on me.

*Heaven. Absolute, utter heaven.*

We stopped using condoms after the fire, but I will never not have a moment of pure gratefulness to feel this woman from the inside, raw and bare. It's a vulnerability neither of us gives easily, except it feels completely natural to give it to each other now.

She rides me, tiny ass bouncing on me as I thrust from beneath her. I grab ahold of her hips, pulling her down hard. We buck and fight together to reach the peak that's looming so close.

"Touch yourself. Get there. Come with me," I grit out.

I feel her fingers dip into the wetness we've made and then move up to her clit. She lets me take over the rhythm, and though I'm overwhelmingly tempted to continue pounding her hard and fast, I don't.

I slow down, staying deep and giving her shallow thrusts. I grab a handful of the dark hair that's hanging down her back, tilting her head to the ceiling. "That's it—rub that clit, feel me inside you. When you come, your cunt's gonna make me come, I'm that close. You want that?"

She nods, pulling her hair slightly but not seeming to mind.

"Do it, Erica. Take us both there." She cries out, hovering on the edge, and I stroke into her a little more forcefully.

"*Yes*," she hisses, going wild. She lifts and drops her hips, setting a new frantic pace, and I can feel her fingers swiping madly across her clit. "Now . . ." she groans, but I don't need her to tell me because her pussy wraps around me like a vice, pulsing waves pulling my orgasm from me too. It's more powerful than usual, built up from her edging me, and I feel like I'm floating, with only her to keep me grounded to the bed.

I grunt, trying to match her pace and drawing as much pleasure out of both our orgasms as I can.

She sags, her head falling forward as I melt into the bed a bit more. "Shit, Lil Bit. If that's your idea of punishment, get used to being thrown over my shoulder."

There's no answer as she turns around and lies down by my side, her head on my chest and my arm wrapped around her shoulder. "Oh, there's more." Her innocent tone should be a warning, but I'm too fuzzy to catch it until it's too late. She teases at the line between my pecs, wandering over to my nipple, before pinching and twisting.

"Ow, fuck!" I shout, cringing away.

She laughs as I rub at my nipple, soothing it. I can't help but want more of that sassy, pleased-with-herself grin. "Still worth it," I tell her with a shrug.

She shakes her head, eyes rolling. "Come here and let me make it better." She acts like she's going to kiss it.

"Why do I feel like this is a trick?" I tease.

It is a trick, but I don't mind in the least because when we finally collapse after round two, both covered in hickeys and exhausted from using each other's body, it's comfortable and natural.

"You and Mama Louise looked like that was an important conversation tonight." Not a question, not pressing me for details, but I want to share them all with her.

"She told me she's holding the farm for me, ready to sell it back whenever I'm ready." My fingers trace patterns on Erica's skin, connecting the freckles even though I can't see them in the dim light of the reading lamp on the nightstand.

"Are you ready?"

So much in three little words. She's asking about a lot more than the farm, and that she will be vulnerable with me this way now speaks to how far we've come.

"I'm ready for a lot . . . with you, with the Bennetts, and eventually, with the farm. But I like how things are now. Never thought I'd say that, but I feel like I'm right where I'm supposed to be and with whom I'm supposed to be."

She snuggles in closer, not saying a word, but I feel the smile as her cheek moves against my chest.

"Even if she is a wrench-wielding badass who can take my head off."

She swats at my chest, laughing. "Asshole."

I pull her back to my side, both of us settling to go to sleep. “Love you, Lil Bit.”

“Love you too, Cowboy.” She’s quiet for one heartbeat before popping off again, “You’re gonna make pancakes in the morning, right?”

# EPILOGUE

## ERICA

I should not be nervous. There's no reason to be, none at all. I've raced Foxy a million times before. Okay, not a million, but hundreds of times for sure.

And each of those times, I sat behind the wheel calm, cool, and collected. Ready to race down the track and let those numbers flash, every time hoping for a new personal record.

Today is no different. Except it is.

Everyone is here. Mom and Dad, Emily and Dan, all the Tannens, all the Bennetts, and all the track guys. Hell, even Todd's back, though he's not racing. The doctor says he still has a few months of physical therapy and maybe even another skin graft before he can drive. But his Challenger is ready when he is, with a properly installed and verified nitrous system, thank you very much.

The crowd is why today feels different. Especially Dad. I know he's proud of me. He's told me flat-out that he is, but there's something inside me that wants to show him just how good I am. Like he won't really believe it until he sees it himself.

I do my burnout and pull up to the staging line. It's me versus Clint, which is going to be a tough race because I've already installed his custom carburetor. But I can still win. I have to —for Dad.

The tree lights up, and I'm gone in less time than it takes to blink. Foxy roars down the track, vibrating beneath me with power. When I cross the finish, I'm in front of Clint.

"You taking it easy on me?" I yell through our open windows over the deafening engines as we take our helmets off.

He smiles easily, teeth flashing through his beard, which is ponytailed up to fit in his helmet. "Nah, just got me today. I'll getcha next time." He's being way too good-natured about losing, which is answer enough.

"Don't take it easy on me because Dad's here. We want to earn those bragging rights." I pat Foxy's dashboard.

He nods respectfully. "You earned every one of them, Rix. But I'll let bracket two know to give it all they've got."

I nod back, satisfied that we're gonna have a good day of racing.

Brody

If it's one thing country folks know how to do, it's tailgate. We've got trucks backed up along the grassy area Ed deems 'the safe zone' and we're sitting in truck beds and camping chairs. Cooper has big earmuffs on, his eyes and smile huge even though Allyson is hovering about while Brutal keeps telling her to 'leave him be.' Marla took Cindy Lou for the day, so the gang's all here.

They all came out for Erica. For me.

Because like it or not, we are one big, happy family.

Mama Louise and Janice sit talking like old friends, and I wonder what they're up to again. But I don't really care.

Because we're all good.

Hell, even Reed and Manuel came. Manuel's wife sits next to him, holding his hand and looking excited. I think she'd get behind the wheel of one of these monstrous machines if she could. Reed is alone, but I've seen him texting a lot lately at the shop and Manuel says he's joined some dating sites.

I'm glad. He's a good guy, and deserves to be happy.

We watch as Erica races again and again, winning in her bracket of gas-powered cars until she's up for the main drag.

Keith stands. His eyes are laser-locked on Erica, tense but powerful. I get up and go stand next to him. "She's something else."

It's praise for Erica, but it's just as much for Keith. He helped her grow into the powerhouse that she is.

"She is," he nods, agreeing. "What're you gonna do about it?" He's acting casual, eyes never leaving his priority, but I know the weight in the question.

"Gonna marry her one day," I say without hesitation.

He chuckles. "If that was your asking permission for her hand, it sucked."

"If you think I'll be asking you, then you don't know your daughter at all," I tell him quietly but intensely. "We'll know when the time's right."

I look back to Erica, who's staging.

"If you don't, I'm sure she'll let you know."

I chuckle, knowing he's right.

We're silent as the lights change and she roars away down the track. Every single time she gets the green, my heart still stutters and stops, my breath locks in my lungs, and I don't blink until I see the red of her taillights and know she's slowing down and safe.

"Best time of the day," Keith says proudly.

I grunt, knowing the best time is still to come.

And when Erica pulls around, getting out with her helmet held high in celebration, I know she's it for me. For however long I get on this Earth, I want every single moment with her, and I'm going to do my damnedest to make them amazing.

She deserves it.

I deserve it.

With everyone cheering for her loudly, Erica only has eyes for me. She runs my way, and I catch her easily, hands under her ass as her legs wrap around me and her steel-toed boots lock behind my back. "Best ever!"

Yeah, she is.

Thank you for reading! Don't forget to preorder Book 3 of the Tannen Boys (Bobby's book!). You can read the blurb here.

# PREVIEW: BEAUTY AND THE BILLIONAIRE

## MIA

The darkness is complete, wrapping around me like an ebony velvet blanket, cool and textural on my naked skin. I can feel it on my goosebumps, the air adding to my trembling.

My body, exhausted from the last ordeal, still quivers as I try to find the strength to move. It's so difficult, the waters of sleep still tugging at me even as instinct tells me there's something in the darkness.

A soft shuffle of feet on the carpet, and I can sense him. He's here, watching me, invisible, but his aura reaches out, awakening my body like a warm featherlight touch on the pleasure centers of my brain.

Arousal ripples up my thighs, fresh heat shimmering with the memories of last time. I've never felt anything like him before, my body used and taken, battered and driven insane . . . and completely, thoroughly pleasured in a way that I didn't think possible.

It was so much that I don't even remember coming down, just an explosion of ecstasy that drove me into unconsciousness . . . but now my senses have returned and I know he's still there, measuring me, hunting me, *desiring* me.

How can he have strength left? How, when every muscle from my neck to my toes has already been taken past the limit?

How can he still want more?

My nostrils flare, and I can smell him. Rich, masculine . . . feral. A man's man who could tear me apart without a second's effort. His breath, soft but shuddering, sipping at the air, savoring the conquest to come.

Another whisper in the darkness, and the fear melts away, replaced by a heightened sense of things.

The moonlight, dim now in the post-midnight morning, when the night's as deep as it will ever be.

The sweat on my skin and the fresh moisture gathering at the juncture between my thighs.

He steps forward, still cloaked in shadow, a shape from the depths of night, ready for a new kind of embrace.

He reaches for my calf, and at his touch, I start to tremble. I should resist, I should say I can't take any more. He's already had his fill. What more can he want?

He inhales, his nose taking in my scent, and the knowledge comes to me, a revelation that I've chosen to ignore.

He wants me to be his. Not just his bedmate, not simply a conquest to have and to discard. He wants to possess me fully, to own me, body and soul.

But can I?

Can I give myself to such a man, a being whose very presence inspires fear and dread?

Can I risk the fury that I've seen directed at others turned back upon me?

His tongue flicks out, touching that spot he's discovered behind my right knee that I wasn't even aware of before him, my left leg falling aside on its own as my hunger betrays me.

My mind is troubled, my heart races . . . but my body knows what it wants.

He chuckles, a rumble that tickles my soft inner thighs as he pauses, his breath warm over my pussy. He scoops his hands under my buttocks, and I feel him adjust himself on the mattress, preparing for his feast.

"Delicious," he growls, and then his tongue touches me . . . and I'm gone.

MIA

The electronic drumbeats thud through the air so hard that I can actually feel my chest vibrate as I look at my screen, my head bobbing as I let the pattern come to me.

I've had a lot of people ask me how I can work the way I do, but this is when the magic happens. I've got three computer screens, each of them split into halves with data flowing in each one. I'm finishing up my evaluations, I've done the grind, and now I'm bringing it all together.

For that, though, I need tunes, and nothing gets my brain working on the right frequency as well as good techno does.

I can hear the door to my office vibrate in its frame, and I'm glad I've got my own little paradise down here in the basement of the Goldstone Building.

Sure, my methods are weird, and I'm sort of isolated considering that I'm in a corner office with two file rooms on either side of me, but that's because I need this to make the magic happen.

Frankly, I wasn't too sure if I'd be able to keep this job, considering the number of complaints I got my first six months working here.

Part of it, of course, is my occasional outbursts—to myself, mind you, and more often than not in gutter Russian so no one can understand me.

That, with the random singing along with my tunes, meant I was labeled as 'distracting' and 'difficult to work next to.'

But the powers that be saw the value that I bring with my data analysis.

So, as an experimental last gasp, I was sent down here, where the walls are thick, the neighbors are paper, and nobody minds that my singing voice is terrible.

It works for them, but more importantly, it works for me.

And here I've remained for almost six years, working metadata analysis and market trends, making people with money even more money.

Not that the company's treated me poorly. I've gotten a bonus for seven quarters straight, and I've always managed my own investments.

For a girl who still has a few years until she hits thirty, I'm doing well on the ol' nest egg.

But I'm pigeonholed. Other than dropping off files from time to time, I almost never see anyone in my day to day work, which I guess is okay with me. I've never been someone who likes the social scene of an office.

On the other hand, I can wear my pink and blue streaks in my hair and not have to see people's judging glares. And I don't have to explain what my lyrics mean when I decide to sing along.

"Another one for the Motherland!" I exclaim as I see what I've been looking for. This isn't a hard assignment, merely an optimization analysis for some of Goldstone's transport subsidiaries. But I prefer to celebrate each victory, no matter how small or large, with glee.

I swipe all the data to my side monitors and bring up a document in the center and start typing. I've already included most of the boilerplate that the executives and VPs want to see, the 'check the box' sort of things that my father would understand with his background.

After all, he is Russian. He knows about bureaucracy.

Finally, just as the Elf Clock above my door dings noon, I save my file and fire it off to my supervisor.

"In Russia . . . report finishes *you*."

Okay, so it's not my best one-liner, but it's another quirk of mine. While I'm as American as apple pie, I pay homage to my roots, especially at work, for some reason. It seems to help, so I'm sticking to it.

Heading to the elevator, I go upstairs before punching out for lunch and jumping into my little Chevy to drive to my 'spot', a diner called The Gravy Train. An honest to goodness old-fashioned diner, it's got some of the best food in town, including a fried chicken sandwich that's to kill for.

As I drive, I look around my hometown, still surprised at how big it seems these days. The main reason, of course, is tied to the dark tower on the north side of town, Blackwell Industries.

Thirty years ago, Mr. Blackwell located his headquarters here in the sleepy town of Roseboro and proclaimed it to be the bridge between Portland and Seattle. A lot of people scoffed, but he was right, and Roseboro's been the beneficiary of his foresight.

I've been lucky, watching a city literally grow with me. Roseboro is big enough now that some people even call this a Tri-Cities area, lumping us in with Portland and Seattle.

I get to The Gravy Train just in time to see the other reason that I come to this place so frequently for lunch wave from the window. Isabella "Izzy" Turner has been my best friend since first grade, and I love her like she's my own flesh and blood.

As I enter, I see her untie the apron on her uniform and slump down into one of the booths. Her normally rich brown hair looks limp and stringy today, and the bags under her eyes are so big she could be carrying her after work clothes in them.

"Hey, babe, you look exhausted," I say in greeting, giving her a hug from the side as I slide in next to her. "Please don't tell me you're still working double shifts?"

"Have to," Izzy says as she leans into me and hugs back. "Gotta keep the bills paid, and doing double shifts gives me a chance to maybe get a little ahead. I'll need it once classes start up again."

"You know you don't have to," I tell her for the millionth time. "You can take out student loans like the rest of us."

"I'd rather not if I don't have to. I owe enough to other people as it is."

She's got a point. She's had a tough life and has seen tragedy that left more and more debt on her tab, and student loans are tough enough without all the other stuff in her life.

And even though she always turns me down, I have to offer once again, just on the off-chance she'll say yes this time. "Still, if you need anything . . . I mean, I've said it before, but you can always come live with me. I've got room at my place."

Izzy snorts, finally cracking a smile. "You mean you want someone to stay up with you until two in the morning on weekends playing video games."

Before I can elbow her in the side, the bell above the door rings and in walks the third member of our little party patrol, Charlotte Dunn. A stunning girl who turns heads everywhere she goes with her long, naturally bright and beautiful red hair, she slides into the booth opposite Izzy and me, looking exhausted herself.

She settles in, sighing heavily, and Izzy looks over at her. "Tough morning for you too?"

"I think walking in the back and sticking my head in a vat of hot oil might just be preferable to working reception on the ground floor of Satan's Skyscraper," she jokes. "It's not like anything bad happened either."

"So what's the deal?" I ask, and Charlotte shakes her head. "What?"

"I guess it's just that everyone there walks like they've got a hundred-pound albatross on their back as they come in. No smiles, no greetings, even though I try. It's just depressing," she replies. "You got lucky, landing in the shining palace."

"Girl, please. I work all by my lonesome in the deep, dark dungeon of a basement," I point out.

Charlotte snorts. "But that's how you like it!"

She's not wrong, so I don't bother arguing, instead teasingly gloating, "And I get to wear whatever and work however the hell I please."

Our waitress, one of Izzy's co-workers, comes over with her order pad. "So, what can I get you ladies?"

"Something with no onions or spice," Izzy replies, groaning. "Maybe Henry can whip up a grilled cheese for me?"

"Deal. And for you ladies?"

We place our orders, and the three of us lean back, relaxing. Charlotte looks me over enviously again, shaking her head. "Seriously, Mia, can't get over the outfit today. You trying to show off the curves?"

"What curves?" I ask, looking down at today's band T-shirt. It's just a BTS logo, twin columns rising on a black shirt.

"Hey, you're rockin' it." Charlotte laughs. "It fits the girls just right."

I roll my eyes. Charlotte always seems to see something in me that I don't. Men don't seem to find me interesting. Or at least, the men *I* find interesting don't find *me* interesting.

Deflecting back to her, I ask, "How're things looking for you? That guy in Accounting ever come back downstairs to get your number?"

Charlotte snorts. "Nope. I saw him the other day, but it's okay. It's his loss."

She does a little hair flip and I can't help but smile. She hasn't always had the best luck with guys, but she never gives up and always keeps a positive attitude about the whole dating game. Her motto is 'No Mr. Wrongs, only Mr. Rights and Mr. Right-Nows.' Maybe not the classiest, but a girl's got needs, and sometimes it's nice to have an orgasm from a guy not named B.O.B.

We eat our lunches, chatting and gossiping and bullshitting as always. It's never a big to-do since we share lunch together at least once a week, if not more, but it's still nice to catch up. Izzy and I have been friends for so long, and Charlotte and I met in college. They're important to me.

"So, when do classes start up again, Izz?" Charlotte asks. "So you can, I don't know, get some sleep and not have fallen arches?"

Izzy snorts. "Too soon, I think. But if I can string together another two semesters—"

"Wait, two?" I ask in shock. "Honey, you're like the super-duper-ooper senior at this point. Seriously, some of the professors are probably younger than you by now."

"Hey, we're the same age!" Izzy protests, but shrugs. "You know, I had a freshman ask me if I was a TA the other day?"

"Ouch, that had to hurt," Charlotte says. "What did you say?"

"I pointed him in the direction of the student union and turned him down when he asked for my number. Seriously, I'm not sure if he even needed to shave yet. I don't have time to teach eighteen-year-old man-boys what and where a clit is!"

Charlotte and I laugh, and I punch her in the shoulder. "You'll get there in your own time, girl. But still, why the wait?"

"Mostly the internship," Izzy admits. "I can juggle classes and work, or internship and work, but I can't do classes, internship, and work. There's just not enough hours in the day."

I nod, understanding that Izzy has plans and dreams. But unlike most, she's willing to sacrifice and work hard to reach hers.

We shift topics, like we always do, until we've covered all the usual topics and my tummy feels pleasantly happy without risk of an afternoon food coma.

Wiping our mouths with our napkins, I glance at my phone, checking the time. "So, Char . . . rock, paper, scissors?"

"Nope, this one's mine!" Charlotte says, giggling as I lean into Izzy, preventing her from moving as Charlotte grabs the check and runs up to the counter.

"Hey! Hey, dammit!" Izzy protests. "I—"

"Should be quiet and let your friends pay for lunch for once," I whisper. "Or else I'll use my secret Russian pressure point skills on you!"

"Oh, fine, since you put it that way!"

Charlotte comes back, and she smiles at Izzy. "Chill, Izz. You bust your ass, and you've snuck us an extra pickle more than once. You're allowed to let me buy you lunch every now and then."

"We could all use some more *pickle*." Izzy chuckles. "Seriously, at this point, I'd settle for a one-nighter. No commitment, no issues, just a good old-fashioned hookup. As long he's well into his twenties, at least," she says with an eye roll.

"Mr. Right Now?" Charlotte asks, and Izzy nods. "Hmph. You find him, send him my way. I keep finding good guys . . . two months after they've met the girl of their dreams. Only single men I find are dogs."

"You've just gotta make sure you give them a fake number and a flea dip, and enjoy the weekend," I tease, though she knows I would never do anything of the sort.

"I'm lonely, but I've got rechargeable batteries."

We all laugh, and my phone rings. I pull it out, checking the screen. "Shit, girls, it's my boss. Says he's got a rush job for me to complete."

"How's he working out, anyway?" Charlotte asks as I finish my drink quickly. "And have you started working for The Golden Child yet?"

"Nope, I've never seen him except for the publicity stuff," I reply honestly. "He's the penthouse. I'm the basement. Twenty-four floors in between us. Anyway, I gotta jet, so I'll talk to you girls soon, okay?"

"Yup . . . I'm going to relax for this next ten minutes before I need to clock back in myself," Izzy says, stretching out. "Gimme a call later?"

I nod, blowing them a kiss, and head back to work.

THOMAS

Looking out over Roseboro, I feel like I'm looking over my empire.

Of course, I'm joking . . . but maybe not so much.

Twenty-five years ago, this town was just a suburb of a suburb of Portland. Though it was already up and coming, I'd like to think that over the past six years I've added my fair share to this place.

I'd finished my MBA at Stanford and set up shop in the growing town, watching the landscape change and cultivating the business interests that serve me best. Because I haven't just watched. I've worked my ass off to get Goldstone where it is today.

Still, I made sure to keep the competition in sight, literally.

My office faces the Blackwell Building, a one-mile gap separating the two tallest buildings in the city. It helps me keep things in perspective. I came to town because I saw potential, even if Blackwell had already created something big here.

But this place is too fertile for him to fully take advantage of. A rose that, if tended right, can provide more blossoms than any one man could utilize.

I watch the morning sun hit the black tower. I'll give Blackwell grudging respect. His design might be morbid, but it's also cutting-edge. All that black is absorbing the solar energy and using it for electricity and heating. The man was environmental before environmental was actually cool.

*Too bad you'll never be that. You're just a wannabe, another young upstart who'll never stand the test of time.*

I growl, pushing away the voice from inside me, even though I know it'll be back. It never really goes away, not for long. No matter how much I achieve, that voice of insecurity still resides in my center, ready to cast doubt and shadows on each success.

The soft ding from my computer reminds me that my ten minutes of morning meditation are over, and I turn back around, looking at my desk and office. It's nothing lavish. I designed this space for maximum efficiency and productivity.

So my Herman Miller chair is not in my office for lapped luxury, or for its black and chrome styling, but for the fact that it's rated the best chair for productivity. Same with my desk, my computer, everything.

Everything is tuned toward efficient use of my time and my efforts.

I launch into it, going through my morning assignments, answering the emails that my secretary, Kerry, cannot answer for me, and making a flurry of decisions on projects that Goldstone is working on.

Finally, just as the clock on my third screen beeps one o'clock, I send off my final message and stand up. Locking my computer, I transfer everything to my server upstairs in case I need it.

I see Kerry sitting at her desk as I leave my office. She's well-dressed as usual, her sunkissed skin and black hair gleaming mellowly under the office lighting, the perfect epitome of a professional executive assistant. While she works for me, she has this older sibling protective instinct. It's not often that I need it, but I appreciate her looking out for me.

"Need something, Mr. Goldstone?" she asks.

"Just headed upstairs," I tell her.

"Of course," she replies, her eyes cutting to her computer screen. "Just a reminder, sir, the governor will be hosting his charity event tonight at seven. I've already had your tuxedo dry-cleaned, and your car detailer called. Your car will be ready and downstairs by three this afternoon."

I give her a nod. Three's plenty of time. "I just sent you a list of other projects to work on, by the way."

"Of course, Mr. Goldstone. I was looking that over, and I got an email from Hank also, the team leader you assigned the Taiwan shipping contract to. He said that he's going to have to take a day off Friday, sir. His daughter's going to college this year, and he promised her that he'd drive her up so she can get settled into the dorm."

I stop, pursing my lips. "What is her name?"

Kerry taps her desk for a moment, searching her memory. "Erica, sir."

"Tell Hank that I understand and wish Erica the best, but if he isn't at work on Friday, don't bother coming in on Monday."

My tone has grown serious, and Kerry's eyes tighten, but she knows Hank is crossing a line. He should've given notice, especially when he's working a contract this important.

He's usually a good employee. But he knew his daughter was starting classes. No excuse for that.

*No excuse for you, you mean. Failure just drips down from the boss's office down to Hank, that's all.*

Leaving the twenty-fifth floor of the Goldstone building, I take the stairs up a level to stretch my legs. Not many people even know about this floor other than the executives. To everyone else, the Goldstone Building has twenty-five floors.

The twenty-sixth is mine. It's my penthouse, and while it isn't quite as large as the other floors, it's still six thousand square feet of space that's just for me.

I strip off my dress shirt, tie, and slacks, depositing everything in the laundry chute before pulling on my workout clothes.

Today's upper body day, and as I go into my home gym, I swing my arms to loosen up my shoulders. They're going to be punished today. Starting with bench presses, I assault my body, pushing myself to press the bar one more time, to get the fucking dumbbells up despite the pain, despite gravity kicking my ass.

*Just like everything kicks your ass.*

The finisher for today is brutal, even for me. The 300 . . . 100 burpees, 100 dips, and 100 pullups, in sets of ten, nonstop. By the time I'm finished, sweat pools on the rubberized gym flooring beneath me.

I have to force myself to my feet because I refuse to be broken by anything, even something as meaningless as a workout that's supposed to do exactly that.

Instead, I jump in for a quick shower and meditate for twenty minutes after. I need to focus because running Goldstone is a mental exercise.

Closing my eyes, I force myself to push all the responsibilities away, to let it all fade into the background.

I push away the flashbacks, the voice in my head, the memories that threaten from time to time, and imagine my perfect world . . . my empire. My perfect Roseboro, deep red petals soft as velvet and eternally blooming, ready to be passed from my generation to the next for tending and care.

I know I can do it.

I *must* do it.

Changing into my tuxedo, I head downstairs to the freshly cleaned limo waiting to take me to this event. The Roseboro Civic Library is one of the newest public buildings in town, a beautiful hundred-thousand-square-foot building in three wings over two floors. The central wing is named for Horatio Roseboro, who founded the city in memory of his daughter, who died on the Oregon Trail, while the other two wings are named for the main benefactors . . . Goldstone and Blackwell. My only request was that the Goldstone wing contain the children's section, and they were more than willing to do that.

Tonight, though, it's the scene for a fundraiser for the governor's favorite charity. Governor Gary Langlee tends to ignore Roseboro most of the time—we're not his voter base—but when it comes time to get money, he'll go just about anywhere he can if someone will cross his palm with a little bit of green.

I arrive at just the right time, ten minutes before seven, in order to get the best of the press. I tolerate the leeches more than like them, but I do understand that the fourth estate has a purpose and a job to do.

And there are legit journalists who I respect. It's just the paparazzi and empty talking heads that I despise.

So I smile for the cameras, giving a little wave and shaking hands with our local state representative before heading into the foyer, where the party has already started.

"Ah, Thomas!" the mayor says, greeting me in that hearty way that really endears him to the locals. "I'm so glad you could make it."

"You know me, never pass up a chance to press the flesh," I reply, making him laugh. He knows I'm lying but thinks that I'm only here because of the press and good PR that Goldstone will get for tonight.

The reality is far different. While Governor Langlee and I might not see eye to eye on most public policies, I actually agree with the goals of tonight's event.

"I'm sure you'll enjoy yourself," the mayor says after a moment when I don't follow up.

Clearing his throat, he looks around. "If you don't mind telling me, Thomas, there's a rumor around town that Goldstone is looking into building a sea transportation hub in Roseboro. I'm not saying I wouldn't appreciate it, but if you are, I happen to know a man who's got about seven hundred and fifty acres just outside of town. It's county land, but I'm sure we could work something out."

That's the mayor . . . a good ol' boy to the voters, a sneaky deal-maker to those with money. The man would sell his grandmother's grave if it'd make him a buck.

*Oh, like you've been such a good son.*

"If we do move on such a project, I'll be sure to keep City Hall informed," I tell him with a smile that turns just a little predatory at the end. "But of course, I would do my due diligence on the property. No use wasting my money when it could be spent on a proper seaport instead of along the Columbia?"

The mayor blanches just a little, which is what I want. A tiny reminder that while he may hold office, I hold the funds that make this city thrive or fail. Or at least a large share of the finances that do so.

Leaving him, I do my best to 'mingle'. I know the faces. I've seen it all before.

A pat on the back here for a friend.

A backhanded compliment for the enemy whom you can't quite man up and call out in public. The icy stare from across the room at those whose families have somehow found the time to engage in feuds despite not having the time to make a difference in the world.

It's all old hat, and while some might find it interesting, I just tolerate it to get my goal here tonight done.

Finally, at nine o'clock, I can't do it any longer. I retreat to the children's section, which is relatively quiet in comparison, and I look over the newest books on the display.

"You know, I'm not too sure if *Long Way Down* really belongs in the children's section," a throaty voice says behind me, and I turn to see Meghan Langlee, Governor Langlee's daughter.

She's wearing a Chanel cocktail dress that fits her like a glove, highlighting a very fit body and a camera grabbing face. A former beauty queen like her mother, Meghan's parlayed her looks into a budding career as a political pundit.

"Actually, I personally insisted on it," I reply, turning away from her and looking at the books again. "While the subject matter might be a little dark and violent, the days of young people growing up needing little more than *The Andy Griffith Show* and reading Judy Blume are pretty much over."

"Hmm, well, I'll say my father would disapprove, but I understand what you mean," she says, stepping closer. "You know, Mr. Goldstone . . . mind if I call you Tom?"

"If you wish," I reply, sizing her up immediately. She must be up to something, she's coming on too hard, too boldly.

It wouldn't surprise me if she's been sent here on a mission. Her father's a weasel and would see no issue with using his only daughter this way.

She takes my arm, as if she expects me to suddenly escort her and be happy to do so, giving me a false coquettish giggle. "Ooh. I've heard your reputation Tom, that you're pretty *rigid* in your fitness routines, but wow, this tux is hiding a *beast* underneath all this worsted wool."

"Clean eating and good habits," I reply, already tiring of her and her lazily flirtatious innuendos. She tries to lead me back to the main wing, and I follow along simply to avoid any issues, but when she sees one of the press and starts trying to angle us in that direction, I pull my arm free. "Excuse me, Miss Langlee."

She looks surprised, anger hiding in her eyes. I doubt she's used to being denied. She reaches out and grabs my arm again, pulling herself close.

"Come on now, Tom. I'm sure we can find a little bit of fun."

I can't tolerate this any longer, and I pull away, my voice tight. "Sorry. I haven't had my rabies booster this year."

I walk away, cursing myself at that last crack. Turning her down cold? That's one thing.

But essentially calling her a disease-infested slut was probably too much.

"One of these days, you're going to piss off someone important," she says threateningly to my back. When I don't reply, she stomps her foot like a petulant toddler, loud enough to cut through the hubbub of the party as she calls out, "Bastard!"

Everything stops, and I nod, glancing back over my shoulder at her with a charming smile. "That's one of the things they call me."

I keep going, and as I pass by the governor, he gives me a dirty look. Reaching out, he puts a hand on my arm.

"You know, my daughter—" he starts, already conciliatory, which makes me think he knew exactly what Meghan's game was tonight.

I don't let him finish. I just shrug him off, ignoring the snapping cameras. I only pause at the door to reach into my jacket and pull out an envelope that I slide into the donation box.

It's unmarked . . . but that's just what I want.

Search Beauty and the Billionaire on Amazon to read the full book. Or click here.

## ABOUT THE AUTHOR

Standalones

The Dare || My Big Fat Fake Wedding || Filthy Riches || Scorpio

*Bennett Boys Ranch:*

Buck Wild || Riding Hard || Racing Hearts

The Tannen Boys:

Rough Love || Rough Edge || Rough Country

*Dirty Fairy Tales:*

Beauty and the Billionaire || Not So Prince Charming || Happily Never After

*Get Dirty*:

Dirty Talk || Dirty Laundry || Dirty Deeds || Dirty Secrets

*Irresistible Bachelor*s:

Anaconda || Mr. Fiance || Heartstopper

Stud Muffin || Mr. Fixit || Matchmaker

Motorhead || Baby Daddy || Untamed

Printed in Great Britain
by Amazon

38297564R00176